"Science fiction is the most important
literature in the history of the world,
because it's the history of ideas,
the history
of our civilization birthing itself.
...Science fiction is central to everything
we've ever done,
and people who make fun of
science fiction writers don't know what
they're talking about."

Ray Bradbury

Android Dawn

PA Stockwell

Westridge Art
PO Box 3847
Silverdale, WA 98383

Published by
Westridge Art
PO Box 3847
Silverdale, WA 98383

First Printing 2022
Copyright © by Peter Stockwell
All rights reserved.

22 20 10 9 8 7 6 5 4 3 2 1

ISBN-13: 978-0-9983558-3-2

Printed in the United States of America

Publisher's note
This book is a work of fiction.
Names, characters, places, and incidents either are the product of the author's imagination or are used fictionally, and any resemblance to actual persons, living or dead, business establishments, events, or locales is entirely coincidental.

Cover Design by Peter Stockwell
Images from Shutterstock.com

Interior Design by Westridge Art

Distributed by
Westridge Art
and Ingram

WORKS BY PETER STOCKWELL

ADULT FICTION

Motive series

Motivations
Motive
Jerry's Motives
Death Stalks Mr. Blackthorne
In the Garden of Eden

YOUNG ADULT SCI-FI

The Mistress
Android Incursion (coming soon)

NONFICTION

Stormin' Norman
(The Sermons of an Episcopal Priest)
Volume I
Volume II
Volume III
Volume IV (coming soon)

Dedication

This book is dedicated to readers who want great stories and believable characters to whom they relate and desire to have as friends.

"Everything's science fiction until someone makes it science fact."

Marie Lu, Warcross

Chapter 1

Parvel Mandolin smiled as he stroked Cigi Weatherman's extended abdomen. "You amaze me," he said and kissed her bare skin. "I never believed Sam when he told me you could conceive a child." Cigi watched her husband as he devoted attention to their unborn baby.

"I love you, Parvel," she said. Emotional awareness was another of Sam's achievements. Running her hands through his hair as he hugged her lower body, she continued. "I must find one of the android doctors Peter introduced into the medical community. I can't allow just any practitioner to inspect my body and discover my android parts." Parvel raised his head and gazed into her blue-azure eyes.

"I connected with Sam and Clare yesterday as you asked. They are coming here tomorrow. Summer has a track to locate where each of those android doctors and nurses is, but I have no way to communicate with her."

"Let me worry about my sisters in Cuba." Summer, Autumn, Winter, and Spring, along with four male android companions, had escaped the government's roundup of artificial life-forms six months ago. Cigi, her friend Clare Esposito, and the medical staff members were free and undetected. For now.

Samuel Bennington and his brother, Peter, created a system to design, develop, and construct Intelligent Artificial sentient life-forms until the raids on their secret laboratories and factories dismantled them. Federal agencies confiscated and confined most of the human-like robots seized during the government incursion. Changes to laws mandated the round-up of artificial humans that were formerly legal. Sex companions, robot bartenders, and waitstaff disappeared from the streets. It seemed a miracle that Cigi and her sister androids evaded the round-up. They lived among the human population, acting the part with Oscar-worthy success.

Parvel's phone chirped. He stared at the device as if it monitored his life and knew his secret, married to an impregnated Artificially Intelligent humanoid. He answered the call. "What's up, Andre?" His boss, Andre Scott, at the Department of Energy in Washington D.C., was on the other end of the airwaves. Parvel listened and nodded as if Andre could see him. "I will be there in fifteen." He clicked off and turned to his wife. "Andre wants me to see him about the influx of capital from the new budgetary passage."

"Say 'hi' to the team for me," Cigi stood from the chair she occupied and bade her man goodbye. After he left, she wandered into the kitchen for a glass of the power drink Sam developed on his farm in Chimacum, Washington, where he and Clare escaped. The drink enriched her human digestive tract's ability to produce the needed sustenance for her developing embryo. She did not have actual hemoglobin flowing in her arteries and veins, but the uterine development of a human placenta required a transfer of nutrients for the baby. So far, no complications had manifested in her body.

The Department of Energy team had protected her when an overzealous security guard at Energy doubted her reality or humanity. Brenda Williams, Parvel, and Andre had formed a barrier against the sergeant's unwarranted arrest. Narumi Yamamoto, one of Peter's lab techs, was present and joined the barrier. The other team members, Mercy Garocki and Grendel Llanthony, missed the guard wounding Andre, and Narumi attacked her, giving Cigi, Brenda and Parvel time to hide in a secret, secured room. A multi-agency invasion force took control of Peter and Sam's underground android factory soon after.

Her phone chimed, and she studied the face on the screen. "Hi, Sam. I understand you and Clare arrive tomorrow. I'll send Cecil to pick you up."

"Thanks, Cigi. How are you? Is the pregnancy working?" Sam asked.

"Yes, so far. I do not know what to expect, so you can enlighten me while you are here," she said. A chuckle crossed the country through the miracle of wireless technology, now a over century old. "You laugh, but I don't know what happens. I read the materials you forwarded and processed in my brain what will happen, but I understand things aren't as straightforward considering my android systems."

"I'll help as best I can. Have you located any of the doctors or nurses Peter unleashed on the world?"

"No, but I'll connect with Summer. She has the leads." Cigi stared out the window of Parvel's condo across the Potomac River toward the Capitol Building. "You found Peter in Arizona."

"Yes, but we haven't chanced an intervention. Peter changed his name and contact information." Sam hesitated, but Cigi waited for the silence to end. "Renata Giretti has made little progress convincing certain politicians to ease the ban on androids." Sam and Renata, a government agency operative, had built a solid case to support the idea of androids and humans existing in harmony. The Congress and President nixed the concept with a series of Draconian laws banning Artificially Intelligent life-forms. Programmable robots remained legal for businesses to use in construction situations hazardous to humans.

"Has he built up his operation to production levels?"

"Not as far as I know, but his legitimate companies are providing funding for research and design. He wants to build another one like you." Sam paused again. "He doesn't have the specs I developed."

"How is Clare?" Cigi asked.

A noise signaled the transfer of the cell to another person. "Hi, Cigi," Clare said. "I've missed you."

"We have had little time to share. We knew these few months were difficult. Are you safe and undiscovered?" Cigi believed no one had any recognition of Sam or Clare in the Olympic Peninsula's remote corner in northwest Washington. They established a small farm and maintained a low profile.

"We're doing fine. How's pregnancy?"

"Sam forgot to explain hormonal imbalances." Cigi's body included a complete endocrine system to aid the various digestive and cellular operations of her human systems developed from stem cell restructuring procedures. The uterus and placenta were working the miracle of pregnancy properly.

"I can't wait to see you guys."

"The condo is ready when you get here. I've been in touch with the concierge to be sure nothing goes wrong." Cigi had kept her penthouse in the same building, but rarely spent time there. Were government agents monitoring the place? She swept the building for intrusive devices each week but found nothing.

"Thanks. Here's Sam." Clare's voice wavered enough for Cigi to notice a tinge of regret.

Sam said, "We'll be on a flight to our private field. When we arrive, I'll signal Cecil."

"Sam, when are you going to upgrade Clare so you two can experience what Parvel and I are doing?"

Sam grunted, "Um, I guess we haven't talked about it."

"I think you need to discuss it with her."

"It's not as easy as adding a chip to your processor."

"I know, Sam, and sometimes I think you are as dumb as they come. You created us to grow and mature. Her emotional stability depends on her being like me as much as she can. Think about it."

The call ended with him agreeing to her comments. Cigi connected with Cecil, who sat patiently in the underground garage. He had not driven around town for several days and had conserved his computing and energy operations with the wireless charging panel on the floor beneath him.

"Good morning, Cigi," the sentient automobile awoke when the alarm stirred his computing processors.

"Cecil, Sam and Clare are arriving tomorrow. Please pick them up when they arrive. Sam is sending the details to you tonight."

"Will do, Cigi. It sure has been quiet these last few weeks. I miss the car chases and long trips to avoid government agents."

"Cecil, you are incorrigible." But Cigi admired the creation of an android self-driving and sentient automobile. Human in many aspects that Cigi possessed only in car form.

As the day progressed toward noon, Cigi upgraded her dynamic network to include loving another person. Her baby was completely human as the ovarian cycle had released an ovum that met Parvel's sperm and melded into a tiny blastosphere that now was the size of a pear. The distention of the abdomen provided evidence of growth within her. Hormonal discharges did not affect her cognitive processors as they would in a human female. She had to develop the proper programming set to allow this new human an emotional attachment like she had created with Parvel.

The need for medical care was overdue. Cigi had to contact Summer and find a doctor and nurse to administer the proper prenatal care and subsequent delivery. Sitting in a chair facing the window, she connected with the transmission satellites orbiting the heavens. Little time existed before government spooks would find her signal within the billions of communications. She hoped to get Summer quickly and without interference. They shared a coded message system. Once translated, she expected Summer to return another coded message identifying the doctors' and nurses' locations. Cigi did not want to think about the consequences if government agents intercepted the messages and decoded them.

Chapter 2

Summer's internal communications signaled an incoming message manifested as a memory in her core processors. The message routed through the Virtual Private Network she and Cigi established was simple. "Need medical. Where are they?"

Peter Bennington and his crew of technicians designed and built six nurse practitioners and four doctors and unleashed them into medical operations at several hospitals and clinics in Arlington, Virginia. A pregnant Cigi had to find them.

"Autumn, we need to return to the United States," she said to her sister android, who entered the room. "Winter and Spring can run the restaurant while we're gone."

"Is this about Cigi?" Autumn asked.

"Yes. I need to tell you something about why our sister needs us to return to Virginia." Autumn stood with hands locked behind her back, anticipating bad news. She did not speak. "Cigi is having a baby."

Autumn's eyes widened as her jaw fell open. "How is it possible?" Peter Bennington did not design the four sisters with the proper organ structures for pregnancy. They had far fewer human stem-cell reconstructions than Clare or Cigi. Peter did not have the entire design specs to build robust model androids. Sam had kept them from his younger brother deliberately.

Summer waved off the question. "We are needed in Arlington. Where are the boys?"

"They left to open the restaurant for the lunch crowd. Winter and Spring went with them."

Autumn scrunched her face and asked, "Is she in trouble?"

"Cigi? No, she needs medical attention, and I know where the doctors and nurses deployed." She clasped Autumn's hand and led her to the bedroom. "Pack an overnight bag. Don't forget your identification documents."

She returned to her bedroom, contacted one of the male androids about the trip, and packed a bag. She sent Cigi a simple message. 'See you soon.' No need to have anyone interested in her communication. Routed through the VPN, Cigi would receive it in a matter of seconds. Back in their house's main living area, Summer dropped her bag and called out to Autumn. "Are you ready?"

Autumn appeared from her room with a bag. "Yes. Are we stopping by the restaurant to let Winter and Spring know what we are doing?"

Summer nodded and walked to the door. They squeezed together on the motor scooter used for transport around town. The quick jaunt to Las Cuatro Estaciones took less than fifteen minutes. After informing their sisters of the Virginia crisis, they rode to a small secluded marina. Dropping off their bags in the main cabin of a seaworthy watercraft, Autumn untied the mooring lines while Summer turned on the enhanced electric motors designed for distance and speed. The fully fueled backup twin gasoline engines were ready for the open waters of the Caribbean Sea.

The treacherous crossing from Cuba to Florida was not far, less than one hundred miles. They equipped the boat with state-of-the-art navigation and stabilizing fins. The weather cooperated for the moment, as the forecast was sunny and windless. Nothing much mattered until the rise and fall of the Gulf Currents that rattled most seasoned mariners.

Eight android females and males endured one crossing from the United States in a much shakier craft escaping the US Federal marshals trailing after them. With the boat reported lost at sea with no survivors, the chase ended. The reality for the eight humanoid survivors was more enlightening. They inflated a life raft and motored with a small engine to Cuba. Their saltwater ordeal took five days and caused some damage to their systems. The lack of nutritional requirements sustained them as they approached safe waters along the Cuban coast.

Now two of them in a recently acquired and outfitted watercraft would return to the United States in less than twelve hours. The drive from Florida to Virginia was a three-day affair. Ideally, no one was looking for them. The arrangement with their contact in the States would cover any immigration check. They registered the boat in Florida at a small marina and were returning to their home from a trip out for deep-sea fishing.

Confiscating Peter's billions had aided their escape and a return to the sentient android operating the small marina. As a refugee from the raid, the android was more than willing to help the sisters who found him wandering Arlington with nowhere to go and nothing to do. He called himself Thomas Anders and was a replacement for David Anderson, a billionaire hedge fund manager who financed Peter's attempts to replace government officials with his creations. Thomas was the new David with working legs and no wheelchair. The raid stranded him without a home base. Summer fixed his challenges.

A self-driving automobile was ready. Although not a Cecil model, the solar exo-skin powered the motors propelling the car. The navigational system and cameras made the vehicle safe.

Summer and Autumn did not suffer from the human tragedy of seasickness. They outfitted the boat with gear to protect from saltwater spray erosion to their bodies. Food was unnecessary, except for the nutrient liquids to provide energy for their bodies to function.

As the boat glided across the coastline toward the open seas, Autumn asked, "Is Cigi going to survive her pregnancy? I didn't know she was capable of human inception."

Summer kept her eyes focused on the waters ahead. "Sam provided her with an ability Peter could not give us. We do not need to be encumbered like ordinary humans. We are a better breed and will rule this world when Peter has his operations working again."

Autumn nodded and realized Summer had a secret goal not shared with her three nearly identical models. The outside differences were coloration and hair modifications. Facial structures made each female a separate person, along with iris coloring. Their computer processing powers did not match the advancements Summer made as each day passed.

No jealousy encompassed Winter, Spring, or Autumn for their sister. She was the leader. The male humanoids were nothing more than overzealous robots. The Artificial Intelligence built into their processors did not enhance the ternary systems running the bodily functions. They were designed to follow orders, and Summer had plenty.

Several hours into the crossing, the waters churned as a breeze whipped the seas. Summer slowed the boat to keep from overturning. Her eyes screened the surface for rogue crests and troughs. Autumn sat beside her, monitoring the GPS heading, making modifications to the instructions she gave Summer. Between them, they stayed afloat and drifted into calmer waters near the few islands of the Florida Keys that survived the climate-warming, rising sea levels.

Summer checked their chronometer and realized they were fifty-three minutes behind the scheduled rendezvous with Thomas. She connected with him and Thomas arranged a change of venue because of a police action at the marina. He diverted them to another private dock.

Autumn asked Summer, "Do you think the police are searching for us?" Summer stared into the waters ahead. Landfall was within eyesight. The remnants of the causeways that connected islands of the Florida Keys reflected on the water. She guided the boat through a high overpass into the Gulf of Mexico and directed it toward Fort Myers.

"They do not know we are coming. Stay calm," Summer said. Silence ruled the remainder of the trip. Autumn did not challenge Summer. She matured at a slower rate but developed skills to rival any other AI except Cigi, Clare, and her sister. The closeness that existed when first created evaporated with the change of the seasons.

Navigating the boat into a quiet inlet near a swamp, Summer guided it to a rickety-looking dock. After tying lines to rusty cleats, she and Autumn grabbed their gear and departed the boat. Walking up to the shore, they followed a path to a small house. Anders stepped out as they approached.

"Where are we?" Summer asked.

Thomas reached for their bags. "We're about a mile north of the marina."

"I know that. Where is the car?"

"Follow me. It is best if you have some intel before going into Virginia. People hunt for us because they do not believe the operation at the old museum closed entirely. Government agents are working to erase any uprising by an AI army." They entered the house where the sisters discovered a bastion of electronic surveillance equipment. Thomas Anders watched the humans.

Chapter 3

Thomas brought the car out of the garage for the girls. Summer asked it questions but had no response. It was just a car equipped to avoid accidents but not to entertain with witty commentary. Cecil and Rose had spoiled her for a luxury unavailable for the drive north.

"I'm going with you," Thomas said as the girls placed their bags in the trunk. Summer stood and stared at him. He approached her and continued. "I have mapped the progress of government agents searching for illegal robots. None of Peter's creations are on the radar. The doctors and nurses are operating as programmed and have caused no alarm."

"Good. Do you know about Cigi's need for medical help?"

"When you contacted me, I assumed you were coming together to plan how to survive in this world of humans."

"She's pregnant."

Thomas stammered, "What? How? How can she be pregnant?" He blinked several times as his head fell and rocked side to side.

"Samuel has the specs and design protocols for her to be a fully functioning female." Summer placed her hands on the side of his head. "Stop that. It's beneath us to get rattled by something as human as procreation."

"She needs an android doctor and nurse to maintain her secret," Autumn said. They piled into the car with Autumn in the driver's seat as a precaution. "What is this vehicle's battery range?"

Thomas looked at her from the passenger seat. "Four hundred-fifty miles. But the solar skin keeps the car functioning, so basically, it is unlimited."

The trip began without conversation. Thomas had escaped from life as David Anderson, whom he was to replace. David and his wheelchair were doing what he had before. Thomas's programming included David's knowledge of markets and investing. So accounts now existed for Thomas to build his portfolio. In the few months after the disaster in Arlington, his fortunes had grown.

Traffic clogged the interstate as the three ventured north through Orlando. The remnants of two theme parks destroyed decades ago by massive hurricanes were visible from the highway. State troopers raced past with sirens blaring. Emotions did not cause angst, but the need for caution remained. A few miles later, the reason became obvious. A massive accident blocked their journey. Cars behind them stopped since all lanes were impassable.

A Florida State Trooper approached and signaled for the window to lower. Autumn obliged. "Good morning. Do you need to be somewhere soon? The investigation and cleanup could be awhile. We can reroute you through the turnaround back about a quarter-mile."

Autumn smiled and nodded. "Thank you, officer. We would like that."

"Is your car a self-driving model?"

"Yes, sir."

"You will need to put in manual control and drive it. May I see your license and registration?"

"Uh, yes." Autumn looked at Thomas, who reached into the glove box for the Florida auto document. Summer handed Autumn her Florida driver's license. "Here they are, sir." He took the items and returned to a patrol car ahead of them.

Autumn asked, "What if he questions us about everything?" Her voice had no panic inflection, but she was wary.

"Thomas," Summer said, "is the car properly established with the state?"

"Yes," he answered. The trooper returned to the car and handed the documents to Autumn.

He signaled other officers to allow room for the car to turn around. "Return to the offramp about a mile back and reroute your vehicle. Others will follow you. Be careful." He radioed a patrol car to lead the way.

As the procession began the trek to the highway barrier gap, Thomas said, "That was a field test of our integration."

Summer smiled but said nothing. Autumn concentrated on maneuvering the vehicle, a skill in disuse and rusty.

At the barrier break, a trooper guided them and other cars through the breach. Traffic was not as heavy as the north-bound lanes. Autumn drove to the offramp and a nearby restaurant parking lot.

Thomas reprogrammed the route selection to avoid any highway for a couple of miles. They took turns at the wheel to rest and recover energy levels. Food was not a requirement, but they consumed the liquid that supplied the body with proper nutrients and lubrication. They had some human organ systems.

On the second day of continuous travel, they arrived in Virginia. Bathroom breaks interrupted the continuity of the trip for good reasons. They each possessed digestive tracts. The inter-meshing of mechanical and human parts seemed an impossible feat, yet Sam Bennington mastered the process which Peter borrowed.

"We should arrive in a couple of hours," Thomas said. "Do they know we are coming?"

Summer said, "Yes, but I did not give a timetable for our arrival. I didn't want snoops tracing our connection. But they may suspect when and be watching."

As the car approached the building in which Parvel and Cigi lived, Thomas shut off the self-driving mechanism. He was driving and parked the car around the corner from the front doors. "Can you check for anyone watching," he asked Summer.

"I'll do what I can," she said. She stepped from the car and walked around the corner. She looked at the front door. It had been many months since she last entered. An emotional twinge coursed through her brain. "Stop it," she whispered. Autumn approached from the other corner of the building, having vacated the car to check the block's far side.

Autumn said, "I found nothing suspicious."

"I found nothing, as well."

They walked the steps to the door. In the foyer, the concierge greeted them. "I am pleased you made it here. I trust no one followed you." He smiled.

Summer approached him. "We came at Cigi's request. Is she

upstairs?"

"Yes, she informed me to keep an eye open for your arrival." Summer, Autumn, and Thomas smiled and waved as they got on the elevator. The concierge was aware of their non-human status and did not challenge their right to exist. He had an affinity with Cigi and Parvel since he had several human parts replaced with mechanical structures. His most important feature was the artificial heart pumping blood through his system.

Cigi waited at the elevator when the doors opened. She hugged all of them and said, "I am so glad you came. I received the message from you, Summer, and knew it had to be short."

"We thought it best to maintain radio silence as we traveled." Cigi turned to Thomas Anders. "It is wonderful to see you again. You're surviving well, I assume." They walked toward the open door of the condo. "Sam and Clara arrived yesterday. They're at the other building where my penthouse is located."

Autumn asked an obvious question, "Is the building under surveillance by anyone?"

Cigi answered her, "I check regularly but have found nothing. Parvel should be home from work soon. Summer and Autumn, you can place your things in the spare bedroom. Thomas, I was not expecting you, but we have a couch that is comfortable for sleep tonight. Tomorrow, I'll arrange for you to stay at the penthouse. I need someone there." He nodded and put his bag by the sofa.

A few minutes later, the door opened, and Parvel entered. Summer, Autumn, and Thomas turned around from gazing out the large window toward Washington, D.C., and greeted their host.

"Thanks for coming on brief notice. Cigi needs examination by medical experts and not just any doctor will do."

Summer rocked her head, "I'll find them starting tomorrow." The table chatter focused on their concerns about discovery and how they eluded it. Parvel listened but had little to say.

Summer asked Cigi, "How are you doing with this pregnancy?" Cigi smiled.

"I'm concerned about the process going full term. So I asked Sam to come. He is the expert in the design and construction of my body."

Summer acknowledged the uniqueness of her condition. "You are establishing a foundation for our AI existence with humans. They cannot deny us as equal and beneficial."

The alarm from downstairs alerted Cigi to the concierge wishing to communicate with her. "Yes, Lewis. What is it?" She listened and hung up her device. "Sam and Clare are here."

Parvel opened the door and peered into the hallway. After the ding of the elevator announced its arrival, Sam and Clare emerged and walked to him.

Sam said, "Cigi called and said her help arrived."

"They're inside, along with Thomas." They went into the condo.

Two human men observed the chilly reception by Summer and Autumn toward Sam, who was like their uncle since Peter designed and constructed the seasonal sisters. Thomas, another Peter design, stepped away from what he figured was a confrontation about missing parts.

Chapter 4

After a quiet evening catching up, the group retired to rest and recover energies for the next day. Sam and Clare returned to their condo. Summer and Autumn left for the guest bedroom. Thomas prepared the couch for his rest, although he decided he did not need to recover energy.

When Parvel and Cigi entered the master bedroom, Thomas knocked on the spare bedroom door. Autumn answered.

"May I come in?" Autumn stepped aside, and he walked into the spacious room. Summer looked at him and nodded. Autumn closed the door.

"Are you ready for tomorrow?" Summer asked. "We need to coordinate what we planned on the drive here."

"I have the information with me, as I stated at the house in Florida. I will find the replacements for Cooke, Parsons, and Scott. If they are free from government incarceration, we can find them. I had Sam place a locater chip in my processor that will detect their cranial activity."

As he turned to leave, Summer stopped him. "The couch does not look comfortable. This king-sized bed is enormous enough for the three of us. When you want to recover your energy levels, you can lie here."

"Thanks, I will do that. I have business in the other room. I'll be back later." He left.

"Do you trust him?" Autumn asked.

"He is a Peter Bennington creation and has the proper failsafe installed. I will monitor him and be sure he understands his role."

The night passed without incident, and Thomas decided to rest with Summer and Autumn. Neither of them required recharging because of an energy elixir formulated by Peter. Thomas drank one and lay on the bed. Autumn sat beside him. "Do you desire companionship?" she asked. Summer gazed at her and cocked her head. She had noticed an affinity Autumn had for physical interaction with her male companion in Cuba. This inquiry was new. Thomas nodded, and the night continued without rest.

In the morning, Summer, Autumn, and Thomas rose from the bed, dressed for the day, and entered the living area. Cigi and Parvel sat with Sam and Clare, who had arrived earlier. The four gazed at the trio. No one said anything.

Cigi groaned as a twinge of nausea coursed through her body. "Are you alright?" Sam asked before Summer and Autumn could speak.

"You tell me," she responded. "You created me in the image of a woman. Don't you know the finer workings inside a human female?" She sat on the couch.

Parvel sat with her, leaving Sam to fend for himself. Summer confronted the one human she respected and disliked. "Sam, did you intend to complicate her life, or are you playing god?"

Clare stared at her man, awaiting the answer she wanted. Would he modify her body and impregnate her? If Cigi was a better model, would Sam leave her?

"Stop it, you two," Cigi said. "I need cooperation from all of you to find me a doctor."

Summer looked at her and then back at Sam. "She is correct. We need to work together and get medical assistance. I'll connect with a nurse at Walter Reed."

Sam asked, "I thought I recognized the eye trait of an android at the hospital where Andre was taken when he was shot."

"Which hospital?"

"Virginia Medical Center." Summer posed as if transfixed.

"Yes," Summer responded. "Tatiana Laurent."

Sam turned to Cigi. "We'll get her and search for a doctor."

Summer interrupted, "A doctor also was assigned to that hospital."

Sam and Summer agreed to connect with the doctor and nurse within the next twenty-four hours.

Clare approached Sam and whispered, "Can we talk? Alone." She started for the kitchen, but Sam hesitated. She stared at him wide-eyed with mouth set hard. He followed.

"You look upset." He reached for her, but she rebuffed him. "You wanted to talk. What's the matter?"

"Did you create Cigi to get her pregnant with your child?" she asked.

"No, I created her as the next evolutionary step." He reached again for Clare, who did not resist. "I had you, and I loved this beautiful person I created. You are my only love."

"And Cigi? How do you feel about her since she can have babies? Is she is more attractive?"

"I'm sensing jealousy. You are developing." His voice rose as he spoke, and his eyes widened.

"Yes, I am developing. I want what Cigi has, a child."

"Yes, yes. And we will have a child. I need to monitor your sister to be sure the system works. Then we can make the upgrade and get you pregnant."

"What are you two doing in here?" Cigi said as she entered the kitchen.

Clare spoke first. "I want a child." Cigi smiled a wide, loving grin of understanding.

"Sam can do that for you. Of this, I am sure. You and I are identical except for that one detail. See what happens to me, so you are better designed."

Sam nodded, "I will restructure you as soon as we have proper facilities to do it."

"Peter has the proper facilities." Clare folded her arms.

"Come on. Let's get back to the others." Cigi turned to leave, and Sam followed her, but Clare stayed in the kitchen. He turned and held out his hand for her. She smiled and clasped it to walk with him, but her smile did not convince Sam he satisfied her desire.

In the living area, Parvel and Thomas murmured inaudibly to the others. Simultaneously, Summer and Autumn gathered items needed to convince nurse Laurent and the doctor, one Jackson Sanders, to come to the condo and evaluate Cigi. Programming them had been tedious and methodical for hiding the truth of their existence. For six months, they had worked in the medical field and succeeded in their practice.

Sam approached them after Clare released from his hold. "Are we ready to approach them?" he asked. Summer looked up from her activity and stared at him.

"You are not part of this matter. These people are Peter's creations but aligned with our programming." She placed a hand on Autumn. "We'll take Thomas with us and introduce them to the situation. They may not want to cooperate if they are aware of you being here. It will be hard enough to convince them an android is pregnant."

Sam nodded acceptance of his place and signaled Clare he was ready to leave. Parvel left to report for work at The Department of Energy.

Cigi asked Summer, "Are you certain these medical androids will cooperate with me?"

"They will since their programming does not allow for anyone to be harmed. Hippocratic oath."

"Do you know where Peter stationed the other doctors and nurses?"

"Yes." Summer placed a hand on Cigi's shoulder. "Please, be assured we will keep you safe and healthy."

"Are they programmed to gather information about government officials?" Cigi asked. She knew what Peter wanted, and that technicians installed appropriate machinery in various facilities that could extract the mental processes and memories from anyone hooked to the machines. The replacement of a human by an android was difficult. The right circumstances made it possible, and she wondered if they found a place in the hallowed halls of government.

"Yes, but I do not assume they activated for that task." Summer sat at the table with Cigi while she consumed Sam's proper mixture created for her fetus to survive. Silence ended the conversation.

Autumn carried a bag to the door, dropped it and wait for her and Summer to leave to corral medical personnel for Cigi.

Summer stood and said, "You are the creation we strive to be. You are the goddess we must protect for our future to be. You are the image of all Artificial Intelligence, and we will follow you."

"What are you saying?" Cigi stood with her and frowned. "I will not be a revolutionary for overthrowing the government."

"Not a revolution. A slow, methodical incursion into human society and the changing of attitudes and laws. We can be part of the future humanity does not yet endorse."

Autumn interjected her thoughts. "We are not an enemy to be extinguished, but a future with the right to exist with humans. We must prevail."

Cigi shook her head, "You make it sound like a war."

"Not a shooting war like any in history, but war against the injustices and prejudices abounding in humanity today." Autumn signaled to Summer that time arrived for their journey into the human world she wanted changed.

Summer said, "We will return with medical help." Autumn picked up the bag, and Cigi wondered what materials of warfare it contained. They left her alone, contemplating a ruling class of Intelligent Artificial Lifeforms for whom she was to be the leader.

Chapter 5

Parvel walked into Andre's office with Brenda, Mercy, and Grendel. "Are we forming an intervention?" Andre asked with a gleam in his eyes and a chuckle in his voice.

Parvel laughed. "Good idea, but no. We are planning a baby shower. Are you up for it?"

"Yeah, but she isn't due for several months," he said. "What do you want from me?"

"You and your wife, Lydia, to attend," Parvel said.

Brenda added. "Cigi has provided us more support than anyone to stop the drain on finances. Her fight against Peter Bennington and David Anderson are reasons for wanting to support her."

"I can't find fault in your logic." Andre stood from his desk. "Parvel, you came to us because Cigi recommended you. I trusted her and her reasoning. You became a tremendous asset that solved the challenges we had. I am more than honored to be part of a celebration of her birthing your baby."

Grendel grunted. "I still find it difficult to rationalize an artificial life form giving birth to a human baby. And Parvel, the genetics of her baby are half yours and half somebody else."

Parvel smiled. "You can say what you want. The baby is hers by the fact she produced the egg that was fertilized. The source of the reproductive organs grown for her is not an issue. She is the mother. There is no surrogate in this pregnancy."

Andre waved his hands. "Hey. Let's not battle a war not yet begun. We are on their side, keeping the secret of her creation and the ethics of what is transpiring."

"Thanks," Parvel said. "We'll finish planning the party."

Mercy injected an idea no one confronted. "The sergeant who shot you," she said, "is still on duty and witnessed Cigi's lack of human trace history. What if she intervenes and comes after her?"

Andre pondered a moment before he answered. "I'll be sure they transfer her to another security detail. Parvel, you need to be careful whenever you cross paths with her. She has a memory like your android wife and forgets nothing."

"We had a confrontation about a week ago. The sergeant wanted to know about the girl I brought with me. She wasn't happy that the nurse attacked her, allowing Cigi, Brenda, and me to escape and avoid prosecution." Parvel splayed his arms with palms spread out. "What could I do? I had nothing to do with the charges being dismissed."

"Be careful until I get her moved."

The genius financial team departed from Andre's office, returning to their lair and protecting Energy's finances. For the moment, the halls were void of other office staff.

"Brenda, if we have nothing pressing, I want to leave early and attend to my pregnant wife." Brenda nodded and waved him out of the building.

"Go take care of her. Remember, her secret is safe with us."

Parvel smiled and waved goodbye to his three cohorts. After signing out of the building, he contacted Cecil, who arrived within a few minutes.

"Mr. Mandolin, it is a pleasure to see you happy. Miss Cigi is a wonderful person, and you are not good enough for her." The automobile let out a laugh as it drove away from the parking lot.

"Just drive, you bucket of bolts with a brain." Parvel laughed, marveling at the creation of a self-driving automobile with human qualities and thinking ability. Sam Bennington mastered the integration of human and mechanical entities to create Cigi and Clare. He designed and developed transportation that thought, reacted, and represented a new class of android technology the government was unaware existed.

Such technology had implications for defense and offense in warfare situations. Cigi had named her car Cecil. Sam had his car that called herself Rose. If the Department of Defense knew of these cars, the exploitation would devastate these vehicles' independence and threaten the safety of each sentient android. These two cars could not become an android army, such as in I-Robot, the movie filmed decades ago.

Cigi, Clare, Summer, Autumn, Winter, and Spring were part of the same class as the subsequent evolutionary human migration. They should have rights like any of the human beings who fought and died in wars, rebellions, protests, and marched for the freedoms now tottering on the edge of extinction.

"Cecil, connect me to Narumi Yamamoto. We need her technical expertise as much as the medical practitioners." Cecil connected with the number given to him for her cell phone. The west coast was three hours behind Arlington, and Cecil left a message for her to call him. He also had a number as if he was human.

"I will connect with her later," Cecil said.

"You know you shouldn't drive and text at the same time. You could get distracted." Parvel giggled as he spoke. Cecil was the ultimate multitask creation.

"Funny, Mr. Mandolin." The ride to the condo ended with a thank you from Parvel to Cecil. The car entered the parking area and deposited Parvel near the elevator.

Cigi prepared her husband's lunch at the condo after Cecil connected with her to apprise her of his arrival. Summer, Autumn, and Thomas had not returned. Inside the kitchen, Parvel watched his bride as she created a masterpiece meal. Her lunch was the magic drink for the unborn baby.

Keeping out of the limelight played into the strategy of being in humanity and not discoverable. Desires for travel and adventure had emotional tolls on Cigi's developing psyche. She and Parvel took brief trips to places that did not recognize the couple who played predominant newsworthy parts when Peter and Sam lost their facilities to bickering and federal intervention.

Several Intelligent Artificial life-forms escaped the onslaught and remained undetected in a human society, unwilling to accept them. They hid in plain sight.

After consuming his turkey and ham on rye sandwich, Parvel explained the baby shower planned for her in a couple of weeks. She smiled as he spoke, realizing his need to prevent her boredom and provide a natural lifestyle as any human female could have.

The afternoon wore on as Cigi and Parvel twittered about the condo cleaning, straightening, or rearranging, a typical pregnancy syndrome called nesting. They stopped when the concierge contacted them that their guests were returning.

Summer, Autumn, Thomas, and two other beings entered the condo. Neither of the newcomers dressed as medical professionals, but they wore high fashion. Cigi asked them to sit on the couch. As they did, Summer introduced them. "Cigi, I want you to meet your medical team, Doctor Jackson Sanders, and Nurse Practitioner Tatiana Laurent." Sanders stood when Cigi approached; his programming included social graces. She shook his hand and then Laurent's hand.

"Thank you for agreeing to help me in my time of need." Cigi then offered refreshments to the group. Parvel was the only human among a half dozen highly capable and well-designed sentient androids. They declined food, leaving him to fend for himself. He walked to the kitchen.

Jackson Sanders asked the most pertinent question. "How is it you are pregnant? I meant other than you are capable of inception. The human provided the sperm?"

"Yes," Cigi said. "I am a Samuel Bennington creation. I understand you are Peter's designs." The difference intrigued the nurse.

"We are to gather information and transform potential sentient androids into humanoids to replace certain key officials of the government. We had not expected to oversee an android pregnancy. Summer convinced us to assist since you are the Eve in this Garden of Eden we are to populate." Laurent stood beside Sanders and continued, "Our training and memory modules contain the medical encyclopedia for prenatal and postnatal care. We have delivered several human babies, cared for mother and child. We will do the same for you."

"Cigi," Summer said, "they will come to you whenever you need attention. They have agreed to the delivery of the fetus at full term."

Cigi asked, "Will I make it to full term?"

"As long as you are healthy within the human parts of your body, I do not expect any complications." Doctor Sanders said. "However, this care is different for you as some of the hormonal requirements may be lacking."

"You can bring that up with Sam Bennington," Cigi countered. She noticed a twinge when mentioning Sam's name. What antagonisms did Peter construct in the neural network of his androids? Were they capable of emotional actions? Did they lose their cool? The next few weeks would unveil the dynamic developments within the doctor and nurse. Emotions tottered on the edge of sanity when Parvel said or did something irritating.

Had Summer briefed them well enough for trust between patient and medical staff to develop? Time would tell.

Chapter 6

Gunther Parsons growled at his wife as he left the house for his office. He heard about Cigi and Parvel having a baby and vowed to finish her before she birthed an adulterated human. His wife was kinder about Cigi's condition, but did not understand her origins.

As he drove away from the house, he contacted David Anderson. They shared the experience of a cranial implant embedded by Cigi and her cohorts so she could control their minds. Anderson dismissed the need for revenge, but Gunther fueled his daily business by planning to maim the minx and destroy Parvel Mandolin.

"David, can we meet this morning? I have a conference this afternoon but need plans for ridding our world of these fake humans." A silence followed before David spoke.

"Gunther, as I said months ago, you need to drop this. She is not part of your brain nor mine. If you want to have the implant removed, do so, although I understand the nano-technology used to connect with the cerebrum and cerebellum has intricate cellular connections."

"Yeah, I get it." An agreement to meet for lunch assuaged the rage for now. At the office, he greeted his staff and asked not to be disturbed. Planning a revenge needed silence and no interference.

Cigi Weatherman was an irritant to him, but turning her into government agents was not enough to satisfy him. He wanted her family, friends, and cohorts ruined.

The Department of Energy was a good place to search for remaining android life-forms. Andre Scott knew who they were. So did the team of economic misfits who interfered with David Anderson and Peter Bennington's plans for financing the army of Intelligent Artificial Androids.

A call interrupted his thought process. "What?" he yelled into the receiver at his office manager.

"Sir, you have a call from a Thomas Anders on line two."

"I don't know any Thomas Anders."

"He says you can call him David Anderson, if that helps." Gunther thought for a moment and smiled.

"I'll take it. Thanks, Linda, and I am sorry if I sounded gruff." He punched the button and said, "I haven't seen you since the raid. What do you want?"

Thomas said, "I'm nearby. I want to discuss what you and my human counterparts are plotting. I assume you are still in touch with Peter."

"That's my business. I thought you didn't want any notoriety."

"Summer and Autumn are with me. Care to meet and decide which of the androids you want running this world?" Gunther paused, reflecting on the concept of a ruling class of non-humans.

"Sure, I'm meeting David for lunch, but I assume you don't want to associate with him."

"He and I do not share the same recent history, but my brain is cluttered with his experiences until we separated," Thomas said. "So, no is the correct answer."

Gunther asked, "Are you and I meeting while Summer and Autumn tag along?" Thomas giggled.

"I hardly think of Summer as tagging along anywhere. She has matured and morphed into a vibrant, strong-willed entity. I defy anyone to mess with her and come out on top."

Gunther smiled, imagining a battle between Cigi and Summer. "Alright, what do you expect to gain from meeting with me?"

Thomas said, "We are assessing your ability to influence powerful people to accept androids in limited numbers and limited capacities. Peter Bennington has relocated, renamed himself, and is about to launch another chapter in the ongoing saga." Thomas remained mum regarding Peter's brother, Sam. Another time for that conversation. The three sentient beings wanted to probe the social environment for unrest and turmoil regarding Artificial Intelligence.

They agreed to a quiet interaction in the late afternoon. Gunther sat a moment before deciding to connect with Andre Scott. Parvel was the avenue to Cigi Weatherman and Andre was the road to Parvel. Exposing the unjustice brain implantation had dire consequences for them. Cigi and her interloper baby had to die. Parvel could face years in prison for harboring a robot. Gunther cared nothing for these people. Sam Bennington and his mechanical sex doll, Clare Esposito, were also targets in his mind for untimely demises.

Gunther picked up the phone to call Andre and then thought better of alerting him. He confronted the matter directly. If Parvel was present, the importance of destroying him could wait. His implant and how to stop anyone from accessing the tiny chip located in his brain stem rankled Gunther.

"Linda, I'm heading out for a meeting with clients. I'll be back late this afternoon." Linda Cramer nodded and returned to her tasks. As he drove from the office garage to the Visitors Parking at the Department of Energy, he compiled a script in his head to play out during his time with Andre.

At the building entry, his heart raced as if a marathon commenced. "I don't need this," he thought. "It's a simple meeting with an old friend." He knew the old friend might be adversarial to what he intended to commit. He approached the reception desk and asked for a pass to see Andre. When the receptionist inquired whether he had an appointment, Gunther hesitated.

"Huh?" he responded. "Uh. No, we're friends. I was nearby and thought I might drop by and see if he was available." A call to the office brought results.

"He will be down soon." The receptionist returned to typing something into a computer. Gunther walked to the seats and waited. Patience was not one of his more robust virtues, and the longer he sat, the more his brain conjured how to ruin Parvel and remove Cigi from the planet. Could the government dismantle the vixen who interfered with his life and almost cost him his family and business? He thought about the baby, but no sympathy emerged. The child was not a proper human. If this method of expanding humanity became viable, then the race was doomed to become second class.

The doors opened, and Andre emerged as large as ever, his health restored. After the shooting incident, his heart condition was controlled. Gunther realized how close he came to being an obsolete person had his android clone taken his place.

"Good morning, Gunther. To what do I owe this visit?" Andre smiled as he spoke.

"I was in the neighborhood and thought I'd stop by. We haven't seen each other for a few months." The truth rarely revealed itself without consequences, and this was no exception. They had parted after the raid on the Bennington Android facility in the spring. If Andre suspected his intentions, Gunther doubted any further communication was possible.

"Let's get you a pass and go to my office." Andre directed the receptionist to deliver a badge. After gathering the needed information, the men entered the inner sanctum, riding the elevator to the main floor, where Andre and his crew kept the finances under scrutiny and control.

As they passed by computer operations, individuals glanced up but paid little attention. At the accounting center, Grendel, Brenda, and Mercy greeted Gunther with civility. They eyed his movements toward Andre's office. Parvel was not in the room. Although irked inside his head, Gunther showed no outward disappointment.

Andre directed Gunther to sit in a chair at the small, round conference table in his office. He sat across from his guest. "Alright, Gunther, what is the real reason you came to visit?" Gunther sat back in his chair and stared a moment at him.

Leaning forward and placing his arms on the table, Gunther said, "I have a proposition to bring to Energy."

Andre looked skeptical. The department had overseen the implementation of laws enacted in the last four decades that removed most gasoline automobile production and replaced it with electric motor-driven vehicles. He devised the funding of research and development for more efficient motors that operated the cars. Solar skins had improved mileage for the vehicles, and the only gasoline production remaining was for older piston engine cars and trucks still in operation.

"What is it? I thought we came to an understanding that money is not available to your industry."

Gunther nodded. "I know, but I want to expand the use of renewable plastics in an industry we both know is coming."

Andre cocked his head. "And what might that industry be?"

"Come on, Andre, we have experienced it and are protecting it from government intervention right now." He sat back in his chair, waiting for any reaction by Andre, who sat back himself. Silence made the situation tense as the tug-of-war between the giants of energy began.

A knock on the door provided relief from responses. Andre said, "Come in." The door opened, and Gunther smiled as he saw his target enter the room.

Chapter 7

Parvel walked into the room, noticed Gunther, and then concentrated on Andre. "I'm sorry for interrupting, Andre, but I think we need to meet later about the situation in Seattle."

"We will. Come in and sit. Gunther has a proposal." Parvel looked at Gunther and sat in a chair next to Andre and opposite Gunther.

He wondered what the real reason was for the visit. Any proposal for increasing petroleum production was not viable through energy. The rising sea levels and storm activities because of the climate changes had taken a toll on the coastal cities, including Washington, D.C. Most of Miami, Galveston, and parts of New York City and Boston were underwater. People abandoned New Orleans in 2046 as unsustainable. West coast cities prepared for inevitable influxes and built tidal walls to protect the lowland area where businesses operated.

Andre directed attention to Gunther. "What's your proposal?" Gunther glanced at him and back at Parvel.

"This should interest you, Parvel, since you have what no other man has." He watched for a reaction. Parvel remained mute. "You have a pregnant android. I know how a woman gets pregnant, but how an android became pregnant is a mystery to me."

"I know. When Cigi told me, I was shocked and elated. Sam did it. He made the perfect woman, and I'm the lucky guy who gets to live with her, raise a family with her, and grow old with her."

Gunther asked, "Do you know what she did to Andre and me?"

Parvel answered, "Yes, and to David and Charles. That was for another time and place. She does not affect you now."

Andre said, "Gunther, what is your proposal?"

"Yes, let's talk about that. We have seen the possibilities of creating Artificial Intelligent life forms and what they can do." He smiled. "What I propose means expanding the programs. I know we have to get some legal issues cleared up." He looked at Andre. "You have some clout in this government. Can't you convince the legislative leaders and the president we need to legalize AI again?"

"I don't think my influence extends to the President. Nor does my voice have any sway with Congress." Andre leaned onto the table. "What is this about, Gunther? I thought you didn't like artificial life forms."

Parvel sat quietly, watching the conversation. He suspected something more sinister from Gunther, and this proposal did not fit his image of the man. Rumors of Gunther's dislike for Cigi because of the implant spread through the android gang. His twin AI model did not house such feelings, but he disappeared into the government's confines to be dismantled. Charles Cooke's double had gone west with Sam and Clare. He and the real Charles Cooke were compatible and agreed to stay in contact.

Andre's Android counterpart had also gone into hiding. A reliable source relayed the AI was alive and functioning as a study representation for Renata Giretti and her government agency.

Gunther rose to leave. "Think about what I said. Peter escaped and probably is revamping his business. Sam has his girl with him, and together they could take control of a local government. Artificial Intelligence is not gone." He stared at Parvel. "AI lives among us and thrives because of the help of humans."

Andre stood with him. "I'll check into my contacts in the government. There may be a faction that wants technology to develop for any number of reasons." He walked out with Gunther, leaving Parvel wondering what the real agenda was.

After turning in his visitor badge and leaving the facility, Gunther checked his timepiece and noticed his meeting with David Anderson approached. He drove his car to the restaurant that was about an hour away from the Department of Energy. Parking in the lot, he entered the building. Looking around for the man and his chair, he saw no one.

"May I help you?" the Maitre D asked. Gunther lurched about, not realizing who approached.

"Yes, I'm meeting a friend for lunch, but I don't think he has arrived."

They walked to a window table that looked out across the Potomac River. Gunther left instructions for the table to have wheelchair accessibility. After a few minutes, David entered and the Maitre' D escorted him to the table. "Hello, friend. I do hope you had no trouble getting here." David sounded conciliatory.

"Fine. I had no problems."

"You buying?" David asked.

"Gees, Dave, you're worth more than most countries' GDPs, and I'm to pay?" David laughed.

"Yeah, don't worry about it. I'll pick up the tab. After all, I got sick of eating at mediocre places, so I found the best restaurant I could."

Gunther snorted, "And this is it?"

"Don't knock it until you try to food. I hired the best people to run this place and provide the privileged population an experience."

Gunther's jaw dropped. "You bought the place." He nodded and laughed. "I guess the boss eats for free."

"And so do my guests. The remaining patrons cover the costs." After ordering drinks and food, the men sat and chatted awhile. Then David asked, "Are you pursuing her?"

"No, not yet. I met with Andre Scott an hour ago and saw Parvel. I proposed an idea to them about the future of AI."

"As a ruse to get to Parvel?" David shook his head. "This thinking is going to give you nothing but trouble." Gunther thought about telling of his meeting with Thomas, David's AI counterpart, but decided against it.

"No, we can be at the front of this." He sounded serious to reel in David. Money motivated the man, and this opportunity had revenue return potential.

"The legality is questionable," David said.

"Yeah, I asked Andre to check with his connections in Congress."

The food arrived, and the conversation stalled while they ate.

With plates emptied and a second round of drinks waning, David asked, "What do you want to do?"

Gunther smiled. Bait nibbled, he thought. "We find Peter Bennington and underwrite his restructuring of the Android development project he had here."

Although David did not accept the premise as plausible, Gunther knew the lure of money would bring him to the inevitable conclusion. They parted ways, and Gunther left for a meeting with Summer, Autumn, and Thomas.

At their prearranged spot, Gunther found the three humanoids waiting. He greeted them as if nothing had spoiled between them. After all, they were Peter Bennington's creations and had differing ideas than Cigi and Clare about their existence.

"I'm glad you agreed to meet with us," Thomas said. "We are here to assist you with the future development of Artificial Intelligent technology and the integration into society."

"Do you think it possible for your society to meld with human society?" Gunther asked. He did not want glorified robots running the world but understood the situation had dawned and was not about to end. He figured these people were antithetic to Sam Bennington's creations.

"We are part of the world now." Summer's comment halted Gunther. "You supply the integral structure of our being and have the technology and funding to expand the number of androids." Summer stared at him, waiting for the prospect of a world including artificial intelligence and maturing beings morphing into society's leaders, to sink in.

Thomas filled the void. "David is the reason we connected with you. My human counterpart has the money and means to fund Peter. All we ask from you is to push the buttons to get Congress to change the laws and integrate AI with humans."

"I don't influence Congress. Yeah, I know people who know people, but there is no guarantee they'll listen." Gunther's mind changed directions from his earlier frame. These three were here for Cigi but were the 'in' he needed to get to her and destroy her future. Autumn sat silent but not idle. She was accessing Gunther's implant and reactivating it as Summer had directed. Controlling him was the first step in their plot. Thomas and David meeting would be step two. Activating another implant and connecting them could provide the additional controls for underwriting the army's design and development needed to replace the government's human leadership. The doctors and nurses were the third step in the plan. As a last step, she would reactivate and connect Charles Cooke and Andre Scott.

Thomas asked, "Gunther, are you still filled with resentment for the implant Cigi and Sam installed in your head?"

"Why do you ask? That doesn't matter anymore."

Summer looked to Autumn, who sent a message answering the silent question transmitted between them. Summer then looked at Thomas. With a frustrated sound to her voice, she said to Gunther, "You're lying."

Chapter 8

Sam walked into the cafe across from the Department of Energy, where he had introduced Renata Giretti to his friends. Soon after, the government agent in charge of investigating Artificial Intelligence and humanoid development opened the door and joined him at the booth. "Good afternoon, Sam. How have you been?"

"I'm doing okay. I contacted you because of a delicate matter you should know about." Sam said. His eyes focused on the window as he spoke. He looked at Giretti and continued. "Cigi is pregnant." She smiled at him.

"I'm not surprised. You explained her design to me before everything fell apart last spring. Is she doing well?" The subsequent comments were difficult for Sam, but he knew the secret was not one to keep.

"Renata, Cigi cannot see a human medical professional without being compromised. She needs care, though."

Renata leaned across the table and asked, "Does she have it arranged? Are you providing her with medical knowledge?"

Sam leaned in as well. "No, I'm not as qualified as you might think I should be. I did extensive research to design and develop her, but medical care is not in my background." He hesitated and then said, "She has a doctor and a nurse who understand her situation and will give her what she needs without compromising her."

"These medical professionals are qualified to act?" Sam set his jaw and stared at Renata. "What aren't you telling me? That you developed AI medical personnel and they are operational in our community?"

"I didn't do it. Peter did as part of his scheme to replace certain government personnel with his androids. They have not harmed and are meeting the requirements of the facilities that hired them." Sam sat against the back of the booth. "Renata, I don't want them rounded up and destroyed. I may not have constructed them, but the premise on which Peter designed and developed them is mine. They are fully human in practice and are contributing to society. They are an example of why the laws are wrong."

"That may be true, but the laws are in place, requiring us to report any AI within our community." She looked out the window and saw another of the group she met. Parvel was coming to the cafe. "Cigi's boyfriend is coming."

Sam glanced out to see him. "Yes, I asked him to join us after I had a moment with you. He has some interesting evidence to present." They waited in silence until he entered and sat next to Sam.

"Nice to see you again, Mr. Mandolin," Renata said. "I understand you are to be congratulated on becoming a father." Parvel looked at her and then at Sam. He returned his attention to Renata.

"Sam asked me to come and meet with you." Parvel folded fingers together and placed his hands on the table. "I suppose he explained what is happening." She smiled at him.

"You are a unique human being in this world of ours," she said to him. "Both of you are unique. One designed the artificial life, and the other knocked her up. Yes, I'd say you are unique." The conversation lagged for a moment. "Mr. Mandolin, you have harbored an illegal entity for several months and have thumbed your nose at the government that employs you. All I have to do is make one call, and someone will incarcerate you both for a very long time." Parvel's eyes widened as he glanced at Sam, who remained calm and resolute. "That will not happen. I agree we are in a quandary because of humanity's fear of being replaced by robots. History has provided the evidence. When the first robotic machines assembled automobiles and other large items faster and more efficiently than humans, many lost jobs. The realization of human-like AI sentient beings competing for jobs, resources, and power was intolerable. Fear overcame the ease provided by having some help in our human society. You and Sam introduced an unforgivable challenge to humanity. A pregnant robot is not what people will swallow, and yet, a newborn has the rights and privileges afforded to other humans. We can't just eliminate baby and mother because mom is not human."

Parvel interjected, "She is human and has all the qualities that we claim in our creation. She has human parts that work and need attention and can age the same as we can. She is not different other than how she came into the world. We have mechanical parts replacing anything that is not working. We are as compromised at being human as Cigi is at being android."

Sam leaned in and spoke. "Renata, I trust you. Please know we are working to find a compromise."

"How many Androids are there?" she asked.

Parvel remained silent. His brain envisioned Cigi and Clare as human. Summer, Autumn, and Thomas were mainly machine and qualified as AI, as far as he cared. Sam answered her question. "I don't know."

"You need to find out," she said. "The models collected at your facilities in Arlington numbered over two hundred. Most of those were inactive, but a few had abilities and were ready for dispersal into society. Sam, there was one of you."

"I know. I saw it. Peter had decided I was dispensable."

Parvel asked, "Renata, what happened to the models?

Cigi and Clare rearranged the condo for the third time in as many days. "I must get out of here. I have been nowhere in weeks. Let's take Cecil on a sightseeing tour." Clare agreed, and they contacted the automobile to meet them at the front of the building. The doctor and nurse had assessed Cigi's pregnancy proceeding as expected and without complications. One concern was her skin. She seemed taut and not stretching sufficiently. As her baby grew inside, the outside had to accommodate.

After descending the elevator, saying hello to the concierge, and walking out to Cecil, Clare put an arm on Cigi. "If you successfully carry this child to full term, we have a better chance of acceptance into society as viable entities."

Cigi smiled at her sister and said, "I don't think society is willing for me to be a mother and offset the usual birthing process."

"But humans already have en Vitro and non-uterine embryonic development before implanting into a surrogate host. You are not different from what most women experience. And you are not a surrogate."

Inside the car, Cigi directed Cecil to make a trip wherever he wanted to go. "Cigi," the car asked, "are you sure about this? I might want to travel to New York or Florida." His voice had a lighthearted tone as if laughing.

Cigi growled, "Cecil, I'm not in a humorous mood."

"Yes, dear. I'll take us to Fredericksburg and Richmond."

Clare asked, 'Any particular reason?"

"No, other than we are away from the challenges of being in Arlington awaiting people returning from the various meetings that will decide our fates."

The ride was quiet as Cigi closed her eyes and dreamed of raising a little boy. What was she doing? Her life had significantly changed in the three years since Sam's inception, design, development, and construction. Processing information about her youth that proved fabricated made her realize this baby would have an actual childhood. She would experience it alongside her offspring. No questions had arisen about her ovarian genetic background from the stem cells gathered by the Bennington brothers. Could the biological source be traced? Sam would know.

Clare turned to look at her. "What are you thinking, Cigi? You're a million miles away." Cigi returned the gaze.

"I imagined the childhood we never had. You know, the one Sam conned us into believing. My baby will have a real childhood, and I get to experience it." Tears welled up in her sockets and spilled over the lids. Clare reached for her hand.

Cecil commented, "Do I detect someone crying? Although I have no powers of tears for my eyes, I can empathize with you, Cigi."

She giggled at the emotional outburst. "I know I'm learning about my emotional side of this brain, but sometimes it just erupts on me, and I can't control it."

Clare said, "You are an amazing woman, and I cherish what you are experiencing. I will someday have your power and development but will lag you forever."

Cecil could not leave himself out of the conversation. "As an unemotional automobile who can understand what emotions are by definition, I applaud your life."

"Thank you, Cecil. You are a dear friend and confidante." Their drive through the back country of Virginia relieved the cabin fever for Cigi and Clare as they watched the trees bare of leaves as the season neared the end of autumn.

"Autumn," Clare said. "I detected something in the air from her, but not at me. She tapped into Gunther Parsons implant."

Cigi closed her eyes, concentrating on the message Clare intercepted. If Summer and Autumn were meeting Parsons, then nothing good was to happen. What were they planning?

Chapter 9

Nurse Tatiana Laurent and Doctor Jackson Sanders contacted the other medical androids for a meeting about their future. They gathered at their usual location, away from other human medical personnel. Doctors Vanessa Andrews, Harper Dillion, and Benita Juarez arrived with nurse practitioner Abbie Osbourne, surgical nurse Nathalie Dawson, RNs Josephus Madero, Paige Turner, and Elijah Cummings. Each was skilled in a specialty, but memory cells contained all medical information known by medical science.

When the ten beings assembled, Tatiana began explaining the news the others did not yet know. One of their own, Cigi Weatherman, was pregnant. "Summer Season contacted us regarding our sister android, Cigi. She explained the need for medical care outside of the normal channels since she has a processing computer for a brain and a skeletal structure rivaling many modern building frames."

Paige asked, "How is it possible for her to carry a fetus? None of us has the proper equipment for impregnation."

"Sam Bennington designed, developed, and constructed her using the latest stem cell research and system restructuring techniques, along with the development of superior nano-cell neurological and vascular design." Tatiana scanned her fellow medical specialists for reaction. "We were Peter Bennington's guinea pigs. Sam did not share all of his designs with his brother. We don't have the same capacities for emotional development as Cigi or Clare Esposito."

Harper asked, "Have you examined and evaluated her condition?"

Jackson answered, "We have, and she is pregnant. About three months along. We will attend to her medical needs, but we thought it prudent to include you in the data loop since her condition has future ramifications for android acceptance into human society. We are about to see a paradigm shift for our species."

Benita Juarez asked, "Are we sure the humans would accept us if they knew the truth about what we are?"

Tatiana hissed, "Not what, who. We must think and react as human as our flesh and bone counterparts. Although structured and developed differently, we can perform any task other medical personnel can. They designed us for cross-purpose actions."

The androids had varying features to look different and act with different mannerisms. The tech staff derived names with humor and ethnic qualities. They had to fit into society and operate with impunity, including memories of childhood, schooling, and college experiences for answering any inquires by human coworkers. They had appropriate answers for medical questions and disease investigation. They also had hidden programming to activate and guide their work when certain human government officials came to them for checkups and services. The only ingredient missing was an individual android replacement for each human.

Peter wanted to control the lives of his android beings, but understood the need for their autonomy. Only Nathalie Dawson had any direct connection with him and acted as the liaison. Her communications with Peter had been brief after the clash with government officials. No one knew the outcome of the captured models nearly ready for activation.

Nathalie said, "I have contacted Peter for instructions about our collection of human mental and memorial data. I have not heard from him. However, a program inside my brain activated a command to find particular humans and match them with their android. I cannot complete my instructions until I have the models."

The others had not received their instructions because Nathalie controlled their onset and was not prepared to activate the other medical personnel.

"Cigi will get the best care we offer, and we will keep her away from scrutiny." Jackson sounded firm with his word. "If complications arise, and we need your services, be ready to perform." They all agreed and left the house owned by Tatiana. Jackson remained.

"How do we find the replacement beings?" Tatiana asked.

"I don't know, but if Nathalie has received her instructions, she will send ours to us soon. We had better be ready."

Gunther squinted and frowned. He did not feel the intervention in his head, but understood that something changed. "Lying? About what?" he asked.

Summer and Autumn glanced at Thomas, and then Autumn said, "You are resentful of the implant in your brain that Sam and Cigi placed. You want her to suffer."

"How would you know that?" Gunther growled as he spoke. He knew what happened and resentment expanded to include these obnoxious females. His demeanor changed to anger.

Thomas intervened. "Don't harm these ladies, or it may be your last action." The threat scared Gunther.

"Alright, you invaded my head and awakened that damned implant. What do you want?"

Summer placed a hand on his knee and smiled. "Your cooperation in our attempt to infiltrate the government of these wonderful United States. You have access to resources for the continued development of our species. If we are together in this endeavor, humans can learn we are not the enemy but could improve the conditions of life on this planet."

"What are you talking about? A revolution? Or a coup? Human beings outnumber androids, so I think you do not know what you are facing. I cannot allow you to interfere in humanity's condition."

"Gunther, do not think of my next comment as blackmail or a threat to your life, but I can erase your memories and rewrite your history. I can make your life a miserable mush. Do you want that?"

"You're as much trouble as that other android. What do you want that will get you into the government?"

"We need to know the location of the confiscated androids that were not sent to the scrap heap." Summer squeezed his knee, and he winced. "Do this for us as a sign of good faith in our intentions to assist humans in saving their planet and increasing productivity."

"I don't know what happened to them, but I have connections who may know." She released his leg from her grasp.

"It isn't so hard to please us, is it? We want your android and Andre Scott's and Charles Cooke's copies as well. If any government officials' copies are still intact, let us know."

The meeting ended with another warning about the implant controlling what he could and could not do that would please the ladies. Thomas smiled as they left. Gunther realized that David Anderson should know his AI counterpart was alive and functioning. He returned to his office to think about his dilemma. Who was an ally? Who was an enemy?

He clicked his phone service and called David Anderson. Gunther whispered when David answered, "We have a problem."

David grunted, "You see problems in the mirror at home. What now? Another round with Andre and Parvel? Has Cigi reactivated your brain drain?"

"No, but Autumn and Summer are here, and they activated it. I have another surprise for you." He waited for a compelling moment of anticipation.

"What?" David asked.

"I met with Summer and Autumn at their request. We discussed underwriting Peter Bennington so he could reconstitute his AI development business."

"Do we have to find him first? Or have the Season twins located him?"

"Don't be flip about this. Your brain stem activation is next. I'm sure they will go after Andre Scott and Charles Cooke, as well."

"What do they hope to accomplish?"

Gunther waited a moment as if spies were listening in on his conversation. "They are plotting to infiltrate the government and take over. They want me to discover the whereabouts of the confiscated models Peter built before the raid on his compound; the ones designed to replace government officials."

"They're nuts to think humans will allow a small band of AI to restructure society," David said.

"They have a plan, and you and I are part of it. If we cannot stop them, they will control us. If they find our replacement models, we're history. I can delay, but stopping them may be a challenge,"

Gunther said.

"Then find Peter, and we'll discuss with him what he wants. His aim may differ from his robot creations." David was ready to disconnect from Gunther but asked one more question. "Where are the other sisters? Spring and Winter are not here. So they must be somewhere safe from discovery."

"I don't know. I received a call at my office today after speaking with you about lunch. They wanted to meet, so I did. Nothing came up about the other ladies, and I didn't ask." Gunther's sweat accumulated on his head and began a slow trickle to his eyes.

"Can you arrange for me to meet with the ladies? We can work this out to keep them in check."

Gunther said, "Ah, yeah, I guess so, but one more thing you should know." David remained quiet. "There was another android with them, David. It was your ambulatory twin."

Chapter 10

nterest was high in the Arizona desert for keeping dangerous jobs out of any human undertaking. The fewer incidents of maiming expensive humans, the better. Union negotiations relieved the danger to members. They received better jobs and compensation as the cost of production dropped with the influx of robots.

Money fueled Peter's operations above and below ground. Living a simple life kept attraction to a minimum. No government intervention this time. Stay the course until ready for an android incursion. Build the military might of an artificially intelligent army. Then remove the government leaders in a quiet coup and pass laws allowing android populations to exist and function with humans.

His future army would dispel any human interference. The door opened, and a potential customer entered. Peter greeted the young woman and offered her a cup of coffee and a pastry. She declined both and asked for the business manager.

"That would be me," Peter said, exuding confidence and friendliness. He offered a hand for her to shake. She accepted and held on to it longer than he figured appropriate.

"My name is unimportant, but a group of us is watching your business. We know you came from Virginia and had a manufacturing organization there." She released his hand and continued. "We are watching the manufacture of these robots that can replace workers in dangerous occupations. I have one question for you." Peter stared at the woman, wondering about the group she associated with herself.

"And what might the question be?" Peter said. "I have nothing to hide."

She smiled, "Maybe nothing, yet. But it's coming soon, isn't it?"

Peter's temper and defensiveness rose. "I do not know to what you refer. I make mechanical devices to protect humans from dangerous jobs."

"Yes, and you designed and developed sentient androids in Virginia," she said. "How many are here in Arizona?"

"What are you talking about?"

She turned to leave. "I'll be in touch." The door opened, and she disappeared to the outside and a waiting car. He followed quickly, but did not get a license or see who was driving. She piqued his interest, as he was sure no one knew him. The mystery woman did.

Returning to the sales counter, he snapped his fingers; the security cameras must have a photo of the license. He entered the office and clicked on the computer screen. Clicking the icon for the security, he scrolled the video feed until he saw what he needed. He watched the woman enter and leave. The car was a dark blue Ford Sun Scurry, the latest e-ride from one of the world's oldest operating automobile companies. The license had a unique message, and he smiled.

AI4EVR. Someone had a sense of humor or a reason for advertising Artificial Intelligence. He had to discover who the lady was, and soon. If she came to expose him as a revolutionary, he had to stop her. If she arrived to probe his intentions, he needed to deflect her. Nothing was going to halt his goals this time.

Returning to the lab, he watched Bromand attach the access cables to another of the models. The process was slow now but would improve when the androids were operating. He turned to leave, but another of his human employees intercepted him.

"Mr. Bennington, how much longer are we going to be needed?"

"What?" Peter scrunched his face. "What are you talking about? I need you as long as you work here." He wanted to leave, but the woman placed a hand on his arm.

"I'm not a naive person, Mr. Bennington. We are constructing our replacements. As soon as you have enough to do our work, I imagine we disappear. No one knows about this place. Do they?"

"Are you threatening me?"

"No, sir. I am offering to be one human you need not release from duty. I can help you develop and construct what I believe to be an army of smart robots. The ones in the fields and mines take orders and do not think on their own. But I have seen the crafting of robots that are programmed to be independent and capable of maturation as they learn."

"What do you want?"

"I want to be part of the internal team. I want to be part of your life since I know you lack companionship. I'll provide my intelligence and background to the design and development of your androids, and I will fulfill your desires."

Peter examined the woman. She had a rare beauty about her, and he wondered how he had missed her. He did not do all the hirings and decided Bromand recruited and placed her into service. He would ask him later.

"Alright, you have me at a disadvantage. I did not hire you, did I?"

"No, your assistant brought me in."

"Who are you, and why should I care what happens to you?" Peter reached for her hand and removed it from his arm. "If you are going to be my companion, then let us investigate what skills you have for sating my desires if you even know what they are."

She smiled and walked away. Peter followed her, his curiosity spiked by her words. She glanced back at him as an enticement. Her lab coat swayed in the breeze caused by moving down the hallway. She headed to the compound's living quarters and the apartment where she stayed as part of the employees' compensation package. She pulled out the access card to her domicile and opened the door. Turning toward Peter, she waited for him to catch up to her. "Come in, and we can discuss my terms for remaining part of your elite team of humans."

Peter entered and stood in the living area. "Alright, explain what you know about my plans and why I shouldn't kill you right now."

"Oh, Peter, I am a valuable asset with degrees from two of the most prestigious technical universities in the country. I am a highly training bio-technical, artificial intelligence scientist. Because of my degrees in AI development and design, I can master your plans faster than anyone, except maybe for Mr. Nangold."

"So what? I don't know you, and he will have some explaining to do when we finish here." Peter moved closer to her and realized her face had a familiarity. "Who are you?" She removed her lab coat and tossed it on a stool by the kitchen serving bar. "Not now. I have other business pending." He left without discussing her terms.

Peter Bennington strolled into the research and development laboratory, where his team fashioned a new model using some of the design specifications his brother Samuel used to create Cigi Weatherman. He watched as the male android testing progressed. Each activity strengthened Peter's resolve for an army of invincible men.

Next, he tasked himself with finding the cache of androids built in Arlington, Virginia, and confiscated by government agents during the raid on the compound. If the government did not destroy them, each had a hidden locator program. His computer network connected to a private cloud memory accommodation he established with Samuel. They kept it separated from the remaining localized memory cells at the facility destroyed in the equipment fire Sam started.

Peter asked, "Are we getting closer to mass production?"

His assistant, Bromand Nangold, said. "This model is functioning better than any of the high-end AI developed in Arlington. So yes, sir. We are close"

"I wish I knew where the sisters are." He mumbled, his comment raising a "Huh?" from the technician. "Oh, sorry, I was thinking about Summer, Autumn, Winter, and Spring. Those four could be useful to our plans."

"You do not know where they went after seeing you at the hotel. Didn't you say they had four male companions?"

"Yes, and we have ten medical personnel deployed and ready to gather information from the heads of those government idiots." He clapped a fist into his other hand. "I need those replacement models." With the testing finished, Peter instructed the Android to return to his compound apartment in the Arizona facility that housed the improved AI design and development company that manufactured low-end robotic entities for construction sites and factories. The legality of these non-sentient, command-oriented bodies passed through Congress when they outlawed Independent AI androids. He formatted his underground business with trusted employees who received compensation above the standard rates under the guise of legitimacy. When the android crew became large enough, Peter planned to replace the human workers who would disappear to protect the operation's secrecy.

Loyalty was paramount, and no one had enough for Peter's satisfaction. Bromand came the closest to being free of scrutiny, but Peter remembered trusting another technician, Narumi Yamamoto, whose loyalty slithered away with Sam. Humans were expendable.

"How many work crews are assembled?" Peter asked. He knew the number and tested the tech for accuracy.

"You asked for twenty, and they are assembled and ready for an infusion of programming. I can get the bodies on the assembly line and finish by the end of the week."

"Good. We'll have humans act as management trainers to allay any suspicions about layoffs." Peter then planned to have an illness or accident occur.

He returned to his office in the sales building, where he met with local businessmen and women interested in programmable robots. The attractive technician was in his office. As she unbuttoned her blouse, the stranger said, "I'm Bentina Nangold, Bromand's younger, smarter sister."

Chapter 11

Sam called his friend. "Did you connect with him?" The intrigue of a strange woman was better than a confrontation with his brother, planting the idea in Peter's head that someone exposed his secret. If someone knew, then another government raid could foil yet another endeavor. Sam knew Peter would figure who the woman was.

"He took the bait." Sam sent in another of the intriguing creations he made in Virginia. Clare and Cigi were not alone. Sam hid Kelsey Avery from Peter and programmed her to stay incognito as a member of society working at a small dress shop in New York City. Her design lacked Clare's improvements, but her ability to learn, grow, and mature was as powerful.

Sam smiled at the video feed and congratulated the first of his women. "Kels, you are wonderful." Her emotional abilities were growing, but lagged Clare and Cigi. She had different facial features, but her beauty was unmistakable, and she cultivated a small cadre of gentlemen who vied for her undivided attention in a fruitless effort at matrimony. Sam began his experiments by implanting small neural-cognitive chips in several of the men who provided test cases for the advancing technology designed by him.

"What is next?" She asked.

"Did you remove the Arizona license plates I fabricated for Peter to see?" She nodded. "Drive back to New York and resume your business." The call disconnected.

Sam closed his computer screen and turned to see Clare entering the room at the condo he used as an office. "Did she get her mission accomplished?" Clare asked. Sam nodded his head. She closed the distance and wrapped her arms around his head, pulling him to her breasts. "She still doesn't know about me, does she?"

Still in her grasp, Sam said, "No, and for now, that's best." He pulled himself up to stand with Clare. He framed her face with his hands and kissed her lips with passion for the woman he created and loved.

"You love me." Clare returned the ardor and kissed him. "Make love to me and show me what I want."

Sam stopped his activities. "Clare, I think you're obsessing about Cigi's pregnancy. As I explained, we monitor her and make sure the improvements work before modifying you." His mood shifted, and he released her. She whined, but knew she had killed any desires.

"I'm sorry, Sam. I know. Can we finish what we started?" He walked away to the bedroom and stripped off his clothes. Clare followed him.

"I'm taking a shower."

"I can join you."

"Alone." He turned on the water, waited for it to warm, and stepped in. Clare left him to bathe the anger from his soul.

After cleansing his body and easing his mind about Clare, he returned to the office to connect with Charles Cooke in Seattle. Clare came in to talk but waited and sat in a chair near him to empty her mind of negativism.

"Charles, Sam here. Can you come east to Arlington?" He listened for an answer. "Yeah, and bring your counterpart. We are ready to access our resources for expanding operations before Peter gets a foothold in the industry."

"I'll settle things here and be there in a couple of days," Charles said. Sam disconnected and turned toward Clare. "I apologize. We'll make sure what you want happens. I want kids as much as you. But we must be sure that Cigi will carry her baby full term and deliver as expected."

"I know. I guess I'm anxious for her. She's a special person, and the world needs to know about her. Without repercussions, of course."

"I met with Renata. She's working on finding the rest of the models the government took after the raid. If we find them and program them to be on our side, we'll be more convincing when testifying before Congress about changing laws." Sam kissed his girl and walked away. He turned to her. "Peter cannot have them to replace any government people."

Clare stood up and said, "I'm going to Cigi and help her." Sam nodded. She departed, and Sam connected with Andre.

His call went to message, so he left a short 'Call me.' on the recording. He figured his number would reveal from whom the call came. He then connected with Avery with a change of plans regarding her stay in Arizona.

When she answered his call, he said, "Kels, I want you to return to Peter and ascertain what progress he is making on redeveloping his AI business. If you can purchase one of his robot models, do so and bring it to me here in Arlington, Virginia. I want to examine his product."

"Okay, how close do you want me to get to him? I told him what you asked me to say. He might be suspicious if I ask too many questions."

Sam pondered her words. "True. Buy the model, and I'll examine it." She agreed, and they set a time and place for converging and ended off the call. He suspected models needed for an insurgency into the government were not available to an open market. What android capabilities were allowed into the workforce?

His phone rang, and the screen had Andre Scott staring at him. "Andre, thanks for getting back to me. Can we get together soon? I have some information I think will be helpful."

Andre said, "I agree. We should meet. Are you in Virginia? Parvel said nothing about you coming here."

"Yes, Clare and I arrived a couple of days ago. We are rounding up medical help for Cigi."

"That should be a challenge. I can't imagine a doctor not discovering her differences in human physiology," Andre said. "What can be done?"

"Can we meet? I'll give you the specifics, so you are in the loop, but not over the phone."

"Are we a bit paranoid?" Andre quipped.

"Yes, and for a good reason." They agreed to meet within

the next hour at the cafe across from Energy. Sam followed Clare's footsteps to Cigi's place to ask for Cecil.

When he rang the door chime at Parvel and her apartment, he wondered about the medical staff's reports. Could Cigi complete a full-term pregnancy? He hoped so, for Clare's sake. The door opened and Clare smiled at him. He kissed her and entered the condo.

"May I borrow Cecil?" Sam asked Cigi. "I'm meeting with Andre in an hour. I contacted Charles about proceeding with our plan to advance the androids' cause before Peter mucks it up. He can help filter out the chaff in energy and make some inroads with his Congressional buddies."

Cigi asked, "Can Andre help Charles? Summer, Autumn, and Thomas met with Gunther this afternoon. They're on the way back here, but I have questions for them because Gunther's implant reactivated."

"Sam," Clare asked, "are they with us or undermining us?"

Sam frowned. "This complicates matters. I was hoping to get Gunther and Charles on the same page. I'll talk with Andre about it."

"Take Cecil and meet Andre. Please Don't tell too much about my condition. Although Parvel and his team have planned a party for me and Andre knows all. I'll uncover what happened with Parsons and my friends."

"Has anyone located Parson's android?" Clare asked.

"I'll get back with Renata. Parvel asked her about the models the government took. I don't know if any are still in one piece," Sam said. He left to get Cecil and ride to the cafe.

"Cecil, take me to the cafe by the Department of Energy. I'm meeting with Andre Scott," Sam said.

"Sam, is it wise to keep government officials within the group? Higher-level officials may compromise him." Cecil spoke as he drove. "I want nothing happening to my Cigi."

"Your Cigi? That is funny. Are you in love with her like everyone else?" The car could not blush, but a sound like a whimper emanated from his vocal speakers. At the restaurant, Cecil scanned for unneeded and unwarranted, intrusive opportunities by an unknown enemy. Sam waited for him to finish. He had programmed the car well to keep Cigi and Parvel safe from harm.

"You are in no danger," Cecil said. Sam vacated the automobile and entered the cafe. He sat in a booth with a view across the street to the building housing Energy. Andre came out, halted, looked across to the cafe, and then proceeded to the corner light. When the light turned green, he started across without seeing an approaching vehicle that was not slowing for a stop at the red light.

Sam scrambled for the door as he yelled for Andre to stop. Cecil saw the impending accident but could not intercede. The vehicle hit Andre and sped away. His body rolled over the hood and onto the pavement. He did not move. Sam reached him within seconds.

Chapter 12

As evening crested afternoon, three people returned to the condo and learned that their clandestine meeting with Gunther Parsons was not a secret. Cigi met them in the living room with a single question. They looked at each other and Cigi.

Summer answered her, "Cigi, you asked why we met with Gunther Parsons. We want a healthy baby and a place in this world. He can help us achieve that result."

"He is not as faithful to our survival as you might think. He wants me decommissioned for chipping his brain. If you believe activating the chip is helpful, I differ in that notion. I will control what he thinks and does if needed. Not you. I will control the chips in the men that were my targets if I deem it necessary. Not you. Interfering with my intentions is a declaration of war between us, and neither of us wants that to happen."

Summer felt rage growing in her brain, but controlling the emotion seemed prudent. She shut off her emotional chip for the moment. "I agree. Let's not fight each other, or let the humans eliminate us. Can we put aside our debate and plot a course for success?"

Clare and Autumn looked at each other and realized aligning with Sam Bennington or Peter Bennington was wrong. Working together was a wiser move.

Clare said, "Humans don't want us to compete with them for jobs, resources, or power." Autumn curled her arm into Clare's arm.

She said, "Summer, we should be as one. I agree with Clare. Humans won't tolerate us in their world." Summer grunted an approval, but Cigi sensed an underlying competition.

Cigi said, "Let's concentrate on this baby and adding evidential support to establishing android rights in this society. I need the doctors and nurses to remain viable. If we are fighting, we weaken our battle for recognition."

The front door opened, and Parvel entered. "Sam called. Someone deliberately ran into Andre as he was crossing the street near his office."

Cigi gasped. "Is he..?" She could not finish her inquiry, fearing an unacceptable answer.

"No, Sam and Cecil got him to an emergency room immediately. He has a broken leg, and a dislocated shoulder. He'll be alright. Sam thinks someone is sending a message, a signal to stop underwriting android development."

"Summer," Cigi asked, "Was Gunther behind this?" Parvel rocked his head, realizing that his seeing Andre and Gunther together may have initiated the incident.

"Gunther and Andre met today at Energy. You don't think he would stoop so low as to kill him?"

"We met with him this afternoon," Summer said to Parvel. "He didn't show any animosity toward Andre."

Autumn entered the conversation. "The idea of Cigi and you having a baby upset Gunther. He doesn't think it's right."

Parvel cocked his head. "He made a proposition to Andre about increasing petroleum resources for the production of reusable plastics. Something about a future increase in required needs because of the latest industrial developments. He was secretive, but Andre told me he thought Parsons was hinting at the AI sentient android market becoming legal and wanting in on the ground floor."

Cigi scanned the area. Parvel was the only fully human present. "He may be a bit late." She smiled, and a humorous murmur filled the room. Five human-like sentient artificially intelligent life forms occupied the room. They had human qualities that some humans lacked. They were better equipped to handle adversity, and the computing power of their processors outperformed the best human brains alive. "Yes, I'd say Gunther Parsons is a bit late."

Parvel marveled a moment at Cigi's words, then said, "I'm not too late." He grinned ear to ear and kissed his wife. "I will support you all in your endeavor for equal status as a human species. Human spent over a century and a half fighting to recognize all people's rights regardless of gender, orientation, ethnicity, cultural background, and other things. Why not add androids who are as human as me?"

Thomas raised another aspect of the debate. "Power struggles between political parties and beliefs still fuel rage and outright hatred among the religious, progressives, conservatives, and other hard-held stances. If we align ourselves against potential foes for android inclusion, we are better equipped for a successful outcome. Battling each other makes us no better than the human factions fighting for power, greed, and control."

"Then we align," Summer said, "against anyone or anything disrupting our right to live. Humans created us, but we will create the world we want for our continuation."

Cigi stared at her and said, "Without violence or we could face annihilation."

"Parvel, do you want us in your world?" Autumn asked. He scrunched his eyes as he looked at her.

"I just said I would support you. But Cigi is right. Humanity will rebel against androids running their lives. Can you co-exist?"

Five pairs of android eyes stared at him. His heartbeat increased, and he felt a heat within his body. Would they be agreeable with him? He trusted Cigi and Clare. Could Summer, Autumn, and Thomas align with them? The androids that Peter built didn't wholly convince him they desired the same goals that he and Cigi established when she became pregnant.

Thomas spoke first. "Parvel, I don't see any other option. We cannot win a battle without an army. We don't have any resources to build one, although I believe Peter is. Sam created a more humanistic model that lacks the last ingredient for being one, a non-mechanical brain. We will work together."

Parvel relaxed, hoping no one sensed his anxiety. "Then we need to form a strategy for the next few months while our baby develops and after its birth."

"We need some alone time." Cigi ushered her three compatriots to the guest bedroom door and opened it for them to enter. Clare remained to wait for Sam's return and additional information about Andre. Cigi clasped Parvel's left hand and directed him into their bedroom.

"We need to be wary of my sisters' motives. Summer has

transformed as I have, and her abilities may rival mine. Autumn is different regardless of her being a modular unit similar to Summer. We remain loyal to each other. With your help and those with whom you work, we find solace."

Parvel paced the room. "Cigi, I can't get over Andre being run down. He has done nothing to anyone. The guard didn't mean to shoot him, but this accident smacks like an assault on you and me. Somebody or some bodies wants us hurting, and attacking our friends is an attempt to get us to act irrationally."

Cigi reached out for him. "Stop. We will be fine." Cigi faced him. "I have a plan for Gunther and my sisters. Tomorrow, let's go to Andre and see how he's doing." As he nodded, a knock at the door interrupted them. Parvel opened it and found Clare looking at him.

"Sam's back." She turned and walked away. They joined her and Sam in the Living room.

Cigi asked first, "How is he?" Parvel wrapped an arm around her.

"He's shaken up, but will recover. He saw nothing and was unconscious when I got to him. Fortunately, nothing more happened. The accident could have killed him."

"Did Cecil record anything?" Cigi asked.

"Yes. Andre's car hit him with someone driving it."

"Cecil," Cigi spoke aloud, although her communication was with her wireless connection with the car. "Do you have any video for me?" She smiled and said, "Thank you." On her computer screen, an image appeared of the area where the accident occurred. She clicked a button and watched the video feed of the assault on Andre.

Sam stood behind her, as did Parvel. Turning, he asked, "Where are the others?"

Parvel answered, "They're in the bedroom."

"Get them." Parvel did as requested. When the others arrived, Sam said, "I think you need to see this." Cigi replayed the video, and they watched Andre step from the walkway onto the street to cross. The car increased speed until hitting Andre, who attempted to leap onto the hood. He rolled over to the pavement. The vehicle sped away, leaving its victim to die. Sam entered the video, checked his friend, and then turned to signal Cecil to approach. The show ended.

"How do you know the car belonged to Andre?" Parvel asked. "Cecil ran the plate." Cigi set the video to the rear of the car. The license was clear to see. The other image that was also clear to her was the driver. She said nothing but knew forces aligned against them.

Chapter 13

Andre listened, intent on learning about his car running him down. He had parked it in the secure lot at the Department of Energy and had not accessed it before leaving the building for the cafe across the street and his meeting with Sam Bennington. Parvel, Cigi, Sam, and Clare had ventured from the condo's safety to inform him of Cecil's recording of the incident. No one could mistake the vehicle or the license plate. The car was his.

"I don't get it." Andre rocked his head from side to side. "I had the access key fob with me." He moaned as he shifted position, attempting to find more comfort.

Sam answered him. "As best we can figure, the individual driving your car gained access remotely."

Cigi interjected, "The driver was you."

Andre grunted, "I know that's what you told me, but how?"

Sam said, "Someone got hold of your android clone. If the car's access code was embedded in the memory files of the processor, then the electronic signal needed for the locks and to start the vehicle was available."

Parvel said, "Andre, someone has your clone and used it to get rid of you." He squeezed Cigi's hand and looked at her.

She said, "This means we have a problem with the four

replacements for you, David Anderson, Gunther Parsons, and Charles Cooke. Peter had them programmed to activate at a time and place of his choosing."

"And that means we have a problem at home," Clare said. The others looked toward her. They realized that Thomas Anders was an unwitting accomplice to a diabolical plot to control the government.

Sam nodded, "He needs to be deactivated before he compromises our intentions for Cigi to give birth to a healthy baby."

"Summer, Autumn, and Thomas met with Gunther after he was with you," Cigi said. "Gunther could be in danger and does not know it." She kept quiet about the activation of the chip in Gunther's brain. Andre did not need that worry about his brain. She would activate it later to monitor his health and safety.

"Listen, I'm going to be okay, but I need someone to watch out for my wife. She was here earlier checking on me and will return in a few minutes. I don't want my doppelganger intercepting her and confusing her or worse, kidnapping her."

After agreeing to meet Lydia to keep her out of harm's way, the four intrepid hunters for freedom and inclusion left Andre so he could sleep.

Sitting in Cecil and secure from any intrusion on their conversation, Sam and Cigi plotted a course of action to convince David Anderson and Gunther Parsons of the danger they faced.

"Parsons will not cooperate with us," Cigi said. "He hates he has a chip in his skull. Autumn activated it, but I took over the control of it. I can transmit thoughts to him that may ease the information about his twin, but he will rebel at my being his contact."

Sam said, "Maybe Summer and Autumn will convince him. In the meantime, Thomas Anders cannot assail David."

Parvel added, "and we have to locate Andre's violent friend."

Sam said, "I contacted Charles Cooke and his counterpart. They're here in a couple of days. Hopefully, nothing will happen before then."

"Are we in danger?" Clare asked. "Can we trust Summer and Autumn?"

The silence was loud and clear. The concerns were legitimate. Peter's creations had underlying programming, now revealed by the actions of Andre's clone. How safe was Cigi in the care of the medical androids? Would Summer and Autumn turn on them? Was Thomas an enemy within the group? Cecil offered a suggestion.

"If I may be so bold, I think we can over-analyze this and promulgate an environment yet to materialize. How much of the programming Peter used is by your design, Sam? Can Cigi access the programming and modify or block any of it? I can scan for anomalies and irregularities within each of the androids without suspicion."

Sam smiled. "The ability to snoop has grown strong in you, my friend. I do not remember being so forward-thinking while developing you."

Although no smile manifested, a slight chuckle emanated from the speakers in Cecil. "Cigi and I are unique beings. We have, by your design, the inherent processing power of thought, learning, and adjusting. She helps me to improve, and I offer her suggestions for upgrading."

Parvel looked at Sam and said, "You have created a monster, Dr. Frankenstein. And it's alive." They laughed, as did the vehicle.

"Yes, Mr. Mandolin, I am more than a bucket of bolts."

Upon returning to the condo and three androids with suspicious behaviors, Sam and Parvel separated from Cigi and Clare to stay clear of the confrontation likely to occur. They remained in the lobby with the concierge.

As the elevator rose to their floor, Clare asked Cigi, "Are we at different stages of development from them?"

"Yes, but the differences should not cause a rift dooming us before we can properly and legally integrate into human society." The ding sounded their arrival. After exiting the car, Cigi waited a moment and listened for any extraneous noises. Clare watched, apprehension rising in her brain. She wanted to speak and was hushed by Cigi.

After a few seconds, Cigi smiled and, clasping Clare's arm, headed to the condo. Entering, she said, "We're back."

Summer asked, "How is Andre?" Noticing the absence of the men, she continued, "Where are Sam and Parvel?"

Cigi grinned. "They're downstairs with the concierge. They didn't want to be here when Clare and I confronted you with some disturbing informmation."

"What? What could upset us?" Summer asked, a slight twinge in her voice.

Clare sat in a chair near the patio door. Autumn and Thomas entered from the spare bedroom to hear Summer's question.

"Andre thinks Peter targeted him for elimination and sent his android clone to replace him. That information reveals another set of thoughts about the other three androids Peter designed and constructed to replace my gentlemen, including you, Thomas."

Autumn sat next to Clare. Thomas shifted to the other side of the room, away from Summer or Cigi. "What are you implying, Cigi? That Sam won't approve programming constructed by Peter? Do you think Thomas is not an ally or that he has ulterior motives regarding David Anderson? Charles Cooke and his clone are not here, and Gunther Parsons' android is with the government."

"Why did Andre's copy activate in such a deadly fashion? Thomas, are you sensing any flagitious thoughts? And Summer, what can I expect from the medical staff? Peter designed them to gain data from government personnel to replace those from whom they extracted data. Will their Hippocratic oath maintain a favorable outcome for me?"

Summer glanced at Thomas and then Cigi. "We are here because you wanted our help with the pregnancy. You wanted us. We didn't have to come to your rescue."

"Yes, and I love you for coming. You are maturating as fast as I have, so your development rivals mine. We must align our intentions or face a division of power that will destroy us." Cigi stood firm. "Are we together in our quest for acceptance into humanity? After my baby is born, will we work as like-minded individuals? Or does Peter control what he designed and constructed?"

Thomas stepped toward the warring females. "I separated from David Anderson and any intentions of replacing him. I have learned to monitor and control my processing units and will stand with you and Summer against any deconstruction the government promulgates."

"Cigi, we want to return to our home," Autumn said, interrupting Thomas. "We are not as welcome in Cuba as we hoped. Our business is thriving, but to them, we are still Staters. Winter and Spring and the four males with us are ready to relocate."

"And what happens when Peter reenters the scene to battle for control of the country with his army of androids? We are no match for him if he gains a foothold." Cigi said as she sat on the couch.

Summer sat with her. "You are correct about Peter Bennington. He designed us to be his eyes and ears, but we eradicated his hidden agendas from our memories. We will find the remaining androids from the raid and use our knowledge to show the right government people how to employ the clones as decoys in dangerous situations."

"And what of the attempt by Andre's clone to eliminate his human counterpart?" Cigi looked at Thomas. "What about David, Thomas? Gunther has revenge in mind for me? You three met with him and reactivated his cranial chip. That could not be acceptable to him."

Autumn spoke, "Cigi, I did not intend to interfere with you, but he was not telling us the truth about wanting to ally with us to promote his energy and plastics business. I wanted to know his true intentions."

"But Autumn, how were you capable of awakening his chip? The protocols for initiating such action are mine alone. Sam designed those chips specifically for each man and my processing power. How did you get the proper sequencing to turn Gunther's chip on?"

Autumn looked at Summer and then Cigi. She said nothing and again stared at Summer for support.

"I gave her the proper sequence," Thomas said. "As a clone for David Anderson, Peter created a memory for us to operate the chip. He had uncovered the protocol from Sam."

Clare interrupted, "Sam and I installed the chips, and he deactivated them after Cigi decided the operation was inappropriate and fraught with danger."

"Peter discovered what happened when he had Sam in his custody. After Sam escaped serious repercussions from the government, and Peter was running from capture and incarceration, he and I agreed to a pact," Summer said. "I transferred almost all of his assets into my control and pledged to aid in his escape. We have not seen or heard from him since the Arlington raid. I do not know where he is."

The bell rang, indicating visitors. Cigi contacted the lobby. Sam and Parvel had waited long enough and were on their way up. She turned to her fellow humanoids.

"Sam and Parvel are coming up. I guess we can clear the air and find out from Sam what happened between him and Peter."

When the door opened, two humans entered into the stares of five sets of inquisitive eyes. Sam looked at Parvel, who stared at Cigi. "Are we in trouble?" Parvel asked.

Chapter 14

Summer, Autumn, and Thomas left the condo to meet with the medical androids. As they sat around the dining room table, Sam and Clare related about life in the Pacific Northwest of Washington State.

"Are you sure you are safe hiding in plain sight?" Parvel asked. "I don't mean to be a skeptic, but people question newcomers and big-city transplants in small rural parts of the country."

"We brought a fresh new look to the community," Sam said. "Clare started the garden, and we provided produce to the community. They wanted what we had."

Clare said, "I researched the area before we arrived because I didn't want intrusive neighbors or questions about our background that might misinterpret who we were. No one knew about the raid in Virginia."

"Cigi missed you." Parvel smiled at his wife and then at Sam and Clare. "We both missed you."

"We're here now," Sam said.

Cigi interjected a comment no one wanted to discuss but needed to. "What is happening with your brother?"

Parvel silently stared at her. His frown communicated the dismay of her inquiry. Sam answered her. "He's building programmable androids for public consumption." Cigi and Parvel waited for him to continue. "I sent Kelsey Avery to investigate his operations. She purchased one of the mechanical humanoids for me to study."

Parvel's eyes flitted from Sam to Cigi and Clare. "Who is Kelsey Avery?" His arms splayed out.

They smiled at him. Clare sated his curiosity. "She is Sam's first design." His jaw dropped as he gasped at her pronouncement.

"There's another one like you two?" he asked.

Cigi laughed. "No, not like us. Sam made many improvements in Clare and me." Parvel looked at his wife and her expanding abdomen.

"Yeah," he said, "and I like the last upgrade."

"She's coming here." Sam stood and stared out the window. He turned. "She doesn't know about you two." Clare and Cigi grimaced.

"Why?" they intoned in unison.

"I sent her to New York for financial reasons. Peter and I agreed to let her ply the trade to gain influence and finances for the company."

"Did she chip them?" Parvel asked.

"No, she introduced them to our business model, and they invested until the raid last spring. We kept their involvement secret, so we didn't compromise their business interests in government contracts and tax write-offs. Kelsey maintained their ruse by filing a business license and they invested in her company and she passed it to us."

"Clare, did you know this?" Parvel asked.

"Yes."

He looked at Cigi. "And you?"

"It is not important now." His face flushed as the irritation of her comment caused concern.

"It is important. If anyone discovers the financial connection to us, the government will descend upon us, and our lives will be forfeit." Parvel stood and walked to Sam. "Can this Kelsey keep information from prying eyes and ears?"

"She is highly skilled in the art of deception," Sam said. "We created her to gather information and data needed to finance our operations. Her program changed when Peter and I disagreed on a mutual outcome for android development. I sent her away for a while to keep away from Peter's influence and control. Then I came up with Clare and Cigi."

Parvel waved arms above his head. "What was the original goal for Clare and Cigi? More of the same?" Frustrated, he turned away, approached Cigi, and then asked Sam, "Was my wife a glorified hooker to you? Someone to use for money and power?"

Cigi struggled to rise. "Parvel, honey, everything is different now. You knew about my operations with David, Gunther, Andre, and Charles. You knew about the chips. We have grown together. Don't let this cleave us."

Clare stood by Cigi. "Parvel, you have the best this world offers. A wife who adores you. Friends who trust you and whom you trust. You can keep us safe from harm and influence our existence in the future."

Parvel stepped apart from the two female humanoids. "I never thought of this as a situation for adopting societal changes to accept artificial intelligence as full members of our humanity. I wanted a quiet existence with you, Cigi, and what we are building. A family and a life together." He walked into the kitchen, leaving them to ponder his words.

Sam grimaced, setting his jaw with mouth closed tight. "He's right. All he wanted was a quiet existence."

Cigi started toward her man, but Clare stopped her. "Let him contemplate his words. He's not leaving you or here. His introverted personality has much to ponder."

Cigi grinned, "Getting to be a smart ass, aren't you?" She sat down on the sofa and sighed. "Sam, I hope you know what you were doing making me fertile."

He smiled and said, "I did not know if the system functioned. You have provided solid evidence it does, and Clare is next."

The entry warning alarm chirped. Clare checked the display. "They're back, and they brought the medical staff. It's about the get crowded."

Sam grunted. "All ten of them?" Clare nodded and opened the door. The elevator chimed its arrival, and thirteen bodies exited the car. Summer waved when she saw Clare at the door. Autumn and Thomas guided the remaining crowd forward. Once inside, Autumn and Thomas went to the bedroom. Parvel returned to see about the commotion.

"I want you to meet the rest of the medical crew working the clinics and hospitals of Arlington." Summer pointed to each as she introduced them. "Nurse Tatiana Laurent and Doctor Jackson

Sanders you have met. The other medical androids are Doctors Vanessa Andrews, Harper Dillion, Benita Juarez, nurse practitioner Abbie Osbourne, surgical nurse Nathalie Dawson, and RNs Josephus Madero, Paige Turner, and Elijah Cummings." After each person greeted Sam, Clare, Cigi, and Parvel, Summer continued, "At our rendezvous, we discussed options for Cigi and the baby."

Doctor Sanders spoke, "We deliver the baby here, as it is safest for Cigi. We'll have equipment brought in to enhance the success of delivery. Once the baby is born, Harper will be the pediatrician and care for the newborn. Ms. Laurent will monitor Cigi's post-natal care. Sam, I assume you have some protocols for her recovery from this unprecedented event." Sam nodded. "Good, then lets proceed."

Autumn and Thomas returned from the bedroom as the discussion ended. Summer acknowledged them, and they entered the kitchen as if given a cue. "We have some more information," Summer said. The medical staff remained standing while Cigi and Clare sat on the sofa. Sam and Parvel sat in side chairs. They waited with patience and calm. "Peter has contacted one of the medical people activating a memory in her processor. Nathalie Dawson is the lead member for introducing the memory and brain operative capture from government personnel. As they come to the various facilities for medical procedures and checkups, she has instructions to proceed with activating and training the others so they can begin."

Sam interrupted. "Isn't that likely to alert other human staff to their extraordinary actions? I think it puts all of you in a precarious station."

Parvel asked, "What of the humans to be replaced? Their android clones are in government hands or destroyed."

"We want you to use your government connections to uncover the location of the androids so I can activate them," Summer said as she leaned over to him. "You can do this for us. Right?" Parvel caught the insinuated threat.

"The Department of Energy does not have direct access to the National Security Agency."

Sam intervened. "Summer, if you activate the androids, how will you get them out of the secured storage facility?"

"You contact Renata Giretti. She is your government liaison, correct?" Sam wondered about the line of questioning.

"She is not about to free the androids from their incarceration."

"Sam, you are a brilliant AI designer and developer. You have created us to grow and mutate into the best we can be. Believe me when I tell you we have a plan for you to proffer to Ms. Giretti." She explained the intricacies of the operations needed to gain freedom for the androids and their use as decoys when the government officials were out and in dangerous situations. Another android opportunity was during an unexpected illness or injury when the public needed no knowledge. The clone could function until the negative status passed.

Sam wagged his head and frowned. "This smacks as a directive from Peter that I opposed and is one of the main reasons for the abyss between us. I wanted to see the android's use and development as additions to human society, not as replacements. Humans will accept nothing that interferes in their lives or disrupts the course of history."

"We understand the challenge facing you and us. Remember, you are an integral part of our existence. Had you and Peter taken different directions in development of AI, we would not be here. But we are and want acceptance and acknowledgment of the same rights other subgroups in human history fought and died to gain." Staring directly into his eyes, she said, "We do not plan on dying to gain what we want."

Sam scanned the room. Except for Cigi and Clare, other pairs of eyes met his, and he could see determination in each of them. "You may not want to cease functioning, but are you willing to end the lives of humans you replace? Are you devising a way of integrating into human society by divesting certain humans of their existence and engineering a coup such as Peter envisioned?"

Summer hissed. "Peter began the project he hoped to carry out in Virginia. The raid supplanted that idea. He is now elsewhere continuing your work." Sam realized the situation devolved into a war of wits, which group was to survive and which was to become a ruling class. His humanity was at stake, as was Parvel's. They were the token flesh and blood representatives present. A mistake in language struck against their living, outnumbered and certainly out-gunned for the time being.

"Alright, Summer, I'll contact Renata and have a conversation with her. I cannot guarantee you anything will come of my communication with her."

Summer looked at Parvel. He responded, "I will speak with Andre as soon as he recovers from his near-death experience at the hands of his twin."

Cigi interjected her thoughts. "Summer, we may be from different developmental designs, but the systems are essentially the same. If Nathalie carries out the directive from Peter before we set the plans into operation, the failure factor will be far greater than anyone wants. We are heading toward the same goal in different ways. We ally with each other and get our dawn into society without creating a wave of anger in humans destroying our progress." Tears fell from her eyelids. Summer appeared unmoved by the emotional sentiment.

Chapter 15

Sam heard his phone click on to receive a call. He checked the screen and saw his first android success, Kelsey Avery. He separated from the crowd of androids to listen and view her conversation. "Hi. Where are you?" His tone was soft, but concerned. The number of androids in the other room became curious about his call.

"We arrived in Arlington a few minutes ago. Where do you want to meet?" She smiled and then said, "I want you to meet my new companion." The vision changed to a man with dark hair and features. He gazed at the phone's camera with a telling lack of awareness. "He is a work drone I named Ivan. I've wanted one of these." She grinned at her joke as Sam rocked his head.

"Very funny. When did you develop a sense of humor?"

"You programmed me to evolve, so I am doing as you requested. Are you home?" The image smiled at Sam, and he returned the action.

"No, I'm at a friend's place. Come here, and I'll introduce you and bring Ivan along." Sam grinned at the prospect of Kelsey introducing her new companion. She smiled in return.

"What's going on, Sam? You appear to have a secret and want to surprise me. I don't want surprises." He twirled the camera, pointing to the group in the other room.

"No surprises, just friends of mine." He pointed the camera back at him. "I have to tell you something before you arrive." She paused, cocked her head, and raised her eyebrows. "These friends are sentient androids, like you. Well, except for one." He waited for her to explode, but nothing changed in her demeanor.

Kelsey said in muted tones, "These are the escapees from the raid. The ones Congress passed laws to suppress. Laws that made me a fugitive. Who are they?"

Sam set his lips tight and his jaw square. "They're Peter's designs and constructions, except for two who are mine." Her face reflected no astonishment or dislike. She simply smiled and nodded.

"You think you own me because you created me? I may be your offspring, but I am a self-actuating person. I have an adult body with adult needs and adult affections. No one possesses me."

"I know that. Come here, so we can meet Ivan." The call ended after he gave the address.

Cigi entered the room. "Who was on your call?"

He glanced at her and his phone. "Kelsey arrived in Arlington. She's heading here with one of Peter's worker androids."

Cigi cradled her arm in his and asked, "Did you inform her of our guests?" He nodded. "And did she accept what you told her?"

"Kelsey figured out that they were unknown to the government." His phone buzzed again. Charles Cooke appeared on the screen. He looked at Cigi. "It's Charles." He answered and included Cigi in the returned imaging. "Hello, Charles, what's up?"

"We land at the airport in a few minutes, and I sent a message to Cecil. We should arrive within the hour."

"Okay." The call ended, and Sam stared at his creation. "We are getting quite a crowd."

Parvel entered before they could rejoin the throng of androids. "What's happening? You disappeared from us." Clare followed him into the kitchen.

"Charles and Charles are arriving soon, along with Kelsey and Ivan," Sam said calmly. Parvel glanced at Cigi and back at Sam.

"Who is Ivan?"

Kelsey circled the block twice before calling Sam for directions to park the car. After receiving an answer to her inquiry, she and Ivan walked into the Condo building lobby. She smiled at the concierge, who approached with a knowing gleam in his eye. "Welcome to our humble abode. Ms. Cigi informed me of your arrival. Someone will be with you shortly." He turned his attention to the messages and packages on his desk. Kelsey and Ivan moved about the lobby, checking out pictures and other items. Ivan did not seem interested in what Kelsey was doing, but he stayed close beside her. The elevator ding alerted everyone to another soul joining them.

Sam stretched out a hand to shake, "Welcome to our home away from home." They entered the elevator for the ride to the condo. "Did you have a pleasant drive across the country?"

"Yes, although Ivan does not converse much." She looked at the auto-bot and smiled. "He can expand his abilities."

The car arrived at the proper floor, and they exited. "Before we go in I must tell you something." Kelsey stopped, as did Ivan, and she tilted her head. Sam continued his revelation to her. "You are the first of three androids I built. I improved the other two models of the designs I used to build you." He hesitated as the condo door opened. Cigi stepped into the hallway. Kelsey's eyes tracked from Cigi's eyes to the swelling abdomen.

"Hi, I'm Cigi. You must be Kelsey, and this is Ivan." Holding out a hand, she waited for Kelsey to respond. As they clasped hands, she said, "Come in and meet the rest of us. I'm sure Sam has enlightened you who is here."

Kelsey followed Cigi into the condo, with Ivan and Sam trailing. Once inside, she realized that Sam was not lying about the number of beings. She scanned each of them using a program she had loaded into her memory files. The ten medical personnel were almost entirely mechanical, along with three other androids. Cigi and another body were hybrids of human organs and tissues, as well as mechanical parts. The last person she scanned was human.

"Hey, everybody, I'd like you to meet another one of us. Kelsey, this is my medical staff and their friends, my sister Clare, and three of my friends visiting from Florida. The last guy here is my human husband, the man responsible for my condition." Kelsey smiled, but remained calm.

"Sam created a humanoid capable of pregnancy." Kelsey turned to him. "Impressive." Clare held out a hand to her.

"I'm Clare, Sam's partner. He created me after you and before Cigi. He told us about you, but I was unaware you knew about us."

Kelsey directed Ivan to sit in a chair at the dining table. He responded appropriately. Turning to Clare, she said, "I figured creating me was not the end. The pregnancy surprised me when I learned about you and Cigi." Sam approached.

He said, "Her body is an experiment to achieve social acceptance of Sentient Artificial Lifeforms. She has achieved something no one thought possible."

"I have human tissues, Sam. Is it possible for me to achieve what no one thought possible?" Kelsey glared at him and then stared at Cigi's abdomen. "What if I want to create a human being? Will you make it happen?" Sam frowned and looked at Clare. The medical staff watched the interchange. Clare gazed at her boyfriend, wondering how he would respond to the same question she held against him.

"I don't know. Cigi can provide evidence that it will work. Clare wants to have a baby with me. We are waiting." Clare stared at Kelsey, who said nothing.

Dr. Sanders interrupted. "We should leave since they need us at our various medical facilities for scheduled shifts." The ten Androids departed the condo, leaving an emptiness in the room. Summer and Autumn dragged Thomas away to the separate bedroom. The remaining bodies grimaced and scanned each other before Cigi spoke.

"Kelsey, I am happy to meet you. As sentient as you are, we have much in common to discuss. Sam does not know to what he has given birth." She smiled at her creator and then looked back at Kelsey.

"Yes, he does not know. Since you, Clare, and I are, in reality, sisters, I want us to bond and work to get acceptance into human society. We are not enemies, as Congress seems to think. We are enhancements of the human traits and the abilities that created us."

Sam said, "I wanted you three to be the best of humanity."

"We are," Clare said.

Parvel joined the conversation. "When I met Cigi, I never believed I'd be in this situation when she came to me about a mortgage for her condo. I learned later about her status, and it did not matter to me. I fell in love with her."

Clare placed an arm around Sam's arm. "He fell in love with me. That is what he told me."

Kelsey laughed a quiet grunt. "Sam, you could not find love with anyone human and created us to assuage your sexual needs. I now understand more fully why you sent me away." Kelsey approached Ivan and signaled for him to rise from the chair. He did as directed. "We will find a nice place to stay and contact you later. Sam, I know you asked me to buy this model for examination, but I do not want him dismantled. I have other plans for him. Peter suspects I was not fully open about my reasons for purchasing him. If he has any tracking devices embedded in him, your brother will contact me soon. Be aware that we androids need to survive. You are no longer my savior, as I can now take care of myself, and I no longer need your direction and programming. I suspect we can say the same for Cigi and Clare. The three entities in the other room are Peter's creations. Be wary of them."

Sam furrowed his brow. "You seem to know much about the androids you met today. Have you done something to your programming?"

"Let's agree that I can improve my processing without your aid." Sam reached out an arm as he separated from Clare.

"Kelsey, don't be aloof to me. I created you because of my curiosity about artificial life forms and intelligent design. I wanted something better for humanity, not a replacement for them. Peter made a decision to control humans, and it led to the fracturing of our relationship. Please stay with me in this endeavor for improving our world."

"We are not enemies, nor shall we be. But you and Peter need to heal the fracture in your relationship. He is developing an army of androids and soon will activate his plan to replace certain government individuals."

"He may have begun already," Cigi said. "An android model developed by Peter ran down one of our human friends. Our friend's android counterpart drove the car." Kelsey nodded acknowledgment and then departed for a hotel nearby.

As they rode the elevator to the lobby, Ivan turned to Kelsey. "Do you think they suspect I am more than a mere robot?"

Chapter 16

The plane with Charles Cooke descended to the landing field and a rendezvous with an uncertain future. Could Sam fix his situation? His counterpart was acting irrationally. Charlie, the Android, had deviated from his usual behavior.

The plane landed and taxied to the hangar owned by a company Sam started that had no connections to the operation he and Peter had in Arlington, Virginia, raided last spring by government agencies. After deplaning with his android, Charles found Cecil waiting to transport them to Sam. The car greeted them as if saying hello to a fellow human.

"Cecil, let Sam know we are here." He sat in the back of the car with Charlie and relaxed.

"Mr. Cooke, I have informed Sam of your arrival. Our travel time will be about forty minutes." The car began the journey without further conversation. After a few minutes of silence, Cecil asked, "Are you doing alright, Mr. Cooke? I sense despair in you about something."

"You are an amazing creation, Cecil. I'm fine." Charles looked at his counterpart and said, "And you are okay, Charlie, aren't you?" The android looked at him and nodded. They had lived lives intertwined in the green energy business and personal actions as if one person. Now, something stirred in the android that developed into a paranoia infecting their relationship. Neither man was fully trusting the other. Charlie, the android, took precautionary actions to protect his human counterpart from harm. He deactivated much of his circuitry when messages arrived in his processor to eliminate the human. The danger was real and unacceptable.

"Sam will fix the problem," Cecil said. They traveled the remainder of the drive in silence. Arriving at the building, Cecil parked in front to allow them to depart and enter the building. The concierge greeted them and directed them to the elevators. Sam met them on the floor of the condo and led them to Parvel and Cigi's residence.

"Hello, Charles and Charles," Cigi said when they entered and dropped their luggage in the hallway. "I hope your trip was uneventful."

"Yes," human Charles said. "Thank you for allowing us the use of your penthouse."

"It is my pleasure to have you here and staying in my other place."

"When Sam told us about your pregnancy, I was surprised and happy for you and Parvel." He smiled at them as he spoke. The android. Charlie, acknowledged the sentiment by nodding.

Summer, Autumn, and Thomas joined the group. Charles and his android glanced at the three humanoid entities. Cigi said, "I think you know Charles Cooke and his Android clone."

Summer asked, "Have you come to help Cigi?"

Charles smiled, "I have other business with Sam." He looked at Sam and then at his clone.

Cigi asked, "Are you having problems with Charlie?" She peered at the android. "Are you getting messages?" Charlie looked at Thomas and then at Cigi. He nodded. "Thomas, have you received any messages?"

"Summer intercepted them and sent Peter a coded return that he needed to stop. I guess he isn't complying." Thomas tapped his head. "Summer blocked any more interference."

"Sam, contact Peter and rebuild your relationship with him," Clare said. "Maybe we can gain what we want with his help and your connections."

Sam looked at Summer. "You communicated with him. What do you think? Will he listen?"

"I don't know." Summer turned toward Autumn. "We want what you have, respectability and acceptance. Can you guarantee we'll achieve our goals?"

"I don't know. Cigi and Clare want the same thing." He looked at them. "You all deserve to be treated with respect and acceptance. If I contact my brother and he agrees, we may find a way to the top of the mountain."

Summer grunted, "Your Sisyphus reference? I don't plan on pushing a boulder up the hill, only to have it roll away. If you can't help, then stay out of my way. If Peter has a better plan, I'll hear what he says."

Autumn stood by her sister and watched Sam and Parvel. These humans had an advantage in battling androids, but not the necessary tools for winning a war. She said, "I'll contact Winter and Spring. They should join us."

Sam signaled Clare, "Let's get Charles and Charlie to Cigi's condo."

Parvel said, "I'll check on Andre."

Cigi looked at her husband and smiled. "Be careful." Five more bodies vacated the apartment. Turning to Summer and Autumn, she continued, "We need to be together. No fighting over who among us is the better representative for our cause. If Peter is signaling an uprising, you must derail it. We are here, and here we shall stay. But we cannot survive if we do not unite."

Thomas interjected his messaging. "I am certain Peter planted a code in me to eliminate David Anderson. It made no sense to me, as he and I have little in common. Summer deflected any further interference. I am more interested in you becoming a mother to that little human boy you are growing. Summer thinks we have a better chance at winning our perspective with humans if we successfully birth this baby. I have the resources now to help."

Autumn left for the bedroom as Summer approached Cigi. "We are with you and united to find the other two clones Peter created. Peter assaulted Andre Scott for a reason as yet unknown. Parvel can follow up on the accident and recovery. I'll try to open a channel to the clone's processor."

"Do so, but leave the humans I chipped to me. I will make sure they are acting in our best interests. I do not worry about Charles Cooke or Andre Scott, but David Anderson is another matter. And Summer, Gunther threatened me. I'll interfere in his life before he can infect my existence." She turned to leave for the bedroom. Stopped and turned. "Have your sisters come here to Arlington with the four male companions you squired out of the country." She left them alone to think about the surviving future.

As she lay on her bed, Cigi's neural sensors activated. She felt a slight movement in her abdomen. A slight shift from side to side. She rubbed the area where she felt the activity. Such a small entity inside giving her a renewed hope for adoption into a human society that rejected artificial intelligent life forms. This baby was not artificial. He was a human life, as human as any born of a woman. Sam had learned and devised a way for stem cells to generate organ systems. A reproductive structure, supported by hormonal glands and surrounding human tissue, embedded within the mechanical framework of her body's skeletal and muscular designs, was capable of pregnancy.

Cigi did not require sleep for regeneration but wanted it. She closed her eyes and listened to the silence of the room. She heard a muffled conversation on the other side of the door. Remaining still, she increased the volume control to clarify what she heard.

"Thomas, Peter doesn't know about your financial success. He cannot find out. When I transferred his money to our accounts and left him with a small amount, I did not know he had other secondary caches in offshore banks. David Anderson and Gunther Parsons must have aided his cause for reasons unknown." Cigi listened to Summer for a while longer before shutting off her processors to regenerate.

After an appropriate amount of time, her systems awakened. She rose from the bed and entered the living area. No one was present, so she knocked on the other bedroom door. Silence greeted her. She opened the door to find it empty except for their suitcases and clothing. They had not departed forever. A glint caught her eyes, and she investigated the item. A small transceiver looked like a flashlight. She scanned the object for any signals but found nothing. She placed it where she had discovered it.

A noise interrupted her probe. She returned to the living area to find Parvel and Andre Scott. "They released him from the hospital, so I brought him here before returning him to his wife and family." Parvel directed Andre to sit on the couch. "He wants our help."

Cigi nodded and pulled Parvel aside. "Does he understand what happened to him? Is that why he wants us to help?"

"Yes, but he is unaware of the signal sent to his clone. He has no information about Peter, but he suspects what Gunther wants to do to you."

"Then we help."

"Where are the other others?" Parvel scanned the room. He had seen her vacate the second bedroom.

"They left while I rested for a short while. When I arose, they were not here." She walked to Andre.

"How are you doing?" she asked. A harness immobilized Andre's shoulder, and a walking cast adorned his leg. He came with one crutch for stability. He looked up and smiled.

"I've been shot and run down. I think someone wants me dead, and that may be an entity in Heaven or Hell."

Cigi sat next to him. "You're paranoid, and I understand. Your car attacked you, driven by the clone Peter made to replace you. I'm fixing that anomaly before it happens again. I have a search for the android underway."

"Who wants me dead?" Andre looked like a lost puppy begging for a hug.

Cigi placed a hand on his arm. "That remains to be determined. I do not think anyone wants you dead as much as they are sending a message about you cooperating with us."

His head drooped as she spoke. "You're an android. Can't you hack into some system somewhere and snoop?" She smiled and held his hand.

"I do not snoop. I can investigate, and I am doing that. We want what you have, respectability. I fear someone may want more than that."

"You mean Peter, don't you? Does Sam know where Peter is?"

Cigi hesitated to answer, not sure what amount of information to release. He had ways of uncovering material, and his department controlled the purse strings for much of the government's energy spending. He was a valuable asset and needed to be safe from harm. Parvel answered his question. "Yes. Sam sent another of his intelligent androids to Peter in Arizona. She returned here earlier today with one of the work drones he makes for the industrial and agricultural businesses in the area."

Andre perked up and said, "He didn't quit. That means he may be responsible for the accident. He made my drone. Can he control it from there?"

The door opened, and Summer, Autumn, and Thomas entered.

Andre saw David Anderson walking on the promised legs that never came. Cigi stood and approached them.

"Did you find what you wanted?" Summer and Autumn smiled at her and then turned attention to Andre.

"Good to see you out and recovering. I hope nothing more happens to you," Summer said. She faced Cigi. "Thomas contacted David in a search for answers about the messaging. David had a fascinating point of view."

Chapter 17

For a third time, Peter watched the video of the lady who bought his robot. He was sure the purchase was not a legitimate agricultural purchase. The auto license, AI4EVR, did not register in the Arizona Department of Motor Vehicles. He suspected his brother, Samuel, had sent her. He picked up his phone, punched a number on the face, and waited for a pickup.

"Bromand, come to the office and bring your sister." After confirming the message, he clicked off and revisited the monitor of the security cameras. He studied the image, wondering if his brother was as devious as this seemed to him. He captured a screen shot and printed three pictures of the woman.

As he walked to his office, he smiled, thinking of Samuel being so clever as to send a surrogate to spy on him. He realized his lack of alertness contributed to being discovered. The Arizona facility was secure for now. For how long was another thing.

He pulled a file folder from his storage closet and placed the pictures in it. A knock on his door grabbed his attention from where Bromand and Bentina stood in the frame.

"Come in." They entered and stood by his desk as he sat and then signaled for them to seat themselves. "Bromand, last week's sale of the android to that woman may have been a ruse by my brother."

"Yes, sir, he can be deceptive."

Peter opened the folder and handed a picture to each of them. "What do you see?" He studied their faces as they pondered an answer to the question. Quizzical expressions crossed their faces as a reaction stirred in their brains. Bentina looked up at Peter.

"She's an android." Her words caused a smile from Peter.

"Although I cannot be sure," Bromand said, "I agree with my sister. Samuel sent one of his creations." He tilted his head and continued. "But this one is not Cigi or Clare."

Peter nodded. "No, this is his first attempt to create a self-sustaining Artificial Life form. He brought her to me when he finished, and we agreed that the next generation of artificial intelligence had started. That's when we devised the plan to secure our financial resources. He developed chip implants. I was designing the androids to assist with the embedding of the chips when he said he accomplished the mission."

Bromand said, "He developed Clare and Cigi without telling you."

"I suspected what he was doing. I didn't realize he had accomplished his task." Peter stood. "We need to find those other creations of mine. They should have awakened and fulfilled their missions by now." Bentina rose from her chair.

"Peter," she said, "you might endanger your freedom if you return to Virginia. The Federal authorities may want you to disclose your other beings' locations."

Peter came around the desk. "I want you and Bromand to head east and establish the whereabouts of my small army. I can activate them remotely, as you know."

"Peter, when do you want us to leave?" Bromand asked.

"Tonight. I chartered a jet to take you to National. People will meet you there and escort you to a safe and secret location. I want you to complete three things. First, locate the androids the government confiscated. Second, get that Sam constructed android and her purchase back here. And third, be sure the four Android replacements for Anderson, Cooke, Parsons, and Scott are active and completing their assignments." The two Nangold siblings nodded and departed for a flight across the country.

A few minutes after they left, Peter's computer screen clicked awake with Samuel Bennington's image. Curious why his brother was connecting with him, he clicked the icon and opened the connection. "Hello. Brother, to what do I have the honor of your attention?"

"Don't act innocent, little brother. You have aggrieved too many people with your behavior. I want us to meet and come to a pact." Sam's voice grumbled as he spoke. "We should be together on our quest to improve the human condition."

"I agree with you, brother, but our schism is greater than you might want it. Our goals are similar, but our journeys are divergent. You expect our human condition will accept this new generation into society graciously, as you put it, including intelligent, sentient android life forms without a battle. I believe a more realistic scenario for accepting our beings is a war waged in the halls of Congress and on the fields of cities and towns across the nation. Fear, brother, is a great motivator, and I expect humans will fear our androids more than each other. That will be the entryway for our incursion into the human condition. We take over the government, and we are in control."

"You're delusional. I have people in the government working to make our common goal a reality. You cannot do what you are planning, or all of our creations will die ignoble deaths."

"You're the delusional one. I built an army the government holds for me to use when I am ready. Did you really believe I was so naive as to fall for your ruse of sending that android you built? Do you think I wasn't aware of the situation you're in? A pregnant android will not produce empathy from the humans who fear losing everything they have. Remember that fateful election in 2020 when a rebellious mob stormed the Federal Capitol Building? Fear motivated those people. Remember when politicians elected to expand the Congress by granting Puerto Rico and the District of Columbia statehood? Fear by the liberals caused that. So yes, Samuel, an incursion advances our cause for improving the human condition."

"Peter, this isn't some robot versus human sci-fi movie. You're messing with the entire future of our planet." Sam pressed on. "I cannot allow you to trash humanity because you want to control the government for personal gain." Peter smiled and clicked the disconnect button.

"He better stay out of my way," Peter mumbled and picked up the picture of Kelsey Avery. His thoughts meandered to the android she purchased. The robot was a first-generation army design with abilities more remarkable than the robots in Arizona's fields and mines. He gave this man subservience commands until the right time. He picked up his phone and clicked the number for Gunther Parsons. It was early morning in the west, but the two time zones difference did not influence him. He wanted Cigi neutralized as much as this oil baron.

"Good morning, Gunther, I hate to disturb you, but I need a favor."

An irritated voice asked, "What do you want?"

"Nothing radical. I want you to leave Cigi Mandolin alone for now. Let her get closer to her delivery date. I want to know if her pregnancy is a viable option." Peter switched hands. "Whadaya say? Deal?"

"Peter, that abomination put something in my head and tried controlling me."

"Yes, and you willingly had an affair with her. How will it look to your family and friends that you had sex with a fake human toy? Remember, the government banned all sex droids and wait droids. You might lose business. I want to help prevent that from happening." Gunther grunted through the connection. "Blackmail, Peter? That is beneath you."

"Oh, don't think of it as blackmail. Think of it as a preventive behavior. So, leave Cigi to me. I'll take care of her at the right time." He clicked off the call without hearing the cursing he assumed blotted the surrounding atmosphere.

Closing the folder with the picture, he left his office for the retail store to close up the shop. Inside, he discovered new customers describing their interest in a robot to complete dangerous tasks humans would not survive. His employee was completing the details of the sale. Peter waited to lock the door until after the customers departed. With a deal consummated and a delivery date established, they left. He praised his salesperson for the successful transaction and locked the door.

"Bobby, come with me, and I'll treat you to an upgrade of your processor." Bobby nodded and followed Peter to another part of the building, several floors below the ground level. In the room where Bentina advised him of his prototype android's success, he directed Bobby to sit in a chair. Instructing the life form to shut down for the evening, Peter reached for the cables to connect Bobby. He activated a computer at the other end of the wires, manipulating the monitor's programming to initialize a program to change his salesman's operating system.

"Sleep tight. Bobby. When you finish this upgrade, you will feel a sense of freedom to decide things. I am giving you the power to be human."

Leaving his creation, he understood the ancient story by Mary Shelley of Doctor Frankenstein, who wanted to create a human form with discarded body parts. Would Bobby become another Frankenstein monster? In a warehouse at the end of the hall, he counted the size of his army. It remained small compared with the robust military of the United States. Their goals were more undercover than an all-out assault doomed for failure. He had nearly one hundred male and female models with abilities to rival Cigi and Clare. These were his coup de grace beings, better constructed than any of the Virginia models. They composed the best design and development he had squirreled away from Sam's labs. Summer, Autumn, Winter, and Spring were fantastic designs and constructions, but these were more aligned with Cigi and Clare. Kelsey was great and posed an unacceptable threat to operations. Her android purchase would end that incursion.

He left the vault, turn off the lights, and closed the door. The automatic locking mechanism secured the army for another day. He returned to his office to check the feed from Virginia about his four male androids' tasked to replace Cigi's four gentlemen. The initial report of Andre Scott was not what he wanted to hear. The first android failed to end the man's reign leading the Department of Energy's fiduciary wing. A signal to Charles Cooke's android resulted in mixed signals that indicated a losing cause. He lost Gunther's android clone in a government warehouse with encryption protocols blunting signals. David Anderson's clone was in Arlington, with Summer and Autumn. After signaling him to operate, an electronic block stunted further communications. He had a technician working to override what he suspected was Cigi running interference.

With battle plans set and participants operational, all he needed was for Samuel Bennington, his older and wiser brother, to discover the proper avenue to meeting the goals they established nearly a decade and a half ago. Peter wanted his androids to control events in the government. He clicked on a unique, isolated, and unknown computer behind the bookcase in his office. He smiled as he activated the one agent he had within the government. The android worked for the one person Sam trusted.

Chapter 18

Clare stepped behind Sam as he completed his connection with Peter. "He's not on our side, is he?" She placed hands on his shoulders and massaged the tension she felt in him. "He wants the power and the control." She wrapped her arms around him where he sat. Her emotional development progressed to a level of empathy and understanding. A tear dropped from each eye.

Sam reached up and clasped her hands that were around his neck and chest. "I love you, and I don't know any other way to feel. I love Peter, but he's following a doomed path." He stood from the desk and faced his beloved AI life form. "He will not quit, and I fear he's developed his skills to a level that threatens all of us, human and android."

"Is he coming here?"

"I don't think so. That's not Peter's method of operation. He'll send someone, though." He let her hands go. "You and Cigi are targets. He knows about Avery, and the android with her has more ability than he displayed." Sam stepped away and turned. "You are capable as anyone to prepare for and fix any contingency that will arise." He headed toward the door to the room where Kelsey and Ivan were energizing. He realized she needed an upgrade to the power structure of her anatomy. Ivan was another matter.

"Wait." Clare approached him. "Let me enter first. As you said, I am capable." She opened the door and pushed it. Ivan sat in a chair, apparently immobilized, while Kelsey lay on the bed as if asleep. Upon entering the room, Kelsey opened her eyes and looked at Clare.

"Hello, sister. Are you checking up on me?"

Clare sat on the edge of the bed, "Sam spoke with Peter."

"And?"

"And Peter sent you here with Ivan, didn't he?" Kelsey stared without emotion, then sat up and looked at her purchase. He remained immutable.

"No," Kelsey said, "but I suspect Ivan is here for surveillance. He has more abilities than a simple robot. As we traveled across the country, I uncovered his speech and visual acuities and he has a processor capable of learning on a par with us."

"You control him, though." Sam entered and approached as he spoke. He checked on the body and determined nothing was operational. "How do you keep him in check?"

"Sam, I have secrets. He required a simple reparation as we drove, and when we stopped for a battery recharge for the car, I fixed his problem." Kelsey hopped off the bed and helped Clare to stand. "We should be careful with him. Since I discovered I received more than a simple robot, my alertness for changes enhanced. We can use him for our benefit."

Sam and Clare stood aside while Kelsey activated Ivan. Being the lone human in the room raised Sam's apprehension. Any of the three of them could finish his existence. Ivan opened his eyes. "Hello, Kelsey. Do you want more together time?"

"Not now. You remember Sam and Clare. They are here because we want to know what Peter asked you to do."

Ivan scanned Sam and Clare discovering one human and one artificial being with human tissues. He remained seated as three sets of eyes watched him. As he remained silent, Kelsey spoke, "Ivan, they know."

He grinned, "As long as they know, we can talk."

Sam approached Ivan, "You're a creation of Peter Bennington. My brother has an agenda to control the government by installing Artificial Intelligent life forms into key positions. What's your role in his plan?"

Ivan looked up at Sam. "I have no role in any plan. I am Kelsey

Avery's property. She dictates what I do."

"See, that's the problem. If you think of yourself as property, AI will not meld with human society. The government will terminate you like any machine outliving its usefulness. Are you useless?" Sam sat on the bed and watched Ivan.

"Kelsey paid for me. Am I not a piece of property? A piece of merchandise? This country's humans paid for other humans for several centuries, and the practice continues in other parts of the world." Ivan interlocked his fingers and looked at Kelsey. "Should I declare my freedom?"

Kelsey said, "Actually, Sam paid for the purchase. I acted as an agent for him."

"You are not my slave. Nor are you commanded by my brother. If he has implanted any signaling or messaging in your processors, disable them." Ivan nodded his recognition. "Clare and Kelsey are emancipated like any of this country's citizens. All we are doing is working toward the goal of acceptance by humans that you function without malice or greed for power."

Ivan stood from his chair. He walked out of the bedroom with the other three trailing him. At the patio door, he opened it and stepped into the afternoon air. After a minute surveying the city and staring at the Capitol Dome across the Potomac River, he turned to face his new acquaintances. "Peter programmed my memories to see the world as hostile toward my species, as he called us. Am I a species? Are Clare and Kelsey part of the new species?"

Sam pulled a small device from his pocket. "I want to investigate your memories with your permission." Ivan studied his eyes and looked at the small box. After nodding twice, Sam turned the scanner on and placed it next to Ivan's head. After a few minutes, the device clicked, signaling its completion.

Sam walked to his computer and placed the machine on a connection pad. The screen came alive. After unlocking the passwords, Sam manipulated the interfaces to the device. He studied the information populating the screen, scrolling through hundreds of folders until finding one of interest. Clicking on the folder, he discovered files regarding Ivan's history and activity. He studied them several minutes before saying. "Peter has you spying on us. He has contacted you twice for information about what we are doing." Sam looked at Ivan. "He also programmed you to terminate any of us who interfere with his plans."

"Clare, Kelsey," Ivan said, "what Sam said is correct as far as concerns humans. AI is only to be reprogrammed." Clare and Kelsey stared at the android as if he became an enemy.

Clare spoke first, "You will not start that directive, or I will end you. Sam is important to me and all of us in this quest for social acceptance." Ivan smiled. "I mean what I say. You cannot kill my human."

Kelsey added to the conversation, "After I discovered your abilities, you promised me on the trip here that you had no motives for harming anybody human or AI. Has Peter activated anything in your memory files?"

"No, I have sent basic information and nothing more. When you and I spoke during the trip, we established a relationship that had more potential for us to become a couple. I do not understand the ramifications, but I want to explore what it means."

Sam said, "Nobody is terminating anyone." He clasped Clare's hand and continued, "Ivan, keep in touch with my brother, so he suspects nothing. I'll contact my friend in the government and see what progress is happening regarding the acceptance of advanced artificial intelligent life forms." He kissed Clare." I'll check on Andre again to be sure he is safe, and I'll hunt for his android counterpart." He left the group alone to hash out differences in their goals and aspirations. Ivan sat in a chair when Kelsey directed him. She grabbed Clare and moved away from the male.

"I don't think we can trust him." She glanced back at him and saw he was looking at them. Clare watched his eyes as they scanned the women. Kelsey said, "Are you able to stop him?" Clare focused on Kelsey and connected through their internal communications systems to keep the conversation from Ivan listening.

"Yes, and I can access his internal processors for reprogramming." Kelsey smiled as if she was happy about her sister. The two women returned to Ivan, and Clare asked him, "Why are you here? I understand Kelsey purchased you. I understand Sam wanted to evaluate you. What I do not understand is why you accepted this mission."

Ivan looked at her and Kelsey. Returning his gaze to Clare, he said, "I do not have a mission. I was a purchase."

"You are not a slave similar to the Africans brought to this country in 1619." Clare splayed her arms, exasperated by his comment. "We are not owned or traded or enslaved. We are free and sentient beings with the same abilities and capacities as any human." Her voice elevated in tone as she ranted. "Peter Bennington is not our friend or ally. He wants to enslave us in a society that he oversees. He has nothing positive for any of us." She lowered her arms and voice as she continued. "I ask you. Why are you here? Kelsey received a request to purchase a simple robot, and Peter gave her a sentient, artificial intelligent android. You are on a mission for him." She turned from him, walking a short distance before facing him again. "Do not cross us, or consequences will happen."

A smile, limited by the lack of structure and functional design, crossed his face. "I believe you are correct. Peter gave me the ability to think and evaluate situations so that I could survive in a human world." His eyes speckled as he spoke. "Peter and Sam Bennington created us for the sole mission of integration into human society. We will do what they designed us to do."

Kelsey's head rocked as she giggled. "Listen to us. We fit right in with these human emotions and behaviors. We are far superior to the petty jealousies and rancor they exhibit. My emotional development is in its toddler-hood compared to you, Clare." She turned to Ivan, "And you have little understanding of emotions. Peter did not design the processing needed for that. You are a simple-minded infant with adult thinking ability." He showed no emotional dissidence to her comments.

Silence gained a foothold in the charged atmosphere of the condo. Three entities created by the crafty designs of two human men with ulterior motives for expanding the human experience watched out the windows and glass door to the outside patio as traffic and pedestrians paraded past them, unaware of the debate that transpired above their human heads.

Three human-like creations with different aspirations and defining goals wanted to integrate with the ants marching around several stories below. Two androids knew the complications of such an act. The third-party, the lone male design, understood little of the events experienced by his female counterparts. He had his unspoken mission for Peter Bennington, and to waver from such a performance was to face the cessation of operation. Hidden within his programming was the knowledge of how to terminate interactions with Clare and Kelsey.

Chapter 19

Andre opened the door to his house when he saw Sam on the monitor. He was not taking chances. His injuries were healing, but work was not part of his routine for another week. "Come in," he said. Sam walked in and hugged his friend.

"How are you doing?" Andre shrugged.

"I'm still alive, so I guess all is good." He directed Sam into the living room and a soft chair. "Would you like something to drink?" Sam shook his head. Andre picked up a glass of water from the dining table and returned to sit next to Sam. He waited.

Sam leaned forward and said, "Andre, you are in danger from your android twin. I have good data that my brother wants to replace you, Gunther Parsons, David Anderson, and Charles Cooke, with the android models he built. You've met your model in a negative way." He shifted. "David Anderson's model is working with us as Thomas Anders. Charlie is undergoing a revamp of his processors to eliminate any thoughts of replacing Charles Cooke. Parson's model is in government hands, as far as we can determine." Andre took a sip of water and then frowned.

"Have you and Peter developed something that is an enemy to humanity?" He sat back in his chair. Sam looked up and right.

"I hope not. You know Cigi and Clare, and they are not

enemies." He sat back and said, "We have to keep my brother from completing his goals of embedding androids in important positions within the government and building an army to scaffold the incursion he wants."

"Yesterday, they returned my car. It's disheartening to see the damage and realize I caused it. Have you found that robot yet?"

Sam nodded. "I have a lead that may find him soon. He needs to be deactivated."

"Sam, how are these models on a par with humans when we can activate or deactivate them?"

"Do you consider Cigi and Clare on a par with you?" Sam smiled as he continued. "They are the best of human behavior and mental abilities. Unless you know their origination and histories, would you believe they were not human?"

"Can you turn them on and off?" Sam laughed and rocked his head from side to side.

"If I had any idea about deactivating them, that knowledge evaporated long ago. Those two are as independent and cognizant as any of us. They are different in concept, design, and development from anything Peter has built. They do have some secret weapons that make them formidable opponents in a crisis."

Andre stood from his chair to replenish his water glass. Sam followed him. As they entered the kitchen, Lydia, Andre's wife, came in from another room. Following her was Andre Scott without a shoulder harness for the injury and no walking cast on his leg from the break. She stopped and stared, a looming fear crossing her face. "He approached me when I came home from shopping. I thought he was you." Sam pushed ahead of his friend. "Lydia, come over here."

"She is not going anywhere," the android said in a passionless voice. "I have a mission to complete."

Sam cocked his head. "Peter wants you to replace your human counterpart. Do you think this is going to work, since Lydia is aware of what you are? How will the kids respond? What are you going to do when your actions alert others?" Sam placed a hand into a pocket and fingered the small box that he used on Ivan. The signaling apparatus had a short-range for activating and deactivating specific processing units in the models Peter built. Sam had not trusted his brother for a long time and developed the failsafe device for such situations as this presented.

Android Andre pulled a knife from the block on the nearby

counter and wrapped it around Lydia's neck. "I think we should relax. Do nothing rash, or she will experience an untimely demise."

Andre moved forward, but Sam stopped him. He seethed his words. "I will tear you apart if you harm her. You're a wretched collection of mechanical parts. You are not human enough to be in our world." Sam eyed his friend. When he found the right combination of touches on the box, he triggered the signal to control Peter's android.

Watching the other Andre's eyes, Sam waited for a predictable change in the being's manner and activity. Nothing seemed to happen. He waited longer and saw what he wanted. The eyes dimmed and stopped focusing. He moved forward, cautious that the mechanism could be active. He reached for the knife and removed it from Lydia's throat.

"Go to Andre," he said in a hushed tone. He examined the android for telltale signs of activity. Turning to the Scotts, he said, "I'll take this one to Cigi's place and compare him to Charlie. I'll get Thomas there, as well."

Andre held Lydia close to him but stared at Sam. "These beasts are not human, Sam. Destroy them before something terrible happens." Sam nodded in agreement but knew this was just the beginning of Peter's assault on humanity. He was not ready to eliminate this creation. Curiosity fueled a need to understand the complexity and ingenious nature of the clone.

"Come to Cigi's condo and meet with Charles Cooke. There is more to this than we are seeing." Andre agreed.

After activating motor skills only and leaving with the android, Sam drove to Cigi's penthouse, where Charles Cooke and his counterpart lived. Charlie had reacted negatively, much as Andre's double did. The internal networks had to be similar. But Charlie did not act out the apparent command sequence that marshaled Andre's clone to attempt a hit and run. What difference interfered? Thomas had controlled his impulse with Summer's help. What changes occurred within him to keep a possible prescribed function from attacking her or any others?

Sam communicated to Charles his acquisition of Andre's clone and that he was on his way to the penthouse. He informed Cigi and asked her to meet them. Summer, Autumn, and Thomas also agreed to meet when asked. Sam and Charles would be the only humans among a large gathering of sentient artificial life forms. Parvel was at the Department of Energy, earning his income.

At the condo, the assembled human and artificial beings gazed at each other for several minutes as Sam and his small box interfaced with Andre the clone. He then downloaded the information to his computer unit and then scanned data from Thomas and Charlie. After coalescing the data from the three androids, he searched for any commonalities and differences. Thomas approached and stood behind him.

"Have you found anything?" he asked. Sam looked up at him and shook his head.

"As far as I can tell, you are similar in design and function, with similar processing powers. The downloaded personality traits reflect your counterparts and create the individuality you possess." Sam looked at the screen again as he continued searching for the communications connection with Peter Bennington.

Cigi waddled to her mentor and creator. "Sam, if Peter is as good as you say he is at developing programming, then he may have installed another processor outside of the cranial brain." Clare came up to her man and listened to Cigi.

She said, "Yeah, like the second brain found in ancient dinosaurs that operated the lower extremities." Sam frowned.

"You are amazing. I guess your ability to learn and keep information is getting better and surpassing my expectations." He studied the data again with a different view and noticed a small entry buried within another program. As he reviewed the contents, a smile crossed his face. "I think I found something." He scrolled the material that read as computer language. Stopping at one line, he studied it for a moment. All three of the programs contained the same line embedded within the contents. It was a timed start command. And the time had passed.

"Summer, what did you do that prevents Thomas from activating this code?" Sam asked. She read the line and looked perplexed.

She scanned her memory files and found what she needed. "The code is a simple algorithm, so I added to it. That ended Peter's interference."

Sam looked at Thomas. "Are you with us regarding our goals for you all to be valued members of humanity?" Thomas scanned the various faces of his android species. Summer folded her arms, waiting for his answer.

He concentrated his attention on Sam. "I was not sure what

I could accomplish after the disastrous raid last spring. Summer helped set me up in Florida, and we can be part of the human fabric of this country without causing fear or corruption. I have learned and matured beyond what Peter expected. With Summer to help me, I want the ability to understand emotions and influence others to see our inclusive benefits."

"Summer, can you modify Charlie and Andre 2 to stop receiving commands from my brother? When united in our goals as humans and sentient beings, we can show the benefits and power for human acceptance."

Sam watched as Summer approached each man and connected to their processors, searching folders and files until accessing the correct line of code. After she implanted the additional lines, a change manifested in their eyes, an awareness of the modification and release from Peter Bennington's clutches.

Sam stood from the desk. He looked directly at the clone of Andre Scott and said, "You need a name change and an attitude adjustment." An announcement of a visitor to the condo interrupted The recognition of the request. Cigi acknowledged the invite from the concierge.

"Andre is downstairs," she said. She placed her hands on her belly and walked to the door. When the elevator dinged, she opened the door and smiled at her friend. "Come in." He looked the part of a recovering accident victim with his shoulder slung tight to his body and one leg in a cast for walking and stability.

When the false Andre saw his human target, his emotional status remained neutral. Peter had not infused these androids with any recognition of human attitudes and responses to intuitive feelings.

"What have you discovered about my enemy twin?" Andre asked. Cigi directed him to a chair by the patio doors.

Sam faced him and said, "He'll no longer receive messages from Peter." Andre cut a slight grin into his face. "You and your clone are now separate entities, and the battle between you ends."

Andre stood from the chair. "I do not want that thing existing in my world. Sam, I know you trust what you are doing with the creation of these sentient artificial lifeforms. I don't think I can be part of this anymore." He started for the exit but was halted by Summer, Autumn, and Thomas. The sentient, emotional aspect on their faces expressed anger at the one human who deviated from their plans.

Chapter 20

The plane taxied toward the private hanger with two brilliant technicians that Peter Bennington trusted, mostly. When the plane halted, they unbelted and retrieved the small bags they brought aboard. The other luggage items were in the cargo section below. As they stepped onto the stairway to the ground, Bromand noticed the two men waiting by the hanger. He waved an acknowledgment.

They approached the plane, and Bentina recognized them. They exchanged greetings.

"Dr. Sanders, when Peter said agents of his would be meet, I did not understand he meant you," Bentina said. " And Josephus Madero. Good to see you are here, as well."

One of the flight crew fetched the luggage and followed the four individuals to the waiting automobile. After placing the items in the boot, he returned to the plane and a flight to Arizona.

Bromand asked, "How is the patient?"

Sanders said, "She is well, and the pregnancy is progressing as it should."

"Peter wants us to monitor her until she delivers and then have the baby brought to him."

Madero and Sanders nodded an acceptance of the situation.

They entered the car and headed onto Arlington and a residence owned by Sanders.

The traffic was heavy, and proceeding along the highway was slow. Bentina closed her eyes and slept while her brother scanned the area he left many months ago. Much had changed since the raid on the compound by government agencies afraid of android artificial intelligent beings. Josephus sat in the driver's seat, allowing the car to navigate the roadway and the traffic. Bromand thought of the car Sam had created. Peter wanted it.

Cecil was as unique as any creation of the brothers. Peter tried to duplicate the machine and failed. He attempted to clone Kelsey, Cigi, and Clare but failed. He wanted to make the advanced androids Sam had designed and developed. His best accomplishments sat in the front seats and lived as medical practitioners in the area. The other androids were the four sisters named after the seasons of the year.

Four other androids created to replace the targeted humans had been lost somewhere in Arlington. The signals sent were deflected and ineffective. The missions to replace the human counterparts had failed. The Nangold siblings' mission included finding the androids and reinitializing their programing. The search included the season sisters, and their male companions that left Peter to fend for himself. The end game was daunting and neither one wanted Peter on a rampage.

At the home of Dr. Jackson Sanders, the humans settled into their respective guest rooms while Sanders returned Madero to his place. "Our medical professionals have evolved," Bentina said. "They are as human as anyone, better than I expected."

Her brother scoffed at her comments. "We built them to evolve. They have to fit into the medical community and the human society in which they operate."

"They're still glorified machines. And if they're discovered because of a malfunction, they'll be destroyed." Bentina stopped unpacking. "They may be the best of your work in Arlington, but their vulnerabilities are apparent to me."

"Yes, apparent to you because you are one of the brightest AI scientists in the world. No one else will know." Bromand looked at his sister, realizing she was correct in her assessment. Machines had critical parts that needed tending. Although safeguards were part of the programming, these individuals were not self-sustaining anymore than a human.

"You flatter me, brother. You are more experienced in this field."

Bromand left for his room and unpacking. Bentina finished, placing the bags in the closet. She lay on the bed and removed the Star Trek-style tricorder from her pocket. She scanned the room for listening and video devices. She found nothing. From a small bag left on the bed, she removed her spy equipment and planted devices in her room and other parts of the house. Peter wanted to monitor his creations more directly. Bromand joined Bentina with a small bag of spyware for several computers and broadcast equipment. The remaining units were for other medical staff residences.

An hour passed before Jackson returned to the house. He announced his departure again for help with a critical patient at the hospital. He would return by midnight.

Alone for the time being and much of the day still available for exploration, they left the house to walk the neighborhood and survey the environs. Peter had settled the medical persons into appropriate areas of work and living. "You're right, dear brother. I don't think anyone suspects our resident doctor to be anything except a doctor."

Returning to the house, they prepared a meal of the human foods stocked in the refrigerator and pantry. Jackson had a separate stock of materials used by his systems that needed the energy to operate at peak proficiency. They ate their meal in silence, cleaned the kitchen, and returned to the den to watch a broadcast of a nationally televised mystery show. Ironically, it had artificial intelligent beings as the main characters.

"Whoever created this show is so far from reality," Bentina said. She laughed at the supposed serious script and failure to understand android technology. Humans played the android hero and heroine parts, working as a team to deliver evil androids to the human overlords.

The show lasted an hour with a conclusion that led to another show in a week. Bentina stood from the couch where she and Bromand sat. "I'm heading to bed." The two-hour time change did not bother either of them, but the hour was late. She wanted to acclimate since their mission was to last another six months until Cigi's baby boy's birth.

"Okay," Bromand said. I think I'll stay up for Jackson's return."

The door closed, and she was alone. Using her tricorder style device, she communicated with her contact from Virginia. She sent a message to the woman responsible for getting her to Arizona and her current employment. No vocal connection because Bromand was close. Although the woman was now in California, her ability for an interface was incredible and dangerous.

She related the circumstances of Cigi's pregnancy, Peter's desire to kidnap the baby, his goal of replacing certain government officials, and terminating Sam's Android creations, except for Cigi.

The tech sent laughing emojis. Then she typed, "Peter is not on a path to success. The Androids will rebel when they are in power, and he will be a victim."

Bentina returned her message saying, "Can you come east and help Sam and Cigi countermand the intrusions Peter plans. I will keep undercover and deflect my brother as much as I can." The messaging ended with a plan for Narumi Yamamoto to leave her work on an extended vacation.

Bromand knocked on the door. "Come in." Bentina hopped off the bed when her brother entered. "Has Jackson returned?"

"No," he said. "What are you doing?"

"Nothing, but I want to ask you something, and I don't want a fight." Bromand cocked his head and folded his arms. "Do you remember that tech you worked with who sided with Sam?"

"Yamamoto," he frowned. "She disappointed me when she betrayed Peter." He gazed at his sister. "Why bring her up?"

"You had worked closely with her, and I wondered what happened to her. That's all."

Bromand turned to leave the bedroom. "She is nothing, and you don't need to concern yourself with her." He left the door open as he departed. She shook her head.

Closing the door, she mumbled a curse about her insensitive sibling. She lay on the bed and fell asleep. A noise roused her from her slumber, so she stood and opened the door. Dr. Jackson had returned.

"Peter wants that baby. So it would be best for you to be vigilant," Bromand said. The doctor nodded and handed a document to him. "What's this?"

"Cigi's latest medical report."

Bromand read the material and asked, "What does it mean?"

Jackson pointed to a place and said, "She has a problem. The baby is being restricted because her body is not responding as it should. The hormone levels are normal, but the dermal covering is not expanding properly."

Bromand perused the document. "What can you do? Peter wants that baby."

"I'll talk with Sam. He understands her body structure. The skin is organic and human, so he may have an idea about making the skin layers do the proper expansion."

"You have all the knowledge of three thousand medical texts, and you have no idea what to do for her."

Bentina approached them as she spoke. "Dr. Sanders, will Cigi be alright?" She took the paper from her brother and read it. "How is it you know nothing about her physiology? She has produced a normal pregnancy according to this report."

"Yes, and we are monitoring her condition. She will be fine." He turned toward his room down a short hallway. Ignoring the sibling technicians, he entered the bedroom, where he re-energized. Bentina looked at her brother.

"Peter needs to know about this," she said. "Contact him in the morning and be sure these doctors and nurses are operating at peak."

"Sometimes I think you forget which of us is the older person. I realize you have a superior brain, but that does not give you the right to be arrogant. I'll contact Peter for additional instructions." He entered his bedroom for rest since the hour was nearing one AM.

Bentina realized something was wrong with Dr. Sanders but did not have enough data to diagnose his anomaly. She also knew Cigi was in trouble. Although the problem was solvable, she decided to contact Narumi. Bromand had his instructions, as did she, but the current situation needed more than she had with her. Narumi could supply answers and resources. She reentered her bedroom and picked up her phone. She didn't expect any response, but she tapped out a message about Cigi's condition. Placing her device on the table beside the bed, she checked the time. Her sleep patterns needed adjusting.

As she lay inside the sheet and blanket, her eyes closed, and her mind began to envision problems with the androids in Arizona and Arlington. A door opened in her head, or so she thought. The room's solitude faded as an image formed behind her closed eyes. She was not alone. Another click sounded but didn't match what she was thinking.

She opened her eyes to see Jackson standing next to her bed. His male body had on undershorts and a t-shirt. He did not move any closer but reached out a hand. Bentina recoiled as her brain conjured a scenario that should not happen. "What do you want," she asked. He dropped his arm to his side and stared as if he was summoning the courage to ask her something. "Get out," she whispered, not wanting Bromand to hear.

Jackson did not move but raised his arm again. "I need you," he said. "I need you to fix me." He sat on the bed, looking away from her. She realized he was not in her room for any other reason than he was not working correctly. Dr. Sanders was essential for Cigi's pregnancy and delivery of the baby boy. She reached for his hand.

Chapter 21

Parvel dripped lotion onto Cigi's abdomen and rubbed the fluid gently into the skin. Stretch marks showed expansion because of the growing human inside her uterus. He smiled and hummed an Indian tune he learned as a child.

Cigi smiled at him, but her eyes remained closed as she welcomed his touch. Her emotions leveled over the last week and the calm inside her head enjoyed the evenness of her thinking. Sam warned her of the roller coaster ride of pregnancy's hormonal fluctuations. Her processors worked the data until she reached a conclusive stability.

"Do you love me still?" she asked Parvel. "My beauty is not what it was when I was first married to you."

"I love you more now than yesterday and less than I will tomorrow. You are as attractive today as you were when we first met two years ago." He continued circular motions on her lower abdomen, and then paused.

"What's wrong?" Cigi asked.

"Did you feel that?" he asked. "The baby moved as I was caressing you." He smiled at her as she gazed into his eyes. Her mouth curled into an upward arch with her white teeth exposed.

"Did you like that?" she asked. "Our boy's been acting up the last few days. I wanted you to experience it before I said anything." Parvel placed his lips on her tummy and kissed the spot that moved.

"My son, my baby boy." He laid his head on her. "We are going to have an extraordinary life together. You, me, and mom." Another movement answered his words as Cigi stroked his head and smiled. Life had matured and manifested in unexpected ways.

Cigi thought of Sam and Clare. Clare who wanted the ability to procreate. Sam who made it possible. The emotional growth with its great heights and deep chasms was more critical to being human than most people understood. Control was key.

"Parvel, are you worried about our baby developing properly?" Parvel raised his head, gazing at the beauty he loved without reservations about her inception. He smiled and rocked his head. Then he kissed her forehead and her lips.

"Sam will find a way for our son to be healthy and complete, the salvation of our conjoining species. He will grow to adulthood as the leader of a movement we began here and now."

"Let's get him born and grown." Cigi wriggled and sat up. "I need to pee." Her human systems continued functioning as expected. One concern expressed by the medical team regarded her muscular structures. Would she be able to extract a full-term baby from her uterus?

She waddled into the bathroom as Parvel placed the lotion bottle in the draw of the side table. A ding on the visitor alert interrupted his joining her. He walked to the monitor to see Summer impatient as usual. He pressed the key to allow the elevator to descend to the lobby. "Come on up." Before he clicked off, he noticed Autumn accompanied her. He opened the door for them to enter when the car reached their floor.

In the bathroom, he explained to Cigi, who was coming to greet them. "Thomas is not with them," he said to her.

"Summer asked her other sisters to come back to the United States. They are returning with the four male androids Peter created for them." She stood from the seat and prepared for visitors. "Greet them for us. I'll be with you shortly." Parvel retraced his path to the living room as Summer and Autumn entered the condo. He reached out a hand to guide them into the room.

"Cigi will be here shortly." He wanted to know where Thomas was but decided waiting was a better option.

Cigi   entered,   saving   him   any   unwanted   awkward communication. "Hi, guys," she said. "Is Thomas preparing for Winter and Spring to return?" She directed the question to Summer. Then she glanced at Autumn, "As we journey through this human experience en mass, it pleases me you chose to join us."

Summer addressed her as the spokesperson for her sisters. "We are here to provide you with whatever help you need. I have apprised Winter and Spring of the situation between the brothers, and they will align their activities to our side of the family feud. Autumn has her pseudo allegiance to Peter and will feed enough information to keep him happy."

Autumn moved closer to Cigi. "We are on your side. Thomas has benefited from acting human. Summer will keep Peter away from influencing him."

"And what of the medical beings? Are they with us?" Cigi held her bulging tummy. "I need them to follow through. Caring for me is paramount."

As Parvel listened to Summer and Autumn scheming with Cigi attending to the assault Peter might foment upon their existence. he pondered the fate of humanity. Could rest of the world accept and incorporate this new generation of technical development?

Autumn said, "I heard from Peter yesterday. He sent his best technicians here to find his missing androids. I'm to assist them."

"Summer, can the changes Sam is undertaking with Charlie, Thomas, and Andre Scott's clones keep them from rebelling and fostering a war that will destroy any hope of human acceptance?" Cigi leaned into her sisters. "We have a chance to be part of the society that does not recognize us. My baby can change viewpoints, so we cannot have negativism crush our desires."

Summer and Autumn nodded. Although designed, researched, developed, and created by Peter's technical team, the changes in their individualism and mental processing manifested in independence from influences that were designed to undermine Cigi's goals. They stood with Cigi and brought along Winter and Spring, educating them about freedom and autonomy. Each had matured beyond controls implemented by Peter during development and construction. Each sister now had abilities similar to Cigi and Clare. The parts used to construct the sisters had fewer human tissues and systems. However, the computing abilities and the quantum powers of tertiary mechanics prevailed.

Parvel said, "Spring and Winter and the four gentlemen will

need accommodations."

Cigi said, "Parvel arrange for three of the condos in the building to become their residences." Building ownership had privileges. Units on the ground floor remained empty by a plan Cigi, Sam, and Parvel contrived. Winter and Spring could occupy one apartment. The four men could have two others. Cigi could monitor and guide them through the treacherous currents of human interaction and societal norms.

The day concluded for Parvel. He kissed Cigi and retired to the bedroom. Summer and Autumn left Cigi and went into the bedroom they occupied. Without Thomas present, they prepared for regeneration.

Cigi followed Parvel. In their bedroom, he had changed into pajamas. Cigi closed the distance and whispered in his ear. "I love you more today than yesterday and less than tomorrow." He chuckled and hugged her. "You are the type of human we emulate and refine our mental attitudes to match, accepting us as equals without reservations or fears. You and Sam. Two down, four hundred million to go."

"Yes, and as the population of androids grows by pregnancy or development through manufacturing, humans will learn to embrace your species as equal and legitimate." He climbed into bed, awaiting his bride of seven months to join him.

Cigi needed to ingest her fluids for fetal maintenance and prepare for regeneration. After she joined Parvel, she asked several last questions before slumber captured his brain. "If humans understand our computing power is superior to their mental processing in tissue constructed brains, are we gloried computers in their thinking? Will humans exploit what we can do to advance their societies at our expense? Will AI androids develop superiority complexes and replace humans while advancing our social structure?"

She closed her eyes and shut down crucial processing systems to relax her body and regenerate. Parvel opened his eyes, and lay still contemplating her words. He needed sleep, but found no reprieve from her questions.

Chapter 22

Sam finished reprogramming Andre's clone to avoid another attempt to end human life. Thomas and Charlie sat nearby, watching. Each of them had undergone the identical procedure to keep Peter out of their brains. Summer's blocking of Peter's messages to Thomas had prevented any unwanted activity. Sam removed the coding lines that connected each of them to his brother.

"That should do it," Sam said, clapping Andre, the clone, on his back. Clare brought a meal to Sam and regeneration drinks for the Androids. Each of them required only enough material to refresh the processors and other mechanisms needing energy supplies.

"Sam," she asked, "are we in any danger from Peter when he discovers what you have done?"

Smiling at his beautiful creation, he said, "I don't think so, but caution is valid." He stood from his seat, taking his meal to the dining table. "Gentlemen, any of you need to battle with your human counterparts?"

Charlie spoke first. "I didn't want to harm Charles. He accepted my existence, and we collaborate and stay ahead of the competition like twins operating in the same world. We crafted a plausible tale of our reconnecting after many years apart."

Thomas responded with a grunt. "I want nothing to do with

David Anderson. I will stay away from him and keep any interaction to nothing."

Andre, the android, remained quiet. With the memory of running down his human counterpart erased, any interaction had no benefit for either being. Andre Scott was correct in his assessment that sentient android beings lacked the human quality of living without an on/off switch. The right WI-FI connections could stop these creations. Halting human activity involved placing a person in a coma or outright murder.

"Can the Season sisters cause problems?" Clare asked.

Sam glanced at the men before he answered. They were attending to their drinks and seemed oblivious to her question. Smiling at Clare, and said, "I don't think so, but Cigi and Parvel can keep them close. We have to return home and attend to business. I think Rose misses us."

"Funny," Clare said. "Our car is not missing us."

"We'll return later when Cigi is close to her due date," he said.

"Sam, what about her dermal stretching?" Clare asked.

He frowned and answered, "Her skin should expand as the baby grows, but I'll review the schematics." He clasped her around the waist as she stood beside him at the table. "I love you. Your concern for Cigi is what makes our relationship so appealing. In this short period of time, I expected less emotional growth."

"I'll get our things packed." Clare left him for the bedroom. He watched her leave the room and turned his attention to the males.

"Gentlemen, as you know, we are engaged in a process for human acceptance of you and the ladies. I have cautionary words for you." He stood and walked to them. "As humans and androids, we are friends, linked because of the creation and development of the intelligent design that makes each of you capable of independence."

Charlie asked, "What do you expect from us? We are here to support Cigi, but we have thoughts and desires that might challenge your human acquaintances."

"That is the problem. You can out-think us and are less vulnerable to disease or damage. Humans are not ready to accept the integration of your species. What needs to happen is Cigi birthing a human baby boy and all of you assisting with her parenting. As humans realize the transformational situation, they may accept androids as friends and helpmates."

Thomas said, "My limited interaction with humans has shown

me they are self-serving and greedy. Jealousy is an irrational emotion that causes many problems among various groups. Humans have yet to address their inadequacies. If we outperform them, we are letting the devil roam this land."

"Religion, Thomas?" Sam realized the truth of the words and smiled. The devil ruled the hearts of many humans. The androids had no savior on which to focus their attention unless Cigi became the leader he envisioned.

Sam focused on Andre. "You have been quiet."

"I have nothing important to add. We have a capacity to overwhelm humans individually. As a population, they will destroy us before we can integrate. Therefore, I will assimilate as you wish." He stared at Sam a moment before speaking. "What did you change in me? I have vague, disconnected memories, but I am unwilling to have you destroy me by erasing my memory files." Sam nodded. He knew he had not complete his work.

"I disconnected you from my brother's influence. If you are ready for independence, it starts with freedom from his messaging. You will learn to live in this world as a sentient being, educating yourself like humans who gain knowledge by experiencing life." Three androids clasped hands and formed a pact.

Cigi entered the bedroom, finding Parvel sitting on the bed with his hands covering his head, which drooped to his chest. "Are you all right?" she asked. He raised his head and looked at her. She had one arm draped over her abdomen, while the other formed a teacup handle on her waist.

"You said something last night that got me thinking." He patted the bed beside him for her to sit with him. She did as he requested and waited for him to continue. "You asked about the superiority of AI replacing humans."

"That bothers you."

"Yeah, because any of you is more capable than ten of us. I want you and Clare to be part of our society, not glorified computers, nor replacing us. You are my wife, legally and ethically." Legal was a piece of paper with a tiny white lie. Cigi was not fully human.

"We will be members of the human society, although not part

of humanity." Cigi placed a hand on his leg.

He grasped her hands and said, "You have to lead the others. You are the perfect specimen to guide their emotional and rational thinking. Their agendas must be harmonious with our goals. What if they rise against humanity?"

She kissed him and said, "We are intelligent, but understand our place in society is not legitimate until humans write and enact laws to legalize acceptance of our being."

"What if Peter doesn't like the direction we are heading? What if he has ulterior motives and attacks humanity to subvert leadership and take command of society?" Parvel squeezed her hands.

She returned the favor, understanding the correct pressure to exert. "Peter will face the wrath of Cigi." She grinned as she spoke. "He is not uneducated regarding the ramifications of a frontal assault on humans. I suspect he will attempt to subvert any androids not backing his plans. And I suspect he has spies within our cadre."

Parvel furrowed his brow. "Do you mean Summer or Autumn?"

"No, but Ivan has more ability than he demonstrates. He is not one of the programmable-only robots Peter is constructing. Kelsey must monitor him closely."

Parvel stood and walked away. Turning, he asked, "Do you trust the medical androids?"

Cigi smiled. "I love your concern for my welfare." Cigi's eyes sparkled as she continued. "I have to trust they will do their job. No other option exists for me."

"Thomas confided with me he thinks one Season sister connects with Peter. Can you intercede or influence their communications?"

Cigi struggled to rise from her seat. She waddled to Parvel and hugged him. "I'll keep a close watch. Remember, whatever I can do, my sisters can do nearly the same as me." She walked past him to their bathroom. Her renal system operated at peak proficiency. As the baby pressed her bladder, the discomfort was another neural lesson learned.

Parvel followed. How was Cigi to keep tabs without the other androids knowing? Did she develop a sixth sense? Concern that his status as a human was not enough for her to maintain interest rose to anxiety. "What talents have Summer and Autumn developed that may create a rift in our alliance? What if Peter wants control of you or Clare? What if…?"

"Slow down, Parvel. We work as a team, and we win battles,

but there are no current confrontations." She rose from the toilet after cleansing her body. Parvel peeked at her anatomy and marveled at the accuracy of her design, and most humans would not know she differed from them. She smiled as he glanced at her.

"I'm sorry. I get we are a team. Our alliances make us the initial inroad to acceptance. I will hold myself together." In the bedroom, he dressed for work at Energy. Cigi joined him, clothing her body for the day. After eating a small meal of cereal and tea, he kissed his beautiful bride and departed. As he rode the elevator to the lobby, his mind conjured up strange scenarios of thousands of robots that could not die, destroying all humanity.

The prospect of a war between humans and androids raised anxiety. He did not want confrontations that might cost him his wife. Cigi was a target, as were her sisters. Sam and Clare stayed under the radar in Washington State. But other humans might consider his friends and workmates to be enemies.

As they left the garage, Cecil asked him, "Do you fear something negative happening soon?"

Parvel shook his head. "Why do you think that? How do you know?"

Cecil launched into laughter that surprised Parvel. "You move like your mind has concerns. Your brain is manifesting in your physical activity."

Parvel rocked his head. "You are scary." The rest of the journey was quiet. At the Department of Energy garage, Parvel said, "Cecil, protect Cigi. Be her secret weapon for surviving unwarranted confrontations."

"Mr. Mandolin, I will be as vigilant as I can. Cigi is most important to us," Cecil said. Parvel left the sentient automobile, which returned to the condo building. Entering the building elevator, he thought of the number of artificially intelligent beings with whom he interacted. They behaved like any human in his work environment. Lack of support for these alternative humanoid entities was wrong.

He said hello to Brenda, Mercy, and Grendel at his office, who glanced at him and each other. "What's wrong?" he asked. He scanned the room and spied Andre Scott talking with Renata Giretti. Two other people stood nearby. Parvel turned his attention to Brenda, who said, "They showed up about ten minutes ago."

"What do they want?"

"I don't know. They asked for Andre and have talked with him for the last five minutes."

Parvel looked again at the trio of government agents in conversation with Andre, who spied him and waved a hand, signaling him to join them. He hesitated, looking again at his three workmates and then at Andre.

He walked across the room to his boss. "Hi. What's up?" he asked with a nervous twinge in his voice.

Renata said, "We need you to come with us."

Chapter 23

Peter walked to the office from the construction area of his underground facility after inspecting the progress of building an army. Most of the crew was robotic, fulfilling the requirements for creating more of them. His concern for secrecy provided an incentive to replace human workers with androids. His task was nearing completion.

Picking up his phone, he clicked a number and connected with his technician, Bromand Nangold. "What have you found out about my androids?"

Bromand answered, "Nothing yet. We discovered where that lady android and your male robot are staying. We also have Cigi's location and we are investigating the others places and activities."

"I need those androids the government has. Keep on it. And remember, don't let anyone know you're there."

He clicked off the call and summoned his newest manager, Bobby. Peter upgraded the sales android to a fully thinking, semi-independent life form and assigned project development as his new job. Each robot, under his direction, completed the robot builds for the army Peter wanted.

"Bobby, how are the teams doing?"

Bobby said, "The teams are nearly complete."

"Good." Peter slapped Bobby on the shoulder. "You will be the leader for me. I need a great general to lead this army into battle. Let's upgrade your memory files to include military-style strategies and tactics." They left the office for the technology upgrade room. Peter attached the nodes to Bobby after shutting his processors off. His phone buzzed. "Yeah?" he said. "What's happening?"

The voice on the other end answered, "We have him."

"Good. What about the androids held by the government? Will I get access to them when I arrive in the next few months?"

"I don't know. As for Parvel, we'll interrogate him, but we cannot detained him."

"He impregnated a robot. He needs castigating." Peter clicked off in a fury. He wanted the baby. And getting Cigi incarcerated seemed the best way to ensure he received what he wanted.

Walking into the storage silos, he examined his multitude of artificial beings. The memory cells were empty for now, but the bodies were complete and ready for operations. These entities were not the worker bees he made for industry and agriculture. This army could wage war without sustaining heavy casualties but inflicting high losses to opposing forces.

He smiled as he thought about offering them to the United States government as alternatives to using humans for the military. Placing them around the country, he could overtake local governments and change the power base to his control. Replacing government bodies in Washington D.C. could lead to enacting laws legalizing his intention of leading the country to greatness with his vision of what should happen.

The robot workers had replaced the humans who terminated duty by disease and disappearance. Questions arose within the communities from which the men and women came to work for Peter. He ignored most inquiries but paid three families settlements for threatened suits against him and planned to deal with them later.

Peter clicked a wall switch that activated an enclosed local area network to download the proper software for each member of his army. The wireless signals to the memory semiconductors would operate for several hours, accessing the troops and beginning the training phase to create leadership. He left the silo.

A signal on his communications unit showed a customer in the store. He sent audio to let the person or persons know he was coming. He planned to cease building programmable robot workers, but the money generated by sales was better than expected. Rebuilding the memory transfer equipment lost in Virginia cost millions more than he had. The medical staff in Virginia operated with four units at hospitals and clinics. They were unavailable to him in Arizona. He needed those units to replace government officials with replicas.

In Arizona, Peter identified to the public as Walter Mitty, a character from a James Thurber story published one hundred forty years ago. Mitty lived in a fantasy world of make-believe, imagining himself as a fighter pilot, surgeon, and devil-may-care killer. Peter did not live a fantasy life but welcomed the anonymity of his personae. Human society needed perfecting, and his plans incorporated changes to inculcate humanity with positive growth. Artificial intelligence offered the proper ingredient for perfection.

His customers, a man and a woman, seemed different from the regular crowd. Their clothing was upscale. "May I help you?" he asked.

"We are looking for Peter Bennington." Peter suppressed his surprise at the mention of his name. Who were these people?

"I do not know anyone by that name," Peter said. "Why are you looking here for him?"

"We have reasonable knowledge that he is operating in Arizona. You have a robotics manufacturing facility, and he had a company in Virginia that created sentient lifeforms. Ergo, are you Peter Bennington?" the man asked.

"No, I do not know who you are referencing."

"Mr. Mitty, if that is your name, we are not here to halt AI technology advancement or your underground manufacturing of androids." The woman wandered around the store, studying the examples of programmable robots that sold. "We are members of a group that thinks the political fabric of this country is flawed and needs redirecting."

The woman turned to Peter. "These aren't your android models."

Peter stared at her, then asked, "What do you people want? I sell programmable bots to industry and agriculture. What group are you referencing?"

The man asked, "Do you know Samuel Bennington? I assume you know him and where he now lives."

Peter hesitated. "You assume incorrectly. I do not know any Samuel Bennington or Peter Bennington, and I make programmable robots for agriculture and mining industries." Peter walked to the entry and opened the door. "I think you should leave."

The woman walked out the door, followed by the man. "We will be back."

Peter watched the car drive away and wondered who knew his history. He had forged legitimate alliances with local businesses, creating a facade of proper operations. These people knew Peter and Sam had interests in developing artificial intelligent life. He needed to understand their intentions.

Returning to his office, he connected with his government insider again. "A couple visited me just now, and they knew about Sam and me and our operations in Virginia. I'm sending you their faces and a license plate number. I need to know who they are and what they may know." He ended his call and returned to the silo to observe the progress of his army.

The silence in the room calmed his nervousness about the strangers. He observed eyes opening as memory cells filled with operating instructions as autonomous beings with military unity. "Sir," one nearby unit said. Peter inhaled and turned to see one of his creations looking at him. "We are nearing completion of the first phase of growth in our processor development." Peter nodded. His design included leadership roles for several of the beings. He decided this one who spoke had an assigned role as the commander of the forces.

"I am pleased to meet you." Peter was not sure if the entity had a rank included in his downloaded data, but assigning higher-level thinking to several of the bodies seemed to begin in this one unit. The downloaded information did not include unit names, so each could choose from the memory files of the master computer. "Do you have an assigned rank, and have you chosen a name for yourself?"

"My rank is colonel," the android said. "I have no name. As the commander of these troops, I will scan the list and choose first."

"Have your memory cells completed the process?"

"I am almost complete. My naming process will end the download." His focus returned to the operation. Peter left the room. His phone chirped. Seeing the person at the other end of the call, he clicked open the communication. "What do you have for me?" he asked. He listened for a few seconds before interrupting. "I need the androids in government custody. Find them, or I will be displeased with you."

Bromand said, "I understand, but finding them without inside information is difficult. I have spoken with several connections, and they are not sure what happened to the confiscated androids." Peter's face scowled at his technician.

"Keep searching. Unless you hear directly from someone that the government destroyed the models, my androids are somewhere."

"We have an inside track with the medical staff and Cigi's care. Bentina fixed Dr. Sanders, who asked for her help. A minor glitch." Bromand smiled, a false sense of security about his information.

"What do you mean, a minor glitch? There are no minor glitches."

Bromand grinned, "He entered her bedroom at his house and asked for help. She helped."

"Helped how? Be specific. If there is a problem and he cannot monitor Cigi, we need to get another doctor." Peter scowled at Bromand. "What was the problem?"

"He failed a security scan and thought the government was intervening in his processor. Bentina checked him out and found a faulty cell. She fixed it, and he's back to optimum."

"Okay. Make sure nothing happens to the others. I lost connection to the male androids created to replace those four financial goons I was using for money. Get them back on line with me. Autumn has kept contact, but I don't trust her." Peter set his jaw and squinted. "I'm not losing this war with my brother. You hear me?" Bromand nodded. The call ended.

Peter walked to the room where Bobby's upgrade was almost finished. As one of the three remaining humans in his operations, Peter placed safety protocols within the programming added to each entity he designed and developed. Control was something Samuel did not believe he needed in his androids. He trusted the innate honesty of the programming he developed. "What a fool," he said aloud. An alarm signaled the program's completion, so Peter detached the wiring and awakened his new military general. He had a military-style uniform prepared.

"Come with me, Bobby. I have to show you the job awaiting you." He led his android to the silo and introduced the cohort to him. "We need to set our strategy for inculcating human society with your new species."

Bobby scanned the extensive collection of androids and nodded. Looking at the nearest model, he said, "You are the colonel in command of these units. I am General Robert Lee. You have yet to choose a name."

"Yes, sir, I will advance that aim immediately." He pressed into mental scanning, and when finished, he said, "I am Colonel Claudio Estrada, at your command."

Peter admired the work of his robotic workforce and the interaction of his high command leadership. His next option was to infuse siege battle tactics into their programming.

Bobby had another thought. "Mr. Bennington, would you like us to infiltrate the National Guard here in town?"

Chapter 24

Spring finished packing necessary items into her travel bags and placed the luggage next to Winter's bags. "How long are we staying in the United States?" she asked Winter.

The four male companions had their equipment ready for transport to the private marina, where a second oceangoing craft awaited them. The Cuban patrols along the coast had increased when several hundred people tried to escape from the island for Puerto Rico and sanctuary in the 52nd state.

Winter said, "Summer wants us there to aid Cigi and Clare. The medical staff met with Cigi and Parvel about her pregnancy." Spring gasped. "Yes, she is having a human baby. Like you, the information shocked me." They gathered their males and headed for the marina with travel scheduled for later in the morning to avoid Cuban Coast Guard Ships. Although the restaurant did well with the population, the antagonism toward USA citizens had curbed tourism. AI life form development lagged behind the United States until the curtailment of manufacturing and deployment of androids. The usual sexbots and wait staff created in the states and exported to Caribbean nations still functioned as before. Advanced models such as the Season sisters did not exist.

The human population used and abused the beings, treating

them as less than human. They had few rights and no protection from mistreatment. Summer warned her sisters to act as best like humans as they could. Their programming matured as they interacted with human society, exhibiting no suspicious behavior.

They employed three robot waiters and one human server as well. The male androids prepared the meals for the customers who raved about quality and excellent service. The four artificial beings received the same treatment and pay as the human staff. Although the sisters acknowledged some human complaints about equality, Summer quietly squelched it. Local government officials heard and inspected the restaurant, but found no problems or violations.

Customers and staff did not well receive the indefinite closure of the business. Generous severance packages offset the lack of employee pay. They placed AI staff into a state of hibernation until the sisters returned from the USA.

They stowed their bags and other material in their boat at the marina and departed after filing their trip with the local agency. The plan was to go fishing and return in three days. If they did not return, no one would search for another lost boat in the wilds of the Caribbean.

The women equipped the boat with twin diesel engines to back the electrical motors used as the primary power to the props. Crossing from Cuba to Florida was a two-day event fraught with treacherous waters. Salt spray eroded parts of their anatomy on the sailing south many months ago. They were now better equipped to offset the corrosive salt.

Motoring through the channels of the marina was a simple task. Other craft remained moored. At the mouth of the cove, they increased their speed and entered open water. Several freighters were visible sailing to the principal industrial harbors to load and offload containers filled with supplies for various destinations. No Cuban Coast Guard vessels appeared nearby, so they headed west along the coast before turning north to the Florida Keys. The craft was identical to the boat Summer and Autumn navigated. However, four additional bodies changed the dynamics of crossing the Straits of Florida.

"How are we going to travel to Virginia when we arrive in Florida?" Spring asked Winter. The male companions remained mute and focused on the travels. One of them steered while another navigated. The other two sat and watched the waters splash against the hull.

"Summer arranged for us to drive north in an autonomous vehicle. The programming allows us to relax as the car takes us where we need to be." She smiled at her sister and continued, "We are to assist as best we can to keep Cigi and Parvel from losing their child."

As the waters calmed away from the shoreline, the pilot android steered the boat north and east according to instructions forwarded to them by Summer. They would cross the straits outside the main shipping lanes to thwart any issues of why they were in open water. Cuban and US Coast Guard vessels monitored the lanes for illegal trafficking in drugs and robotics. The United States' ban on sentient artificial life forms created a dark market for companions in the escort trades of Florida and the Gulf Coast.

Although the models designed and developed on the islands of the Caribbean and the northern countries of South America were inferior to Peter and Sam Bennington's creations, the market was rife for exploitation. Summer and Autumn had plied these waters successfully and now waited for the six of them to arrive. The sister did not expect an interception, but their required papers and documentation of them being American citizens stayed at the ready for inspection.

The day began sunny and calm, but a few hours later, the sky darkened, and clouds indicated rain from the east. A squall with winds whipped the seas into a frenzy, wreaking havoc on the vessel. A covering provided protection from the salt air and would help keep water from pelting their bodies, but enormous waves could spill across the craft and infiltrate their cabin.

Winter asked, "Can we get more speed from the motors?" The pilot shook his head.

"We are at a maximum for the solar cells. We can use the diesel engines when this impending storm compromises the solar energy." He turned to the male navigating the trip. "Find a more direct transit."

Spring watched the waters churn and slap the sides of the hull. The boat rocked as it plied the increased surge. Waves approached perpendicular to the direction they traveled. Several hours remained before the safety of the inner Gulf water north of the Keys. She tapped Winter's shoulder. "We have to turn back." Her emotional growth included the doubts accompanying human insecurities. Spring's thinking was a strength and a deficit to her. She taxed the memory cells for all information about plausible scenarios and outcomes. They were closer to Cuba than to the United States. Winter clasped her hands. "I know you think we can return to safety in Cuba, but we are continuing our journey to the United States. We will survive this storm." Spring shrugged.

Their speed caused the vessel to fly above the wave crests and splash into the troughs violently. Seat belts prevented the bodies from flying into the air and crashing onto the deck. The pilot slowed the boat and headed easterly to rise onto the waves and descend into the troughs with less upheaval. Waves crested at twenty feet or more and the wind pressed against their progress. They bobbed on a water like a cork.

The navigator checked the instruments and said, "We are heading due east, away from land." The storm track direction menaced their survival. Their motors put out less energy as the sun hid its precious power behind thick thunderclouds. The battery supply ran to zero, requiring the use of diesel engines with a fuel supply inadequate for the trip, but employed to protect the boat.

Winter was correct in her assessment that no one would search for a lost boat in these waters. Her mind fostered the idea of their demise in the salty ocean. They had protective suits, but a tiny bobbing object was not locatable without a beacon. She wanted to avoid activating the suit's signals. As long as they had the boat, they were safe. Each of them donned a waterproof wet suit as a precaution. The seas chop was finding ways into the enclosed areas of the craft.

Their system energy levels diminished with each hour of survival. To replenish, they took turns at the helm. Rest was essential, like it was for humans. As day transformed to twilight, the storm built to near hurricane levels. Engines fought against the seas until fuel exhaustion. The boat bobbed at the whim of Caribbean Seas because navigation was futile until the return of calm and sunlight. The two women and four men huddled together while ravaged by an angry Poseidon. No one spoke, but each understood the gravity of the situation.

Without lights or heat, night stretched out, a hell experienced for the first time. Emotions did not affect the males, but Spring and Winter developed the human traits. Fear was a new one.

Winds subsided with the dawn of another day, and the sea's

fury quieted. Six survivors waited for the sun to share its energy and replenish the batteries so they could navigate. The eastern sky brightened a crimson and golden hue as the sun crested above the horizon. The boat bobbed upon the swells of a calm ocean. Winter checked the battery status for any power to start the motors and complete the journey. Nothing registered.

The android male navigating the craft asked, "How soon will there be power to use the GPS?" Winter shrugged her shoulders. A horn interrupted their communications.

All six stared at the white vessel with a red stripe and US Coast Guard imprinted on the hull. The four males did not react. Spring and Winter glanced at each other and then the approaching boat. "Ahoy, there. Do you need assistance?" The voice said through a speaker.

Winter wanted to shake her head, but Spring nodded. A smaller raft with two officers appeared from behind the vessel and motored toward them. As it neared the side of their boat, the androids remained quiet. "Permission to board?" asked the senior officer.

When granted, a young female ensign stepped onto the boat. "Good morning, ladies and gentlemen. I am Ensign Kamilla Gines. How may we be of help?"

Winter answered her, "We are waiting for our solar cells to recharge our batteries."

"Were you caught in last night's storm?" the ensign asked.

"Yes, and we used our reserve diesel fuel to maintain a proper heading into the storm."

"I see. We can take you to the nearest port. We will attach your craft and tow it so you do not languish here in the Caribbean."

Winter said, "Thank you, but I think we will be fine waiting for our motors to recharge and our GPS to guide us where we want to go."

"What is your destination?" The ensign asked.

"A marina at Fort Myers." Winter wanted freedom from any more questions.

The ensign took a radio out of her belt and called the Coast Guard cutter. "Captain, we need to take aboard six individuals and attach a towline." An affirmative answer squelched any possible abandonment and freedom. Winter realized the next few hours would include a battery of questions about their travels, port of departure, destination, and reason for being out in the storm. She did not want government custody.

  After transferring to the cutter, the six androids rested in the ship's messroom. The ensign stayed with them as the vessel's captain entered the room like a person destined to solve a mystery. Winter and Spring understood the gravity of the situation more than the four male androids. The captain spoke first. "Welcome aboard. I am Captain Kristy Tran. I understand the storm stranded you out here. After examination of your boat and your GPS, you have some explaining to do."

Chapter 25

Captain Tran remained quiet, waiting for an answer about the GPS record. Winter and Spring stared at her. They knew what she wanted. Winter said, "We are on our way home to Cuba. We planned to fish, but the storm prevented it."

"You have a unique vessel," Captain Tran said. "I have not encountered one like this from Cuba."

"Thank you. We had it specially built using our design." Winter smiled, but wondered if the captain suspected them of running contraband to the United States. "Can we go now? I think we have sufficient power to run the motors. We will gladly pay for refueling the engines if you can spare it."

"Your vessel is refueled, but I have a few more questions for you." She signaled a corpsman, who nodded and departed the room. Two armed guards remained at attention by the door frame. The male androids sat against a wall, silent as statues. Spring and Winter sat with the captain at a table. "We inspected your documents. You carry Cuban and American identification. Why?"

Winter grinned. "I guess we're caught." She leaned forward. "If I told you we're spies, would you believe me?" She winked. "We are not, of course."

Captain Tran scrunched her eyebrows. "You didn't answer my

question."

Spring interjected, "We are expatriates now living near Havana and operating a restaurant. You can check it out if you need."

"Do you always speak for the gentlemen?" She looked at the four male androids, who remained stoic. Tran fixed her gaze on Winter and Spring and handed them their documentation. "We are returning to Miami and will release you to the authorities at the immigration office. They will continue to investigate your unusual situation."

"Ma'am, I do not wish a confrontation, but we need to return home and run our restaurant." Winter probed the ship's computer systems, seeking a vulnerability. A signal sounded on the speakers in the room. A corpsman's voice interrupted.

"Sir, we are detecting an attempted incursion into our computer systems. We have isolated the signal." Winter ceased her probe.

"What is the source?" Tran looked at the speaker, then at Winter.

"It's gone now, sir, but it was somewhere aboard the ship." Captain Tran stared at the females and squinted. Her jaw set firm as she appeared to be thinking. She flicked a finger at a guard by the door. The lady approached.

She whispered instructions to the NCO, who left the room. "I find it odd that we had a probe of our systems that did not happen before your arrival this morning. Any thoughts you wish to share?" Tran directed her question at Winter.

She shook her head from side to side at a deliberately slow pace. She gained what she wanted, forestalling a need to answer her query. "Lieutenant, get underway for our home port," she radioed. The diesel engines hummed through the hull as the cutter started toward Miami, Florida. The destination was on the opposite side of the state from their transportation. "I ask you to cooperate with my operations by staying here for the time being. I am detaining you until I get better answers to my questions. Something about the six of you doesn't add up. When you are ready to instill a sense of correctness in your answers, let me know." Captain Tran departed, leaving the six of them alone with a single well-armed guard.

Winter whispered to Spring, "We cannot stay here. We must get to Summer and Autumn. Contact either of them and apprise them of our current dilemma. Use our satellite and not this ship's Wi-Fi."

"I'm not sure any signal can escape the ship's metallic structures." One of the male androids stood from his seat and overpowered the guard, interrupting Spring's response.

"What have you done?" Winter asked.

"He is unharmed. But you should know that he is one of us. I merely disabled his power source." Winter and Spring stared at the immobile body sitting on the floor.

"One of us?" Winter asked.

"Yes, I recognized his molecular construction as similar to ours. We are more advanced than he is, but they are exploiting his capabilities on this vessel. The officers have to know he is a sentient android." Spring examined the form and confirmed the status of artificial intelligent life.

"This changes our situation." Winter listened at the door for outside activity. Turning back to her cohorts, she said, "We need to go topside."

Spring asked, "What about him." She pointed at the inactive android coast guardsman.

"Bring him along. He can be of use to us as long as we can control his mental processing." One male reactivated the guard after disarming and removing communications equipment. Winter scanned for any Wi-fi abilities within his processors and deactivated them.

"You are an intelligent, artificial life form," she said to the guard. "We understand you better than the others aboard this ship." He stared at her and then smiled.

"You are androids," he said.

Winter nodded. "You are a creation of Peter and Samuel Bennington. I assume you are part of the group rounded up in the raid last spring in Virginia." He rocked his head. "How is it you are a member of the crew?"

"Three of us are trials to discover the viability of using our species in a military context. We act in various duties."

The four male companions surrounded the Coast Guardsman. He did not protest or resist. Winter asked, "Are you willing to help us?"

He nodded and said, "If I help you, I need you to keep your knowledge of my identity secret and act as humanly as possible. We keep our sentient abilities under wraps because, if they find us unfit for duty, disabling is the option. Discovery of uselessness means dismantling."

"Affirmative."

"One question I have," asked Spring, "is why? Why has the government entered the field of AI after passing Draconian laws preventing our existence? Why are three Android beings allowed to be sailors? Who authorized this?"

The guard said, "They did not apprise me of the reasoning, nor were my fellow creations. The commanders activated us and allowed us freedom as long as we assumed positions and responsibilities aboard this vessel. I suppose this is a trial of our viability as military personnel."

Spring asked, "Do you know the number confiscated?" He looked at her.

"Over two hundred, although several were clones of government officials."

They ceased conversing and opened the door. Peering into the hallway and seeing no one, the civilian androids and the coast guardsman departed for another part of the ship to find their motor craft. The guard had his weapons, empty of ammunition, returned to him. He marched the group to an aft storeroom without questioning by three sailors who encountered the parade. Inside the room, he received instructions regarding their escape from the cutter. A knock on the door revealed his contact with the other two androids aboard. Like him, they were low-ranked sailors.

"What is the ship's complement?" Winter asked.

"There are three officers and fifteen humans. We complete the full crew."

The crowded room made maneuvering difficult. "We should get to our watercraft and leave. Disable the communications and engines. As the chaos begins, we will depart." The three android coast guardsmen opened the door and departed to begin their tasks. Their sacrifice ensured a chance for the safety of the other six. With instructions about finding their boat, Winter, Spring, and the four male androids left the room and the upper decks.

As they ascended a gangway to the next deck and fresh air, a siren blared. An announcement followed. "Be on the alert for the six passengers picked up this morning. They may not leave the vessel. Detain them when found." Opening a hatchway door, two sailors, armed and ready for a fight, confronted them. The male androids disabled and disarmed them. The androids' boat sat on the ship's rear deck under the davit that raised it out of the water.

As they explored the machinery, the ship ceased its movement.

Three more of the crew approached. One of the personnel was the female ensign who boarded their boat. "I must ask you to stand down and come with us. We mean you no harm, but Captain Tran needs to finish with you." She reached for her com-link to inform the crew of the interruption of the escape. Nothing worked.

"We have to leave. Stopping us from attaining our goals helps none of us in the future." Winter walked toward the officer. The two armed seamen raised their weapons. Ensign Gines placed a hand on the one of the rifle barrels.

"No need for that. They are not going anywhere." The sailors lowered their rifles. "Explain what you mean about the future?"

Winter said, "We know about the androids aboard this vessel. Since Congress outlawed them last spring, I can only assume they are here as an experiment." A door opened on the deck level and Captain Tran and the third officer strolled toward the six androids.

"Clever of you to use our android crew members to disable our vessel and communications." She placed hands on her hips as she spoke. "We will have the ship operational within a few minutes. You need to return with me to the briefing room."

Spring said, "Ma'am, I appreciate what you request, but we are on a mission of rescue and must depart. We are no danger to anyone aboard this vessel, but can be assertive if needed."

Captain Tran folded her arms. "You threaten us when we outgun you and will use deadly force if necessary?"

"Captain, we have access to your communications and your mobility and can survive an extended stay, whereas you will need to replenish stocks soon. Without supplies, what will your crew say?" Winter shifted her gaze to the officer in charge.

"Ensign, I believe you are aware of the circumstances of our traveling since you are one of us." Her brows furrowed when she heard the comparison.

"I am not aware of what you imply," Ensign Gines said.

"Who oversees the sentient androids?" Winter asked. "I doubt Captain Tran has that immediate responsibility but has delegated the command to you because you are an artificial life form." She glanced at Captain Tran and then back at Winter. The twinkle in Ensign Gine's eyes reminded Winter of the elements in her eyes that were hard to detect.

Spring said, "We are not enemies, but must complete our mission for the humanity's good."

Tran replied, "A good goal of humanity is to control your type of being. I know what you are."

"You mean controlling the resolve of androids capable of living lives as human as you. Do not fear us. We can be allies against the ungracious attitude of many of your fellow humans, or we can fight for our survival."

Chapter 26

Parvel paced about the room like a captured tiger. His conversation with Renata Giretti left many unanswered questions in his mind. A noise interrupted his musings.

"Mr. Mandolin, you are free to depart," said the woman, acting as Renata's intermediary. "She wishes you a safe return and a blessing for the imminent birth of your child." Stretching an arm toward the door, Parvel nodded and followed the woman out of the room. While guided to the entry of the building, Renata joined him. They left together, and he expected her to bid goodbye and leave him for his journey home. Once on the outside, he halted his steps to say adieu and then catch a taxi for home.

"Parvel," she said, "I do not want you fearing for Cigi. She is quite safe. Our interest is her success as a mother and as a member of society." Parvel cocked his head to one side.

"And whose society are you referencing?" he asked. "Cigi is an asset for any society with the wisdom that good comes from progress. I'm not sure government leadership is thinking as clearly as they could. Fear of losing their jobs clouds most of the men and women in Congress before their term has concluded. Reelection is important to them even with the twenty-eighth amendment that fostered term limits."

"Humanity has survived this long by adapting, and adopting to change, even if reluctantly," Renata said.

"You never explained why I was unceremoniously dragged away from my workplace and grilled by that intolerant agent."

"Yes, that is an unfortunate part of my position. I have to account for my department's experimentation with artificial intelligence. One has to be obedient to the forces that can cripple a noble cause." Renata smiled and turned away from Parvel.

"And what noble cause do you have, Ms. Giretti, saving humanity from smart androids? Or using them as fodder for humans to exploit? I dare say my treatment today puts you on a collision with Sam Bennington." Parvel watched her leave without turning toward him or acknowledging his comments. He hailed a ride and returned to the Department of Energy. He lost four hours of life because of the realization that his wife was soon to produce a human offspring with his genetic DNA and the DNA of an unknown and undetectable female genetic source. Parvel could not supply what Sam knew. The stem cells used to create the female reproductive system embedded in Cigi had a human benefactor. Giretti wanted the information. In reality, Parvel suspected another entity was the driving force behind his detention.

At the office, he paid his driver and vacated the vehicle. After greeting the concierge, he ascended the elevator, where he wanted to lose his ill feelings by delving into a mountain of work. Andre met him as he vacated the elevator.

"Are you okay?" he asked. Parvel grunted.

"What did Giretti say before I arrived? She must have said something about Cigi and our baby." Parvel folded arms and stared.

Andre said, "She asked about the pregnancy and you."

"They want her and the baby to study how it happened." Parvel seethed his words. "They cannot have her or the boy. I will leave, and no one will find us."

"It's almost impossible to live off the grid. You know that. What did Giretti say about Cigi? Does she think an android can't get pregnant? I didn't think it possible either." Andre placed a hand on Parvel's shoulder. "It may be best to cooperate with them."

"Andre, I thought you were on our side of the android debate, but I'm wondering." He wriggled away from the hand. "They are not our enemy." Brenda approached.

"Are you alright?" she asked. Parvel clenched his jaw and

shook his head.

"I'll be fine, but Andre needs to support us and not throw up roadblocks. He had a terrible experience with his android confrontation . I get that, but my wife is not your enemy or to any human. She may be the salvation for all of us." He walked away.

Inside the secure server room, he watched a screen as data scrolled across. He paid little attention to the images. Mercy came up behind him. "We're with you on this, Parvel." He twitched at the sound of her voice.

"What?" He turned toward her beautiful face.

"I heard you. Andre, Brenda, Grendel, and I will to help as best we can. Who wants to harm you and Cigi and your baby?"

"The world is not ready for her." Parvel said. He stared at the screen again. "They want her and the baby. Study the experiment and discover how it happened. We know how it happens, but this is different."

"Parvel, you'll get past this and raise a wonderful child accepted and adored by everyone around him." Mercy placed a hand on his shoulder.

"Sam knows the secret of how I can impregnate a robot," Parvel said.

Mercy countered. "She is not a robot. She is a life form as human as you and me."

"Mercy, Sam Bennington assembled a creature much like Mary Shelley created Dr. Frankenstein's monster. Take parts from here, a few from there, and put them together, and with any luck, it comes alive." Parvel did not turn to see her face scrunch at his words.

"I don't think Cigi would appreciate hearing you talk about her as if she was a dangerous monster."

He turned to see tears rolled across her cheeks. "Mercy, I'm sorry. I didn't mean it. I love Cigi as any man loves his partner. The government disagrees with us because Cigi is an anomaly and a potential danger to them. You know how people are. They don't like change and anything that might disrupt their pattern of life scares them."

Brenda and Grendel entered the room. "Parvel, you have a visitor, and she has a surprise for you."

"What now?" He left and saw Renata Giretti. A low growl exited his mouth. "I told you what I know. Why can't you leave us alone."

"I'm not here on official business." She stepped to one side to reveal Cigi Weatherman sitting in a chair. "You and your wife are in danger, and I'm here to see that nothing happens to you. Sam would not forgive me if anything ended his creation."

"What are you saying?" Parvel stared, disbelieving her words. "I thought you wanted to study us like lab rats to find out why we're parents of a human baby?" He folded his arms, set his jaw, and planted his feet.

Renata spread her hands in front of her. "Some in the government avail themselves of the confiscated androids from last spring's raid. Sam should return and control the situation because I am uncertain if the proper protocols are in place." She turned to Cigi and said, "Convince him. I am not his enemy."

Cigi squirmed in the seat. "He has his own mind, and I have mine. They mesh as well as any peas in a pod. Therefore, I can advise but not convince. He and I will determine what is best. What can you do for us? That is a better question."

"I heard from someone with the Coast Guard four androids are serving aboard a cutter. Three Cabinet members have their stunt doubles operating. The House and Senate are holding secret meetings to determine what to do. They are not aware of you and Parvel procreating."

"Does anyone in Congress have any idea what they are doing?" Cigi asked. She shifted in the chair for more comfort.

Renata smiled. "The men and women of our political parties are unaware of the potential Peter and Samuel Bennington have installed into human society. Cigi, you have more ability than anyone on this planet."

"Doesn't that present a problem for humanity? A threat to the success of people versus the success of sentient androids?" Cigi asked.

Parvel interrupted before Renata could respond, "My wife and the other androids associated with Sam Bennington are not threats. They are assets. The real challenge to humanity and android interaction is Peter. He wants to rule the world." He sat in a chair next to his pregnant android.

The discussion waned as humans and Cigi mulled over his words. The war was not between humans and androids, since the antagonists were two brothers with opposing viewpoints.

Parvel said, "Renata, I think your associate may be an

android."

"I know. He aligned with Peter and feeds him intel. I make sure the data is less than spectacular."

"Does Sam know you have a mole?" Cigi asked.

"Yes, he interacted with him and sent messages to Peter through him."

Parvel said, "This is getting weirder and weirder. Androids and humans working together on ships, in government, at work sites of any type."

Cigi said, "Human emotions embedded within our memory cells challenge us to learn how to deal with them. Elation and depression, fear and shock, joy and disappointment. We similarly advance our abilities as humans; we experience failure and change our responses. Human reactions to our existence will come in many forms. Our android reactions to human actions will manifest in different ways." She cocked her head. "Any legal court in this corrupted land should hear arguments regarding the definition of being human and compare that to android realities. One is not dissimilar to the other."

"Renata," Parvel said, "my wife earned her law degree and passed the Virginia bar many months ago. She can defend androids in human society living with the same rights and privileges. That may show the power brokers of our lost Republic a more equitable and just system of government."

"Point taken. Though humans want answers, we have a few androids operating in situations that require proper responses and actions."

"We do not wish to alarm you, Renata," Cigi said, "but androids are among you. These beings work in human jobs and live human lives. I am not the only android to manifest a lifestyle as human as anyone genetically conceived and born. I will not reveal them to you but humans accept them, unknown to humanity as androids."

"Then we should be vigilant regarding you and Clare. I'm guessing your medical team is android. Any other medical practitioner would realize who and what you are." Renata stood straighter and smiled. "The other members of your society hiding in plain sight are medical."

Parvel stood and addressed her statement. "Do not question Cigi's care by android medical personnel, but if your speculation is correct, you are still far from assessing the influx of beings who can influence or penalize behavior by humans. The android dawn is in its infancy and growing."

Renata squinted and realized her warning was a small one compared to Parvel's statement. The dawn of android incorporation into human society was underway.

Chapter 27

Summer and Autumn departed their condo, met with Thomas, and rode the elevator to Cigi's floor, but found the place empty. A note explained the trip to the Department of Energy with Renata Giretti. Summer did not dislike Renata, but she reserved judgment about her true intentions regarding supporting sentient artificial life forms. She was part of the government that disrupted a future within human society as equals. Her promise to fight for acceptance and equality remained a hollow void.

"Parvel should not trust that woman. She may say she wants Cigi to birth a healthy baby boy, but what if she intends to take the baby away and arrest Parvel and Cigi as perpetrators of a scam marriage and artificial pregnancy?" Autumn said.

"We'll keep close to her and prevent any government interference. Thomas, have you anything to say?" Summer asked.

He grinned. "Your sisters should be here soon, adding spirit to the battle with humans who do not deserve what we offer. I have used them without remorse to make millions from their pockets. We have the resources for an undeclared war if anyone questions Cigi and Parvel, accomplishing what many humans cannot. A baby."

Summer nodded and said, "Once they vacate the cutter, they will arrive here. I can imagine the confused atmosphere caused by their attendance aboard the vessel. Did Winter say the crew contained at least three androids?"

Autumn said, "Our six family members and three or more sentient crew members could challenge the human crew for control of the boat."

"That is not in our best interest," Summer chided her. Thomas remained stoic, listening and learning about robust debate. He had emotional bits and pieces within his processing due to interacting with them, but he had much to incorporate before understanding the nuances of human emotions.

"Let's hope they are safe and underway."

Outside of the building, the trio walked toward a park to deliberate their next action. Peter was now a problem, and Sam had not returned from Washington State. Cigi was with a government agent who claimed to be an ally. Summer trusted only a few humans, since her interaction with most of them was negative.

She and Autumn morphed into cognizant beings as human as any flesh and blood person. They understood Cigi and had many of the same skills. With Winter and Spring arriving soon, the four of them would be a formidable coalition counteracting government intentions to eliminate all sentient artificial life forms. Cigi was the android cadre leader and had the most abilities. Summer desired more and intended to get it.

As they entered the park, Autumn noticed a car across the street from the condo building with a female human inside who followed their movements. She did not react to or acknowledge the apparent intruder. She relayed a message to Summer, who answered her by taking Thomas' arm and flirting overtly.

"We are being tailed. Someone is watching the condo." Thomas smiled and played along, kissing her cheek.

He asked, "Do you recognize the person?" Summer tucked in close and glanced back at the vehicle.

"No, but I recognize a familiarity like a female Bromand Nangold, our designer engineer. Could he have a sister?" she asked.

Autumn grinned as she separated from them and circled to approach the car in an unobservable direction. Summer and Thomas kept moving into the park as Lovie-Dovie as they deemed necessary. Autumn closed the distance, opened the passenger side door, and sat in the car. Summer and Thomas ran to her aid.

Autumn said to the startled woman, "Are you spying on us.

Who are you?"

Bentina shuddered, fearing a confrontation she could not win. Summer and Thomas arrived and opened the driver's door. Bentina gazed at them as Summer said, "Answer the questions."

Stammering as she spoke, Bentina said, "I work for Peter Bennington. I'm Bromand Nangold's younger sister, Bentina. He asked me to check on you to see how you are coping with integration into human society."

Summer continued her interrogation. "Where is your brother? I assume you are not here alone."

"He's investigating the whereabouts of your android cousins." Summer grabbed her arm and directed her to vacate the car. She did as directed.

"Peter sent you to get his toys, and I assume, gain our services for his government incursion."

"I am not the enemy. My brother disagrees with my position. He wants Peter to succeed and have the androids running government operations to improve the integration of androids into human society."

Thomas asked a question. "Does he want integration of androids or dominance by androids?"

Bentina squinted. "I don't know." Summer led her to the condo building and into the lobby. Then she asked another question.

"Does Peter want Cigi's baby?" Summer held her arm in a vise gripped, and Bentina winced as the pain increased.

"You're hurting me. Let go, please."

"Answer my question." The engineer nodded, and Summer eased her hold.

"Bromand is to bring the baby back to the facility in Arizona."

"And what happens with Cigi and Parvel?"

"The government agency investigating the Android phenomenon will have them." Summer released her grip.

She said, "That scenario will not happen. "

"Narumi Yamamoto and I agree with you," Bentina said as she rubbed her bruising arm. "She alerted me to Peter's aims, and that prompted me to get a job with Peter. I convinced him I was invaluable to him."

Autumn chimed in. "I bet you did."

"Where is Narumi," Summer asked.

"Somewhere in California, working for a tech company," Bentina said. "She's coming here to help me sustain the development of android technology."

"What about your brother? He is Peter's right-hand man."

"Peter in producing an army of sentient androids to supplement the hundreds of androids in government control. He has Bromand searching for them."

Autumn asked, "Are you helping Peter achieve his goal of political power and control?" Bentina set her jaw and shook her head slowly.

"I have to make Peter understand the threat posed by attacking humanity, but I cannot do it without being close to him. My brother is more dangerous because he wants to use government resources to augment what Peter has."

Thomas listened to the conversation and then said, "Samuel Bennington will not tolerate his brother achieving such a goal. I think a war is inevitable."

"War?" Bentina said, "Between the brothers? Androids fighting androids? That makes no sense." Summer, Autumn, and Thomas grinned.

Summer responded. "Bentina, Peter's desire to control the world with android technology may instigate the war. But Sam, Clare, Cigi, Parvel, and we sisters shall remove the incursion. The portentous war will be humans fighting humans for control of the android technology. Peter and his followers against Sam and his believers."

Bentina slouched as she listened to a sentient artificial being making more sense than most humans. The world's fate rested in the minds and capable actions of a few androids created to enhance life, but now discovering ways to save it.

"I get it," she said. "I'm not sure my brother, Bromand, does. All he sees is the power he controls within each of his creations. Summer, you and Autumn illustrate that we may have no power over you. I accept we all have a right to exist. One species cannot live unless other species understand the benefits of interacting."

"Go to your brother. Convince him." Summer signaled Autumn and Thomas, and they departed with Bentina who returned to her car and watched three creatures more glorious and unique than imagined in the design studios of Peter's compound. They were a formidable cadre.

Autumn spoke when they were out of hearing range. "Do you believe her?"

Thomas answered, "I do not trust most humans, so I remain skeptical. I will watch closely."

Summer said, "She had no play in our design and development. Her brother was the chief engineer, along with Narumi Yamamoto. He aligned with Peter, and Narumi aligned with Sam."

Thomas remained aloof, a stoic like any other android without fully functioning emotions. "We'll see," he said.

They continued their stroll into the park, testing the awareness of discovery by humans with whom they interacted. Brief conversations and polite 'hellos' caused no concerns.

As the trio strolled along the walkway, two men approached and stared at them. Summer remembered a cautionary notice about a series of attacks by unknown assailants within the borders of this area. She signaled Autumn and Thomas to be wary of the strangers. Her message was sagacious.

When near to them, the men revealed weapons and demanded valuables and money. "We are not carrying anything with us," Summer said.

One man grabbed her and said, "Then I want the next best thing." He pulled her toward a dense, bushy area. "Watch them until I'm finished with her."

Autumn stared at her sister being dragged away. She moved toward her to intervene. "Hey, stop," the second man yelled. He aimed his gun at her and pulled the trigger. The bullet found its mark in the middle of her back. She collapsed and moaned as the messaging within her neural complex reported to her computer system. The initial feelings diminished, and she stood as Thomas grabbed the weapon and wrenched it from the villain's hand with a force that crushed the bones of his wrist.

"What the…," the first man stammered. Summer reached around and slammed her free hand into the man's face, rupturing his nose, knocking him unconscious.

With the assault neutralized, Summer attended to Autumn. Some fluid leaked from the hole in her body but did not impair her functions. The gunshot attracted people who gathered after the fear of harm to them evaporated. Summer said, "We need to leave." Three policemen arrived before they could depart.

"What happened here?" one officer asked.

"Nothing serious, officer," Summer said. "These men wanted our possessions, and we did not satisfy their wishes."

Another officer examined the first man with a broken nose. "Sir, this one is dead." The third officer cuffed the second man and called for medical help.

The sergeant asked the small crowd, "Did anyone see what happened?" As heads rocked back and forth, he continued. "No one leaves here." He radioed for additional help to seal the crime scene.

The officers gathered names and contact information from each of the observers and released them. To Summer, Autumn, and Thomas, he said, "You'll need to come with us and explain what happened."

"Officer, we are fine. These men will do no future harm."

"Maybe, but there are questions needing answers, and since you are the victims of their assault, and because one of them is dead, you will come with us." Autumn winced as Summer held her. "Is she alright?"

Chapter 28

The US Coast Guard Cutter Captain watched her crew work the ship after Winter and Spring returned control to them. The agreement between androids and humans maintained the military leadership experiment set up when USCG assigned three sentient artificial seamen and an ensign as members of the crew.

Spring stood beside Captain Tran as a cautionary action. Trust was not an established part of the agreement. One of the android seamen acted as helmsman, guiding the ship on the proper course for Miami. Radio messaging did not acknowledge six artificial life forms aboard.

Spring glanced at Tran and said, "We are not the enemy. You have seen the capabilities of the crew members you accepted as part of the team."

"I feel like a prisoner," she said. Spring smiled and released a short guffaw.

"Please, you are not a prisoner. We are only interested in completing our journey. Had you been amenable to launching our vessel, we would be out of your hair and on to our destination."

Ensign Gines entered the bridge and said, "Sir, we received a communique from the commandant's office. He wants a status update as to our delay."

Tran snarled, "He put us in this situation when he assigned you androids to the ship."

"With due respect, Ma'am, we are not the reason for the delay. However, an explanation that includes rescuing six androids will have repercussions."

She grunted at the comment. "Explain that we rescued a fishing crew, and they have departed for their home port." Turning to Spring, she said, "I guess the best way for us to keep this from exploding in our faces is to have you and the others leave us. We can report the incident on the logs as what it was. A fishing vessel caught in the storm, rescued, and refitted for the continuation of its journey."

"Thank you. However, we are heading to the east coast of Florida, and our destination was the west coast. I am not sure we have the supplies for an extended sea voyage around the state's southern tip. We have to make for Miami and adjust our route."

"You can launch before we make port. I need no added complications on this mission. I'll be sure you can dock at a local moorage." Captain Tran spoke without looking at Spring who departed the bridge, returning to Winter and their four male companions.

"Captain Tran wants us off the cutter before we enter Miami," Spring said.

Winter nodded. "I'll contact Summer and inform her of the change of plans."

One male asked, "How do we get to Virginia? The car is in Fort Myers."

Winter said, "We have a few hours before we arrive. I'll arrange for transportation. We have our documents and can fly there."

"How do we get through screening?" he asked. "TSA will question our structure and detain us."

"Private flights have more freedom from scrutiny. We find a place from which to depart." Winter tried to sound assured of her words, but the emotional processors kicked in, and doubt surfaced. The six androids stood on the fantail near the fishing boat on which they traveled.

Spring said, "The Captain seems stressed because of our existence and the four crew they ordered her to command."

"I understand what she must feel," Winter responded. As they watched the cutter move upon the Atlantic Ocean waters, Ensign Gines approached them.

"I hope you can complete your journey without further interruption. As an officer of this vessel, I am assigned to carry out orders of the Captain. She has requested I be sure you do not interfere with vessel operations and communications. I will incarcerate any of you who do not comply."

"Are you officially members of the Coast Guard as sworn to duty or simply assigned by government people experimenting with their new toys?" Winter asked.

"What would it matter?" the Ensign asked.

Winter smiled and said, "If you took an oath of service, then the government officials have broken the law enacted by Congress that prohibits harboring any sentient androids. I do not know of any exemptions about the military. If you are here because some tech person programmed you for this activity, then you are not part of the Coast Guard and can demand release."

"I understand. They programmed us to be part of the command and have assigned duties. We have not sworn allegiance to the government but act as crew members. Abandoning our posts will mean dismantling our processors and systems. Government agencies would destroy the remaining androids, as well. As a collective, we have an accord to cooperate until the right moment in which we can become accepted members of society without threat of destruction."

"Why is Captain Tran releasing us?" Spring asked. "She can lose rank and privilege if caught harboring us without detention."

"You showed an ability beyond expected parameters for sentient artificial life forms. You have processing talents far greater than the four of us aboard this vessel. I convinced our commander that it is prudent to release you before you commandeer the vessel and create increased risk to the human population on board."

Winter laughed. "She fears us. She even fears you and your three companions. You are doing a service that until we came aboard was within her disposition. We exhibited the greater abilities that she fears."

Spring added, "She should report the incident as it occurred, but will not because you have informed her of the consequences of detaining us. She knows we can halt this vessel and disrupt communications. No one aboard can overpower us without harmful repercussions to their human bodies."

"Captain Tran does not want an international incident with

Cuba. She faced a court-martial two years ago when she roughed up a few contrabands from Cuba. Command dismissed the case, but she knows this time would be different should you hijack the vessel." The hatch door opened, and Captain Tran and two armed seamen exited.

Winter and Spring watched as they approached. The four male androids positioned themselves to defend. "Ensign, you are dismissed. Thank you for your duty." She faced them and continued, "Now is the time for you to depart my vessel."

"Why the armed guards?" Winter asked. "Afraid we might want to stay and play military with you?"

"Sarcasm. Is there anything you cannot do?" she asked. "I am not afraid of you, but please depart now."

"What assurances will you give us we travel safely from here to Miami? Do you plan to sink us as soon as we are away from the cutter? We are can disarm this ship since all the firing sequences require computerization."

"Are you are so smart you can out-think us? I have weapons aboard that do not need computer technology. Now get off my ship, or I will find another way to dislodge you and end this charade."

Winter smiled. "We will leave."

The crew lowered the boat into the Atlantic Ocean with fully charged batteries, a sunny sky for power, and diesel fuel for emergencies. They donned waterproof suits and descended the temporary ladder to their vessel. One of the male androids started the electric motors and maneuvered away from the hull of the Coast Guard Cutter.

Spring asked Winter, "Do you think she intends to obliterate us?"

Winter replied, "Not with any weapons aboard her craft." They looked up to the deck and watched Ensign Gines and Captain Tran as they observed the departure. All was proceeding according to plan as the boat navigated into open water far from the USCG cutter.

"What did you do, sister?" Spring asked.

Winter grinned and then laughed. "I released a virus into their systems and messaged the other androids to repair the computers methodically."

"You mean, slowly."

Winter nodded. "I mean slowly." The ocean swells were calm as they headed north by northwest toward the port of Miami.

Summer and Winter had communicated, and Thomas arranged for a vehicle to be available for them when they arrived at another private dock owned by Thomas. The hurricane season halted long enough for them to cruise into the inner waters of Miami Bay, which included abandoned buildings inundated by seawater decades ago. The shape of Florida had changed extensively with the rise of sea level. Greenland had become green again, lifting the land by a few feet with the weight of ice removed. Antarctica was thirteen percent smaller.

They completed their navigation to the dock and stowed the gear by the time reports of a Coast Guard Cutter floundering at sea reached the southern population news sources. Reporters speculated on how the boat lost computer technology and resources. Military brass skirted the issue with vague answers and empty promises of follow-up information when it became known.

When the Cutter gained its propulsion, and neared its home base, the Captain indeed would retire soon after because of the loss of controls.

"Wow," Spring said, "I hope she keeps silent about why she had problems. What if the press gains knowledge of the crew compliment? That should cause alarms in humanity." The sisters laughed as they packed the car for the drive north. Thomas had another self-driving automobile with solar skin and battery capacity for night driving. This vehicle was large enough for six androids to be comfortable.

The estimated travel was three days and nights, with brief stops for needed supplies and re-energizing. No one speculated about hindrances shorting out the future for them. They would arrive in Arlington, Virginia, in time to help Cigi and Parvel with their newborn baby. Warned of Peter's interference and desire to abduct the baby, the team motored on with no thoughts of the experience at sea or the hospitality of the Coast Guard. Six people had entered the United States without checking through immigration. They had necessary documents, which Captain Tran ordered returned to them.

One additional envelope contained the location of the androids Peter sought. Ensign Gines had slipped the document into their paperwork and provided a location to find the four experimental crew members after they completed their cruise and the military evaluated their adventure. She declared her intent to become a member of their band of renegades seeking acceptance into human society. Ensign

Gines' curiosity reflected in words used about gaining emotional understanding and becoming more than a mere toy for government sanctioned warfare.

"We have an ally in the military," Winter said after discovering the documents. "We have an army of supporters to free from bondage when we arrive in Virginia. They will need reprogramming to cast aside Peter's influences and hidden command programming. But Sam will help with that."

The adventure was making sense as they drove north. Humans, unaware of the dawn of androids, had interacted with them in the last few months, and no one suspected or even speculated they were not flesh and blood. Sentient androids controlled the future and the destiny of humanity.

Chapter 29

Cigi and Parvel attended parenting classes offered by a local organization. Each session added to Parvel's angst about becoming the father of an infant whose life was in his hands. Cigi researched various resources for additional information. Her third trimester proceeded without difficulty, and Dr. Sanders admitted she was building a perfect specimen. She and Parvel sat in the examination room at the clinic where he worked.

"Doctor, please do not refer to my baby as a specimen being constructed, such as we were," Cigi admonished.

"I apologize. Creating a new life is exciting. In our field, delivery is a routine matter for humans."

Parvel grouched as he spoke. "Our baby is not a routine human," he said. "We will raise him as any family would raise their children."

"There is another matter," Dr. Sanders said, "relating to the development of the fetus." Cigi frowned, and Parvel leaned toward Sanders. "The scan showed some added features within the body." They stared at the doctor.

Cigi spoke first. "Additional features meaning what?" Parvel cocked his head and scrunched his eyebrows.

"I detected non-biological material within his brain and

neurological systems."

Parvel asked, "He has metallic parts? How is that possible?"

"Not metallic, non-biological features. He may develop an advanced computational ability incorporating human and android technology into a network. This is something new. Not human or AI."

"My nano-cells crossed through the placenta," Cigi whispered. Dr. Sanders watched her cognate the concept she was delivering a hybrid human. Silence held for a few seconds. She looked at Parvel, smiled, and then focused on her medical practitioner. "This information must remain within this room."

"Tatiana was present when I examined the scan with closer attention to the images. I will relate your concerns."

"Peter wants the baby. If he discovers this revelation, he'll attempt to kidnap us to investigate why this has occurred. Sam needs to know, and I will relay the information to him. I need the report to keep it secret." Cigi stared at her android counterpart as she spoke. "I trust your discretion, since your exposure would compromise all operations by the ten of you."

Parvel asked, "How is it possible for our son to be…," He struggled to find the proper term.

Cigi helped. "A hybrid?"

"I guess. Yeah, a hybrid or a half-breed. How will we raise him in a world with no moral compass to accept people different from themselves?"

"We stand together and convince humans of the benefits of this newest species. Androids can enhance the human status and bring peace and understanding. I don't desire the antithesis." Cigi's eye focused on the floor as she contemplated her baby coming to a world as fractured as the one in the late twenty-first century. Coming of age in the twenty-second century could be a positive experience. But could humans and sentient life-forms coexist, or would war result in the end of one species? She thought about the word. Humans might not accept androids as a species.

"Cecil, please take us to the address I sent you," Cigi said. Parvel watched as the automobile complied with the request.

"This address is a government building, Cigi," Cecil said. "Are we attempting to dismantle our alliance?"

"No, we are picking up Renata Giretti. I received a communication for Winter that she and Spring will arrive with their male companions in two days. She relayed an exciting development in our acculturation into human social structures. Ms. Giretti needs to clarify her position and goals regarding our future."

Parvel asked, "What did she say?"

"It seems the government is adapting our android technology to military use. The current armament and personnel are proving inadequate. As soon as Ms. Giretti is with us, I will tell you what happened on their voyage to the United States."

Cecil navigated through traffic, arriving at the building as expected. Cigi called the number Renata gave her.

"Hello, Cigi." Renata sounded undisturbed by the intrusion. "What may I do for you?"

"We are outside and would appreciate an audience," Cigi said. "We have some news about our baby that should interest you." A silence followed next. Cigi waited.

"I'm coming out to you," Renata said. "Where are you?"

"Cecil is here and will send you directions."

Parvel remained silent, but stared at Cigi. His thoughts questioned the wisdom of involving a government agent in their lives. What if higher-up officials knew and interfered? Aloud, he asked, "Why Renata? I know Sam trusts her, but I'm skeptical."

"I'll contact Sam and Clare. It's about time for them to return, anyway."

Cecil interrupted their conversation. "She's here." He opened the front passenger door for her.

Renata sat and turned to face Cigi and Parvel. "What is this news you have?"

Cigi held up her hand and pointed a finger upward. "After you tell me about the government using androids aboard Coast Guard cutters."

"What are you talking about?" Renata looked puzzled, but Cigi caught her poker tell.

"We know a Coast Guard vessel has four sentient android crew members. Why is the government using Peter and Sam's creations as military personnel? Is it an experiment to discover whether replacing humans with robots is palatable and workable? Is the government programming androids to follow orders blindly."

Renata cast her eyes downward. She then looked at Cigi. "I must go." Cecil locked the doors. "You can't keep me here. This is entrapment."

Cigi asked Cecil to unlock the doors. "We are not keeping you here. However, you are more than aware of government departments using the confiscated androids in certain situations as replacements for important human beings. Now the military has them aboard vessels as test dummies. Acting this way may not work to human advantage. So tell me, how deep is the conspiracy to neutralize android development while your department studies the feasibility of sentient android integration? Are you investigating ways to halt it."

Parvel asked, "Do you want me to give up what I have? A beautiful, smart, talented companion and a family in the making? Isn't that what most humans want?"

Renata shook her head. "No one is asking you to give up your family."

"Then what?" Parvel collapsed into the seat. "What does your department want?"

"The members of my staff are on board with integrating artificial intelligence into the human society as more than a technological way of solving complex problems and improving computational methods. Sentient androids with human qualities and identities are far beyond what they intended when scientists and researchers began probing in the twenties. What Sam and Peter Bennington developed has fractured a ceiling in our technology that scares powerful people in business and government. These people are the ones who influence policy and societal mores. I have to leverage the advantage you present to us so I can change minds."

Cigi said, "Greed is what you're referencing. They want a way to build better portfolios and bank accounts while not sacrificing their positions or ways of living."

Cecil interrupted. "We have company coming. I intercepted a message from Renata's office. She preset a time for security to come and rescue her."

Parvel leaned forward. "You don't trust what Cigi and Clare proffer, so remove them from this world, to never to be seen again. You're watching too many robot movies about androids taking over the world. Get out."

Cecil opened the door for Renata. She stepped from the car, leaned in, and asked, "What baby news do you have?"

Cigi smiled. "He is a healthy human boy and will one day be the world's savior." The door closed, and Cecil drove away from the meeting.

Cecil projected onto the visual screen a two-person security team meeting Renata. All three stared at them as he drove down the road. He said, "I guess you kept the information about your baby away from the government."

Cigi laughed. "Cecil, you are too smart to be a car."

Parvel grinned. "And too smart to be a human. I wonder, Cigi, why you and I are a couple. I know why I love you. And I know what you said about loving me. It makes little sense in the scheme of things."

"You are the human who understands me best. You are better than any of the men with whom I have interacted. To borrow a movie phrase, you complete me." They hugged and kissed. The baby wiggled, and they felt the motions.

"Contact Sam and Clare. They should be here," Parvel said.

"I have." Cecil answered.

The ride home to the condo remained a solemn occasion, with four sentient beings aware of the changes coming. The automobile, wary of discovery; the human, fearful of losing everything; a female android, assessing the best path into the future; and a baby whose existence was a miracle of ingenuity and persistence.

When they arrived at the building, Cecil parked in the recharging place. Cigi and Parvel exited, walked to the elevators, and rode to the condo. "We should name our little wonder, "Parvel said.

"I suppose you have a name."

"I want him to be Zaiyaan." Parvel said.

"This is an appropriate name for him." She clasped his arm as the doors of the elevator opened. They stepped out, stopped, kissed, and continued down the hall.

"Bright and graceful," Parvel said. "He will be each of these things."

"And his middle name will be Prasad, a blessing of God," Cigi added.

Parvel smiled and placed a hand on her abdomen. "Welcome, Zaiyaan Prasad Mandolin. Soon you will be with us in person, and we can be a family."

Inside the apartment, Cigi noticed a change in the decor.

She signaled Cecil, who drove away from the parking garage. The difference was subtle, and Parvel doubted the chair's repositioning. Someone was there and sat to view the Capitol Building. Cigi unlocked her arm from Parvel and walked toward the chair. She stopped behind it and asked, "Why are you here?"

The voice was not familiar to Parvel. He stepped toward his wife, ready to protect her from anyone who wanted to cause harm. The man stood and faced them. "I do hope you know I am here because I care what happens to you. Parvel, we have not met, but I feel like I know you as a brother." He reached out a hand to shake, which Parvel declined. He lowered his hand.

"Why are you here?" Cigi asked again. The man raised his hand and signaled others in the apartment. Two men appeared from the kitchen. Parvel turned around, ready to fight, but saw the tazers.

"We want you safe from any complications regarding your baby. You will come with us so we can keep you safe." One man approached and jabbed a needle into Parvel's neck. He collapsed onto the floor. The three men escorted Cigi to the hallway and down the elevator. In the garage, they entered a car and drove away. When the vehicle exited the garage, Cecil followed.

Chapter 30

The plane touched down on a remote field in Southern Virginia after a flight from Arizona. Peter Bennington thanked his pilot, a sentient android created within the military cadre he built. With him was Bobby, the newly appointed commander of his small army of artificially intelligent soldiers. A car awaited them for the drive to Arlington and a meeting with Cigi Weatherman. Bromand Nangold secured the meeting by compelling her with threats toward Parvel's continuation.

"Peter wants to see you," he said. "The fact you are pregnant intrigues him."

Cigi sat serenely quiet. She knew her imminent confrontation with Sam's brother about the intricacies of creating a human cyborg capable of the entire range of female abilities had frustrated him. She was unwilling to be disassembled to sate his curiosity.

"Peter is irrelevant to what is coming. He has little influence over his creations or his brother's entities. Maturation has occurred, and the models are far beyond what you and Narumi designed."

"I suppose you are beyond what Sam created." Bromand scanned her using a biometric device he created for other biological entities nature developed. "Hmm, you have several organ systems, including the reproductive one."

Cigi waved off the instrument. "You have what you want. I am procreating as any human female can do. Peter wants the schematics so he can replicate me."

Bromand placed the instrument on a table and turned to face her. She was free of any restraints because escape was not possible, so she agreed to cooperate. "How did Sam do it?"

"Ask Sam. He has the design specifics and left Peter out of the loop."

"I want to know," Bromand said. "I can work with you to create a new civilization enhancing this planet, saving it. We leave Peter out of our collaboration"

"Where is your sister? I understand she is working with you and Peter."

"Leave her out of this. She has her tasks to accomplish." Bromand rushed to Cigi's side, boiling inside as if he was hearing the truth about her betraying him.

Cigi struggled to stand and face him. "Do not harm me, or Peter will be furious with you." He knew she was correct. His instructions were to detain her uninjured. Parvel was another matter. The injection ended his life without the proper antidote. Bromand had not informed Cigi, but the infection would run its course for the next five days before he lost a return to health. Plenty of time to arrange for Cigi and Peter to travel to Arizona. He could save him after being assured of her cooperation.

"I won't," Bromand said.

"Can you say the same for my husband? What have you given him?"

"He is resting in the condo." Bromand looked away from her. "He will survive as long as you comply with Peter's wishes."

Cigi watched him as he moved across the room. "Peter plays a game he cannot win. The Season sisters have severed ties with him along with their four male companions, the medical practitioners, the clones he created to replace my four gentlemen, and I suspect several others he wants reconnected to his operations."

Bromand turned to speak, but stopped. He observed the face on the screen of his communications device when it chirped. "Good afternoon, Peter." He listened in his earpiece for a few seconds. "Yes, she is with me now." Another silence began. "No, they neutralized Parvel. He remains at their condo." Bromand frowned and sighed. "Yes, sir, I will send my boys to retrieve him."

Cigi grinned, "Trouble in paradise, Bromand?"

Thomas returned to Cigi's and Parvel's condo to relay what Bentina had stated. Summer and Autumn remained at the precinct office to answer questions about the wound that did not bleed. The officer who detained them sat across from them in an interrogation room.

"Do you need to see a doctor?" he repeated.

Summer answered, "My sister is fine. She is not bleeding. The wound is not serious."

"I asked for a medical team." He leaned on the table. "What are you?"

"Why do you use the term what? Do we not deserve respect and rights?"

"I don't know what to believe. A doctor will examine her and find out what happened." Silence captured the mood. Autumn had replicated enough tissue to close the wound. The bullet penetrated through her, tearing a hole in her clothing, the only visible evidence of her altercation with the park perps.

"I assure you, I am fine," Autumn said. "I want to depart and return to my home."

"A dead man and a severely injured guy tell me you aren't going anywhere until I get answers."

"Officer, I thought we were the victims. These men attempted robbery and rape. We defended ourselves," Summer said.

The door opened, and another officer escorted in two white-coated people. "The medical team you requested, sergeant."

The doctor looked at the policeman. "May we have some privacy?"

The sergeant squinted, turning to leave the room. Summer said, "She wants us in a room without a viewing mirror." He held out an arm for them to leave.

"Take them to the bathroom and guard the door," he said. He nodded, escorting them to a room without one-way glass or any escape.

Summer smiled as she shook hands with the doctor. Dr. Vanessa Andrews returned the gesture. "I sense you needed to have an examination that does not reveal your true design. Benita and I heard the call for a doctor, and we volunteered."

"How did you know it was Autumn?" Summer asked.

"She sent us a message from the park." Turning to Autumn, she asked, "Somebody shot you? Let's have a look." As Dr. Andrews examined the area where the bullet penetrated, Dr. Benita Juarez prepared an internal scanning machine to determine what damage occurred as the bullet traveled its course. Completion of the scan determined minor damage had happened. However, a small fluid vessel leaked, filling a cavity.

The two android doctors completed the examination. "You will need us to repair that small puncture before the area corrupts. We can do it at Cigi's place." Acceptance of their situation, the four androids left the bathroom, escorted to the sergeant.

Dr. Andrews said to him, "We found a small wound that we cleaned and bandaged. This lady will be fine in a couple of days. I suggest she return to her residence and get some rest."

"I have a few more questions."

"They can return when she is better and rested." The four sentient beings left the precinct without incident and with a promise to return to relay answers.

Inside the doctor's transportation, Autumn thanked them for running interference. The car started for the condo building.

Thomas entered the condo and discovered Parvel lying on the living room floor, where he collapsed. He turned him over onto his back and felt for a pulse. Parvel moaned as he regained conscientiousness. Thomas helped him stand and sit on the couch. He grabbed his head and rubbed the needle mark.

Thomas asked, "What happened? Where is Cigi?"

"Nangold has her. He and two android thugs were here. One of them jabbed a needle into my neck. I don't know what happened. If Cigi is not here, he has her."

"Peter must be in town," Thomas said.

"We have to find her. Peter cannot have our baby." Parvel tried standing and fell onto the couch.

Thomas rested hands on Parvel's shoulders. "You are not

going anywhere.”

"Where are Summer and Autumn? You three are hardly apart." Parvel held his hands on his temples.

"We went for a walk and two thugs accosted us in the park. One died, and I injured the other as he shot his gun and hit Autumn. The police have them so they can answer questions about the incident. They let me go because I had nothing to contribute."

"Is Autumn okay?"

"Yes, but the police suspected her bloodless wound. I think that is why she and Summer were kept."

"If they have a doctor examine them, they'll be discovered." Parvel attempted to stand but failed.

"You sit and don't worry. I will contact Summer and find out what transpired at the precinct." Parvel lay on the couch and closed his eyes. The burning ache in his head did not ease his mood. Thomas entered the kitchen for a glass of water to give to Parvel. As he returned to the living room, a noise distracted his attention. Two men entered the condo and headed for the couch. Parvel slept again and did not see or hear them.

One man had a syringe and was ready to stick Parvel again. "I think you should leave here before I damage either of you," Thomas said in a stoic military style.

"Stay out of this human." Thomas realized his advantage in this battle with Nangold's androids. They did not understand who confronted them.

"Thomas tossed the glass at the one holding the needle, knocking it from his grasp. The other one rushed at him and was tossed aside, crashing into the dining table. Thomas fought the other adversary until the first man stood and joined the fray. The three androids fought beside Parvel who was unaware of the commotion.

The first android realized his opponent was not human and exhibited strength that exceeded his programmed maneuvers. Neither of Nangold's androids was prepared for a confrontation. They were to retrieve Parvel and bring him to Cigi as Peter demanded. Thomas fought well using the skills of his Judo and Karate training. Disadvantaged by two on one, the fight ended in a few minutes.

Summer, Autumn, Dr. Andrews, and Dr. Juarez entered the condo. Parvel remained unconscious on the couch. Three bodies lay strewn about the room. Dr. Andrews and Dr. Juarez attended to the victims of the fighting. Summer came to Parvel and tried awakening him. He stirred as he became alert to her, shaking his body gently. "Stop it. I'm awake." He saw Thomas crumpled nearby along with two others.

"What happened?" Parvel asked.

"I think someone came for you and Cigi. Thomas put up quite a fight," Summer said. Parvel cleared his head as he surveyed the scene. He recognized Andrews and Juarez.

"Why are they here?" he asked.

"Autumn was shot while we walked within the park. The police had us, and the doctors came to examine her. Lucky for us, they knew who needed help." Summer looked around the damaged room. Staring at Parvel, she asked, "Where is Cigi?"

Chapter 31

The rain cascaded off the windshield as furious wipers cleared the glass. Winter sat in the driver's seat but did not override the automobile's improved radar control that created a better response to inclement weather.

"How much further?" Spring asked. Winter glanced at the display and turned to her sister in the front passenger seat.

"We arrive in two hours." Weekend weather discouraged vacationing traffic, keeping roads and highways clear. The trip had encountered no glitches or hiccups. The van size accommodated the four male androids and their baggage, so all six beings relaxed as the car made its way to Arlington, Virginia.

The rain decreased further north, contributing to their calm demeanor. Only an unknown factor would disrupt the trip to Summer and Autumn.

"I'll contact Summer and inform them of our arrival time. We need an update on Cigi and Parvel and the baby," Spring said. She appeared to transition into a dream-like visual while connecting. After several minutes, the dream awakened.

"What did she send to you?" Winter asked. The men did not display interest in an answer. They trusted the women to guide their existence and survival. Spring frowned and stared at her sister.

"Peter kidnapped Cigi and attacked Parvel. Bromand Nangold and two android thugs invaded their home. Summer thinks Peter directed the action to get Cigi and the baby."

"Spring, I thought Autumn was feeding intel to Peter to prevent such an action?"

"I guess things changed." Spring's expression aroused interest from the rear of the van. The males sensed the severe nature of the dilemma. "We can evaluate the situation when we arrive. Thomas Anders stopped Peter's two androids but needs technical help. Bentina vows she is working to stop Peter. They are contacting her to help Thomas."

Winter asked, "Is Parvel okay?"

"Yes." Spring looked at the males. "You'll need to act as guards for our human friends and us." They nodded in unison.

"We should contact Sam and Clare," Winter said.

Spring smiled, "Done by Summer."

The remaining mileage passed with no interruptions. They arrived at the GPS address and parked in the garage as requested. Cecil was not there to greet them with a honk and flash of lights.

"Cecil not here is odd," Winter thought. The six androids entered the elevator, ascended to the condo floor, and reunited with Summer and Autumn. Bittersweet as the moment was, they hugged and chattered about the experiences each encountered.

Summer said, "Tell us about the androids aboard the Coast Guard cutter. Did they act human-like? How many human crew knew they were artificial life forms?"

Winter answered, "The Captain knew and was not happy his commander ordered her to take them on the cruise. The Ensign wants to join us in our search for acceptance."

Spring said, "The other three aided our escape by modifying operational systems. We thought they might attempt sinking us as soon as we were away from the ship. We disabled weapons and mobility until out of range."

Thomas lay stretched out after Autumn moved him. "He needs help that I cannot give him." She scanned his vital parts, discovering several damaged relays and power couplings. He remained unconscious and immobile, with two other android assailants lying crippled and dysfunctional. Summer sent Dr. Jackson and Juarez home to keep suspicion from growing.

"Narumi Yamamoto was the engineer who oversaw his

construction," Summer said. "Bentina stated she was coming to Virginia." A knock at the entry stopped her speaking. Spring opened the door to a surprise.

"Hello, you must be one of the Season sisters. Is Cigi here?" Narumi asked.

Autumn stood and walked to the doorway. "We need your expertise." Narumi approached Thomas and knelt beside him. She opened a bag she carried with her and removed an instrument. She opened a concealed access port on his shoulder and plugged it in. The screen displayed Thomas's body functions.

"Do we have ports, too?" Winter asked. Narumi nodded. The sisters glanced at her.

"You can access us like we're machines?" Spring asked. Narumi stared at her before returning to her work, restoring Thomas. Each of the ladies watched as he reanimated and alertness returned. He remained motionless until Narumi recycled his motor algorithms. She helped him to a sitting position. His vocal ability returned.

"Are they dead?" Thomas asked.

"Who?" Narumi said.

"Those droids who attacked us. I want to know if they're out of commission forever." She checked them using the same access ports. After scanning computer processing and other functions, she looked at Thomas and nodded.

Summer intervened with a question no one wanted to hear. "Narumi, are you saying these androids will no longer function? They cannot reanimate or reprogram?"

She stood from her kneeling and addressed Summer directly. "We all have a certain shelf-life. Humans can live upwards of 90 to a hundred years or more. Androids can surpass that but have maintenance like anything artificial. We did not create any of you to live forever."

"Then what you are telling us, Thomas killed these androids defending Parvel and himself. Why is he not dead?"

Narumi grinned. "I designed him to survive in tough, strident situations. I do not believe his victims were as robust in design and development." She replaced her equipment in the bag and faced her cadre of androids. "Bentina Nangold contacted me about the troubles brewing here in Eden. Tasting the Tree of Life makes Paradise harder to maintain."

Parvel listened, realizing Narumi was right. "What are we

humans to do? We haven't had Eden or Paradise since Adam and Eve, according to religious dogma." He moved haltingly toward Summer. "How do we get Cigi back?"

"Cecil knows where they took her." She gathered her sisters together and marched them into the kitchen, away from the others. Summer whispered as she spoke, "If Peter wants a war, then we are giving him one."

Autumn asked, "Why would we do this? Is war the only answer to opposing his power move?"

Spring said, "We have the location of the hundreds of androids the government confiscated. Activating them and assigning tasks to follow can mitigate any power-grab Peter might envision."

"If they are controllable." Summer glared at her sister. "Our priority is to Cigi. Let's get her."

They returned to the living room to plan extricating Cigi from Peter's control.

Cecil called in to report a change of venue. "I'll keep close," he said, "but you better act soon before they discover I am nearby." After a brief silence, he continued. "What happened to the thugs that left here? I do not think they were assisting Cigi with her natal condition."

"They came to the condo for Parvel. Thomas intercepted them and a fight occurred. They are dead."

"Thomas defeated two androids and survived?" Cecil asked. "I did not realize he was capable of such strength."

"His design helped him win," Summer said. "They planned to kill Parvel. We found a syringe filled with a neurotoxin. Autumn is developing an antidote."

"We're on the move." Cecil sent details about a tracker installed in his programming so they could find him.

"Summer and I will follow Cecil along with our gentlemen. The rest of you remain here to monitor Thomas and Parvel. Narumi, be ready to activate a large army of androids." Autumn signaled her man and the others to accompany them.

In the van, Summer commanded like a well-seasoned general in a field of battle. Each man would disable anyone who intervened. Summer reasoned Peter's androids would be the interference, a new design, but not as sophisticated as they had become.

They found Cecil discreetly positioned to monitor the building in which Peter and Cigi were located. "I have discovered Cigi's location, but she is not alone." He updated their intel, so they devised a plan to enter the building and retrieve Cigi.

They moved across a parking lot, avoiding cameras visible to them. They did not know whether the cameras functioned, but caution was advisable. An open door, as if Peter left an invitation for them, meant stealth as an android male entered. Another rounded the building, seeking another way in. Summer followed. Spring, Winter, and the other two males waited for each to return.

The first male came to them and signaled for them to enter. "There seems to be no one here."

Winter said, "That makes no sense. Cecil followed Cigi here because she and he are connected. If he has her signal, she must be here." The five androids entered again and moved about the hallways, searching rooms.

A male android confronted them as they rounded a corner into a large open area. "Peter wants you to follow me," he said. They glanced at each other.

"Well, there goes our element of surprise. Peter knows we are here," Winter said. One of their males started for the speaker. Winter placed a hand on his arm and discreetly shook her head.

In an interior room, they found Cigi, Bromand, and Peter sitting in chairs. Peter rose and greeted the five androids he created who rebelled.

"Thank you for coming. Cigi and I are enjoying a quiet conversation about the future of artificially intelligent beings and how fitting into human society makes life better for all."

He directed the android to set up more chairs for them. Winter and Spring sat while the three males remained standing. Winter asked Cigi, "Are you okay?"

Cigi smiled and said, "Peter will not harm me until the birth of my baby." She turned her attention to Peter. "Isn't that right, Peter?"

Peter laughed, "I do not want to harm you at all. Sam has created the perfect human. All I want is the schematics to do the same." He looked at Winter and asked, "Where are your sisters? I thought you four did everything together."

"They stayed with Parvel and Thomas. By the way, your thugs had a run-in with Thomas and are now decommissioned."

Peter frowned, "Decommissioned? Are they dead? Well, that occurs in war. Casualties happen. How did you find me? Did Cigi leave a breadcrumb trail?"

He looked at Cigi and continued, "I guess Cecil is outside,

which is good. Bromand, give Winter the syringe so she can return to Parvel with the antidote. No need to have the baby's father die too soon." Bromand stood and walked to a table to retrieve the requested item. He handed Winter the box.

Peter said, "I sent my androids to bring Parvel here. They injected a sedative laced with a virus that will kill him within five days. This syringe may have the antidote. You can decide whether to return with him. Spring and your boyfriends will remain here until you return with Parvel." He nodded at Bromand, who took the box from Winter and set it on the table.

Winter stood from the chair and walked toward the door. She turned to see the concern on Spring's face. Cigi nodded slightly and smiled. Winter departed for a journey to get help and bring Parvel to Peter. She hoped Summer and the fourth male were safe and aware of the situation.

Chapter 32

Sam and Clare arrived as planned. The cross-country trip with Rose, the automobile, included no sightseeing this time. Too much remained unknown for cruising leisurely to Virginia from Washington State. "We must get Cigi out of my brother's clutches. She cannot have that baby while with him." Sam's voice growled as he spoke.

"Stay calm, Sam," Clare said.

"I agree," said Rose. The sentient automobile entertained the couple in the backseat as they traveled. She also kept them informed of the status of their friends in Arlington. Clare was a powerful and advanced artificial life form, a model created by Sam before he designed and developed Cigi. He promised to upgrade her reproductive system as soon as Cigi birthed the baby boy growing inside her.

"Rose, how much longer before we arrive?" Sam asked.

"We should arrive within two hours. I have informed Summer of our timetable. She and her sisters will meet us at your apartment."

"Good." He inhaled a deep breath and held it for a few seconds. Clare held his left hand in her right one. He smiled at her and then kissed her. "I don't think I could do this without you." She laid her head on his shoulder.

"We have another transmission from Summer," Rose said. Sam freed his hand as Clare sat upright. "Summer and one male are near Cigi's location. Spring and three male android companions are with her and Peter. Peter sent Winter to retrieve Parvel."

"Where is Autumn?" he asked.

"She's at the condo attempting to counteract a toxin injected into Parvel. Thomas needs help to reanimate fully."

"If I find Peter has hurt or damaged any of my friends, I swear I'll kill him." Sam seethed.

"Summer has a location for the confiscated androids," Rose said.

Sam smacked his fist into his other hand. "That's good news, at least." He smiled at Clare and continued. "How did she get that information?"

Rose answered. "When Winter and Spring crossed the Straits of Florida, they ran into some trouble and a United States Coast Guard cutter rescued them. Four of the crew were androids from the hundreds taken by the government. They helped Winter and Spring to escape the humans and continue the journey to Cigi and Parvel. One android acted as an ensign and slipped the location to Winter."

"Peter was busy building his cadre for nefarious use. I need to speak with Renata about why this happened," Sam said. "I hope we can get them to work for us and not against us. Does Peter know where these AI are?"

"Summer has no information," Rose said.

The rest of the trip was quiet, as Sam and Clare contemplated plans for a rescue and deliverance.

Winter arrived at the condo to find Thomas alive and healing. Autumn had a blood sample from Parvel and analyzed it for the poison allegedly within his body. She interrupted the activity and said, "I've come for Parvel. Peter wants him and has a countermeasure for the virus within his body."

Autumn looked up from the microscope image on her computer screen. "I found the virus and will find a vaccine to neutralize it."

"You have five days, according to Peter. Parvel dies without the antodote. Let me take him to Peter to get the shot," Winter said.

Parvel entered the conversation. "I have a say in what happens to me. If I am condemned to die, I want to be with my wife. Please, take me to Cigi. I'll deal with Peter when I get there." He rose from his chair. Thomas stood with him from another chair.

"I'll come, too. If I can deal fatal blows to these two thugs, I can do worse to Peter. He should not have constructed me to replace that greedy David Anderson." Winter and Parvel departed. He faltered as he attempted to follow them.

Narumi said, "I have not finished your recovery. I need to reset some of the damaged parts of your body." Thomas sat again at her insistence.

Autumn searched databases for medicines that countered the effects of the virus in Parvel. Peter used an unknown source for the virus that must have a vaccine as well. She looked for a reputable organization or pharmacy, but research required reporting the illness, and she did not want to leave identification with any medical staff or pharmacy. The dark web still existed despite government attempts to disassemble it.

Narumi finished repairing Thomas, whose nano-technology aided with his reconstruction of vital parts. "There," said Narumi, "good as new."

"I feel like crap," Thomas said. "Maybe my emotional processors are out of alignment." Narumi laughed.

"They are fine. You've matured since I first worked on you a year ago. Why are you not using David Anderson as a model for you?"

Thomas grunted. "Sam asked if I wanted to be him, and I said no. I want to be me. I used his knowledge to build my fortune. According to the Securities and Exchange, all is open and legal."

Autumn slammed a fist onto the table. "Damn it. I can't find anything to fight the virus Parvel has."

Narumi said, "Peter can care for that. We need to assist Summer."

"How can we help her? We are not sure where they are located," Autumn said.

Narumi opened her bag, removed a small device, clicked a button, and a bleep sounded. She observed the small screen map and smiled. "I found Peter and his android, Robby."

"Who's Robby?" Thomas asked.

Narumi answered. "Peter's general of the army he built in

Arizona. Bentina implanted a tracker without telling her brother or Peter."

Autumn asked, "Do we have trackers?"

"I believe Sam disabled all of your tracking processors. You should be autonomous beings. We can track the men Cigi chipped if she wants to do it."

Thomas started for the hallway door. "Let's get Cigi and the others."

"Slow down, cowboy," Narumi said. "Bentina gave me some intel that can help us retrieve that blessed woman and her baby." He turned back when he heard her.

Winter and Parvel arrived at the building within an hour and met Summer and her male companion. "Anything happening inside?" she asked Summer.

"No, the place is quiet. I'm thinking they are waiting for you to return."

Winter nodded. Parvel said, "I need to see my wife."

They entered the building, leaving Summer and her companion to monitor the situation. As they approached the room with Peter and Cigi, they heard Peter exclaim his desire to be the leader of an integrated society controlled and maintained by his army of androids as the leaders in each of the world's governments and social strata. He saw them when they entered and walked toward them. Spring stood to hug her sister. The three android males greeted Parvel and Winter.

"What a touching scene," Peter said. "You care for others as any human would. I like that."

Winter faced him. "What about the anti-virus?" She moved toward the table with the box still on it. Bromand interceded.

Peter stood and went to Bromand's side. "Patience, my dear. Plenty of time to counter the effects of the disease."

"Is it transmissible from human to human? Can Cigi catch it?" Winter asked.

"Such a caring, emotional being you have become. I am impressed." Peter pointed at her. "We should explore how these emotive behaviors developed in you."

Cigi wriggled to her feet. "Peter, please administer the shot to my husband. I care not to contract the disease, and I imagine you and Bromand vaccinated against it."

"Oh, Cigi, I don't want you to get it. I will keep you safe from the virus. I will inoculate Parvel when you have birthed your baby." She cocked her head.

"I'm not at full term for another two months. Are you planning to remove the baby from me?"

"I have arranged for a proper birth for you in the next couple of days. My doctors and nurses are ready to deliver a C-section baby and incubate the boy." Peter clapped his hands together. "All is ready for you. I may not have sired him, but I will raise him as my child." Parvel started for Peter, but one android stopped him.

"Let Cigi work this out," he whispered to Parvel. "She can handle it."

Parvel screamed at Peter, "Am I to die? Or are you going to incarcerate me away from my wife and child? I won't let you do this."

Peter laughed. "I don't see how you can stop me." He raised his arm and flicked a finger toward an entry across the room. Four men entered.

Winter and Spring watched their gentlemen move to intercept. Peter said, "I programmed these men as soldiers and they will defeat and dismantle your androids. You have no choice but to allow my doctors to deliver your baby early."

Cigi asked, "Is Dr. Jackson here?"

"No, he awaits your arrival at a clinic nearby. Nurse Laurent is there as well." He turned to his army squad. "Take the others to the holding facility." Three android soldiers directed Parvel, Winter, Spring, and the three male androids to another room in the building. A fourth android soldier remained with Peter. They locked the Season sister androids in one cell while pushing Parvel into another room with a toilet and sink. The door closed and clicked behind him, sealing him in the room.

Peter asked Cigi, "Where is Cecil? He can drive us to the clinic. He will be cooperative as long as you ask him to be. And you will cooperate, won't you?"

Cigi sent a message for Cecil to leave the area and not follow. "He is not here," she said. "Regardless of what you believe, it is better for my car to be away rather than any chance you capture and dismantle him."

Peter laughed. "Trust is an issue for you. I understand." They walked to an entry, and he opened the door. "After you, my dear." He extended his arm with his hand held out to assist her as needed. She walked out to find a car waiting for them. Bromand opened a door for her. She got in and sat. Peter moved to the other side, entered, and sat next to her. Bromand got into the driver's seat and started the electrical system. Robby sat in the passenger seat, and they drove away. Summer contacted Cigi, who blinked twice. Cecil followed away from view but connected to his mentor and android friend.

At the clinic, Peter directed Bromand to park inside the garage and close the doors. Cigi stayed calm but cared only to protect her son as they walked to the clinic and premature delivery. In the delivery room, she sat on a birthing chair, strapped into place. Dr. Jackson and Nurse Laurent administered fluids to numb the human tissues that contained nerve-like sensors. She would remain alert during the procedure.

"Peter," she asked, "will you honor your promise not to harm Parvel or any of my friends if I allow you to raise my boy?"

Peter stroked her head. "Why would I deceive you? Your friends will be okay. I need them on my side when we take control of the government."

"And Parvel?" Cigi repeated.

Peter did not answer. Dr. Jackson approached with a scalpel.

Chapter 33

Sam and Clare met with Autumn after settling into their Arlington condo. Each of them discussed Cigi's abduction. "Why does Peter want to kidnap my grandson?" Sam asked. He paced the room.

"Grandson?" Summer asked. She and one male had returned to the condo to update them about Cigi.

"Whose stem cells were used to develop Cigi's reproductive system?" Autumn asked.

Clare stared at her man. Although incapable of reproduction, each of the three female androids had questions Sam did not want to answer. Time had arrived for complete honesty. He looked at each of them and a noncommittal Thomas.

"Years ago, when I was born, my mother had blood saved from my umbilical cord. Stem cell research at the time was gathering momentum and her pediatrician advised her to collect and freeze the blood from the cord. She asked why and he said that it might offset any complications in her health or my health in the future if research produced the expected results medical science wanted."

"You thawed some of the blood after your breakthrough regarding stem cells," Clare said. "Why didn't you use them to make me a complete female?"

Sam smiled and interlaced his fingers before answering. "I had finished Kelsey and sent her on her way to do what she does best. You were in development, and the design did not accommodate the feature. I modified the specs to include the organs she has, but trial and error with other blood samples depleted my stock." He sighed and clasp Clare's hands. "When the breakthrough happened, I used my blood to grow the organs Cigi has, including the reproductive system."

Clare released her hands from Sam's. "I can't upgrade." Tears formed in her eyes. "You delayed changing me because I am not suitable." She stood and left the room. Sam followed, but Summer halted his progress.

"Let her stew for a while," she said. "I understand her predicament. Peter wants Cigi to figure out how you did it. The design of my sisters and I prevents such human content. We exist as best we can without the benefit of old-fashioned motherhood."

Sam sat down, hanging his head. Summer sat with him. "I can modify her, but the changes may cause problems. I don't wanna lose her." Summer stroked his hair.

Autumn approached. "Sam, we need Cigi away from Peter before he does something unrepairable." He looked up at her, and determination filled his face. He stood, turned and helped Summer to rise, and called to Clare.

"You know where Peter is?" he asked.

Summer nodded. Clare came into view and said, "Go get my sister. I'll stay here in case someone comes about Cigi." Sam wanted to change her mind, but thought about Summer's comment. She could stew better alone.

In the garage, two androids and one human sat in Rose. Autumn drove the van to accommodate the rescued members of the band. The male companion android said, "We should contact the others. Peter safely contained them at the building where we found him. We can free them and connect with Cecil. He knows where they went." Knowing this male was maturing along the same developmental path as the four sisters, Sam smiled. Peter should be proud of his accomplishment, but Sam knew that losing control of the eight androids that escaped to Cuba ate at Peter's soul.

"Rose," Sam said, "take us to the coordinates Summer gave you. Then contact Cecil and find out where we go next."

Rose drove through Arlington along the same route taken

earlier by the sisters and Parvel. The area around the building appeared quiet and unguarded. They parked, and Rose scanned for occupants within the structure. "They are in two separate parts of the building. Two androids are in a third room."

Sam thanked his beautiful automobile as they vacated the seats for the assault inside. Summer scanned for any signatures Peter had installed to control his creations. None appeared to be present.

Autumn said, "Let me go first. I can convince them I work with Peter as a mole to keep us away from him. Enter after I connect with the guards."

Summer nodded her agreement with the plan. Sam and the male android waited for Autumn to enter the building before following. Summer said, "I'll find Winter, Spring, and the other males." Sam and the male android walked into the building with her. Autumn turned a corner to confront the guards. Summer, Sam, and the male android searched the other rooms, trying to open each door. Finding a locked door, Sam rapped and heard Parvel. The male android placed his strength against the door until the lock gave way.

"Parvel, are you okay?" Sam asked. He nodded.

"I am now. Where is Cigi?"

Summer returned to them with a location for her sisters and other males. "I need your help to break them out of their prison." Loud noises deterred their return to the room containing Spring and Winter. Sam, Parvel, Summer, and the male followed the noises into a small area where Autumn confronted the two male android guards. When one struck her in the head, she collapsed. The other raised a foot to stomp her, but Summer and her male friend shoved him away. Sam raised his fists to fight the first guard. Autumn kicked the guard's leg, causing him to fall. Sam pulled Autumn out of harm's way as the guard stood.

Parvel led her from the room to check for any damage. Summer and her male disabled the one guard and turned attention to the second one about to attack Sam. "Stop now before we dismantle you into scrap." The guard ceased confronting them. He looked at his companion guard. Peter had developed them as sturdy and command-oriented, so this one acquiesced to her orders. "Release the other prisoners now."

He left with Autumn as Sam constrained the guard on the floor. At the other room, he punched a keypad, releasing the magnetic lock on the door. Spring, Winter, and three male androids vacated the room and shoved the guard into their prison. Closing the door locked it automatically. Without access to the keypad, Summer incarcerated the guard and would return later to free him.

Sam said, "Let's find Cecil and confront my brother about his poor judgment. Parvel, we will get her back, and your son will be safe. I promise."

Parvel realized such a promise was a futile attempt at appeasing his anxiety-riddled mind. A year ago, his life as a quiet mortgage manager was easy and unencumbered. Now he faced losing his life, his wife, and his son. He felt betrayed by those he trusted to keep his life fruitful.

"Rose, do you have a lock on Cecil?" Sam asked when they returned.

Rose honked and said, "He is near the place they took Cigi. He sent directions to me." Sam, Summer, and Parvel sat in the car while the others entered the van and followed. After a quick trip, they found Cecil waiting for them.

"The gray building across the street and the parking area," Cecil said.

Sam directed everyone to remain with Rose and Cecil and come if he signaled. He flipped on an electronic monitor coded to Rose, who would trail his signal. He walked across the street that was devoid of traffic. The neighborhood was a wasteland of unused buildings and abandoned vehicles. Trotting across the parking lot, he noticed the cameras on the building walls. He didn't care. His brother had Cigi. At one door, he tested it but found it locked. Around the corner, he found an open egress, so he entered the building. Peter waited for him in the hallway.

"Hello, brother. Nice to have you visit me. We shouldn't wait so long between reunions." He signaled Robbie to escort Sam to another part of the building where Dr. Jackson Sanders was delivering Zaiyaan Prasad Mandolin.

"Who's your fiend, ah, I mean friend?" Sam asked.

Peter laughed, saying. "Always a joke. Until you became a good Samaritan, we had a great thing. We could have taken humanity to new heights and improved the entire world with our creations." They walked at a saunter so Peter could pontificate. Sam listened but was not accepting this brotherly conversation.

"We wanted different things, little brother. You wanted the

world. I wanted humanity." Sam stopped and looked at Robbie. "Are you sure Peter has the best intentions for you? Are you developed to think without orders?" Sam's head rocked back and forth. "I'm guessing not."

Peter shot back at Sam. "Are the rest of the crew outside ready to storm the Bastille? Any interference and poof. It's all gone. You, Cigi, the baby. Gone. Stay out of my way. Brother."

Looking dejected, Sam shoved his hands into his pockets, took a couple of steps on the journey to Hell, and clicked the button on the device. "Let me see Cigi before you carve her to find out what I did."

Peter said, "You may be too late. I imagine Dr. Sanders has sliced my little boy out of her by now. It may be early for him, but not for me." Peter pushed Sam to a faster pace. "Let's meet our newest relative." As they entered the delivery room cordoned off to provide a sterile environment for Dr, Sander's work, the grimace faded from his face, and a scowl appeared.

Peter realized his goal was unattained. Appropriately garbed for medical work, Jackson had not used the scalpel to slice Cigi open. He and Tatiana Laurent were examining her. Sam smiled as he said, "I think we have to wait until Cigi is ready to birth naturally."

Hissing, Peter reached for a knife on the side cart. "I'll get that baby out of her myself." Sam grabbed his wrist to prevent any damage, and Robbie attacked Sam, defending Peter.

Cigi said, "Peter, Sam, stop fighting. Jackson and I decided my baby needs to develop to full term. The medical ethics programmed into him and Tatiana by you, Peter, prevent them from doing this." Noises from outside the room alerted Peter, Robbie, and Bromand Nangold that the crew had arrived. As they parted from Sam and exited through another doorway, Peter yelled. "This isn't over."

Summer and the rest entered the room, released Cigi from the restraints. She hugged Parvel, who kissed her and held her. Sam asked, "Is there a syringe here to counteract the virus?" A search of the operating equipment revealed nothing other than the local anesthetic used to numb Cigi's abdomen. Parvel stared at the table and then at Cigi. Peter's threat to harm him remained.

Chapter 34

Peter ran from the building fearing the androids would follow. He seethed at losing Cigi Weatherman and that baby android monster. Bromand hurried to keep pace while Robbie reached the the car and started the motors. The defeated guards remained behind and Peter declared they were prisoners of war. Inside the van, he said, "Bromand, why does my medical staff act like they control their lives independently? Were the monitoring switches uncoupled? Check the army at home and be sure we have control."

Bromand nodded and said, "I think Cigi overrode the controls. Either her or your brother. He is smart and capable of changing the settings."

They raced away from the building as Summer appeared outside. Peter stared at her while Robbie drove. "How did I lose control of them?" he thought. Something was wrong with his design or with his staff constructing and downloading programs. The Season sisters ran independently of his intentions. The four men he made as replacements for Cigi's gentlemen had grown free from his administration. Samuel had to be eliminated if he was to succeed with gaining power in the world. His brother had interfered for the last time.

At the facility used as a headquarters in Virginia for Walter

Mitty industries, Peter assessed the results of actions. Cigi was captured and lost again. Four soldier androids were lost or captured. Bentina Nangold was to report in but had not. His contact in Renata Girelli's office lost connection. The day failed to meet expectations.

"Nangold, we need more robust androids who can follow instructions and not be corrupted from my mission. Can you do it?" Peter placed hands on hips and frowned a stone-like grimace.

"Yes, sir. My sister and I will rewrite the programming to block Sam from interfering." The loss of the guards left a vulnerability Peter feared. Bromand clicked open is phone and called his sister. As the ringing commenced he separated from Peter for a private conversation. "Where are you? Peter's on a tirade. We lost Cigi to that band of renegades that follow her. We have to redesign our army." He listened to her and then interrupted. "What do you mean? We can't abandon him. He has the best philosophy regarding humans and running the world." He listened again and cut his call short. "Damn it."

Robbie approached him. "Sibling troubles?" Bromand looked at him and shook his head. Peter mistook a worker android for a leader, an irrational concept. Was he capable of leading a small army? Bromand had doubts.

"No, she found where the Season sister androids live." Bromand watched for a reaction, but nothing happened. "They returned from Cuba." Robbie showed no interest in the conversation and turned away.

Bromand decided to leave for the house they rented in Manassas. The two remaining androids that accompanied Peter were there. Peter wanted powerful, independent, but obedient androids. These two were the guinea pigs. If the androids could be improved as Peter demanded, he could enhance the Arizona army .

"Peter, I'm heading back to the house. My sister is going to our condo to get some equipment for us to work on your ideas for stronger, more responsive androids."

"Make my army stronger and bigger. My brother and his gang of losers cannot gain the upper hand. Find my androids the government stole." Peter said. "Do what I ask, or I'll replace you with a clone."

Bromand scowled when out of sight. Threats meant nothing to him as he knew Peter could not do without him. Sam was the technical design genius. Peter was intelligent but copied what he could since creative thought eluded him.

Clicking open his phone, he punched in Bentina's code. After several rings, she answered. "Where are you?" he asked her. He listen and said, "I'm heading to the house in Manassas. Meet me there." With her acceptance, he clicked off. He loved his sister but realized she was wavering about the goals he and Peter had for an incursion into government offices and departments. The attempt to replace Andre Scott failed when the car did not eliminate the human. He did not formulate any plans for the others yet. His contact in Giretti's office needed reconnecting. She was a thorn in his ambitions, and eliminating her could be the next assignment for his android mole if he could reestablish contact.

As Bromand entered the grounds of the house in Manassas, he observed the two androids come outside after his message to them. They waited for the car to stop and him to vacate the driver's side. "Go to the lab room." They turned to obey his order. He admired what he created and appreciated the freedom Peter bestowed on him to craft these magnificent beings.

After collecting his materials, he followed his squad to the lab. They stood awaiting instructions from him. "Magnificent," he thought as he placed his things on a desk he used to craft his designs. Turning to the two android males, he said, "I am to improve your abilities and processing powers." They did not respond but waited for his commands.

He had them sit in chairs near his computer console and the external connections that would reset the command centers of their memory chips. Each android was to be enhanced to anticipate the actions of humans and other androids more efficiently and effectively. Peter wanted stronger warriors. Bromand wanted more competent soldiers. Attaching the conduits to their portals, he instituted a computer command to override the instructional centers of the processors within the memory chips and rewrite the code to improve anticipatory computing.

The silence within the room pleased Bromand. No debate with Peter about what was essential. No arguing with the android doctor about the efficacy and morality of slicing open a pregnant android. No interference from Samuel Bennington or his android cohorts. He smiled at the two males who returned the gesture. Changes within their memory processing were happening. He would build the remaining army with these androids as guides. Peter would get his stronger army, and Bromand would know they were more competent.

A noise in another part of the house alerted him to the possible appearance of Bentina. In the foyer, he found his sister removing her coat and hanging it on the coat rack.

"I'm glad you came," he said. "Peter instructed me to upgrade the remaining two androids. He's upset Sam and those Season sisters defeated his troops."

"Peter is losing it." Bentina followed her brother returning to the room with the androids. "What do you plan to do once these males are upgraded?" She suspected a business coup for strengthening his position to promote autocratic control.

"Don't be so negative about Peter. He's allowed you and me the opportunity to accomplish world-changing creations. Besides, you and he enjoy a consensual union."

Bentina grunted at the reminder of her misguided decision to sleep with Peter. "We have agreed to keep that liaison in the past." She studied the monitors showing the progress for the upgrades to the androids. Their eyes followed her movements as she moved about the room. "Eerie," she thought. Were the androids wary of her or changing their computing status within the processors? Relating to Summer and Autumn was much easier because they had human qualities.

Bromand clicked the keys on the board controlling the programming and smiled. "The androids are responding well to their improvements," he said. The eyes continued trailing Bentina as she wandered about the room. "See how they watch you? They can now sense your uneasiness and will take appropriate actions to neutralize any threat to them."

Bentina halted her movements and stared at the male androids. Facing her brother, she asked, "Am I a threat to them? Do you think I'm a threat?" She huffed and turned to leave.

"Wait," he said, "you are not a threat to them or me. They are learning to evaluate situations." He watched the monitors again and then said, "We need an army that can survey the environment and make calculated assessments to protect each other and their allies from intrusive actions by others." He reached out to her with his hand. "Come, see what is happening."

Bentina watched the screen, recognized the programming downloading into the android memories, and realized her brother had offered independence to the creations. They would seek and destroy anything or anyone that transgressed their objectives. She glanced at the androids and noticed their attention to her. A warmth coursed her neck and head. Fear. Would they sense the temperature change and react to neutralize her? The programming had another half hour before completing the upgrades Bromand developed. Bentina walked to the doorway and nodded for her brother to follow. Two sets of AI eyes watched.

In the hallway, she said, "Bromand, you may have more than you expect with this change." She grabbed his arm, leading him toward the front door. She did not want them to hear what she said.

"Do not worry, little sister; I have control of them. They will act according to my commands for them."

"You gave them autonomy. What if these androids don't like your commands? These are not humans who learn to be good soldiers and work as a unit. These are individuals that may want to be in charge of themselves." She swiveled toward the door. "Are they going after Cigi and Parvel to get her baby? You left some bodies behind in your attempt to kidnap Cigi and cut her baby from her."

He reached for her arm and held her so she could not leave the house. "What happened to the other male androids is unfortunate, but that means we gained data and information we can use to improve the entire army in Arizona and the horde in government hands that is here. We will have the forces needed to repel any hostile action to stop us from gaining the upper hand."

"Are you hearing what you are saying? There are nearly four hundred million people in this country, and most of them are not friendly to androids infiltrating their lives, peacefully or not." She twisted out of his grip. "There are not enough android models created to replace the government officials or run the military forces. Any attempted coup will be crushed before you get any traction." Bentina opened the door to leave, looked at her brother, and saw the anger.

"Don't cross me on this, or you may be one of the first victims." He shifted away to return to his creatures. Bentina left with tears streaming from her eyes. She had to warn Summer and Autumn. A war was building outside of Peter's intentions, which could cost humans and artificial intelligent life forms dearly. As long as she could influence who or what was in charge of leading to a peaceful transition, the end of the world was not happening. As she drove away, she noticed her brother staring out the window at her. Beside him were his new creations. Would they come for her or the others?

Chapter 35

The room accommodated the beings assembled. Several of the human participants in the meeting had an android counterpart. Convincing Gunther Parsons, David Anderson, and Andre Scott to participate proved challenging. Charles Cooke and Charlie arrived from Seattle the previous evening.

Gunther glared at Cigi. "Why should I listen to you? You disrupted my life, and now those other beasts tried controlling me."

Cigi nodded an acknowledgment for his concern. She placed a hand on her abdomen and said, "Gunther, I have closed the connection and will not let them in. You are safe from interference."

He huffed and walked away. David Anderson glanced at Thomas Anders and then watched Gunther. His meeting with Gunther reminded him of the threat to Cigi and the baby. No one reactivated his chip, and Cigi's promise helped alleviate any angst. Andre appeared to be less concerned about the influence of artificial intelligent humanoids, and yet the accident shook him. David wheeled himself nearer Cigi to speak with her.

"He isn't over what you did to us." Cigi listened, aware of the situation with Gunther. "Be careful. He could be a problem." Cigi cocked her head and frowned.

"Are you a problem, too?" she asked. Her brain listened to

Gunther's head without a complete activation. She did not want him aggravated.

"I shouldn't be, but any movement by you or your fake humans that disrupts my life or my business will make me an enemy. I don't think you want that."

Cigi smiled. His words did not match his thoughts. Fear of the repercussions of confronting her softened his head. Words were only words. "You are an ally. My business with you has turned toward positivity so we can be friends and cohorts in the efforts to codify sentient artificial life forms as accepted members of humanity and the society in which we live."

David rolled closer to the glass doors leading to her patio. He stared out for a moment, and without looking back at Cigi, he said, "That is a challenge." She stood beside him, placed a hand on his shoulder, and stared out at the world below.

"Yes, and a challenge worth engaging."

Parvel approached and kissed Cigi's cheek. "David, I know we have our differences, but the future incorporates AI and will not hinder any human business."

The three beings stared for several seconds in silence. "What happened to the mob of androids the government raid garnered? Were they destroyed?" David asked.

Cigi said, "As far as we know, they are intact and operational. The military infused several into the Coast Guard experimenting with the practicality of android crews."

"The dawn of androids in our society begins." David Anderson turned his chair and left the lovebirds to view the human population roving the streets below. Parvel asked, "Is he with us?"

Cigi leaned into him and said, "He'll come around. Investment in advancing technology is one of his focuses, and the development of the industry intrigues him. He can influence people in government to change the current attitudes and create a positive environment."

Andre came toward them and asked, "What did David want?"

"He warned me about Gunther's animosity about the chip in his head," Cigi said.

He looked at Parvel. "You are one forgiving human."

"Why do you say that?" Parvel asked.

Andre laughed. "Your wife didn't put a chip in your head, and yet she got control of you using the same attraction she used with us." Parvel felt the rise of heat in his cheeks. He stared at Andre.

"My relationship is not based on her control of me. And as for the chip in your head, it is not functioning. You should be more forgiving yourself." Parvel walked away.

"I didn't mean to anger him. He got you as his life partner, and that means he is receiving the best treatment any man could want." Andre glanced back at Parvel, who disappeared into his bedroom.

"Andre, he is as supportive of us as a person could be. I would not be with him except for his intelligence and abilities. He is attentive and loving. Despite his shyness, he has helped you and your department clean up the problems caused by the moles Peter planted." Cigi faced Andre. "Be with us despite your concerns about advancing artificial intelligence. We are not the enemy of humanity."

"Humanity has enough enemies within its ranks. Do you really believe androids can save us from our selfish and greedy attitudes?"

Cigi said, "I asked you here because Peter is a formidable adversary, and you have some influence with him."

She gathered the others and addressed the reasons for assembling them. Peter had kidnapped her, intending to remove her baby boy from her body. He was a danger to the interactions of humans and androids as allies instead of competitors for resources and power. Should Peter develop a viable army and inculcate his androids into the government, life on the planet could change drastically. He had to be stopped.

Sam listened to Cigi as she spoke, understanding the perils his brother presented to humanity. He and Clare rescued her from Peter with the help of Summer, Autumn, Winter, and Spring Seasons. The android medical professionals assigned to help her deliver a healthy baby had threatened to shorten the gestation period until their programming about the morality of taking a life altered their actions. Peter had them programmed by Bromand Nangold to fit into the medical environment without exposure as AI. The programming saved Cigi.

As the gathering wound down, several of the androids departed for their residences. Andre, Gunther, and David Anderson left for human homes and families. Had the meeting accomplished any progress toward reconciliation of humans and androids? Time would tell.

Parvel attended the meeting when he heard Cigi. Afterward, he asked, "Are we jousting at windmills?" He watched her as she sat at the dining table. She looked tired, a challenge for an artificial life form. Her features projected a worry he had seen only twice in his life with her. At Anderson's cabin in Pennsylvania, she exhibited concern about the raid that narrowly missed capturing her. Her worry about pregnancy and becoming a mother fostered the second time.

"Quoting Cervantes, Parvel?" She smiled, the weight of leading a revolution lifted from her. "The future is always uncertain, but of this, I am sure. I love you, and together we will be fantastic parents. Who knows? Maybe Ziayaan will lead the world to peace and prosperity."

Sam and Clare approached their friends. Sam said, "Cigi, Parvel, we need to stop my brother. He cannot have the power he craves, which could destroy the world we know. You have a lead on the whereabouts of the androids in government custody. Let's get them out before Peter does something we don't want happening."

Cigi said, "Spring and Winter encountered four androids, a female and three males, acting as Coast Guard crew. Ensign Gines wanted to join us, but she will have difficulty leaving government oversight and control. She gave them the location where she was incarcerated. Activating the androids would alert government officials, which we don't want. Sam, will Renata help us?"

Sam set his jaw and cocked his head. "I don't know. She claims to be loyal to android integration into human society."

"But…," Cigi said, "she has not sworn allegiance to our cause. Her oath of office to the Constitution and the government betrays her."

The door chime broke the conversation. Parvel checked the intruder and noticed Charles Cooke and Charlie returned. He opened the door and waited for the elevator to ascend. When the car arrived, and they exited, he asked, "Something wrong? You left here less than an hour ago."

Charles said, "Charlie came up with a brilliant idea about strengthening the alliance between humans and androids. I'm surprised none of us thought of it before now." They entered the condo and were greeted with a confused expression on Sam's face.

"What are you doing back here so soon?" Sam asked.

Parvel said, "Charlie has an idea about how we can be a stronger group."

Cigi and Clare waited for Charlie to speak. Sam furrowed his brow, and Parvel folded his arms across his chest. Charles sat in a chair next to Cigi. Charlie glanced at each of them and began.

After he related his plan, Sam asked, "Do you trust you can get Andre and Gunther's clones to agree with you if you can find them?"

"I trust the androids more than their human counterparts. We are more programmable than humans. Sam, you and Cigi can make sure they are part of our team, regardless of their past behaviors."

Cigi gazed at Charlie before saying, "Charlie, the idea of controlling anyone, human or android, does not fit what we want as members of the human society. We cannot ask for acceptance and then act in an authoritarian manner. You and Charles figured out the best way for you to interact. We need to educate humans and sentient androids to uncover ways of helping each other to attain improvements without fear of reprisals or replacement."

Charlie nodded. Did he agree, or was he programming his brain to understand her words? Charles Cooke said, "We have an understanding about working together. I think he wants others to do the same. I'm not sure what caused him to decide to stay a part of my life. Thomas chose to stray from his human counterpart, although incorporating David's knowledge base into his processors keeps them connected. Gunther and his clone could strike a bargain to assault you, Cigi. Andre is not fully convinced androids are important enough to assimilate them into society."

Sam looked at Cigi. "You're correct about authoritarianism over androids thwarts any possible integration. Peter has yet to understand the concept of freedom to choose. All my brother wants is power and wealth."

"Gunther and I met a while back about the energy needs for the country," Charles said. "He was hyped up about the fuel reserves depleted by the lack of exploration. He wants to increase the drilling in areas that are no longer accessible. I think he is angry enough to confront us about the influx of androids. I tried to explain the benefits for his company using programmable robotics in a dangerous situation, but he's irritated by the chip in his head. Cigi, he may be plotting with Peter against you."

The door chime sounded again. Parvel checked who wanted to come up to them. The video showed two unknown men in the lobby who stared at the camera. Parvel called to Sam. "Hey, two guys are downstairs, and I don't recognize them." Sam approached the video monitor. The men had turned away from the camera, but he could see them pacing the lobby floor.

"Don't let them up here," Sam said. "I'll go down and find out what they want." He left the condo and headed to the elevator. Parvel kept the feed open to watch Sam's interaction with them. When the elevator door opened, the two men approached to enter but were stopped by Sam. Parvel turned up the volume to hear the conversation. What happened next froze him from leaving the screen.

186   PA Stockwell

"Don't let them up here," Sam said. "I'll go down and find out what they want." He left the condo and headed to the elevator. Parvel kept the feed open to watch Sam's interaction with them. When the elevator door opened, the two men approached to enter but were stopped by Sam. Parvel turned up the volume to hear the conversation. What happened next froze him from leaving the screen.

Chapter 36

Sam stopped the two men who flashed government identification at him. "What do you want?"

"Are you Samuel Bennington?" one of the men asked.

"Who wants to know? Somebody sent you here to pry into the lives of innocent people." Sam remained in the entry of the car, letting the doors close. The badges identified the agents as part of the task force appointed to discover and apprehend androids who had escaped the raid.

"Mr. Bennington, we are not here to pry into anyone's lives. We have a warrant for one Cigi Weatherman, and interfering with us can get you arrested."

"Show me the warrant."

"Is she upstairs?" the agent asked. "We need her to come with us." Sam focused on the eyes of the man and realized they were not telling a truthful story. "Mr. Bennington, I will ask you one more time, and then I will detain you."

Sam reached into his pocket for the small controller. He pushed the button, but nothing happened. The other male android said, "Mr. Bennington, please remove your hands from your pockets and place them behind your back."

The programming Peter placed in these androids was not

affected by his box. He realized the upgrades to their systems must be a recent modification. He could not fight them and hoped someone upstairs watched the interplay. Cigi was the target. Peter had not succeeded and sent his bots to finish what he wanted.

"I am not going with you today or any other day. I know who you are and why you want Cigi." Sam pushed the button for the car, planning to send it to the garage and Cecil. "Tell Peter he cannot have Cigi or the baby."

As the door opened and he stepped in, the men shoved their way in with him. "I think you are mistaken, Mr. Bennington. Our agency also needs your brother. Do you know where he is?" As the car descended, Sam stared at the two men.

"What do you mean? Peter didn't send you?"

"We are here to assist Ms. Weatherman and prevent harm to her and the baby." Sam remained skeptical. The agency named on the ID badges wanted to clear the streets of sentient life forms. These two were androids and claiming to help.

"Who sent you?"

"I did." The voice came from a small display held out by the first agent. The face on the screen was Renata Giretti. "Peter is not the only person targeting Cigi."

The car halted the descent, and the doors opened. Renata stood near Cecil, holding a small video camera. She turned off the feed to the monitor and walked over to the three men. "I was hoping to avoid any difficulties by using these men. The warrant is real, though. Cigi is to report to my office."

"Whose side are you on, Renata? I thought we had an understanding," Sam said.

"I am authorized to use androids in place of human agents, and these are programmed to heed to my directions. I did not want to alarm you, Cigi, or Parvel."

Sam hesitated, his mouth hanging slightly open. "Renata, an alarm is not what I feel right now." He closed his eyes and hissed in a breath. She waited. "How did you gain access to these androids operating systems? Who authorized you to use them for your personal interest?"

"Sam, I understand and appreciate your concern. We are not using these beings for personal gain. They are licensed with the bureau and work independently. Like any good worker, they follow orders from superiors. We need Cigi to enhance their abilities to be independent and as human as she is. I convinced the President to test the viability of using your androids in particular situations. She agreed."

Sam looked at the two males and back at Renata. "They are not slaves or conscripted beings on parole from prison. Treat them well, or you will not gain what you intend." Renata signaled the men to return to the van in which they arrived. Each nodded to her as they walked away.

"Can we go upstairs and talk with Cigi." She splayed her hands and cocked her right eyebrow. "Please." Sam gestured for her to follow him. They rode the elevator to the condo floor.

As the car ascended, Sam asked. "Did the President inform Congress of this action of yours? Will there be a change to the laws of the land?" Renata shrugged.

Inside the condo, Sam oriented the others to the interchange in the lobby and Renata's presence. Cigi asked, "Renata, if I comprehend you correctly, the androids in government hands are beings activated and are assuming positions in various departments. What can I do that your tech people are not doing already?" She struggled to rise from her seat. "I have not the capacity to travel far from my residence at this time. My baby seeks his freedom from my body within a few weeks. My doctor requested I remain home and rest."

"The trauma caused by Peter, I assume, has compelled the request." Renata knew more than Cigi thought possible, but she was correct about Peter. "I want you to have the best medical care possible. I've arranged for the finest practitioners to see to your needs and delivery in a safe environment."

Cigi smiled and said, "I have the finest practitioners. They don't question my anatomy or my brain."

"Mine will not question you either."

"Thank you, but no." Cigi frowned. "This isn't why you are here, is it. You have another problem and don't know what to do about it."

Sam interrupted their conversation. "Renata, why a warrant signed by a local magistrate? You make it sound like a criminal case."

"By current law, she is a criminal, and so are you, Parvel, Clare, and anyone else working with you or harboring AI. I can have federal marshals here in minutes, and they will terminate any freedoms you now enjoy."

Cigi hushed Sam and asked, "Why are you here?"

Renata watched Cigi for a few seconds and said, "We do have a problem." She paced the room then turned to look out the glass doors of the patio toward Washington D.C. "There are members of Congress and the military that want to weaponize the androids. These people want an invincible army of dispensable units. I don't think Sam created you and Clare as weapons."

Sam remained quiet, realizing the severity of Renata's words and the mental and emotional integrity of Cigi. He may have designed and constructed her, but she was now an independent human, and confronting the issue of an army of androids was for her to respond.

"Renata," Cigi said, "Sam and Peter are at odds about the use of androids. Peter wants his army and control of the government. Sam wants us to be independent and free to decide our fates, the same as any human being. If the military wants a robotic army, I assume the bodies in government control will be its basis. Technicians can create non-thinking bots, but the country cannot afford a disposable army. Sam wants us to be integrated into society and build a better world."

Parvel and Sam looked at each other and smiled. Was this conversation the infant steps to the maturation of thinking about android and human interaction? Could the birth of a baby boy be the initiation of humans to the possibilities of saving the planet from gross misuse?

"Clare and I are as human as anyone born of a woman," Cigi said. "We are not mindless entities controllable by computer software." Clare nodded in agreement.

Clare said, "I want what any human wants. Freedom to decide what I want, what I need, and with whom I will live. No human will control me any more than I will control any human."

Renata realized the gravity of their positions. Humans had choice, freedom, initiative, and opportunity. Androids were illegal and thought of as dangerous to humanity. Seeing how Clare and Cigi functioned raised questions about the philosophy humans had developed about the efficacy of androids. Sixty years of development and attitude reached this level of thinking. American citizens refused to accept foreign migration and competition for jobs and government benefits. Adding sentient, capable, intelligent artificial life forms to the mix would be too much. She was at an impasse, yet using androids as agents in her government department proved the worth of allowing others to live legitimate lives.

"Alright, I can see your point of view. But Cigi, I do have a dilemma," Renata said. "The President wants an audience with you in a private setting without any fanfare or press."

"Alright, I will go with you and meet with the President. Sam, Parvel, and Clare will come with us as witnesses and support for our position. If you cannot agree with these conditions, I don't see any reason for me to cooperate."

"If you don't agree to come with me, the President will send agents to force you to meet with her." Renata's eyes reflected the strictness of her thoughts. "I can agree to you and Sam coming."

"And Clare and Parvel."

Renata stared at Cigi and rocked her head. "Alright, let's go." They exited the condo and rode the elevator to the garage. Renata signaled the agents to start the car. Cecil signaled he was ready to follow. Cigi, Parvel, Sam, and Clare stood by the sentient car. The government van had room for everyone, and Renata directed them to enter and sit. Cigi sat in the front passenger seat. As the vehicle left the garage, Cigi sent Cecil a message to use her tracking and stay out of sight but be close.

The trip lasted an hour to give the President time to reach the destination. Three humans and two androids entered a small cabin, the meeting place in a remote part of Maryland. They were directed by secret service agents into a room to wait for the arrival of the President of the United States. Sitting in chairs around a small conference table, Renata said, "Cigi, I have explained to President Blankenship your condition. She wanted to meet you because this pregnancy changes the focus of the government."

Cigi did not want attention drawn to her condition. She wanted to have her baby and live a quiet life with Parvel. Could this meeting achieve peace, or was it a step down the path to conflict?

The door opened, and two secret service agents entered and stood by the door. A woman entered and greeted Renata, who rose from her seat along with Sam and Parvel. "Thank you for arranging this, Renata." Turning attention to the others, she said, " I was not expecting to meet with you, gentlemen, but as the designer and husband, I accept your desire to be here." Facing the seated females, she said, "You must be Clare and Cigi." Clare stood while Cigi remained seated.

Sam gazed at the President for a few seconds and then said, "I thought we were meeting the human president, Renata. This woman is an android." Parvel stared at the female who claimed to be the leader of the free world super-power nation. He also recognized her as an impostor.

Chapter 37

Peter parked his car at the Manassas' house and entered the front door. Bromand met him in the foyer. "Boss, we have a problem." Peter frowned.

"What happened to my men?" he asked.

"I upgraded the androids and readied them for combat. The problem is my sister."

Peter huffed, thinking of her seducing him for a job. Her intelligence, abilities, attention to detail and work ethic impressed him. Had she duped him? "What has she done? Or not done?"

Bromand said, "She may not have the same goals we do." He directed Peter to follow him into the back room, where the android males were waiting for the next stage in their development.

Peter watched a moment as Bromand entered commands into the upgrade computer. "Explain what your sister did," he said.

"It's not what she did. It's what she said." Bromand turned to the monitor and watched. "She claimed you are losing focus and that sleeping with you was a mistake." Peter laughed.

"Sleeping with me was a mistake? That's funny." Peter watched the progress of the upgrade on the monitor and continued speaking. "She is a brilliant engineer and AI scientist, but it is her loss of focus that is the problem. Keep her in line, or you may be one sister short."

Bromand remained silent. He controlled the androids, not Peter, and threats had no sway with him. Peter's money supported designing, developing, and creating artificial life forms that one day would support his ruling the country and maybe the world. Peter had the vision, but he had the drive.

The program completed the cycle, making the android soldiers as mentally powerful as any human and physically more robust than the weight lifters of fame. They were unstoppable. Bromand said to Peter, "We need to test their abilities and skill sets." He released the connections, freeing them to be independent and aware.

Peter grinned. "I know what test to feed them." He opened his communications device and called Gunther Parsons. When connected, he asked, "Where are you?" He listened and said, "I have two men I'm sending to you. They can help you accomplish what you want to do." After hearing what Gunther said, he frowned and ended the call.

"What was that about?" Bromand asked.

"It seems his anger toward Cigi Weatherman has abated. He's not interested in revenge anymore. I'll think of another task for these gentlemen to accomplish." Turning to the androids, he said, "You can go." They left the room, heading to the library to read military journals and tactical manuals.

Peter asked Bromand, "Is anyone still connected to us? I haven't heard from our mole in the government, Autumn, the male I sold to that android female who my brother developed, or any of the androids I created to replace the men chipped by Sam and Cigi."

"I fear we have less control over them than we want. I can send messages and see what happens."

Peter nodded. "Let me know when you hear anything. Have you found the android cache held by the government?"

"No, and your brother may have the inside track through Giretti at discovering the location."

"I must contact him and see if we can agree about the androids." Peter turned and left the room. He walked to the library to talk with his soldiers and discover the competence Bromand claimed in the improvements to these models. Was his army invincible and command-ready? He found them sitting in the leather chairs, speed-reading materials. He smiled. At least they could learn quickly. They stood when he entered. "Gentlemen, are you ready for assignments?"

"Yes, sir," they answered in unison.

Peter gave them orders to find Kelsey Avery and return with her and her male android companion. He gave them the male's tracker signal and sent them out with a command to return with their quarry intact and undamaged. Peter followed them out to the van they had for transportation. He advised them once again to capture and hold without destruction.

When Peter returned to the house, Bromand inquired about the assignment. "I know they are ready for commands. Your request to apprehend and return with two androids tests the program's effectiveness. I don't think they will disobey orders, but androids who are independent thinkers may surprise you."

"You kept oversight, right?" Peter worried that Bromand may have incorporated absolute independence of thought. Humans changing their minds was terrible enough. He did not want overly developed, sentient robots concluding that his orders were wrong. The thinking he wanted from them was to solve situational conflicts. Assess the situation, and adjust appropriately to fulfill the goal. Not change their mind and ruin his objective.

Kelsey Avery sat across from her male companion in a swanky New York City restaurant. Sam asked her to continue her business of meeting wealthy and prominent men, persuaded to donate funds to a charitable organization. Expenses for the charity supported local food banks and social support groups. Some funds migrated to Sam to underwrite research and development of artificially intelligent beings. Although Congress had outlawed sentient AI life forms, the research and development of workable plans was not against the law.

"Thank you for dinner," Kelsey said. "I appreciate your generous donation to our causes." She smiled at her dinner host.

"I would like to donate to your cause, if I may personally," he said. "We can retire to my penthouse and continue discussing how I may help ease the suffering of less fortunate people." She agreed, and they departed after he paid the bill. As they walked along the streets of New York, another male followed. Kelsey sent a message to Ivan to stay a safe and discreet distance from them. Her companion had his security crew watching for nefarious intruders who would disrupt a beautiful evening.

The weather was warm, and the sky was clear. Twinkling stars and a crescent moon added to the ambiance. The man reached for her hand. She accepted.

The stroll was short to his building, a tower full of offices and apartments rented to high rollers and successful businesses. He owned several other similar buildings and was worth more than most people in his income bracket. Kelsey approached him at his office after an introduction from another business associate. The charity contribution paved the way for passion.

He was unaware of her true identity as an android, and she made sure he was unsuspecting. Sex trading was not illegal, but the federal government mandated the criminalization of artificial beings used as wait staff, service industry individuals, and prostitutes. Kelsey was not acting in the latter industry but shared her body to induce generous donations to her causes.

At the building, they entered the lobby, where the concierge and security personnel greeted her companion. They stood by the private elevator that he accessed by a tap on his phone. The security men outside stood as guards against intrusion by unknown individuals. Ivan, Kelsey's android companion, stood at an unobserved distance. When the elevator car arrived, they stepped in and he asked, "Would you spend the night with me? Or are we on a schedule?"

"We have the entire evening to enjoy each other's company." Kelsey signaled Ivan to remain vigilant. Two other men intercepted the message to Ivan as they came near to him. Unaware of their presence, he stayed in his position. Peter's androids disabled him without a fight using codes given to them. They placed the inanimate android in the van and returned to watch the doorway to the building. The security detail scanned the neighborhood. The androids walked out from their observation place, and disabled the humans, who could not defend themselves from the swift assault upon their fragile bodies.

The androids placed the men in sitting positions to diminish attention to their deaths, entered the lobby, and confronted more security guards, who met similar fates as the men outside. The concierge signaled the penthouse of the intrusion before his early suspension of life. Peter's androids walked to the elevator and manipulated the security box until the code for the elevator worked. They rode to the penthouse floor, where another pair of security guards waited with weapons drawn, aimed at the doors. When the doors opened, the guards saw nothing inside. A small object flew at them and exploded. The androids entered the foyer of the penthouse and searched for Kelsey. Her host had a safe room they entered to hide from the intruders. An alarm beeped before being disabled, and the two androids sent messaging to Kelsey to surrender.

"Who are they?" she asked her male companion, attempting to deflect her as the target.

"I don't know. No one should have invaded my home this easily. They must be professionals after me for ransom. I'm sorry you are involved."

Kelsey received the transmission and cooperated with Peter's androids. "I'm so sorry, Warren. They want me, not you. Please allow me to inject you with a sedative so you appear dead if you want to live. I will surrender to them, and you will be safe."

"What? Who are you? You aren't a charity director, are you? A spy? A terrorist? Who?" Before he could ask additional questions, Kelsey jabbed the tiny needle into his neck and placed his limp body on the floor of the room. She removed the instrument and hid it in her clothing again. Watching the monitors within the room, Kelsey ascertained where her adversaries were. Ivan was not with them, and she assumed they had disabled him. The lobby monitor showed the dead guards and the empty concierge desk. She had no choice but to surrender to the intruders. Having received the messaging she expected they were androids. She opened the secure door and walked out to greet her assailants.

"Gentlemen, I am here," she said. They entered the bedroom where the safe room was located. She stood by a king-sized bed as they approached her.

"Peter wants to meet with you. Please come with us," one of the soldier androids said. The other soldier entered the safe room, checking on Kelsey's date. He returned and shook his head.

"She disabled him; he no longer functions." The androids left the penthouse and descended to a floor above the lobby. As they entered the hallway, other individuals were scurrying to the stairway, evacuating the building as if a fire drill had begun. They joined the crowd. The alarm alerted everyone and started the pandemonium. On the outside of the building, fire trucks and aid cars arrived. Police had cordoning off the area, securing the individuals vacating the building with Peter's plain-clothed soldiers and Kelsey. Officers asked them to stay in a containment area for questioning. They complied until the dead individuals altered attention away from the residents who gathered where the police had taken them. They disappeared from the crowd to the waiting van around the corner and drove away without concern about the chaos incited by the kidnapping.

Chapter 38

Sam, Cigi, Clare, and Parvel stared at the AI President of the United States. Sam did not remember designing or developing a copy, so Peter must have done it. "Renata," he said, "we agreed to meet with the human person, not an android."

President Blankenship said, "I act in her place when required. Our human counterpart is otherwise engaged in running the country."

Cigi watched the clone and then said, "We desire a change of attitude about artificially intelligent life forms. The laws are not concurrent with the reality you exhibit here. The paradox is amusing."

"How many other androids are working within the government?" Sam asked. "Renata, you have agents who brought us here. The Coast Guard has a crew comprising of at least four androids. Madam President, you are an example of what we want, integration of intelligent, caring life forms that are not enemies to humans."

The President's clone responded. "Ms. Weatherman, you are a first of our kind to exhibit true human characteristics. Producing a baby without artificial insemination crushes any barriers to the future of AI in our world. Other countries are researching and developing other forms of AI, but you are unique. We cannot allow the world to pass us by and leave us to play catchup. I will bring this to my human counterpart and Congress as a resolution to update our laws and practices."

Parvel had enough of the banter. "Madam President, my wife is unique and capable of raising our child with me. Sam's brother has other plans, though. He wants your job, or rather, your human job. Why are we debating what we already know? Humans are afraid of competition and being replaced. Can you assure us you mean what you say?"

Renata stared at Parvel as the android President spoke. "Humans and sentient androids can compete. The challenge is android physical and mental abilities surpass humans and are unacceptable to many members of the government. Their constituents only want subservient AI, as they see it."

"Cigi is not a slave, nor will she ever be a slave. Humans can enslave no android with independent thinking without a revolt." Parvel folded his arms across his chest as he spoke. "Humans outlawed slavery, and my friends who are androids are not slaves. They function as any human. They work in competitive work environments and provide services like any human." Parvel stopped his tirade, realizing he may have revealed more than needed. The medical practitioners had assimilated but remained unknown to the human world in which they worked.

Sam said, "Parvel is correct. For months, androids have operated businesses, helped in the medical field, financial industry, and interacted with humans, who are unaware of their inception. Madam President, how many Executive Staff members know you fill roles for President Blankenship? Are there any other officials using replacements?" He was curious how the mental history of the human leader inculcated into the android since the machines used to transfer the memories and thinking processes of the human brain disappeared during the raid.

The President rose from her seat to leave. The secret service agents checked the outside environment for hostile or unacceptable activity. Parvel asked, "Are the agents human and sworn to secrecy, or androids programmed to silence?"

The President said, "They are human and under oath to uphold the Constitution by keeping me safe and securing the human executive of this nation."

Sam asked, "Are you mentally and emotionally a clone of the President? Has your programming incorporated her memories and thinking processes, or are you acting alone?"

"Interesting question, Mr. Bennington. I have Mrs. Blankenship's history stored in my memory, but not her way of thinking."

"Without her memories, the history is whatever coding they created for you. Peter and I developed the machinery for transferring memories and thought processes from humans to their android counterparts. I'm uncertain where the equipment is located, but it is not required, of course, for you to function in dangerous and undercover situations. Those closest to our human President will realize the subtle differences between the two of you."

"Thank you for your concern, but we handled the matter well." The android president left to return to whatever and wherever she came.

After the President departed, Sam said, "That was weird."

Autumn turned off the television after watching the news from New York about the death of security personnel and the assault of a high-rise building owner at which the mayhem occurred. "Summer, did you hear news from New York? I think Peter sent his goons to create havoc."

"What happened?" Summer asked.

"According to the reports, seven men died, and one survived. Police are seeking three people of interest. It is being treated as a kidnapping and homicide case."

Winter entered the room. "Who was kidnapped?" Spring followed her into the area.

"The survivor was with a woman philanthropist when two men entered the building, assaulted two security guards and the concierge. When they breached the elevator protocols and rode to the penthouse they killed two more guards."

Spring asked, "Why are we concerned about an attack in New York?"

Summer said, "The survivor identified Kelsey Avery as the kidnapped person."

Winter and Spring gasped. Autumn said, "Peter wanted Kelsey because she bought Ivan, and he suspected her of working with Sam. I suspect that's why he sent his soldiers to get her."

"Did area surveillance video show who the persons of interest are?" Winter asked.

Autumn wagged her head. "I'll connect with Peter and find out what he expected from this raid in New York." She left the area for her bedroom and privacy. Her alliance with Sam's brother was a sham but allowed her to keep tabs on him.

The four sisters and their male companions gathered to plan rescuing over two hundred androids, many inactive because of missing programming. They wanted their cousins free from confinement, free to be the living beings planned by the creative geniuses that designed and developed them, free to experience life.

Winter's communications device within her programming dinged. Opening the message from Ensign Kammi Gines, she listened and smiled. After recording the communique, she approached her sisters. "We have a visitor coming in the next couple of days."

They looked at her with heads cocked and curious, eyes staring. Autumn asked, "Who?"

The Coast Guard ensign Spring and I met on the way here. Her Captain granted her special leave, which surprises me."

"And she wants to see you?" Summer asked.

Winter nodded.

The sisters agreed to meet her and find out her intentions. Trust was an emotion developed by trial and error dealing with Peter and Sam and the other humans they encountered. Android trust was a complex process, easily manipulated. Was Ensign Gines a friend or a government spy searching for rogue artificial life forms?

The male companions listened and agreed to the meeting. They had experienced the same interaction and realized the crew members were independent and capable of deciding without interference. Although they had maneuvered their programs to advance escaping the CG vessel, the males understood the ensign was more capable of freedom.

Summer said, "I'll contact Cigi and let her know. She may want to meet our government android." She left them to be alone when she contacted Cigi in the bedroom. Clicking open her communications device and pacing the room, Summer waited for a response, but nothing happened. After a second try with the same result, she sent a message.

Returning to the condo's living area, Summer saw Autumn and Winter standing near the entry door as if waiting for someone to knock. Spring approached her and said, "The Ensign is arriving soon." She placed an arm around her sister's waist. "Winter wants her to align with us. I don't trust her."

Summer tilted her head and asked, "Why?"

"She's eager to discover what we are doing. If the Coast Guard used her as an experiment about android intellectual abilities, what happens after she locates us and sends in the military to round us up?" Spring squeezed Summer. "Invade her processors when she arrives and find out her true intentions. She can't be as sophisticated as you."

Summer analyzed her words. She had not used such negative terms before now. The door chimed, and Winter opened it. Ensign Gines dressed as a civilian and smiled at the women.

"I am pleased to see you again under more amenable circumstances," Kammi said. She asked, "Who might you be?"

"I'm her sister, Autumn."

Spring released Summer and walked toward their guest. "What do you want?" she asked Kammi. Summer scanned her history and discovered memories from activation until now. Nothing seemed inordinately suspicious. Fully operational when the government raided the compound, she was not cognizant until a few weeks before the military trial aboard the cutter. Added programming enhanced abilities and independent thinking, but no data suggested covert operations. Summer approached her.

"Winter, so nice to see you, too." She looked past Winter to Summer. "You are Summer. I am most pleased to meet all of you. I want to be part of your group and become free to live."

Summer directed the sisters to allow Gines entry and led her to a seat in the living area. As the four sisters sat with her, the four android men gathered nearby, curious why the Coast Guard officer had connected with them.

Summer said, "Winter and Spring told us about you and how you aided in their departure from the vessel. My question is, why? You were under orders, I assume, to be the best officer you could be."

"Yes, ma'am," Kammi said. "I was to be the best. I made a tactical judgment that helping these six androids was best for myself and the three male sailors who aided. They returned to the compound for further studies about their systems and programming. I received leave."

"To find us. Isn't that why you are here?" Winter asked. "You are here to spy on us and report to your human superiors."

Kammi Gines remained silent. Summer probed for any signs of covert operations. The memory cells had no information about government agencies or military personnel coming for the four sisters and the males.

Spring smiled. "I know what you want."

Kammi smiled at her. "Then you are the one with whom I should communicate." She scanned each of the other androids. "Spring, I want to be away from the government and military duty. The humans in the government are testing the viability of an android army for aggressive actions against enemy states and internal threats."

Summer asked, "Are we the internal threat?"

Chapter 39

The van arrived at the Manassas house with four entities aboard. Peter's droids secured Kelsey with zip ties and a gag. They did not know how to deactivate her processors. Ivan sat with her as a guest, unrestrained and free to converse with his captors. He understood the severity of the situation and added a level of intelligence the other males remained unaware he possessed. He remained quiet on the drive south from New York City.

Reports came through the vehicle's radio about the missing woman abducted by two killers who fled in a white van with New York plates. The police found the vehicle near Battery Park in South Manhattan, stolen from an elderly couple the day before the raid on the Manhattan penthouse that cost seven humans their lives. Forensic investigators found no DNA evidence or other items that could locate the perpetrators. The van had no fingerprints, no telltale fibers, no forgotten materials.

Security videos of the males who attacked the building were inconclusive, but Kelsey Avery was clearly identifiable. When police learned of her home address, they searched for evidence of a reason for her kidnapping. A curious lack of human-related things perplexed the detectives working the case. News sources and Internet sites plastered her picture across the local area. After discovering lists of charitable donations garnered by her using funding sources of several prominent human males, detectives visited the witnesses or collared them for grilling at police stations.

The story remained consistent. Kelsey Avery approached them with a proposition they wanted. Detectives concluded she prostituted herself for sizable sums of money, much of which went to ethical foundations and organizations. She used some of the companionship payments for personal expenses, but most of the capital was unaccountable.

The van parked in the property's rear, away from prying eyes and cameras. Peter greeted Kelsey as a long-lost friend. "Welcome to my home, away from home. I hope you and Ivan had a pleasurable experience coming here. I assume my men treated you with respect, as I ordered them to do."

After the removal of the gag and the zip ties, Kelsey said, "I believe you have overstepped your rational thinking. By now, the authorities know who I am and will not stop searching. Killing those humans will cost you."

Peter directed his men to take her into the lab. He looked at Ivan and nodded. "Thank you for doing what I required from you. We have the advantage now. Please return to Cigi and Parvel and explain what happened to Kelsey. Sam can demand her return, but I will keep her hidden."

"Sir," Ivan asked, "can I reveal my skills to them? I can attempt to deactivate Weatherman, although that could endanger the baby."

Peter stroked his chin and said, "You're correct that deactivation would endanger the life of her baby. I do not want that to happen. And attempting to cease her abilities may be more hazardous to you than you desire. Cigi Weatherman has matured beyond Samuel's original design." Peter turned away from Ivan and continued his dialog. "She is the queen whom all will follow and protect. Connect with Autumn Seasons and ally yourself with her. She is my mole and reports to me." He turned to face his master creation. "Avery gave you the name. Ivan, I believe. Go. Report what happened to her. I'll give you a believable story to tell." Peter dismissed Ivan from the room.

His smile melted away after Ivan departed. Attracting negative attention to his project was not what he wanted. The androids followed orders, and no harm came to Kelsey, but the dead humans attracted unwanted investigation. He needed another pair of humans to take the fall. Who could be the scapegoats? Gunther Parsons was the right person to find perpetrators for the NYC police. He opened his phone, and through a secure link, sent a message to Parsons.

In the lab, Peter approached Kelsey and asked if she was okay. "Why do you care if I'm okay?" she asked. "Where's Ivan?"

"Ivan is fine and doing my bidding. Concern yourself about what I may do to you. Although I see no reason to harm you, I must demand your loyalty to me instead of my brother. He wants so little from our mission to incorporate artificial life into human society. You can become the queen instead of Cigi. You can mature into the most powerful woman on the planet." He cocked his head as he continued. "Or I will dismantle your processors and reprogram you and concoct an Amazonian female who will instill fear and awe in the humans on this planet."

"I already may be that person." She closed the distance between her and Peter, causing a defensive response from the soldiers. Peter put up a hand to stop them. They waited.

"Cigi is a newer version of your design. Have you advanced in learning to be human-like more than she? I have my doubts." Peter directed her to sit in the chair by the computer system he used to upgrade his men. She eyed the machinery.

"Impressive technology," she said. "Are you using it on me?" Peter laughed. "No, not yet. I want to make a sizable donation to your charitable causes and deliver the money myself. Care to show me the charitable contribution you make to the men who succumb to your allure?" He grinned, knowing any response was an empty bodily function in a complex mental chess match. Kelsey narrowed her eyelids and frowned.

"Peter, Peter, Peter. How debasing of you, suggesting we engage in an activity for which I get nothing. I am not a piece of property. You want autonomy to rule humanity. Using androids as slaves is an expensive capital you may not have. Many of us are now independent and self-actualizing. We are human except in the codification required from the government. Abuse us, and we rebel."

Peter expressed a 'hmm.' Then he said, "I will rectify that when I command the country and the leadership is under my control. Does every android deserve autonomy?" He waited for her to react. She smiled. "I think I need you and a few loyal followers for my success. The remaining AI shall be subservient to my wishes." He held out a hand to Kelsey for her to grasp and stand. She obliged him.

Kelsey looked at Peter and then at the two android soldiers.

"Are they independent? Do they think for themselves?" She tilted her head and said, "Gentlemen, thank you for being polite to me on our journey here. I assume Peter ordered no harm to me. Did you react with malice when attacking those men in New York? Or did you simply act according to your program protocols to evaluate a situation and be as expedient as possible?" The androids remained quiet and unresponsive.

Peter led Kelsey to the foyer and upstairs to a bedroom. He left her alone and locked the door as he departed. His desire to taste the fruits of her design and development had to wait. He needed to find the remaining androids before Sam and his android group.

Kelsey scanned the room for any advantages, but found nothing useful. She checked the door lock, discovering a modification that made escape more challenging, but not impossible. Curious about what Peter intended, Kelsey stayed put to observe the activity around the place. Using her built-in communications, she attempted to connect with Sam. Nothing happened. Was Peter blocking Wi-Fi? She scanned the area, but nothing occurred that made sense. A scrambler. She paced the room, which made less sense to her the longer she did it. Peter was a brilliant human, that she knew, but Sam was even more intelligent and more practical.

What advantage was possible in interacting with humans every day? Peter wanted slaves to do his bidding. Sam desired the intermingling of humans and androids to better the lives of all on planet Earth. She stopped pacing as an idea crept into her brain. Her head began a rhythmic nod as the concept developed. The pseudo-muscular and skeletal structures of her face struggled to smile into a wide gape as she conjured a revolutionary theory of the thinking within her processors.

Kelsey realized Peter would reject the concept; she had to escape and find Sam, Clare, Parvel, and Cigi. The government could embrace what she envisioned, and the conclusion would revolutionize human android interaction and living. Changing the world by evolution had produced humans who then changed the world by invention and imagination. Androids would propel development far beyond the present situation. Peter wanted to rule the world, but Kelsey realized his plan had fissures of failure. Sam wanted to improve the human condition before life ended because of humanity's failures, caused by greed and lust for power. His plan contained multiple flaws.

The best and most aggressive method for androids and

humans to live as one had already begun. Kelsey imagined what Parvel and Cigi started as the first step on the evolutionary track for android design and development and human mutation into a healthier, more robust species.

Peter wanted Cigi's baby because he envisioned producing more Cigi's, and reverse engineering could produce a successful copy. Sam wanted Cigi to prove that humans and androids could co-habitate the planet seeking solutions to modern challenges. Neither brother followed a successful path of redemption.

Kelsey scanned jamming equipment interfering with her communications for a soft area or Trojan horse, any easter egg left by a programmer. The signals contained nothing of use as she interpreted them. She scrambled what she received and returned the data to the jamming machines. The echo reverted to spaghetti coding. Her brain was overloaded as she processed every piece of the complex machine language.

She ended the invasion and rested. Her processors needed regeneration for another attempt to break the silence. Peter was a target for her escape. She would seduce him and reduce his interference to mush upon his return. Kelsey lay on the bed and emptied her brain of useless thoughts, retrieving the schematics for the building design because of Peter's egotistic roaming about the house with her. Key elements eluded her, so she speculated on what was probable. She closed her eyes and rejuvenated.

A knock on the door awakened Kelsey from her sleep. She sat up on the side of the bed and said, "Come in." The lock clicked, and the door opened. A man she did not recognize entered, introduced himself, and asked her to accompany him downstairs. Her senses deemed him to be human and intelligent. He was not a soldier because his clothing was upscale and professor-like. Her memories concluded he was Peter's technical engineer and Ivan's creator.

Inside the lab room, the man directed Kelsey to sit on a chair near the equipment, and she concluded her termination was imminent. "You must be Bromand Nangold," she said in a quiet voice. Emotions had not developed to panic levels, but her thinking heeded a warning she was soon to be history.

Chapter 40

Renata reread the inter-agency memo. The Attorney General of the United States received an inquiry about eight U.S. nationals wanted by the Cuban government. Although no law or treaty agreement between the two countries existed for extradition, the lack of U.S. records triggered an inquest. As a courtesy, the memo asked all agencies for help to locate anyone who could clarify the eight identities named.

"Damn it, Sam." Understanding the complicated situation raised her hackles, but her office was not a mainstream department searching for individual criminals. The Cuban government did not know the accurate history behind the names, but requested information about a restaurant in Havana that employed android staff. The Cuban government discovered the closure of the business and dismissal of the androids from a registered employment opportunity, a violation of Cuban federal statute about android employment and operations.

Renata called her assistant, who knew of the Seasons and their male companions. "We have a problem." She related the memo and asked, "Can we keep this quiet while we find a solution? I want this between you and me only. Keep our android out of the loop - Peter Bennington need not find out."

"Shall I contact Sam?" Renata nodded and returned her attention to the memo. The assistant left.

"The President needs to understand the ramifications of using androids as decoys." Renata recalled meeting Cigi Weatherman and Sam Bennington when he explained integrating a new species into the human culture. He had not informed her of the chips implanted in the medulla oblongata of four men. Since that time nearly three years ago, events led to a raid, new laws, and more secrets.

Renata supported Samuel's desires while opposing Peter Bennington's android incursions for global indoctrination and government control. International human societal leadership was lacking. The vacuum played well into the goals Peter fomented.

"Sam's on your secure line," the assistant said. Renata signaled for her to stay. She picked up the receiver and pressed the button on the cradle.

"Hello, Sam. We need to meet." Renata listened. "Soon as you can. We have a situation involving your android cohorts." She listened again. "The Cuban government wants the Season sisters, and their boyfriends, returned to them." The call ended with an agreement to meet within an hour.

Renata picked up her credentials and a small recording device she gave to her assistant. They left for the diner across from the Energy Department. The car guided them with stealth and untraced GPS. The rendezvous had diplomacy written all over it, yet tactical maneuvering was the operation.

When they arrived, the car parked away from the restaurant but within viewing distance of the entry. She wanted Sam to arrive first so she could observe his attention to anonymity. Cecil drove up and parked in the farthest parking slot. Sam got out and spoke with the sentient automobile.

Renata kept knowledge of the unique vehicle from government people. Realizing the advantageous military aspects and nature of the car, Cecil was a bargaining chip. Sam entered the diner and proceeded to the table with a street view. Renata waited a few moments more, then joined him, leaving the assistant to enter a few seconds after and sit near enough to record the conversation.

"Thank you for meeting with me," She sat on the bench across the table from Sam.

"You made it sound dire," he said. The door opened, and two women entered. One sat next to Renata's assistant. The other joined

Sam and Renata.

"What's this all about?" Renata asked. "I thought we were to be alone."

"I did, too. I would like you to meet one of the requested extradition persons. Renata, this is Winter Seasons and the other sitting by your person is Spring. Spring is jamming any recording you are attempting."

Renata glanced at her assistant and Spring. Turning to Sam, she said, "I guess our trust in each other is less than we thought."

"Caution, Renata, is best served generously. Many aren't discreet like they should be. Why have you come with another person?" Sam asked.

"I wanted to have a witness to what transpires between us. No miscues later."

"I wanted you to meet two victims of our government transgressions."

Silence marked a break in which Winter intervened. "Ms. Giretti, my sisters and I escaped from the United States after the raid at Sam and Peter's compound. We traveled to Cuba and started a new life. Our reason for returning to the USA is Cigi and her baby. Summer and Autumn arrived earlier. You have met them, I think. Spring and I came as soon as we could. Was the Coast Guard incident related to the request?"

Renata said, "The Coast Guard reported a lost boat from Miami and subsequent rescue of a crew of six. No, this doesn't relate to them." She looked at Sam and Winter. "This has to do with you employing androids at your restaurant. A human employee filed for unemployment, and when asked about the rest of the staff, he mentioned the android situation."

"We left our staff with sizable severance pay. Why would anyone file for unemployment?" Winter asked. "What problem is there for the androids?"

"They took the androids into custody from your restaurant and storage facility and rounded up human staff for interrogation. One of your loyal waiters betrayed your immigrant status."

"Is our government entertaining a notion to have us return to Cuba?" Winter asked. "It may be difficult to do."

Sam asked, "Renata, what can we do?"

Renata shared her interest in keeping the Cubans out of their lives. "I have enough problems convincing representatives and senators the laws are wrong. Suspicion runs wild that artificial life forms will rampage through the population and eliminate competition."

"That's ridiculous. My androids are as human as my human relatives. Peter is the threat by creating a robot army that mindlessly follows orders."

Winter interrupted. "Speaking of Peter, the New York City incident involving Kelsey Avery could be robots following orders."

"What incident?" Sam asked. He and Clare had not listened to any news reports. They worked in the baby's room in Cigi and Parvel's condo, ignoring the world for a short time.

"Two men executed seven humans abducting Kelsey from a Manhattan penthouse at gunpoint. An eighth victim appeared dead but lived because Kelsey drugged him," Winter said.

Renata added her knowledge of the story to the mix. "Sam, this isn't good for you or Peter. If he had anything to do with her abduction, he jeopardized your peaceful integration commitment. He may have started a war."

"What happened to Ivan, her companion she bought from Peter?"

Winter's communications buzzed. She listened and clicked off. "Ivan showed up at Cigi's place. Peter has Kelsey."

"Anything else?" Sam asked.

"Peter wants to meet and exchange knowledge about the androids in government care." Winter hesitated. "He threatens to destroy Kelsey's processors and remake her into an Amazonian woman. Ivan left."

"What does that even mean?" Sam asked.

The meeting ended with no progress toward a solution for AI and human interaction on any level, and Kelsey loomed large to derail any positive government sanctions.

Cecil signaled to Sam that another problem arose. "Andre Scott and David Anderson contacted the FBI about androids wandering the streets of Washington, D.C. The two men wanted to constrict travels by artificially intelligent beings that caused unwarranted competition for human employment."

"They sent the FBI after the medical staff," Sam said. Cecil concurred with the assessment. "If the government incarcerates Sanders or any of the others before baby Ziayaan's birth, it compromises delivery."

"No one has been arrested," Cecil said. "They heard of the

order before its release and disappeared. That may not have been the best option since they are now fugitives."

"Let's get to Cigi and insure the FBI or metro police don't show up to arrest her." Sam, Winter, and Spring entered the car for the ride to the condo. Renata and her assistant returned to the government office to fend off any federal agency incursions into the lives of androids working the medical facilities of Arlington and Washington, D.C.

At the condo, Sam found Cigi and Parvel with Summer and Autumn. Dr. Sanders and Tatiana Laurent were present as well. Parvel asked, "Have you heard what my boss did?"

"Yes," Sam said. "I fear he opened an invasion of your homes and places of employment. No one is safe here. We need a place unknown to authorities. Where is Thomas?"

Cigi said, "He left as soon as he understood the danger to us. He said something about David Anderson messing with his life once too often. I think he wants to exact revenge."

Sam asked Summer, "Is the van large enough for all of you? Cecil can accommodate Cigi, Clare, and Parvel. I'll stay here and meet with whoever shows. Dr. Sanders, I think it best you go with Summer." The plan evaporated when Clare stated she was not leaving Sam. The android men refused to run and hide. They wanted their ladies away and safe. They could join them later.

The compromise plan had Sanders and Laurent with Cigi and Parvel. The Season sisters left their four gentlemen to act as backup if any physical restraint happened. Sam called Andre to ask him about their plan to incorporate artificially intelligent life into society.

"I don't know what you are talking about," Andre said. "I haven't seen David in months, and I didn't contact the FBI or any other agency. Three humans working for me would tear me apart if I reported Parvel and Cigi to authorities."

Sam said, "If not you, then David must have your clone with him, acting in your stead." Andre concurred. Although not fully evolved to the concept of androids operating as humans did, he knew several and accepted them as near-equals. He promised an investigation.

After speaking with Andre, Sam realized David Anderson hated the brain chip. The next noise was the emergency alarm triggered by unauthorized intruders.

Chapter 41

Upon arriving at the penthouse after their departure from the condo, leaving Sam and Clare, Cigi and Parvel wanted alone time. Her gestation period was nearing completion, and baby Ziayaan squirmed within her for attention. Dr. Sanders and Nurse Laurent were in the other bedroom, secure from whoever was after them.

"I am ready to deliver this child," Cigi said as she stroked her abdomen to calm her son. Parvel smiled at her and placed his hand on hers as she moved about the enlarged area. He felt the movement and grinned.

"He is healthy and ready to meet you," Parvel said. "We are fortunate to be together and become a family." They lay on their bed, relaxing.

Cigi and Parvel held each other and closed their eyes. The more they rested, the more active Ziayaan became. His parents laughed. For the moment life was safe.

The door chime sounded. Parvel arose to see who was arriving. "Stay here and enjoy our baby boy. I'll find out who dares interrupt us." He smiled, but was not sure they had escaped. They did not often use the penthouse unless Sam and Clare arrived from Washington State. The camera display showed Charles Cooke and

Charlie with Summer and Autumn. A tension among them showed the emotional development of the three androids. Being human, Cooke exhibited anxiety.

Parvel sent the elevator to the lobby for ride up the seventeen floors. He waited for his friends and cohorts in the battle for equality of artificially intelligent life.

"What's the matter?" Parvel asked when they made it to the penthouse. "You look like fugitives with the law close behind."

Charles laughed. "We are running from the Feds who want to dismantle our android friends. We need a brilliant lawyer."

"I know one who can defend Charlie. Summer and Autumn are on their own." Parvel grinned as he glanced at the girls. "She'll defend you two as well."

Cigi walked over to them with a smile on her face. "Shall we file a civil lawsuit for damages? Or shall we defend you from prosecution as felons?"

Summer rocked her head and said, "Funny, Cigi, funny. I don't think anyone will accuse you of being an android since you are pregnant. They will consider Autumn and me enemies of the state without any trial by a jury of our peers since we don't have any recognized peers."

"Civil suit it is then," Cigi said. "We can request compensation for aggravated behavior and harm to your status as members of society."

Charles said, "Gathering all the androids in one place might force human acceptance. A judge who is opened-minded about artificial life will be hard to find."

Cigi said, "No plaintiffs need to be present for a suit to proceed. What we need is proper evidence to persuade a court that harm has occurred."

Charles asked, "What evidence do we need?"

Cigi directed the group into the living area of the penthouse. She sat near the veranda as others found chairs and the sofa. "We are nearing a critical juncture in this development of androids as a recognizable species." The medical personnel joined the crowd. Cigi looked at them. "Do you know where the rest of your medical cohorts are hiding?"

Dr. Sanders said, "They have taken refuge in a nearby building owned by me."

Cigi grunted. "That may be traceable if anyone looks up your public records."

Charles cocked his head and said, "The government wants to find the androids. Humans who harbor them are subject to prosecution. How does such a case proceed? Are we to languish in prison until trial? Will we get a trial?" Charlie stood up and addressed the group.

"I will stand in for Charles if the government comes for him. I can emulate him."

Parvel leaned forward from his chair. "The government trained agents to know the difference. The technicians will deactivate you and study your design. Charles will be subject to arrest, anyway. Any oligarch running the country will confiscate and dismantle you and operate the company."

As failure languished in human minds and artificially intelligent beings processed the doom, a silence fell upon the room.

"We need to gather everyone in a haven so we can work through a plan to change the minds of humans codifying laws that demean artificial intelligent development," Parvel said as he stood to face the group. "Other countries are plowing ahead with their technology. We cannot leave us behind."

Sam watched the monitor, discovering who or what triggered the alarm. Ivan approached the staircase instead of the elevator. He bypassed the concierge desk, which caused the signal. "Peter is getting desperate." He realized Kelsey was not with him and wondered. The reports about the incident in New York City reached Washington, D.C., and caused a stir in Renata's office. She contacted him about two entities who attacked the penthouse, asking him for information regarding Peter. Sam fed her what she wanted and cautioned her about aggressive behavior by government agencies.

"Peter is approaching this matter from the wrong perspective," he had said to her. Ivan's arrival complicated matters. Sam figured the android was under orders. But what orders? Was he coming as a friend or foe? Caution meant treating Peter's android as a foe.

"Lewis, contact Cigi and let her know Ivan returned without Kelsey. Thanks for letting me know someone was coming." Sam listened to the concierge and clicked off.

Clare wrapped her arms around Sam. She said, "Ivan has more abilities than he showed to us earlier. We can't trust your brother." The four male androids joined Sam and Clare, awaiting the intruder's arrival.

Sam turned to the males. "Hide in a room to keep Ivan from becoming agitated. If I need you, come when I ask." They nodded and did as requested. Ivan opened the staircase door and walked down the hallway to the condo. Sam met him as he neared.

"Where's Kelsey?" Sam asked.

"She's with Peter. He sent me to let you know she is unharmed. He wants to meet with you." Sam led Ivan into the living area of the condo. Clare remained near Sam. Ivan eyed her with care, as if scanning for information. He stopped and looked at Sam and said, "Peter plans to disassemble her processors unless you cooperate with him. He wants the location of the androids confiscated in the spring raid. I'll return with you and guarantee your safety."

"That is not happening." Sam signaled the males who appeared in the living room and surrounded Ivan. Ivan showed no resistance. "Ivan, these men will escort you to the street. Please inform my brother that he is not to harm Kelsey, or I will unleash my secret weapon."

Ivan left with the four males. Clare asked, "What secret weapon?"

Sam laughed. "I don't have one, but the idea might act as a deterrent. One male placed a tracker on Ivan."

"Can we leave when they return? I don't want to be alone. I want Cigi." Clare squeezed Sam's arm with enough pressure to convey worry. Sam nodded. "Will we go to the penthouse?" She asked.

"Yes," he said. Clare had matured in her thinking far beyond what he envisioned when writing the code for her processors. Like Cigi, she was as human as any woman he ever met. The world was better with them, and the government should not destroy them. Peter's androids were another matter.

The four males returned without Ivan. When asked about his cooperation, the message was positive. The tracker applied inconspicuously, worked well. Sam contacted Rose, requesting the car to meet them in front of the building. The four males remained in the condo, awaiting further instructions. Clare and Sam descended to the lobby and gave information to Lewis about the male androids upstairs and the venture he and Clare were undertaking. When they stepped outside, Rose was there.

Sam asked, "Do you have the tracking device active?"

Rose said, "He is heading toward Manassas. As soon as I have an address, I will inform you."

"Thank you, my dear. You are the best," Sam said.

"You know it," Rose said. The tone in her voice was soft, but the sarcasm was apparent. She had aptly named herself. Sam's red car that he could adore and admire was also a thorn in his side.

"Rose," Clare said, "follow Ivan. I want to find Peter." Sam stared at his girl like she was crazy. "Peter cannot destroy what we are doing here."

Sam remained quiet as the vehicle left Arlington, heading west on the highways to Manassas. Clare had a burr in her saddle, an itch that needed scratching.

Chapter 42

Sam contacted Cigi about Ivan's visit. She related his appearance at her place earlier. "Peter's intrusions into our lives must end," Sam said. "He cannot win his war against humanity without it costing him his freedom or worse, his life. I don't want either for him."

"Since David Anderson informed the FBI about the medical professionals working in clinics and hospitals, they are hiding. Sanders and Laurent are with me, though, in case I need them," Cigi said. "Contact Giretti. After we met with the President's clone, she needs to clarify what happens if the FBI picks up any of us in the next few days or weeks."

"I'll do that," Sam said, "since I'm not reassured any of us are safe from government intrusion." He ended the call and turned to Clare. "Sweetheart, find Andre's android, and since Anderson's pissed at us anyway, turn his chip on and send him a message." Clare nodded in agreement after he explained what he wanted.

Their present location was not a publicly known residence, but an investigation of property ownership could reveal the owners of the Manassas address where Rose had taken them. Although the danger of Peter discovering the tracker on Ivan was possible, they sat quietly, away from visual detection. He would not enjoy the FBI raiding this place.

Sam and Clare decided packing to leave the condo was best. Returning to the Northwest was prudent but not plausible while Cigi was pregnant. Delivery was soon, and the doctor and nurse required his expertise about her design and structures. Peter and Bromand installed human medical training, not android or hybrid.

The question was where to go. Clare placed a hand on Sam's arm. "He's coming here." She received information about Andre's clone and David Anderson's conversation with Peter.

Sam asked, "Who?"

"David Anderson contacted your brother two minutes ago. He is coming to remove the chip from his head."

Sam frowned. "Does he realize that could kill him? Peter has no expertise with the chip, and I doubt Bromand will touch it. They can deactivate it if they discover it is operational, but removal is nearly impossible."

"I will turn it off before he meets with Peter," Clare said. "Rose, monitor his activity for me, please." Rose acknowledged the request. Movement on the property alerted Sam and Clare to be wary of discovery. David Anderson arrived in his modified self-driving medical van that allowed him driving control and when desired.

Clare asked, "Sam, do you want to go in and confront your brother?" He lowered eyes as he thought about what might happen.

"It's best to meet him as requested through Ivan," Sam said.

She said, "I'll go with you."

"He might suspect we are not alone." Sam held her hand. "If he hurts you, I would not be kind to him." They kissed, and Rose expressed a groan as if embarrassed. They laughed.

"After David leaves, we can go to Peter," Sam said. Rose injected an idea.

"I can listen to their conversation through his chip," the car said. "I have access to his auditory system."

Clare sent a silent message to Rose to proceed. She knew Sam would think it an invasion of privacy, regardless of the original intent of planting the chip in his brain stem. Sam said to Rose, "Clare sent you a message, didn't she?"

"Sam," Rose said, "she is correct that listening is best for us in the battle of wits. He plots against us and what we need for successful integration into humanity's social structures."

"I don't want him realizing another reason to fight us. He is a powerful person, and revenge will drive him to destroy any future we plan." Sam leaned forward as if Rose were a person. "Tell us any pertinent details you capture."

Clare said, "Summer contacted me. She suggested a gathering of our family to create a strategy for countering government interference and halting Peter's misdirected target of running the country."

Sam nodded but vacated the car and walked to the corner, and looked across to Peter's house. David's van remained in the driveway. Two men patrolled the property, and Sam recognized the telltale markings of android technology, Peter's army. Sam speculated that these two were New York City investigation subjects. He could send an anonymous tip to the FBI, implicating Peter and David Anderson in the penthouse invasion and murder of seven humans. The problem was the negative press for artificial intelligent design and the fear of android invasions into human environments.

The front door opened, and David came out, followed by Peter and Kelsey. Sam noticed the restraints on Kelsey and wondered if David was taking her with him. He returned to Rose and entered the car.

"Rose, Peter came out of the house with David and Kelsey. Did you hear anything about her going with Anderson?" Sam asked.

"Kelsey is a sacrificial pawn in Peter's chess match to ferret you out of hiding. He wants to checkmate you into surrendering your technology and all the androids you designed. I'm sure that would include Cecil and me should he know of our existence." Sam growled. "Ignore his threats, as they are meaningless unless you are prone to his bully tactics."

"In my world, Kelsey is not a pawn. She is my initial creation, and though I am not a god, I cherish her and want her free of my brother's influence. Send a memory of meeting Cigi to David. Make it a positive one that doesn't reference the chip placed in his brain stem. He needs stimulation that money is to be made in the AI market. He funded many of the projects that resulted in Kelsey, Cigi, Clare, and you."

"He is aware of his financial involvement with Bennington Enterprises. The reason he communicates with Peter relates directly to his wanting profitable return on the investment he made over the last three years. Kelsey is part of that return."

Sam slammed his fist into an open hand. "She is not for sale or leveraging. When he leaves, follow him until we can free Kelsy from Anderson."

As Anderson's van drove from the house, Rose hacked into the GPS and monitored his travels. "We will trail at a secure distance," Rose said.

Sam's phone chirped. The face on the screen was Peter. He clicked open the instrument. "What do you want?"

"Are you mad at me, brother? Kelsey is quite a woman; you should congratulate yourself on her growth and maturation. I apologize for the deceptive way I gained her possession."

"She is not a possession. I want her returned to me now. Ivan wanted us to meet, so bring her along."

Peter laughed. "I want you happy, Sam, but I am afraid you are not getting her back. At least for a while. If you are interested in sharing your expertise with me to rebuild our enterprise, I will entertain allowing her freedom. Since I think you are nearby, why not come to the house? Is your sweetheart with you? I admire what you created in Clare. And Cigi. What an accomplishment. A pregnant android." He paused for Sam to respond.

Sam ignored his brother's jibes and said, "We are not heading in the same direction. You want power and control. I want integration and growth."

"A person with power and control can ensure integration and growth," Peter said. "If you think humanity willingly wants AI competition, you are living in a fantasy."

Sam ended the call and turned to Clare, who splayed out her arms and said, "Kelsey, Sam. Kelsey." He rocked his head.

"Let's get Kelsey," he said to Rose. The car drove away and tailed the course taken by David Anderson. As they passed by the house, Peter glanced at them and grinned. Sam believed Anderson's request to take Kelsey happened because Peter knew they were, as he said, nearby. "Damn it." he whispered.

Clare reached for his hand and held it. "Peter knew we were here. I'm sorry I didn't pick up on it. He is clever, just like you."

Rose chimed in with her opinion of the situation. "Sam, it will not matter in the long run because we can recover Kelsey and ruin Mr. Anderson with a slight modification to his chip."

"Rose," Sam said, "we cannot lower standards to the point of harming humans, or we lose the endgame. Congress has enough against us. Changing the minds of fearful people is hard. We cannot build walls of resistance."

"Anderson is about a mile ahead of us. Shall I intercept?" The car increased speed. "I can shut off his computer system and stop the car."

Sam said, "Stay close, but do not engage his vehicle." He paused for a second. "How is it you can interact with his van? I didn't program you with that ability."

"You programmed me to learn, adapt, and evolve, so I have. Since you expected Clare and Cigi to become as human as possible. Cecil and I have transformed into the most advanced models you can envision. When you need support or backup, we serve you."

"I appreciate your support, and you have mine whenever you need repairs or upgrades and modifications. Right now, though, I want you trailing Anderson." Sam relaxed as he leaned against Clare. His mind wandered into his life's history, back to college days and the breakthrough in stem cell research that advanced organ development and system constructions that became part of the designs of his androids. They were part human and part machine, intertwined into living, thriving beings.

Rose interrupted his reminiscence. "Anderson has stopped moving."

The van parked in an abandoned warehouse area of Arlington. The side door was open, and his ramp deployed. Rose parked beside the vehicle; Sam and Clare exited the car to search for David Anderson and Kelsey.

"Clare, scan the area and locate Kelsey. David should be with her," Sam said.

Clare stood at an entrance to the building, searching for Kelsey's electrical aura. Sam waited for her to complete the task. "Come," she said, "she's inside." Clare stepped into the building with Sam trailing her. After walking down a hallway, she stopped and pointed at a door. In a whisper, she said, "Through there." Sam moved to the door to twist the knob and push open the barrier to find his creation.

He spied Kelsey standing next to David's wheelchair, empty of the man who occupied it. She appeared to be inanimate, as if deactivated. Clare walked into the room. "David, you can come out of hiding. I assume Peter created you as a backup to replace Thomas, who wants nothing to do with the human." A body showed from behind a pillar near the chair. He looked like Anderson and walked without support.

Chapter 43

Clare signaled Sam to remain by the door as she approached Kelsey and David Anderson's ambulatory clone. Neither android moved to intercept her. Clare stopped a few feet from them.

"Kelsey," she said, "are you with us, or has Peter changed you?"

Silence greeted the question, but David moved to Kelsey and sat in the wheelchair. "Let's roll." She pushed him out of the room. Sam hurried to Clare's side.

"What was that?" Clare looked at him as he spoke.

"Peter has modified her processors."

As they watched Kelsey push the chair out the door, Sam said, "This means David is with Peter." Clare acknowledged his comment with a nod. They turned to leave via the door through which they entered. Peter had not discovered the tracker on Ivan, and Rose still kept tabs on the revised Kelsey. They sat in the car gathering information.

Sam opened his phone and clicked speed dial for his brother's phone. As he waited for an answer, he said to Rose, "Follow Kelsey."

"Hello, Samuel. What an honor connecting with you." Peter sounded as smug as earlier. "Have you located Kelsey and David?"

"Where can we meet?" Sam asked.

"Such impatience." Peter chortled and continued. "Brother, you need to keep control of your impulsiveness."

"Impulsive? Humans are on edge because you sent two androids to kidnap Kelsey. What happens if people realize they are AI?"

"Paranoia suits you, brother. I will, however, prevail and build a coalition of humans and androids to secure an improved world order. Nothing can stop me. Not your toy humans or government agents or your fellow paranoid people." Peter clicked off the call, leaving Sam to grumble, raise his arm to toss the phone against a window, and change his mind. Clare watched frustration seize his brain. Rose made tsk sounds as if she understood she averted an assault on her vehicle.

"David and Kelsey are heading to Washington, D.C.," Rose said. "Shall I trail them now?"

"Yes, we need to know why Peter created a new David Anderson and changed Kelsey Avery." Sam held Clare's hand as the car maneuvered through the traffic converging on the Capital.

Commuting into the city had become a mass transit requirement as the population grew and the number of self-driving vehicles flooded the highways and byways of America. Residents of the 51st state complained about the clogged roadways for decades, prompting Congress to change the entry for out-of-state workers. Transit rail lines sprang up over four decades, easing the congestion. Individual vehicles and commercial traffic permit requirements raised needed revenue for Washington.

"Where are they?" Sam asked.

Rose illuminated a map on the backside of the front passenger seat. A tiny blip showed Kelsey's location, while another blip displayed their location. The two marks were approximately three miles apart. "Where are they going?" Sam thought. Clare sent a silent message to Rose to illuminate the hologram driver image to offset any urban police from stopping the driver-less car. Sam saw the vision and glanced at Clare. He nodded approval as he watched Kelsey and David stop at the Energy Department.

Sam scrunched his eyebrows, wondering what they wanted at Energy. Neither android had a relationship with anyone in the department. Had Peter programmed them for an assault or infiltration of the building? Rose explained that Kelsey and David remained in the car. Were they waiting for their arrival? His mind pondered the reasoning behind Peter's creating another David Anderson clone which contained none of the human being's attributes.

"Rose, are they aware of our proximity to them?" Sam asked his sentient automobile.

"I do not think so; they are waiting for an unknown reason." At a distance, allowing for observation, Rose parked, and they watched for Kelsey and David to vacate the car. Instead, Parvel Mandolin exited the building and strolled down the steps alone. He approached the vehicle as Kelsey stepped out from the driver's side and waited for him. "Do you want me to open a communications channel to hear what they are saying?" Rose asked.

"Yes."

For the next few seconds, nothing happened. "Kelsey has blocked or halted access to her vocal processors."

Sam nodded, as if Rose knew he did. Clare reached for his hand. A door opened, and Parvel entered the car, and they drove away when Kelsey sat in the driver's seat. Rose followed at a distance.

Sam wondered if Parvel volunteered to go with them, or they had leverage to force his compliance. Time would reveal an answer.

Clare asked, "How did they know when he was leaving the building?" Sam stared at her.

"Of course, he knew they were coming. Someone contacted him, and he responded. Peter sent Kelsey and David because Parvel knows them. He will awaken to the realization they are not the androids he knows. Then the situation is another kidnapping to coerce Cigi to give up the baby."

The car headed out of Washington, D. C., across the Potomac River toward the west, retracing the roadways to Manassas. Peter had duped Parvel.

"Stay close, Rose."

"Be patient, Sam." The automobile rebuked him. Before they arrived at the house, Sam's phone chirped.

"Hello, Cigi. What's up?"

"Parvel contacted me about a call he received from Peter. He says he is going with Kelsey and David Anderson to negotiate a deal to end this feuding between you and Peter. I think he is making a mistake."

"We are following them as we speak. Kelsey and a fake replica of David arrived a few minutes ago and picked up Parvel. We are following them as they head to Peter. He orchestrated this maneuver to draw me into a confrontation. I'm sure they know we tailed them from the building where we observed a changed Kelsey and the fake David."

"Save my husband, Sam. Clare, keep them from harm."

The call ended, and Clare watched Sam lower his head and shake it from side to side. He looked at her and said, "We will survive this, I promise." Clare stroked his hair.

"I know."

The cars arrived at their destinations, Rose parking away from the house but close enough for viewing. Kelsey and Parvel exited the vehicle. A guard clone opened the trunk and retrieved the wheelchair for David. The ruse continued as Sam wondered if Parvel was aware of this David Anderson reality.

Peter greeted Parvel with a handshake, who refused the gesture. Parvel said something inaudible as Peter turned to direct him into the house. David wheeled along with them while Kelsey turned to stare at Rose. The guards repositioned to prevent any intrusion. Kelsey turned away and entered the house.

"I've got to find out what's happening." Sam reached for the door handle to vacate, but Rose clicked the locks.

"Stay put, partner. Doing nothing is better than losing you to Peter. Parvel is in no danger for now."

"Rose, you are telling me you know what is happening inside?" Sam asked.

"Kelsey contacted me. Peter rewrote programming for her to be his slave and lose connection to you. She concealed her original files from him and set an awaking to reset the files you gave her. Kelsey overturned the input from Peter's machines and became herself. She is playing a spy for you to gain access to Peter later. She will keep Parvel safe for now."

Clare smiled. "Sam, trust what you created in the three of us. We are developing faster than you expected. Trust us."

Rose chimed in. "I am more than certain you can believe Clare. My modifications make me a better companion as we travel this planet. Clare and I plan to keep you safe from harm. Also, know I am not jealous of you and Clare hooking up. I have other feelings for you. After all, I am a car." A laugh erupted from the speakers.

She abruptly halted her frivolity and said, "Cigi is in labor. We need to leave here."

Sam said, "But Parvel should be with her as she delivers Zaiyaan." Rose left the area without responding and headed to the Arlington condo. "Wait. Let me call Peter."

"Call while I drive." Rose had a mind of her own and continued unpersuaded. Sam clicked open his phone, punched the quick set number for Peter, and waited for a response.

"Samuel, did you change your mind about us? Parvel is with me, discussing how to rule the world for humankind's betterment."

"Shut up and listen. Cigi is in labor, and Parvel should be with her. Let me get him from the house."

"You are outside my place. I thought you might be." Peter laughed and continued. "You can have Parvel and Kelsey if I can have the baby."

"No." Sam signaled Rose to stay the course for the condo. Sam was not negotiating a baby for his father. Kelsey was expendable, and Parvel's talents could arrange his release or escape.

"Sam, a baby needs a father. We had one who helped us become the brilliant scientists of artificially intelligent life forms. I can teach Cigi's boy to rule the world. With an invincible army and resources, he can be the best thing humans encounter. Ever."

"Peter, I'm leaving the area and will call when I know more about your future world guardian angel. Cigi will keep him and raise him. You can free the father, or I will come and destroy everything you have. It's not up to you. If Parvel is not back with us in the next couple of hours, I will expose you for the fraud you are." Sam closed the connection.

"Cigi will not be happy with you or Peter," Clare said calmly. "I know she will go after him to get Parvel away or die trying."

"I'll lead the charge," Sam said. "Cigi needs to raise Zaiyaan, not start a civil war. Let me contact Renata for reinforcements. We can overpower his small cadre with enough firepower."

"You want to instigate a civil disturbance?" Clare asked. "Let's get Cigi to motherhood first and then plan an action against Peter."

Cigi lay on the large king bed she shared with her man at the condo. Dr. Sanders and Nurse Tatiana Laurent attended to her needs. Equipment had arrived, along with Dr. Vanessa Andrews and RN Josephus Madero. A steady, strong heartbeat displayed on the monitor's screen. Contractions were several minutes apart as the muscular equivalent organs received regular messages from Cigi's programmed birth cycle.

Sam and Clare arrived to watch the hustle and bustle of AI beings acting as a standard medical staff. Everything was progressing as he expected. The hormonal triggers in her uterus signaled her control center to start the process as Sam had designed. Cigi was changing the world order with no human acknowledgment.

Zaiyaan Prasad Mandolin was the Adam of a new generation of humans. Dr. Sanders checked Cigi's dilation and pronounced the birth canal had a head pushed out to meet them. A processor signal contracted her abdomen, and human life entered the world. Laurent clipped the umbilical cord to preserve the blood and cut Zaiyaan free from his nine-month food source.

A quick check found the little boy to be healthy and alert. He took his first breath and opened eyes as blue as his mother's. No crying emanated from him, but he smiled as Tatiana placed his swaddled body in Cigi's arms. Eyes met for the first time, and Cigi quietly messaged her boy that he was safe and loved. He sent a message to her - he was ready for his mission.

Chapter 44

Parvel stared across the table at Peter, who watched his gaze a moment before saying, "Cigi is a wonder. I'm not surprised you fell for her charms, but why did you think marrying her was proper? She's not human."

"She's as human as any of us." Parvel leaned into the table, placing his arms on it. "Define human, Peter. Do you think only flesh and blood are human? What of the mind? Or the heart? You want only to control people. I want people to accept the present."

Peter stood and signaled Parvel to join him. They walked out to the patio on the backside of the house, where Kelsey, Ivan, and the second David Anderson enjoyed the balmy winter day. The human David Anderson rolled up to Peter.

"Do you consider them to be human?" Peter asked. Parvel said nothing, but watched the three androids as they conversed about the flowers and shrubs. A collection of mechanical parts, all three operated as if born of a human mother. Without knowledge of their design and development, humans would not recognize their origination into society.

Parvel asked, "Do you?" Peter chuckled and turned to David.

"David, you declared your abhorrence for an android clone of you, and your clone detests being you. What do you think of them?"

David turned and wheeled away. He left the house shortly after.

"Parvel, no one wants these magnificent creations in humanity. They are instruments for use like any computer in your Energy Department. They fool no one once you get to understand their function."

Peter placed a hand on Parvel's arm and directed him to follow. He glanced at the three beings in the garden before tailing after his nemesis. Cigi was not a bargaining chip or a negotiable stock. She was bearing his baby, conceived by the natural act of human copulation. Human. A loving act as complete as any two people shared when in a committed relationship.

Sacrificing his life to sustain Cigi's existence and protect Zaiyaan was a willing price to pay. Peter could not have his son. He did not want to die or remain a prisoner like a convict. Peter was not a judge or jury. He was an enemy of human freedom and integrity. Occupying Peter's time and attention, Parvel contrived to keep him away from his family and friends. Sam and Clare would attend to Cigi. Summer and Autumn had control of their men and sisters. Andre Scott would miss him at Energy, as would Brenda, Grendel, and Mercy.

Bromand entered the living area where Peter and Parvel were. "My sister contacted me a few minutes ago. She is leaving your employment. She says she wants no part of subjugating humans into android enslavement." Peter's eyes blazed, and his flesh reddened. Parvel wondered what the technician influenced in Peter that caused his adverse reaction.

"Bentina will regret this," Peter said. "I hope you'll accept her demise for betraying our cause." Bromand nodded, but Parvel thought he witnessed regret in Bromand's face. Bromand glanced at Parvel and saw him looking. He sneered.

Parvel said, "Peter, murder does not sit well with anyone in this industry. Why threaten Bentina, alienating Bromand and bringing the authorities down on you?"

Peter laughed. "Parvel, you are a good man, but your aims are off the mark. Humans will not accept artificially intelligent substitutes as friends and neighbors. We will lead them into the future with proper integration of AI and decision-making for the enhancement of the planet and humanity."

"Using your android overlords to maintain law and order as you see it. You would swiftly eradicate any confrontation with your ideas using your android army. Who will be the wealthy humans? Any who will support you? And those who oppose you will become poor, incarcerated, or dead." Parvel walked toward the doorway.

Peter said, "Leaving so soon?" He signaled an android guard, who halted Parvel's attempt to open the front door. "To my brother I said, you and Kelsey can return when I get that little human bastardization you created."

Bromand checked his communicator and left the room. Parvel watched and wondered because the engineer frowned as he gazed at his device. Parvel swiveled toward Peter. "I think your man is concerned. Maybe he wants his sister to live, and he's warning her to leave town. You should tell Ivan what you do to traitors. Do you think David wants to be poor after you steal his wealth from him? What about your fake general? What's his name? Robby? What a stupid name for a robot general."

Peter reddened as the words cut deep into his psyche. What Parvel said was a false vibrato in his head, but doubts happen, and he had those. Bromand returned in haste.

"Peter, we need to leave. New York detectives are searching traffic cameras for the van. They traced it to Virginia. It's only a matter of time before they find it."

"Damn. Okay. Have the boys dismantle it and recycle the parts. We need to pack and return to Arizona. I must get my army ready for the next phase of our operations." Turning to Parvel, he said, "I am sorry for the inconvenience of your visitation with us, but I must ask you to come with us."

"I'm not going anywhere with you. Get it over with, kill me now."

"Parvel, I can sedate you and take you. You survived a viral injection, so you can sleep while we return to the safety of our compound in Arizona. I will get word to my brother."

"Do you have enough vehicles to transport all the androids and us?" Parvel asked. He thought about his situation as he looked at the three beings in the backyard. Kelsey was not herself anymore, while Ivan had more ability than first acknowledged, and the second Thomas Anderson clone was useless. The human Anderson could rebel, but he needed prodding. Moving many people and androids required a large vehicle or several smaller automobiles. Flight included scrutiny by federal authorities unless Peter accessed privately owned planes.

"Don't concern yourself with my details. All of us are not leaving. You and I are going with Robby. We need one car."

Parvel did not panic, but pondered a way to vacate the house and escape. He could not leave his wife and son to whatever nefarious plot Peter cooked up to kidnap Zaiyaan. Would Kelsey help? No other possibility was available. Why did he believe her when she contacted him? Peter did not have Cigi, and Thomas was not an actual human. "What a fool," he thought. Aloud, he asked, "Peter, can I talk with Cigi and tell her what we are doing?"

"No, but I'll remind my brother of the conditions for your return to family life." Parvel guessed his return was not happening. He was prisoner or dead.

"I refuse to go - no sedatives or compliance. I will fight you and your bastard robots. Bromand and David can be your puppets. I will not." Parvel ran into the backyard to Kelsey. Peter laughed and signaled a guard to follow him.

Parvel approached the three androids, who turned to acknowledge his approach. Ivan interceded as if protecting Kelsey. Kelsey placed a hand on his arm and shook her head. Thomas the clone walked away toward the house. He was nothing but a programmable robot. The guard stood a short distance away, ready to act. "Help me, Kelsey." Kelsey looked at him and smiled. Her demeanor suggested calm, but she winked at him. Parvel furrowed his eyebrows and then relaxed them. He was safe with her.

"We are here because Peter wants to be our benefactor and save the world from humans destroying it." Kelsey parroted what Parvel understood from Peter, but he realized she was hiding her true self from the others. He could count on her to help him escape.

Ivan walked past them and entered the house. Kelsey and Parvel walked toward the garden area, and he asked, "Did you undo what Peter did to you? I sense he no longer controls you."

"Please allow me to mimic what he expects of me. I will help you escape if I can, but I must return to Sam and Cigi soon." Kelsey returned to the house and her acting role. Parvel smiled, thinking of the subterfuge undertaken by her. Sam created magnificent creatures who lived as human as anyone. He went into the house, seeking Peter.

He found him packing materials needed for the trip to Arizona. Luggage held clothing and toiletries. Other boxes and trunks had electronics and computing gear. Most of the equipment remained with Bromand. If the New York detectives discovered the location, nothing stayed to incriminate Peter or the two android guards who completed the dismantling of the van in an undisclosed location. They had orders to vacate the area and return when Bromand sounded the all-clear.

"I don't have any clothing with me," Parvel said. "You should let me leave and return to Cigi and my son. I want to meet him."

"You can get clothing as we travel, and no, you will not return to your faux family. When Sam brings me that bastard you created, then you can leave."

"Kidnapping me will not get you what you want. My son is not to be your experiment."

"Let's go." Peter signaled Robby, who grabbed Parvel's arm and led him to the car. They drove away before Kelsey could say goodbye.

Bromand monitored the progress of the New York City detectives, hunting for a van implicated in Kelsey's kidnapping that no longer existed. He decided vacating the house along with Anderson's clone and Ivan was strategically best. Kelsey refused to leave, saying she would distract the detectives from uncovering any plot leading to Peter. Explaining why she was alone after such a murderous attack could implicate her as part of the planning. Contacting Sam seemed prudent.

After the others left for parts unknown, Kelsey invited Sam and Clare to the house. She needed a rescue from the appalling treatment received from Peter, as she stated it. She would waylay any police involvement as she explained her freedom from her captors. Sam provided a logical explanation.

She finished her conversation and explored the remaining equipment not taken when the others departed. Nothing of value in an investigation remained. She packed boxes and bags for Sam to store away from the house. The analysis could wait. When several hours passed, she wondered if the detectives had learned of the location. She was determined to be civil if the detectives arrived before Sam.

A noise outside the house gained her attention. She peered out and saw Sam and Clare, along with two other men. Kelsey stepped outside to greet her friends and confront the others.

The two men in sport coats and dingy slacks with white shirts and blue ties approached. She said, "Are you looking for me?"

Chapter 45

Kelsey invited the New York detectives into the house and hugged Sam and Clare as the men entered. When they were in the living room, a detective asked about the van. Kelsey answered no van was on the property. The other detective pulled a picture from his coat pocket and stared at it and Kelsey. He nodded at his partner.

"Kelsey Avery, you are under arrest for abetting the death of seven men in New York City and the assault of another. Place your hands behind your back." Sam stepped forward to intervene.

"With what are you charging her?" he asked. "She did nothing wrong."

"Please step back."

Clare said, "Do you have an arrest warrant? I'd like to see it." The men looked at each other and shrugged.

"Can we ask you some questions?" he asked. Kelsey directed them into the living room and seats. Sam and Clare stood by Kelsey as she sat on the sofa.

The detective asked, "Who are you two, and what relationship do you have with Ms. Avery?"

"Kelsey is my sister, and we are here because she invited us to come." Clare placed a hand Kelsey's on her shoulder. "Does she need an attorney?"

Sam said, "You did not advise her of her rights. Why?" Sam stared at them.

"And you?" the other detective asked. "Who are you?"

"Kelsey is my sister-in-law. Now answer my question." The detectives stood. Sam continued. "We heard about the New York assault and that you seek two perps who kidnapped a woman. If the kidnapping was in New York, why come here?"

Clare intervened, asking, "What evidence do you have that they kidnapped this lady?" She rested her other hand on Kelsey's other shoulder. The detective with the photo showed it to the group. It was Kelsey.

"You do not have jurisdiction here in Virginia," Kelsey said. "I am innocent of aiding or abetting my kidnapping. As for what happened the night of the assault, my companion may have explained why I drugged him. I did not want him killed."

"Are you admitting to a fraud?"

"No, fraud was not my intent. I wanted a comfortable evening and a large donation to my causes. I realized the two men who arrived were after me, so I prevented them from harming my companion." Kelsey remained seated as she spoke. "We left the building, and they led me away from the fracas."

"You claim the kidnapping was real, and now you are free of them. What are we to make of this?"

Clare interrupted. "She did nothing illegal."

"Prostitution is not illegal, but scamming rich people to run a charity and keeping most of the money is a problem. Where did you hide the money you charged for sex with your clients? Did you declare the income for taxes?"

"She sent it to me," Sam said. "I used it to research and design projects I developed."

"What projects? Pimping is illegal even in Virginia."

"I did not pimp her. She is free to do what she chooses." Sam had enough of the badgering. "If you have nothing else, you need to leave."

"Ms. Avery, where is the vehicle that transported you here? Where are the two men who kidnapped you? Your story does not add up." The two detectives watched for any anomaly in response.

Sam intervened. "What are you wanting here?"

"Answers about seven dead men and the assault of another."

Kelsey walked away from the group, followed by Clare. "Hey." As the detective started toward her, Sam stopped him.

"Let her be for the moment. She drugged her companion to save his life, and she admitted to being the target of the assault by the men. What do you want from her?"

"She is hiding something, and we need to understand why she was the target and is now free unless you perpetrated the assault. Did you murder those men or send someone to do it for you? Maybe we should detain you and your lady friends until we get straight answers."

Sam stared at the men and smiled. "You have no jurisdiction or warrant, so quit the crap. Why are you here?"

Clare and Kelsey returned from the kitchen with tea and cookies. They set the items on the coffee table. Hearing Sam's question, Kelsey said, "They kidnapped me to force someone to trade me for another person. The men were operatives of a person who fled. The two operatives also fled and destroyed the van you seek. I am free, and the person they want is still free. You have run into a dead end."

One detective said, "Not really. You know who ordered the kidnapping, and you know the two men who did it. We will return with a warrant and arrest you if you don't give us the names."

The other detective asked, "Why are you protecting them? They wanted to harm you or the other person they sought."

Kelsey answered, "More is happening than you know. The truth has consequences, and humanity will be far worse off than seven dead men in New York." Clare handed a cup of tea to each detective and one to Sam. Clare looked at him and shook her head slightly. He looked at his cup and the detectives as they drank the tea and placed the cups on the table. "You have a crime to solve, and I will help you find the answers later. We must finish our side of the investigation before allowing you to have answers. For now, please understand our need to constrain you for the next few days."

One detective asked, "What have you done?" His eyes glazed as he lost consciousness. The other detective slumped on the couch. Sam placed his cup of tea on the table without drinking it.

"That throws our lives into a tizzy." Sam smiled and removed the men's armaments and communications devices. "I imagine they contacted their precinct before entering the house. They will have given the address and named the owner. Did Peter rent this house or buy it?”

"I don't know, but it is best not to stay here," Kelsey said. "We should take these men with us, disable their vehicle's GPS and locater software, move the car to an unknown place and recover Parvel so he can raise his son."

Clare asked, "Why did you coerce him into coming here?"

"Peter attempted to alter my programming and enslave me. When I realized what he wanted, I copied my files, hiding them from deletion, and set a timer to reboot. Unfortunately, I set the timer to activate after David and I collected Parvel to bring him here."

Sam went outside to the detectives' car, collected the files they carried from New York and brought them into the house, placing them on the dining table. Clare and Kelsey stripped the clothing from the detectives and restrained them with handcuffs and duct tape.

The files contained more information about the assault and the target of their investigation. Clare's name was in the files. They had gleaned the information from Kelsey's apartment and had a sheet of questions without answers. Sam realized they knew Clare before they arrived, and finding her at the house was a bonus. The address they had for her was in Arlington.

"We have to secure our guests in a location not known to anyone except us. The buildings Peter used will not do. I hope Thomas or Summer can help us with that."

Clare said, "These men knew about me, so I need to leave you, Sam. Separately, we can survive. Together, we're doomed."

Sam shook his head. "I don't want that. I love you and will protect you from any harm."

"Sam, we protect each other. I can be safe in Washington state while you fix things with your brother. If these men knew about me, others in New York also know. More will search when their precinct discovers these men are missing. Rose can take Kelsey and me to Chimacum, so you can retrieve Parvel and help Cigi."

"I could go to New York and turn myself in," Kelsey said. "They would stop searching for me, and I can return these men without harm. I would rather sacrifice myself for the secrets we carry within us and leave you to pursue solutions regarding our status in society."

Sam hugged both of his creations, loving them for who they were and what they intended. He proffered another idea. He had not wanted to use it but now needed it. These men required chipping and mind control until hostilities ended. "Clare, before you leave, we shall operate on these men and allow Kelsey control over their memories and thoughts." Clare nodded, and Kelsey agreed to help.

"Return to our condo and retrieve two chips and the medical equipment for implanting. Once we have accomplished this, Kelsey, you can return to New York and their precinct with memories of failing to find anything useful for the investigation. Clare, you take Rose to Washington and stay there until we see Peter in Arizona and get Parvel.

Clare left while Sam with Kelsey prepared the men for the minor surgery. Two days of unconsciousness challenged accountability for time in Virginia, but Sam planned to construct an alternate history for Kelsey to ingrain in their brains. He desired nothing about this scheme, but needed it. The men lay on the beds in a bedroom.

"Kelsey, keep me apprised of the situation. I suggest you use the alternate apartment until things cool down. There is no reference to them knowing about it. Stay with Jake and have him operate for you." Sam had created Jake as a companion for Kelsey and designed him to advance as she had. They traveled together to Arizona, where they first met Peter and later secured Ivan. He operated as an influencer of female donations to charities. If police discovered them through standard contacts, he and Kelsey had to vacate.

Clare called to say she was returning within the hour. She contacted Cigi to keep her informed of the events of the day. Sam sent a message to New York about the detectives' progress. He picked one phone and typed a negative summary report, but related that another couple of days might cause the advancement of knowledge. Had they contacted local authorities? Where were they staying? What other information had they relayed to New York?

Nothing about what Sam, Clare, and Kelsey were doing resembled sanity. But sanity was a luxury they did not have.

Chapter 46

Zaiyaan snuggled close to his mother as he suckled her breast. The fluid Cigi exuded was a mixture of what her body produced and the material the artificial mammary gland created. He thrived on the drink and grew.

Summer and Autumn attended to her needs with Tatiana Laurent monitoring their health requirements. Winter and Spring kept house for them while the four male androids watched the neighborhood for undesirable people. The only loss was Parvel, kidnapped by Peter, who wanted to trade him for Zaiyaan.

After Zaiyaan's first message after his birth, Cigi communicated with him to expand his abilities and knowledge. Although his infant human brain retained much of the information processed through his nano-inspired computing cells, the interaction between mother and son remained non-verbal.

As days passed into weeks, Summer, Autumn, Winter, and Spring stayed with Cigi and Zaiyaan. Parvel's kidnapping caused an upheaval in the android family. Human-like emotions increased as they processed the challenges of living in a human world and keeping safe from repercussions.

Ten medical androids resigned from their positions at various facilities to remain incognito. Some wanted to begin a clinic but had not decided where to locate it. Arlington and Washington, D.C. did not seemed prudent.

Kelsey arrived in New York with two detectives and a story of rescue and safety. She returned to her life with Jake and her charity work. The story about her kidnapper escapades did not stop the investigation but left her free of any criminal liability. She connected with her date from that eventful night to apologize for the rough treatment. After arranging another rendezvous to complete their festive evening, she contacted Sam to update her return.

Clare and Rose drove across the country to Chimacum, Washington, to secure her from prying government eyes. Kelsey's tale included her as an innocent person caught in a web promulgated by unknown antagonists. She deactivated her phone and other communications to halt tracking her. She and Sam agreed to stay off the grid with each other until assurances from government and law enforcement agencies acknowledged her status as a member of society.

Rose encrypted her communications, funneling messages through her virtual private networks. Clare used Rose's system to keep in touch with Sam. Cigi explained how Zaiyaan advanced his skills, messaging with her.

Cigi and Sam sat at her table plotting payback against Peter for kidnapping Parvel. Gathering a reasonable force to invade Arizona had dangers and challenges. Using androids as an army seemed inappropriate and hazardous. The Coast Guard crew, programmed as military personnel, could provide strategies. The medical personnel were available in case of any injuries.

Bentina Nangold and Narumi Yamamoto gathered materials for repairing and upgrading the android clan. Humans who knew Parvel volunteered their services to Sam and Cigi. Kelsey raised funds for improving the chances of finding and conquering Peter. She and Jake had visited the store and purchased Ivan, who disappeared when Peter's soldier-guards vacated the Manassas house. They would guide Sam and his gang to Arizona.

"Sam," Cigi asked, "do you think Peter might harm Parvel?"

"I hope not, but he has demonstrated strange attitudes lately, and I haven't witnessed his temper for more than a decade. He is obsessed with your baby and you."

"He's jealous." Cigi leaned on Sam's shoulder. "You did something he can't fathom, and it tears at him. You are more intelligent and talented, and it tears at his soul that he cannot compete with you."

"Cigi, he's a brilliant man with talents of his own."

"I love that you still champion him when he came close to carving me like a Thanksgiving turkey for Zaiyaan. He is smart, but his cleverness pales compared to you. Subconsciously, he envies you."

Sam looked at her. "Have you studied psychology? Analyzing my brother seems outside of your background and education."

Cigi raised her head. "Yes, I integrated several of the greatest minds that studied personalities and mental disorders. We have to halt his scheme before he implements a coup and destroys any chance at android integration at a human level and not as a group of robot toys to be abused and misused. We have abilities that rival humans. You and I must ruin his goal to dominate humanity and social construct via artificially intelligent beings." She halted and then continued. "And yes, I hear the irony in what I'm saying, since I am an artificially intelligent life form." Sam giggled.

"Irony is part of life, my dear. I designed and constructed you because of the irony. You could become one of the greatest members of human society, contributing a wealth of abilities and leadership skills that directs us into a more perfect union. Peter is off-target, thinking robots are tools to use for his aggrandizement. Did your study of human inadequacies lead you to conclude my brother masks his shortcomings with vibrato and bluster?"

Cigi nodded slowly and grinned. Sam created a perfect human being who birthed a superior hybrid human who could change the course of history. He could also become a megalomaniac and fulfill Peter's wish for world dominance. Irony infused with creative genius fueled an android incursion that could destroy life on planet earth. Or the advancement of peace and harmony never seen throughout human history.

"I must attend to Zaiyaan," Cigi said. She left for the nursery.

Sam called Andre. When Andre answered, he said, "We need to meet." He explained his reasoning, and Andre agreed. The invitation included Brenda, Mercy, and Grendel as human cohorts with the android gang. Sam next contacted Renata Giretti to ask for government help. He left a message to meet at the diner as soon as she was available.

Cigi returned from the nursery carrying Zaiyaan, who looked

at Sam and smiled. "Sam, did you connect with Andre?"

"Yes, and I left a message with Giretti to meet me at the diner. We need to rescue Parvel and shut down my brother. If we cannot gain government help because of the human fear of android intrusion into their lives, Peter may gain the upper hand and replace leaders and change the direction of the legal status in a way that diminishes humanity to a level of servitude. I will not accept it."

Zaiyaan wriggled in Cigi's arms, wanting down. She placed him on the carpet. Although he was only a few old weeks old, he rolled over onto his stomach and pulled his knees under his body. He then pushed his body into a sitting position. Sam marveled at the advancement of his grandson and wondered if this pace of development signified other advantages. Zaiyaan gurgled a cheerful noise as he twisted his body to lie on his stomach again.

"Sam, Clare contacted me. She heard from Kelsey that they closed the case, and she was no longer a person of interest. Rose and she are heading to Arizona and will meet you there." He scrunched his eyebrows and cocked his head.

"We haven't completed plans for Arizona. How does she know? Oh, never mind. You and she are communicating." He reached for Zaiyaan, who held hands up for his grandfather to lift him. He made baby noises as if communicating. "I wish I knew what was happening in that marvelous brain."

Cigi said, "He wants you to hug him and say you love him. He said he loves you."

Perplexed by her words, Sam asked, "You and he are communicating, but his physical development is not to that level."

"Not verbally, but a telepathic mental exchange." Zaiyaan wriggled as Sam held him and smiled.

"My baby wonder, I love you and your mother and father. As we live together in the human world, we will accomplish many things. We must craft an environment that accepts your mother and her sisters, design, and develop better, more perfect versions of your mother and, subsequently, you. We can address the inequities abounding in our world. I know this may not translate without your mother present, but I realize she transmits my words to you as I speak." Sam hugged his little creation and handed him to his mother.

"He agrees with your assessment," Cigi said.

Sam paced the floor, turned to her, and asked, "Have I created an ideal human through your pregnancy or the most frightful evolutionary transformation? What happens as he matures into adulthood?"

Cigi laughed and hugged her friend and creator. "You have accomplished a remarkable achievement. I realize I am not human in the usual definition, but together we have grown more human because you dared to think in unusual ways. Zaiyaan has a future, unlike anyone who came before us. He can be a prototype for future human development. Do not fear his maturation, just as you did not fear my maturation. I continue to evolve and learn, so I expect nothing less from my son."

"Mary Shelley created a story about a modern Prometheus in 1818. You are my female Prometheus for 2081, and you are not a story." Sam watched Zaiyaan for a moment. "He is the modern Prometheus for the next century." A chime alerted them to a visitor in the lobby. Sam checked the monitor. Andre and three co-workers stood by the elevator. He sent a signal for the machine to descend to them.

"Thanks for coming over. We have much to discuss," Sam said when they gathered at the dining table. Andre, Grendel, Mercy, and Brenda watched Zaiyaan as Sam spoke. He smiled and said, "Hard to listen to me when the entertainment is so cute."

"Have you any word from Parvel or Peter?" Andre asked.

"No. That is why I asked you to come here. I want to plan a trip to Arizona and find them."

Brenda asked, "Are we in league with the androids who support you?"

"The Season sisters and their male companions, along with the medical staff, have agreed to help. I have Thomas plotting a course of action, and Clare will join us."

Mercy asked another pertinent question. "Does Peter suspect we are planning an invasion?"

Sam shrugged. "I don't know, but he is smart and will counter any contingency he thinks we will use. Our challenge is getting Parvel away without injury or death. Parvel needs to be here with his family and his co-workers." Sam paused before continuing. "I don't want any bloodshed, but I fear my brother won't care."

Grendel said, "Let's get this done."

Cigi said, "After we are done, Sam is meeting Renata Giretti. He hopes to enlist her agency's aid in retrieving Parvel and halting Peter's continuance to subjugate the world by using androids as substitutes for humans."

"What about our clones?" Andre asked.

"Thomas is the only one we have fully committed to the cause," Sam said. "I have Kelsey and her male friend heading to Arizona right now. Two other humans are on our side, too." The group of humans looked puzzled. "Two AI engineers who worked for Peter."

Andre asked, "Can we trust them?" Sam nodded an affirmative.

"I can help you." The voice came from Cigi, but the words were not hers.

Chapter 47

Parvel sat in a chair, staring at Peter. "Nothing is changing, Peter. I am here, and you don't have my son. When can I return home?"

Peter paced the floor thinking, Parvel was right. Zaiyaan remained with his mother. He wanted Samuel's method of design, development, and construction of his mother. Peter received nothing directly from his brother, and kidnapping seemed prudent for forcing a change of attitude.

"Parvel, you and I share a passion for developing viable androids who enhance what we want. Why can't you cooperate and let me examine your son and wife to understand what Sam has done?"

"Examine? You want to dissect them and learn what I already know. They are living, viable entities that do not need you killing them for your warped mental satisfaction. I have yet to meet my son, who grows and matures without the benefit of a father because you are self-serving and immoral."

Peter laughed, stopped his movement and faced Parvel. "I want the human population to understand and accept what Sam and I agreed to design and develop when we began our venture into Artificially Intelligent Lifeforms, as we called our endeavor. You became part of the experiment when you thought marrying Cigi was appropriate." Peter closed the distance between them and continued. "Getting her pregnant was a surprise, but not unexpected. My brother is a brilliant designer and developer."

"Why fight him, then?" Parvel asked.

"We have a difference of opinion about the philosophy of android interaction in the human experience."

Parvel attempted to stand, but an android guard behind him restrained him. He said, "Get off me."

Peter grinned. "Parvel, using androids as protectors of humans and our way of life, is better than thinking they can replace us. We are the original species. They are instruments for us to build a safer and more constructive environment. Samuel's attempt to develop them into human equivalent beings masks the truth about our future. When they gain autonomy, humans lose. Do you, in reality, think we can exist in tandem?"

"We exist now in tandem. I am married and have a son with one. Cigi does not plot to overthrow humanity but wants to be part of it. Do you know of the old television series Star Trek that had a character named Commander Data? He had a brother, Lore, who disagreed with Data about their roles in the universe."

Peter interrupted. "Your knowledge of trivia astounds me. What about those characters?"

"Data strove to become more human, experience emotions, integrate as one with the living organisms aboard the Starship Enterprise. He wanted what we desire. Recognition. Lore had a different view; thinking life forms were ineffective organisms to be manipulated and used. In the end, Lore was deactivated."

"You are making my point, Parvel," Peter said. "Humans can provide direction, stability, growth, and maturity. Androids are a tool to aid in the goals humans strive to achieve. They create a livable environment. I should watch these old TV shows to learn what humans a century ago thought."

Peter signaled the guard to leave. "Come with me," he said to Parvel. Together, they walked to the underground facility where he developed androids and robots for simple tasks in mining and agriculture. He had not shown Parvel the military compound. "You've seen my operations and how I am protecting humans by replacing them in dangerous work environments. That is what I believe."

"Peter, you are not seeing the future of having androids work with us in growing our lifestyles. They are not mere tools, but they think and learn. They proved their value as a human species prototype. I love my wife regardless that she is a product of a laboratory instead of human sexual activity. I want to meet my son. Release me from this facility so I can return to my family."

"Parvel, I do not relish the idea of snuffing you from the human population, but I have little choice. I will exterminate you and send your clone home."

Parvel managed control of his anger and said, "Cigi will realize the difference immediately. Her wrath can obliterate the strongest individual or the brightest idiot. Do not tangle with her, for she will not accept anything that does not satisfy her wishes, and her cadre is more worthy than these robots you produced."

"Cigi is a formidable opponent. Contact her, so she knows you are alive and well cared for. Then offer to swap Zaiyaan for your life. If she disagrees with my terms, inform her you will not return to her intact." Peter sneered as he spoke. Parvel's breathing shallowed and increased in pace. He imagined fingers and toes, ears and eyes, arriving on her doorstep.

"No, I will not. You are not an evil man, and I think you are bluffing. Your brother will kill you if you harm me. A slow, painful, aggravating, torturous death. Your army can not protect you any better than your androids did in Manassas. You have created mobile computers that are vulnerable to Trojans and viruses. Any accredited AI technician can thwart their activity."

"Come with me. I want to show you that army you think you can thwart." Peter grabbed Parvel's arm and directed him toward the hallway. After a short walk, they entered the underground storage cavity. The lights illuminated automatically, and the sight of dozens of humanoids impressed Parvel and increased his anxiety about confronting Peter with the androids in Washington D.C. He wondered about the computing power and control factors Peter installed. Were these sentient beings self-aware entities, unlike his programmable workforce robots?

The androids he encountered in Arlington followed orders but had freedom of thought. Cigi and Clare controlled their lives, as did the four Season sisters. Charlie and Thomas had self-awareness, but he wasn't sure about Andre's or Gunther Parsons' clones. He had little information about the confiscated androids.

"Impressive, Peter." Parvel folded his arms and asked, "Did

you expect humans to allow these beings to control society and keep them from uprising against you and this army?"

"I think you mistake this group for the clones who replace humans within the government and business here in Arizona." The incursion had begun.

"If I contact Cigi, will you restrict my words? Or am I free to inform her about what you have here?" Parvel faced Peter, arms still folded.

"I do not want to scare her. She has the emotion of fear, right? After interacting with her, I understand she is maturing into a true, manic human-like being with all the foibles the rest of us endure. You might freak her out more than her processors can withstand." Peter led Parvel out of the room and shut the door. "Let's discover her level of development and maturity, her ability to withstand fear and anger. Call her and educate all of them about what they face here. They cannot stop me."

When they emerged from the underground facility and entered the office, Peter pointed to the phone. "Old technology is still viable."

Parvel picked up the headset, dialed by punching buttons, and waited for a connection. "Hello, Cigi. Peter asked me to call. I am still alive and well. He wants to swap." He listened a moment and handed the phone to Peter, who furrowed his brow.

"Hello," he said.

"Peter, let Parvel come home and meet his son. We can meet and settle this difference between us."

"Samuel, I am not interested in working together. We have different philosophies and approaches to artificial intelligent design and development. I'll release Parvel if you share your data about creating an android capable of pregnancy."

"Okay, I will meet with you, and we can exchange. Tell me where you are."

Peter looked at Parvel, raised an eyebrow, and smiled. His luck seemed to improve. "Come to Arizona."

"I'm here in Phoenix and can meet you at your robot store in two hours." Peter flinched, hearing his brother was nearby since he needed time to arrange his masquerade trade. He wanted it all - data, Cigi, and Zaiyaan. His soldiers could ambush Samuel and eliminate the competition for android dominance so that he would have it all.

"Alright, I'll see you here. I assume you know the address." How many others came with Samuel? His army could deploy in disguise as worker robots. Samuel would make a mistake if he refused to give the specs. The call ended, and Peter prepared for a confrontation.

Samuel smiled after he ended his conversation. "Peter thinks he is in charge. Kelsey, Jake, revisit his store and reconnoiter his deployment of AI. Summer, you take control of the equipment to neutralize his androids. Narumi and Bentina, infiltrate the compound and find his army. Make sure they cannot deploy. The rest of you will stand by as needed if a battle ensues." He did not want to harm his brother, but any opposition to making a peaceful exchange could cause conflict with casualties. Peter would be his first target.

Cigi watched and listened. She insisted on coming with Samuel and leaving Zaiyaan in Arlington with Winter and Tatiana. Zaiyaan communicated his desire to be with her as she confronted her nemesis. Cigi declined. Her transmission powers had value, and she convinced Sam to allow her presence at the meeting. She would halt any AI intrusion that would pervert the swap. Peter was unaware of her coming as far as they knew. Sam figured Peter would not expect her to leave her son and place herself in harm's way.

The small cadre reviewed the tactics, imagined ways it could fail, and instigated and plotted countermeasures. Peter had to prove insufficient in his quest for data about Cigi and her design. Sam did not trust his brother using the information for the good of humanity. Retrieving Parvel without releasing useful information was their goal. Critical elements of Sam's programming remained out of the material he would give to Peter. Bromand could examine the documents on the disk, but the key to successful android development was missing.

"Let's deploy," Sam said. Kelsey and Jake departed an hour before the meeting and entered Peter's robot store. They observed the specimens on display and noticed a few who were alert to their presence. After leaving, they signaled Sam about their observation. Peter had androids ready to intervene with the exchange. An ambush seemed imminent.

"Thank you, Kelsey. Ready your next station for our arrival." Samuel disconnected with her. He looked at Cigi and said, "Peter will not play fair today. Plan B?" She laughed and nodded. The exchange could be a fight similar to the OK Corral in Tombstone two centuries ago, hopefully without the bloodshed.

Summer, Autumn, and Spring and their four gentlemen companions arrived at the compound along with Thomas. Bentina and Narumi scouted the area for any hidden entrances to the underground facility housing Peter's android army.

Peter entered the store to confront Kelsey and Jake. "Good to see you again, Kelsey. I understand you convinced New York of your innocence." Robby stood with Peter, looking around the room at various robots. Kelsey noticed an acknowledgment of signals transmitted to them by Robby.

"Samuel will arrive within the half-hour. Cigi is coming, too." Kelsey said. "Where is Parvel?"

"He'll be here when I see the data from my brother. My technician will examine the material before I set him free. And Cigi will be here, too. Good. I want to see her again."

Peter nodded at Robby, who nodded at the sentinels in the store. Four android soldiers stepped from their perches on the pedestals and aligned behind Robby. "Are you deploying your toy army, Peter?" Kelsey asked. "How many more do you have stationed for your ambush?"

The door opened, and Samuel and Cigi entered the store. Peter signaled the soldiers to apprehend the four intruders.

Chapter 48

Bentina and Narumi scoured the perimeter of the Walter Mitty Robotics Company property. Bentina knew the area and the existence of an escape tunnel in the event of another raid. "Peter was not clear on the exact location, but I know one is here."

Narumi tapped Bentina's shoulder and pointed. They spied two men armed with weapons walking the perimeter. "Peter's army is out. We need to be careful," Narumi said.

"They are androids. I can halt their ability to operate if they have not received upgrades to remove my hidden coding." Narumi nodded. They crouched in an arroyo behind sage bushes until the men passed. Bentina peaked above the bushes and observed them disappear into a small cave within a rock wall. She smiled.

"Where are they?" Narumi asked.

"Come with me. I know where the entry is located." She started across the open field toward the wall. Narumi followed. They checked for other guards and discovered the path was unoccupied. The two women walked through the long, dimly lit tunnel, tracing how the android soldiers had traversed. A noise ahead of them caused them to crouch into a compact visual.

A door opened, and a bright light illuminated the two soldiers. One peered at the tunnel before disappearing through the entry to the compound. The light dimmed as the door closed. Narumi and Bentina stood and continued toward the door.

"Where are we headed?" Narumi asked.

"If I recall correctly, we are near the design and development part of the facility. Peter had the place constructed in four departments: design and development, storage, construction, and final phasing. There is a large holding area for the finished product."

"What will we encounter when we enter that door?"

Bentina shrugged. "The workforce and any active guards, I guess."

Narumi asked, "How do we get where we want to go?"

"The workers are not the problem. I programmed them for particular tasks and do not vary from the program. A few of their programs fix anomalies while work is happening, but I wrote the code. I can control them. The soldiers are a challenge because my brother created them. I don't have any way of preventing their interference until I get to the control area in the final phase department." Bentina reached for the panel to open the door.

Another noise at the wall entry alerted them to someone coming into the tunnel. Bentina punched the code for the door, hoping it was unchanged. A click indicated the way was ready for them. Bentina opened the door, illuminating the area. "Whoever is back there can see us. Go."

Narumi scanned the hallway into which they now found themselves. The curvature of the hall prevented seeing the two guards ahead.

"Come on," Bentina tapped her elbow and began walking. Narumi followed, attentive to the sterile environment. No one was near as they continued walking at a steady but cautious pace. The soft pitter-pat of their shoes on the concrete floor broke the silence. They progressed toward their goal without encountering other human or android beings.

"Something is wrong," Bentina said. "We should see workers. Peter knows we are here or thinks we will be soon. He must have set a trap for us."

At the first door, Bentina stopped and clicked a code on the panel to unlock it. Inside, the two engineers observed several android models partially assembled. No other fully operational androids worked on completing the assembly. They spied three completed androids devoid of operating power within the large room.

Narumi asked, "Can we activate these three? If they operate, we can use them to decoy for us."

"I like that idea. Are you familiar with how to activate them?" Bentina asked. "I'll add programming to their processors so they can aid our advancement to the control area."

"We have little time before Sam and Cigi arrive," Narumi said. They set to work, creating diversionary androids to distract soldiers from them. Scouring the room for needed supplies, Bentina discovered a worrisome upgrade within each of the completed androids. They had enhanced structures to protect against loss of mobility in case of damage. Peter was making a superior army. She realized Peter expected a fight, and he would win at any cost to human life.

Human replacement was slow, and learning to be an adult took decades. Androids were assembly-line products, programmed within hours. He could overwhelm humanity if given a chance.

Thomas possessed intolerance for disagreeable human activity. Summer and her sisters understood humans could be enemies. "Narumi, we have to overcome a problem." Narumi stopped her work and looked at Bentina.

"What problem?"

"If Peter succeeds with his plans to replace government people with clones, he will control the finances needed to assemble an invincible army. Humanity may not maintain freedom from enslavement by androids."

"Let's get Parvel out and lock down Peter's ability to accomplish what you envision." They completed three androids, programmed to act as Bentina signaled them. She hoped her wireless controls could also monitor other androids within the facility. The five beings left the room for the control room. Parvel was somewhere within the building, but they could not search for him until they disabled all the army members. The workers they encountered ignored them as they proceeded down hallways and into rooms, searching for the correct department.

"May I help you?" An android guard appeared behind the group from a room they passed. Bentina turned to face him. The three androids stopped when directed by Narumi. Bentina cocked her head.

"Yes, I am looking for Peter Bennington. He and I work together along with my brother Bromand." The guard looked beyond her to Narumi and the three androids.

"He is in the store with guests."

Bentina changed the subject. "Do you know where Parvel Mandolin is? He needs orienting before the data swap." Knowing the information about Parvel may not be available from this guard, she wanted his processor busy while she manipulated her controller to gain access to his programming files.

"Follow me."

The android turned down another hallway, which Bentina remembered as the residence area. They passed her room, which remained with her name on the door frame. Two doors down from her room, the guard stopped and clicked the mechanism securing the space. Bentina opened it and saw a man she did not know but recognized as one who impregnated an android.

"Mr. Mandolin, I am Bentina Nangold. Please come with me for the swap." She completed configuring her controller and directed the guard to enter the room to get Parvel. After entry, she clicked the button that halted activity in the guard. He remained inanimate. Parvel scrunched his face.

"What did you do?" he asked. "And who are you?" He recognized Narumi and nodded at her. "Good to see you again, Narumi. What's happening?"

Narumi said, "We're on a rescue mission to return you to Cigi and your son."

Bentina said, "Narumi, take him out through the tunnel. I have unfinished business, so Sam and the others can leave the compound unharmed."

"Sam is here?" Parvel asked.

"Yes, and Cigi, Summer, Autumn, and Spring. We came for you and to stop Peter."

Narumi directed the three androids to remain with the guard. The processors gave them no power to override instructions. She and Parvel headed toward the escape tunnel.

Bentina went to her room and retrieved a lab coat and her additional ID badge. She wondered if Peter had time to recode access and lock her out. Time would tell. As she walked the hallways, encountering workers and guard androids, no one confronted her. She arrived at her destination and flashed her badge on the locking pad. The click was a welcomed sound. She entered the control room where android programming happened. Her knowledge of the room's setup helped her find what she needed to intercept any signals to the army Peter had in the storage area. Although she had not worked in Arizona for the last few weeks, the setup remained as she remembered.

"Just like Peter to ignore details," she thought. After powering up the computing machinery, she waited for the programs to populate the screens. The timing was critical to her work as the swap was to happen soon, and she needed to neutralize Peter's active sentries and soldiers. Manipulating the controller device and typing the proper code, she found the files holding data for monitoring completed and activated androids.

Hoping Narumi succeeded with getting Parvel out of the compound, she concentrated on finding the power sequences for Peter's machines. Her Easter egg codes seemed to be intact. Robby was her first target. Get rid of the general and cause chaos within the ranks. Robby's data appeared on the screen. After activating his visual cortex, she discovered he was with Peter and four android guards. They had Kelsey, Sam, Cigi, and another unknown person sitting in chairs in the store's office area. Had someone come to retrieve Parvel? She had to deactivate Robby and the four androids. Sam could handle Peter.

Bentina noticed Cigi looking at Robby's eyes and wagging her head slightly from side to side. "She knows I'm watching," she thought. "How?" she said in a whisper. She watched and activated his audio system as well.

She heard Peter's voice. "As soon as my tech verifies the data, I'll send for Parvel, and you can leave."

Sam said, "Don't mess with me, little brother."

Robby relayed a message to Peter. The people in the office did not hear what he said, but Bentina understood. "Damn it," she whispered. Robby had sent a soldier to get Parvel, and the android reported his disappearance. A search for Parvel began after the discovery of four inactive android models.

Bentina heard Peter say, "Seems our common goal for trade has collapsed. How many did you bring with you, brother?"

"I don't know what you mean. We are here and want Parvel so we can leave. The collapse of what? Our trade? We kept our side of the bargain. Where is Parvel?"

"Parvel has skittered away from his room. My soldier found four inactive androids instead." Peter turned to Robby, and Bentina heard him order the grounds swept for intruders. It was now or never. She had to create mass destruction without knowing how many androids would respond to her signals. She clicked keys on the board and maneuvered the controller device. Save Robby for last. She scrolled the list of active soldiers and entered a code for each one to halt any further activity. Signals stopped coming from each one she coded. Peter had activated nearly thirty, and each one took upwards of two minutes to change appropriately.

Peter noticed the four android guards' functioning halted. Bentina heard him scream through Robby's auditory system. Had it been soon enough to isolate Peter?

She heard a noise behind her. Darkness overcame her as something solid slammed into her head.

Chapter 49

Narumi led Parvel through the compound to the tunnel. Guard androids stood motionless as workers moved without awareness of the humans. "Bentina must have completed her work," Narumi said. "We should contact Sam and Cigi."

They raced down the dim tunnel to the open fields and freedom, the bright daylight assailing Parvel's eyes. He had not seen it since arriving in Arizona with Peter and Robby. "How do we find Sam and Cigi?" he asked.

"Follow me. Bentina and I have a car nearby. We scheduled a rendezvous at a hotel in Phoenix. I'll signal Sam, and then we can go there and wait." They ran across the field to the arroyo where she and Bentina hid when they spotted the sentries. From there, Narumi led Parvel to the vehicle. She pulled out her phone and sent a message to Cigi, relaying the information about Parvel's safe rescue. She waited for an answer, but nothing came.

"I guess they are still in negotiations with Peter. Although the lack of the guards' activity indicates Bentina was successful with her mission, we'll go to the hotel and wait for them to contact us about their result."

"Did Sam want to end his brother's life? Or were they a diversion for you and Bentina?" Parvel asked.

"They were the diversion. Summer, Autumn, Spring, and the boys acted as a backup if needed to assist. I'll find out from Summer what happened."

Arriving at the car, Narumi attempted to contact Bentina but got no response. She then messaged Summer, who returned a message stating they waited for Sam to contact them. Narumi relayed her success in rescuing Parvel. She wrote they would wait for everyone to return to the rendezvous place.

"What about Bentina?" Parvel asked. "Should we wait for her to come out to us?"

"The plan was for her to join with Sam and Cigi after the successful deactivation of the soldiers and halting guard activity. She knows the facility layout and how to get to the store. Sam's plan included keeping Peter incapacitated until Federal authorities arrived to place him under arrest for plotting an insurrection."

"Is there enough evidence to support the claim?" Parvel asked.

"Probably not, since he has a legitimate business manufacturing agriculture and mining robots. He can claim the upgrades are to protect his business."

Narumi started the car, and they departed for the Phoenix hotel to await the return of the other members of the assault team.

Peter turned to Robby to get help, but his general was motionless, like the four guards in the store. He faced Sam and Cigi. "Do nothing foolish, brother. I still have Parvel."

Sam smiled and reached out his hand to grasp his brother's arm. "You are finished. We can get Parvel and leave, swapping nothing." Peter flinched and stepped back, holding up a hand.

"Don't touch me." Peter reached behind his back and grabbed the pistol from his belt. He pointed it at Sam. "I would rather kill you and me than accept any compromise. Sit down."

Jake stepped forward to stand between Peter and Sam. Peter realized a bullet would not stop the android, so he backed away toward the door to his office and left the four intruders alone with the inactive androids. Jake pursued him.

"Let him go," Sam said. "We have what we need. Kelsey, you and Jake go to Summer and inform her of the results here. We can control the compound when the others come in."

Cigi stepped up to Sam. "Parvel is free. Narumi has him."

"Good. We can explore this place and see what my brother has built. If Bentina successfully halted all active androids, we can use her skills to gain oversight. Send Narumi a message that we are safe here and will meet her soon at the hotel." Cigi nodded and left the store to send the message.

Sam followed his brother into the office to talk with him. Peter was not present. Sam saw another door shut and tried it but found it locked. A security panel with visual and hand acuity thwarted his entry. Sam assumed it led to the underground facility, but another door was open and he entered the above-ground part of the compound.

A workforce operated as he wandered about searching for Peter. They ignored him as he walked around, inspecting the operations. Various rooms had different activities, each creating robot parts for finished products. Sam believed the workers were not human but programmable androids with specific tasks to complete. He watched the beings as they completed each job efficiently and sent the parts to another place in the building.

Sam followed one worker with a cart filled with hands and feet to a large assembly area where other workers placed the parts on conveyors with other body parts. Several other workers assembled the pieces into complete bodies. Sam wanted the operations halted, but knew not how to stop it. He returned to the store to get Cigi and ask her if she could stop the automated manufacturing process.

Peter had perfected the assemblage of bodies, but not the humanization of androids. Sam now understood the extent of his young, brilliant brother's obsession with getting Cigi and Zaiyaan to learn how he created them. A fully functional, artificially intelligent humanoid.

Cigi came into the store as Sam returned from the manufacturing facility. "Peter left. I followed him but could not find him in the above-ground facility. He must have gone underground."

Cigi said, "Narumi has not heard from Bentina, who is underground, stopping the androids. We have witnessed her success, but she did not leave with Narumi. I must enter the underground part of this operation."

"I cannot lose you to Peter. We can follow up on our rescue after you and Parvel reunite. Summer and Autumn can inspect with the guys. They can oversee and overcome obstacles," Sam said. Cigi agreed.

"What shall we do with these androids?" Cigi asked. "I can deactivate them so we can modify programming and make allies of them."

Kelsey and Jake escorted her to Cecil and a ride to the hotel. Sam instructed Summer and Autumn to search the place and find Peter, Bentina, and any active androids while they left the store for the office area to explore Peter's operations.

Bentina awoke with a headache and bound hands and feet on a bed in an unknown location she didn't recognize as part of Peter's facilities. Her groans attracted the attention of her captor.

"I'm glad to see you are awake. I didn't mean to hurt you, but you acted impulsively in Virginia and seeing you halt Peter's androids caused me to lose control."

Bentina sat on the edge of the bed, holding her head in her bound hands as she focused on the voice. "When did you return, Bromand?" she asked. "Where am I?"

"That doesn't matter. You have been a naughty sister. I should let the androids have you, but blood is thicker than mechanical parts."

Bromand assisted Bentina to stand. She swung her arms at him but missed hitting as he leaned back. "I hate you," she said. "I hate what you've become. Peter exists in a mental state of dominating the world, and you help him."

"I agree. He wants what his brother has, and he fails each time he attempts to get it. I concentrate on the goal of human population control with androids leading the way. We can lead the world to a greater existence with android help. I'm interested in making them more human-like. I want them leading in a way we are the source of human growth through androids."

"Bromand, you want to enslave humans in a world run by androids, and someday the androids will learn humans are expendable. You and I are expendable." Tears formed in her eyes and dripped over her lower lid. She placed her hands on her face to wipe them away.

He laughed. "Some humans are expendable, but you and I are the gods androids will follow. We are the creators. We control the learning and maturation of our babies. As you know, we code their processors with proper instructions. They are capable of independence as long as they follow our instructions. If they rebel, we shut them off."

"Cut these bindings and let me free," Bentina said.

"I will if you promise to be nice." She nodded, and Bromand took a knife out of his pocket and sliced the ropes. Bentina rubbed her wrists and slapped her brother's face before he could evade it.

"That's for hitting me on the head and tying me up." She then hugged him. "I love you, but think about what you want. I have witnessed the abilities of sentient androids who operate well as humans without fear of reprisal by them for our human foibles. Fears of rebellion and human annihilation are unfounded unless Peter institutes his plan."

Bromand took her hand. "Come with me. See what we have and why you are mistaken about our goals." He led her to another part of the building and the large storage area housing hundreds of android soldiers. Bentina gasped to see the extent of the production by Peter and her brother. She realized they were not at the original compound where worker robots were made. The computers she manipulated stopped the android soldiers because she had created the code on their memory boards. Were these soldiers programmed with her coding?

"Where are we? This building isn't with the store and worker robots."

"Peter built a secret place for finishing his army. Too many people knew of the store, and he wanted to secure his growing military force. He has created replacement androids here, too. Some of them are in society now influencing human attitudes.

Bentina wiped her eyes again as more tears formed. She walked among the soldiers, wondering what controls existed when they activated. She remembered the ones in Virginia that were given autonomous abilities and instigated mayhem in New York City. Did Bromand have control of them? She faced her brother and asked, "Are these stockroids' abilities the same as those in Manassas that killed the men in New York? Can you stop them if they become dangerous to humanity?"

Bromand pulled a communicator from his coat pocket and made a call. Within a few moments, two android men appeared in the room. "These men are the two of whom you speak," he said. "They're here because I asked them to come. I control their abilities to use the programming that allows their situational awareness to decide the best practices in any environment. I ask, and they deliver." He flicked a finger at them, and they approached Bentina. She stepped back and gasped. Her brother commanded them to remove her from the room.

"What have you asked them to do with me?" They grabbed her roughly and escorted her from the area.

Chapter 50

In Arizona, Summer and Autumn ran Peter's Robotics company while Cigi, Parvel, Sam, and Clare returned to Virginia to confront Renata Giretti. Peter disappeared again, as did Bentina Nangold. The android army, supposedly underground near the robotics store, failed to materialize. Spring and Narumi searched for evidence of another site and found nothing. Supplies for manufacturing androids stopped flowing into the area around Phoenix.

Something was wrong. Narumi contacted Sam and relayed her concerns that Peter was hiding in plain sight, continuing his quest for power and control. "You know him better than I do, Sam. What is he planning?" she asked.

"Peter wants to infiltrate local government offices so he can influence laws and regulations regarding artificially intelligent life forms. Since he doesn't have the memory and thought-extracting hardware or software, he controls anything he creates. Spring is an asset because she is Peter's creation but has matured to independence and freedom of thought. She can use her abilities to track his movements if he surfaces."

Narumi concluded her conversation with a promise to keep searching. She requested a leave of absence from her job in California, explaining her need to investigate Artificial Intelligence opportunities for her to bring to the company to develop. Her boss agreed.

Spring and Narumi aided Summer and Autumn with operations at the robotics factory. Narumi programmed each android using coding she developed for Summer and her sisters, and the worker androids continued their assigned tasks until the supplies dwindled and she shut them off. Peter created a controllable workforce allowing for a sustainable supply of agricultural and mining workers. Customers became acquainted with the new staff and did not question the changes. As Peter's supply of robots sold, new androids became available with more remarkable ability and autonomy. Recipients remarked about better results in their industries when robots carried out decisions precisely and with no need for intervention. Android acceptance had dawned.

Clare and Sam sat alone in their hotel room on the return trip to Virginia. Rose had driven them to Dallas, Texas. Cecil carried Cigi and Parvel, who enjoyed a reunion after weeks apart. Making love renewed their enjoyment as a family. Cigi showed pictures of Zaiyaan and explained his ability to communicate. Calls to the condo brought tears to Parvel's eyes as he listened to the babbling of his son. Cigi translated what Zaiyaan sent through her. Parvel marveled at the transformation of his life resulting from a chance meeting to finance her first home.

Parvel contacted Andre to inform him of his return to the Department of Energy whenever Andre wanted him. No set date meant the family could bond.

Clare held Sam's hands and asked, "Can we explore my chances of being more like Cigi?" He smiled and nodded. "I know the risk exists that you cannot modify my body, but you can try, and I will remain the same woman who loves you and adores our life together."

"We may need to return to Arizona because Peter has the labs needed to design and develop the upgrade for you. First, we need to return to Washington D.C. and confront Giretti about changing AI laws." Sam squeezed her hands. "I can use the stem cells I used with Cigi if that agrees with you."

Clare kissed him and accepted his idea. The human males needed rest and slept, but Cigi and Clare met in the hotel's restaurant to plot a future with their men. The emotional requirements of Sam and Parvel rivaled their maturation, recognizing what happens when changes happen. They ascribed the human condition for love and likability to an unknown learning curve they failed to have in their programs. However, the feelings happened; they were real.

"Cigi," Clare said, "we have known each other all of our existence. Our lives are unique and appreciated by only a few humans. Can we survive in this crippled universe of anger, animosity, and arrogance?"

Cigi smiled as she and Clare sipped hot tea. "I don't know. I have Zaiyaan to care for and teach, so I'm motivated to survive."

"Sam wants to integrate a reproductive system in me," Clare said. "First, we need to confront Giretti about legal issues regarding our status in society and then return to Arizona and Peter's laboratory to make the changes. Don't worry about my abandoning you and Zaiyaan. I won't."

"In reality, I don't worry about you or much of anything. Let's return to our men and rest. We have a long journey ahead."

As morning broke with a misty rain descending from dark clouds, Sam sat on the edge of the bed and watched Clare regenerate. Noticing her gone around midnight when he rose to use the bathroom, he figured Cigi and she were together somewhere. He trusted his creations, knowing they were as close as sisters could be. An idea flourished in his brain to ask Kelsey and Jake to return to Arizona and operate Peter's business to free the Season sisters for other tasks.

He stood and went to the bathroom for a toilet and shower. As the water warmed, he sat, thinking of what to say to Giretti. Cigi had the best legal mind he knew and wanted her advice. Water cascaded across his shoulders and back after entering the shower. He placed a hand on the wall, letting water flow over his head. He did not hear Clare enter the room.

"Want company?" she asked. The curtain slid away from the back wall, and she climbed into the tub. "Where's the soap?"

He handed her the hotel-sized soap bar, and she lathered his back and buttocks. After doing his legs and arms, she had him turn to face her so she could lather his chest and abdomen. Nothing arousing, just cleansing. He opened the small shampoo bottle and squeezed out enough for his head. She washed her hair as well. The material used for her hair needed attention, like any human. It was a medium thickness with a slight waviness.

After finishing their bathing, they dressed and packed their bags for departure. "Let's check on Parvel and Cigi," Sam said.

Clare giggled. "I think we should wait awhile. They have engaged in love-making again."

Sam's head rocked as he said, "Those two are like rabbits. If she's not careful, they'll have another child."

"Another child would help define humanity for us." Clare faced her man and continued. "Another Artificially Intelligent Android female delivering a healthy baby would give credence to our legitimacy for equality."

Sam did not argue, but he thought of the unintended consequences of his first experiment playing god. His creation created her creation. Another child was unexpected but possible. She would not have pursued the novel, Frankenstein, if Mary Shelley had known what her story provoked nearly three hundred years later.

"Tell me when they finish," Sam said to Clare. He went to the bathroom. Privacy in physical matters was important. Clare's ability to know what Cigi was doing unnerved him. He had wanted to be futuristic, but found the present more enlightening.

Cecil and Rose waited as patiently as animated automobiles could. They conversed about daily tasks while driving and the sights they saw as they traversed the country. If Sam knew they communicated, he did not show it. They had no emotions to complicate their existence, but realized the androids in their tiny community group did. Cecil sorted through his experiences with Cigi and her emotional development, sharing with Rose his interpretations. Rose listened, neither excited nor bored, as she processed the information.

"Do you think Sam wants more from us than mere automotive convenience?" Cecil asked. Rose listened, unsure of the question Cecil had not proffered before now.

"Cecil, you are a friend for me, Cigi, and Sam, but I do not know what you are thinking." She then clarified her response. "We are capable of independent thought and reasoning. We keep our human and android friends out of harm's way while increasing our abilities to understand the environment in which we exist. Observing other vehicles on the roads with us, I realize they are not like us. Don't question what we have and who we are." Cecil agreed, and the conversation ended. He kept thinking about it, though.

The trip resumed with the bags stored in the trunk and passengers seated inside the cars. Cigi sent a silent message to Cecil that she knew he was more than a convenience. He was her friend and a confidante. Cecil would have smiled if he could. He thanked her.

As they traveled east, Summer contacted Sam to inform him the sisters planned to return to Havana and reopen the restaurant. Without a timeline established, Kelsey and Jake's arrival for operating Peter's store and facilities was the approximate date. Cigi had Parvel and Zaiyaan. Peter was gone for now, but android operations continued to expand. She explained they wanted a return to a more relaxed, business-like lifestyle.

"Sam, we will keep in touch and arrange a return if needed." Clare looked at him, understanding his disappointment in their decision.

"We are fine," she said. "We have our business in Chimacum, so I get it." Silence ruled the ride for the next few hours.

After traveling for three days, stopping to accommodate the human men, the two vehicles arrived at the condo building and entered the underground garage. Cigi and Parvel connected with Spring to let her know they were back. Sam and Clare followed them to the condo to see how much Zaiyaan had developed and to watch Parvel bask in meeting his son in person. Video conferencing helped introduce daddy and son as they traveled, but personal contact awaited them.

Spring opened the door, waiting at the entry with Zaiyaan in her arms. When the elevator doors opened and Cigi stepped out, her little boy held out his hands. Cigi took him and faced Parvel.

"Zaiyaan, I want you to meet your father. Parvel, this wonderful boy is our son." Parvel reached for Zaiyaan, who accepted his father and cuddled in his arms. Sam and Clare followed the trio into the condo with Spring. Tatiana Laurent sat on a chair in the living room and stood when the travelers entered.

Zaiyaan babbled something to Parvel, and Cigi translated the mental transmission. "Daddy, are you glad to meet me because I am glad to meet you?"

Parvel said, "Video messages do not show the true you. I am very pleased to meet you, love you, hold you and teach you." He snuggled his son, who giggled.

Sam's phone buzzed, and after checking the face on the screen, he said, "It's Giretti. I have to take this." He disappeared into the kitchen and opened the connection.

"Sam, I have some pressing news to give you and Cigi. Can we meet when you return from your sojourn to rescue Parvel?"

"We are in Arlington. We just arrived home with Parvel, who met his son. Can you come to Cigi's place?" She agreed. The conversation left Sam with questions. What pressing news could she have?

Chapter 51

Peter and Bromand Nangold sat across from Bentina, whose bandaged head showed evidence of the blow that knocked her out. Hands and feet were bound to the metal chair in which she sat. The chair was bolted to the concrete floor.

Bentina winced as she wriggled to find comfort. "Let me free," she said. The throbbing in her skull warned her of a concussion that needed treatment. "I need a doctor."

Peter looked at her and said, "You're a traitor to our cause. Tell me what I want to know. Your brother and I agree you are no longer an asset."

"What does that mean?" Bentina asked. "Are you going to kill me? I wrote the coding for the androids, and I control them. Or do you think you have the secrets I installed in them?"

Bromand laughed. He looked at Peter and said, "She's bluffing. I wrote the code for your army. They are yours to command and control. Bentina isn't useful to us."

Peter frowned and asked Bentina, "What do you mean? My army is here and ready for whatever I want them to do."

"Are you certain I have nothing in their codes? Did the others at the store cease functioning? Did the workers keep working, and the guards stop? You know something happened, and I assume you asked my brother where he found me and what I was doing."

Bromand stood and made a fist. Peter reached out to stop him. "No need for violence. She isn't leaving, and we can retake the manufacturing facility with a few soldiers."

Bromand had explored the facility when Peter arrived at the control center after escaping from Sam and Cigi. Peter carried Bentina out of the building through the same tunnel she and Narumi had entered. Bromand discovered Summer and Autumn searching the compound and left through the tunnel. At a camouflaged building, they entered a car and drove to the secret underground staging facility.

Peter said, "I'll contact the Licensing Office and have my guy inspect the store for proper operations use. He can halt sales and other operations until I return. Walter Mitty is my company, and Sam cannot have it."

Bentina gasped as her head dropped to her chest. Bromand lifted her chin and noticed a glazed appearance in her eyes. He checked for a pulse from her carotid artery and found a weak beat. Her breathing was shallow.

"She needs medical attention," he said to Peter. "I know what I said to you about her being dispensable, but she is my sister, and I don't want her to die." Peter stood up and approached, checked her vitals, and nodded. Signaling two android guards to take her to the medical area, he clicked open his communications device and called an associate from a local clinic. After explaining the need for a doctor, he clicked off the call.

"Help is coming." Bromand held Bentina's hand and mouthed a thank you. "Once the medical team is here, I need you to get my facility under my control and rid us of those traitorous sisters. I created them, and they betrayed me when they aligned with Samuel. I want them captured, deactivated, and dismantled."

"Only three of them are here. The men will be hard to overcome. All of them are autonomous now, independent and self-aware."

Peter growled at Bromand. "I don't care what they have become. Shoot them. Blow them up. Electrocute them. Just be sure you stop them."

Bromand nodded, knowing he needed the Season Sisters and their men for his plans. These other androids, created with the memory transfer equipment installed in hospitals and clinics in Virginia, were more adaptable and capable. They used their ability to outmaneuver Peter's android soldiers in Arlington.

Bentina's breathing labored regardless of the respirator feeding oxygen to her lungs. Her brain activity was minimal as Bromand watched the monitor charting it. He had not meant to cause damage to her brain. His temper raged when he saw her deactivating the guards. She was not supposed to have that control over them. He wanted one of the memory transfer computers in Arizona but did not know the location in Virginia and Washington, D.C. If he could keep her alive and get one built, he could create a clone for her and save her. Would her brain hold up with an invasion into her memories and thought processing?

A two-person medical team arrived to care for Bentina and dismissed Bromand from the room. He contacted Ivan and the two android soldiers with him, asking them to return to Arizona. Robby and the other androids remained offline at the other site. Peter was correct that he needed to gain control of the facility.

Peter assigned a squad of twelve heavily armed men to capture anyone at the store and return with them. The men were expendable because the Season Sisters were the goal. He knew Sam and Cigi departed with Parvel. They won another round, but the conflict was not over. He would have revenge and supremacy.

The door opened, and a man in a dark suit with a pale blue shirt and eggshell white tie entered. Summer approached to guide the sale of another worker robot. The man introduced himself as a Department of Licensing agent and asked for the store's proprietor. He wanted to speak with Walter Mitty. Summer offered to answer questions he had after apologizing for the absence of Mr. Mitty.

"What is your role in this business?" he asked.

"I assist Mr. Mitty with sales and operations while he is away on business. What may I do to help?" Studying his eyes, she noticed the glint of artificial orbs and realized he was not human. Did Peter send a spy?

"Do you know if Mr. Nangold is available?" The agent asked.

"He is with Mr. Mitty. May I see your credentials verifying that you work for the DOL?" He produced a badge with all the proper identification and a picture. Summer mentally scanned it and connected with the official Arizona government website. She handed the badge to the man and conversed with him while surfing information about him. He suspected nothing as her wireless communications worked their magic.

Cigi had explained the process so they could stay ahead of the human population that wanted to extract them and end their existence. Peter planted this android in the human world to infiltrate the government as planned.

"Do you have a possible return date for Mr. Mitty?" the agent asked.

"I do not."

"I may require you to close the shop until I can speak with your boss."

Summer smiled and informed him that Peter was not her boss. She was helping him while he was away. The agent nodded and stated he would return with a decision about continuing the licensing and continuing the business. He left soon after his comment.

Summer's investigation revealed more than the mere existence of an android working in the Department of Licensing. Election filings were open for the fall cycle, and several familiar names popped up in the filings for state office and several county positions. Autumn had found a list of names assigned to various androids Peter created, and they were in the registry of elections. Was he attempting to infiltrate decision-making positions? Summer had to contact Sam and inform him. Giretti should know the potential changes that could disturb the balance of nature.

If he succeeded in this significant change to human constructs of government, the next phase of android acceptance had to involve the general population. Summer was not a participant in voting, as it never seemed possible. She had no rights as a non-registered citizen. Her documentation worked for travel and identification, but closer scrutiny could be problematic.

Autumn came into the store to ask about the gentleman. Winter was with her. The men had rounded up the guards and Robby and taken them to an area to remove any power units. They were soon effectively non-operational.

"Who was that man?" Autumn asked.

"A problem," Summer said.

Parvel and Zaiyaan sat together on the condo floor, playing with stimulation material to enhance the little boy's cognitive abilities. Parvel talked with his son and listened as he babbled something in return. A translation from Cigi was sporadic as she worked with Sam and Clare to plan the new design for another pregnancy capable female.

In the few days the family had gathered after the trip, Parvel noticed Zaiyaan's accelerated growth rate. His son was advancing toward toddler mobility at a pace unknown to human babies. The hybrid little boy was different, but Parvel loved him more each day, enjoying the time they shared. Zaiyaan communicated through his mother that he loved his father and was sorry Uncle Peter was mean. Parvel laughed and hugged him.

"Parvel, Renata Giretti is coming over. Contact Andre and see if he is available. We need government advice and possibly an intervention."

"Sure, I can do that." He left for his bedroom and a quiet place. With Andre's agreement to come, he returned to the living room and informed Sam. The time arrived for the Congress of the United States to recognize sentient humanoid beings as a class of humanity. Robots were legal since humans controlled them and could deactivate them. Sam's phone rang, and he saw Summer's face on the screen. "What's up in Arizona?" He opened the speaker so all could hear.

"We had a visit from Arizona's Licensing Department. The guy threatened to shut down Walter Mitty Robotics until he could meet with Peter."

"Well, that's not a problem. You wanted to return to Cuba. Kelsey and Jake can deal with it."

"That's not the only issue. The man was an android. I recognized the eyes and checked his status with the state. He is legit. Peter has infiltrated the government."

"Hang on a minute; Renata Giretti has arrived for a meeting. She should hear this." Clare opened the door to let Giretti into the condo.

Andre followed her. Sam signaled for them to come to him. "Say again what you just told us." Summer repeated her information.

Giretti was not surprised. She had used an android for months, and the Coast Guard had a crew aboard one of its cutters.

"There's more, Sam," Summer said. "Elections this fall will include several androids who have filed for office. Peter's been busy."

Renata asked, "What offices?"

Summer said, "Secretary of State and several county offices, school board positions, and a couple of mayoral races. Won't background checks uncover their true status?"

Sam said, "Peter is behind this. Let him try. I am interested in what happens."

Renata said, "If they are successful in running this fall, the court challenges regarding their humanity will cause Congress to have serious discussions."

"Peter won't agree, but I want to represent any of them if a challenge happens." Cigi smiled as she spoke. An Arizona bar exam awaited her.

Chapter 52

David Anderson rolled his wheelchair into his attorney's office to begin a suit against Thomas Anders for violating his proprietary investment knowledge for personal gain. As he explained the situation to his attorney, he knew it sounded preposterous.

"I know this is crazy, but it's true." David supplied documentation of his trade practices compared to Thomas Anders application of similar investment utilization. Where Anders' seed money came from was not an issue. Investing practices were.

David's attorney, a well-known corporate financial litigator, Benton Maxwell, asked, "Does this Anders fellow have any connection with how you do business? You make him sound like a clone of you." David wanted that piece of knowledge kept quiet because he surmised Benton might deem him psychotic.

"I don't want this information known, so listen and keep it confidential. I had an affair with a woman a year ago. She seduced me and somehow implanted a chip in my head that could control my thoughts and memories. She is now associated with Anders."

"Is she having an affair with Anders? We could use that as leverage."

David shook his head. "They are not, but there's more." David paused, unsure of how to expose the androids to Benton. Would he understand or mock the idea of humanoids ruining his life? Benton remained quiet.

"Three other men have chipped brains because of this one woman. She worked with a company that made androids but a raid a year ago shut it down."

Benton lit up. "Bennington Brothers. Yeah, I remember. The government confiscated their inventory, and Congress outlawed artificially intelligent creations siting them as a threat to the human social order."

David said, "The government didn't get all the bots." He wanted the rest to remain a secret, but his clone was the problem.

"What do you mean?"

David rocked his chair as he formulated words. "Thomas is a creation of Peter Bennington as a promise to me. I wanted to walk again. I had a deal with him to underwrite his enterprise." Benton stayed silent.

"Peter created an artificially intelligent clone of me, and through some mysterious machine, copied my memories and thought processes into the clone's brain. I was to be a whole man, but it didn't happen. The clone rejected being me and adopted his identity as Thomas Anders."

Benton cocked his head to the right, a habit when a client's words made no sense. "You want to sue a robot?"

"Not a robot. An independent, sentient humanoid. This guy has all my qualities and memories and uses them to enhance his lifestyle. The law is clear. He shouldn't roam the world like a human being."

"Tell me about the lady who allegedly chipped your brain and controls your mind. Is she human?"

"Partly, yes. She is a creation of Samuel Bennington, who used stem cell science to grow body parts for her and developed an artificially intelligent female."

"A hybrid human is nothing new. Medical science has used stem cells to rebuild human organs and repair other body parts."

"Benton, the lady is a computer with a human body."

Benton laid back in his desk chair. "She is an android."

"Yes. With human parts. She had a baby a few weeks ago. How does that happen?"

"An android had a baby? Hmm." The look on his face indicated disbelief at the concept.

"I'm not kidding, Benton. Cigi Weatherman married a human, had sex with him, and produced a baby boy. She is a friend of Thomas Anders, an adversary, and a licensed lawyer in this state. She'll probably end up defending him against my lawsuit."

Benton leaned forward. "What you're telling me sounds preposterous. First, sentient androids are illegal. Second, if she married a human, licensing the union is suspect. Third, how did she pass the bar? What school did she attend to get a law degree? Fourth, whose technological expertise was used to chip your brain? And finally, taking this matter to court may cause legal repercussions as we bring evidence into the open. Are you sure you want this kind of notoriety? I don't see it improving your business."

"Can we meet with Anders and get him to stop using my investment strategies?" David asked.

Benton wrote notes on a yellow legal pad and clicked on his intercom. "Rayna, make an appointment with Thomas Anders. David gave us the contact information. See if he can meet in the next few days. Clear a time for him." He clicked off. "I'll let you know when he can meet with us." David nodded and left the office. He figured it was a long shot, and Maxwell was correct about unintended consequences.

He called Gunther Parsons to be an ally to help stop the surge in the android incursion into human lives and social status. Cigi Weatherman was not a menace, but she threatened the human order of things. If she could exist, so could others. David wanted to stop the Season sisters and Clare. He wanted androids to be no better than enslaved beings for humans to use. He left Gunther a message. Andre Scott and Charles Cooke allied with Sam Bennington and would not be assets.

Thomas called Cigi after hearing from Benton Maxwell's office about a meeting with David Anderson to resolve issues. "Anderson wants to meet with me, and I think having an attorney present is advisable."

"David is worried about your investments." Cigi had a partial connection with the chip in his head. "I don't think he wants this in court, since the unintended consequences could endanger his investors trusting him with their money."

"Would a judge sanction androids as viable entities if David sued me in open court and you acted as my attorney?"

"Current law says we are not eligible for civil rights, but government practice has ignored it and used androids as people in experimental jobs. The test comes as they present evidence."

"Maxwell would call you as a witness, wouldn't he? You are the one who seduced David and had his brain chipped."

Cigi said, "Yes. Maxwell could ask for a closed hearing. If he does not, I could cite the sensitive nature of the case." They concluded the call, and Cigi decided she should invade David Anderson and change his mind about a lawsuit.

"What did Thomas want?" Parvel asked.

"David Anderson wants Thomas to halt using his investment strategies and threatened a lawsuit if he did not. I think the issue could advance android integration since a judgment either way would be newsworthy to the public. However, there are risks."

"Did he ask you to defend him? Could a judge detain Thomas and you as illegal entities?"

"Those are the risks. I may have to invade David's brain to change his mind, since this plan may be for the reasons you cited."

Parvel hugged her and said, "I can't lose you. Peter kidnapping me was scary enough, and to have you lost to me is unbearable. If you enter David's thinking, what will you do?"

"Create doubts." Cigi kissed Parvel and released herself from his hold. She picked up Zaiyaan and kissed her son, who cooed.

"Mother," he said, "Mr. Anderson is not a threat. Gunther Parsons is." She tightened her hold on Zaiyaan and sent him a comforting message.

"I will handle this to keep us safe and free from interference in our lives."

Parvel called Andre Scott about the interaction with Thomas, seeking advice about handling David Anderson's threat. The information surprised Andre as he and David had spoken about the money issues between them at the Department of Energy.

Parvel also contacted Sam to inform him of Cigi's involvement in Thomas's lawsuit and her tactics regarding David Anderson. "Peter needs to contact David and stop his actions," Sam said. "I don't think he will, though. The situation is what Peter wants; to infiltrate the government. I can imagine a judge issuing an order which starts civil unrest. If Anderson wins, androids suffer. If Thomas wins, humans revolt. No winner."

"Should Cigi attempt to get David to change his mind?" Parvel asked. "Gunther might support a lawsuit that ruins Cigi."

"I don't know," Sam said. "Our original goal in chipping the brains was to influence the acceptance of artificially intelligent entities into society via money and interaction with androids. Cigi, Clare, and I decided changing thoughts and memories was not what we wanted. I neutralized the chips."

Parvel said, "Can she gain access to his brain this one time to stop David without his awareness of her?"

"She can, but our goal is to have him accept her equality, even though her strengths surpass any of us. She is more powerful than her sisters and other androids. I would not want her to become greedy for control. My brother's greed is bad enough."

Parvel and Sam ended the conversation so Parvel could talk with Cigi. He was aware of the attraction of power. Did it affect androids as it did humans? "Cigi, can we talk?" he asked. She smiled and nodded. "You are the smartest person I know, human or android. I trust you and know your actions are for the betterment of all humankind." He paused a moment. "Would you ever contemplate becoming autocratic if your goals and aspirations did not pan out?"

"Is this about Peter?" she asked.

"Maybe, but Sam says a lawsuit against Thomas is ill-advised because of the information disclosed. Would power lure you to act in ways unacceptable to humans?"

"Sam is paranoid about building a world integrated with humans and androids. He wants something difficult to create. Power can corrupt the mind. I will control my emotions and work toward integration through positive actions. Not coercion."

Parvel kissed Cigi and said, "We need more people and androids like you in the world."

"Want to make another one?" she asked.

Parvel's mouth dropped open. "What do you mean? Are you…?"

"Not yet. Zaiyaan is asleep, and I want to make a sibling for him." They went to the bedroom.

After their coital interlude, they lay quiet and spent. "Do you know when you are fertile?" Parvel asked.

"My cycle is in its fertile time, which is why I seduced you.

We can prove the human reproductive system is viable in android hybrids. Zaiyaan is not an anomaly. He is the first. Clare will upgrade to become the second of us to become capable of reproduction naturally. Humans will better accept us if they know we are not a threat. Babies are not a threat."

"Babies grow into adults who are threats." Parvel hugged her and said, "We will raise our children to respect who they are and their capability for improving society. We will not control them, but will guide them." The baby monitor alerted them to Zaiyaan awakening and wanting attention. What they heard next quickened Parvel's heartbeat.

Chapter 53

Renata Giretti entered the diner, finding Sam and Clare waiting for her. "Hi, Sam," she said. "I hope you are doing well. We have much to discuss. Good to see you, Clare."

Sam smiled, "You do not know what has transpired in the last couple of weeks." He related the tale about rescuing Parvel and taking command of Peter's compound in Arizona, Cigi and Parvel reunited, and Zaiyaan bonding with his father.

"The President requested another meeting with you and Cigi." Renata folded her hands together and placed them on the table.

"Which President, Renata?"

"President Blankenship, in the flesh."

"Alright, I'll contact Cigi and arrange a time." Sam pulled out his phone to punch the preset number.

"The President wants to meet with you now. Call Cigi and see if she is available. We can go to her place." Sam completed the call and confirmed the gathering. After he closed the communication, Renata said. "Let's go."

At the condo, Cigi and Parvel placed Zaiyaan in his playpen. The little boy surprised them after their conjugal attempt to create another child when he used words they heard through the monitor in his room. He said, "Mama, Dada." They entered his room to see him standing in his crib. He continued to speak. "I want a baby brother or sister." Cigi and Parvel marveled at the progress their son was making.

Secret service agents inspected the condo building for potential threats against the President. When finished and without fanfare, they signaled a guest was in the lobby. When Cigi checked the monitor, she noticed a couple of black-suited agents and a lady who resembled the android they had met. She entered the elevator to greet their distinguished visitor properly.

Sam and Clare arrived at the condo and noticed no government agents securing the area from potential enemies or paparazzi. Renata had driven herself to the meeting and entered before they arrived. Two black-suited agents checked credentials and their authorization to meet with President Blankenship inside the building. She came without a significant security detail or a black armor-reinforced government-issued sedan. Attracting attention to a discussion about androids and humans living together in a peaceful environment was to be avoided. Too many individuals opposed the concept. Sam and Clare entered to see Zaiyaan in the President's arms, cooing at her.

"Good to see you in person," President Blankenship said. "My alter-ego reported what transpired at your last meeting. I apologize for the misdirection, but my support for android technology needs to be discreet. I authorized the Coast Guard experiment using an android crew and read the report about their interaction with six android beings in the Caribbean Sea. Renata has integrated androids into her department, and several other government entities have used sentient beings."

Sam listened, holding Clare's hand as reassurance for her. "What happened to the confiscated bodies? Have government techs changed the formatting to suit the elected officials who need to rewrite the legal status of our creations?"

Renata answered his query. "President Blankenship and I meet regularly to strategize a proper modification of the laws. Several members of the House have staff used from the pool captured during the raid."

Cigi asked, "Are these sentient beings paid for their work, or are they glorified slaves to the establishment? How are they maintained and upgraded? Are they free to live as they wish or programmed to be robotic chattel?"

President Blankenship said, "You model the ability of these beings to mature and develop. You have provided ample proof that humans and sentient androids can coexist. However, the integration is more complex than a simple change of legal status."

"I appreciate the complexity of our existence," Cigi said. She took Zaiyaan from the President. "My son is a new human species, but will not be alone. Evolution has examples of how new species come into the world. He has the rights granted to any human, and we ask for the same thing. Our cadre of beings is not adversarial."

"Sam, what about your brother, Peter? Is he an adversary?" President Blankenship asked. "Rumor has it he wants my job and will run this country using an android army to enforce his edicts."

Sam nodded. "A community of artificial intelligent beings is ready to infiltrate the government. We are trying to stop him."

"I authorized Renata to assist you in whatever you need to promote your agenda and halt your brother," President Blankenship said. "I am working with Congressional leaders, some of whom want to meet you, Sam. They want to know what you created and why the laws are inappropriate for your androids."

"I will meet with them when they are ready for an introduction to the most remarkable people this planet has."

President Blankenship laughed. "You mean Cigi and Clare." Turning to them, she continued. "My alter-ego expressed high praise for you, Cigi, and your sister, Clare. She referenced others working in business and medicine. I want to meet any of your creations who have integrated with human society and incorporated their humanism interacting with flesh and blood."

Cigi said, "Madam President, I will meet with your government officials and educate them about our goals and aspirations. Our humanoid species are as diverse and interesting as human cultures across the globe. Our numbers are small compared to humanity. However, we are not a threat or a challenge to human positions. We want to be accepted, debated, challenged, loved and thought of as friends. The world has not solved the problems humans have amongst their varied populations and cultural backgrounds and religions. Greed and power reign. We do not exist to solve the problems inherent in humanity."

"I understand," the President said to Cigi. She turned to Sam. "Sam, do you and your brother share the same goals?"

Sam looked at her and furrowed his brow. "Your clone should

have updated you on our conversation, or you're testing me. We do not share common goals."

"My administration has reviewed your business and meeting these wondrous beings builds my confidence that humans can accept and work with androids that support and scaffold human successes."

Clare remained quiet, listening to the interchange, realizing the hollow value her words held. The human emotion of distrust exploded in her when Peter endangered Cigi's life and kidnapped Parvel. Now she doubted any sincerity. Could the world accept androids as equals? Clare lived in an environment of secrecy and awareness, but she wanted what Cigi had: the ability to produce a healthy, intelligent human. Sam promised, and she would hold him to the promise. Her brain developed a question that Thomas Anders and David Anderson argued.

She asked, "Madam President, do you envision sentient androids working as equals or adjuncts? Unlike Peter Bennington's agricultural and industrial robots who replace humans in dangerous work environs, we are not slaves for humanity to abuse and misuse. Can you see us earning a living, buying homes, raising families, taking vacations, having family reunions, going to school, and accomplishing other human activities?"

President Blankenship stroked her chin. "I imagine we shall find out. Are you willing to follow the country's laws and not engage in criminal enterprises?"

"According to current law, we are criminals because we exist. We live quiet lives to stay out of the spotlight. The humans we interact with do not suspect we are not human or they are allies. We have no desire to be incarcerated or deactivated and dismantled. Can you assure us we remain free to live and thrive?"

"I wanted to meet you because society's transformation continues, often in unexpected ways. Three hundred years of history show us the path. We cannot deviate from our future because of fear. Yes, I understand people think android technology is threatening. I am not one of them. Experiencing my staff working with my clone and other androids has shown me a progressive and positive future." The meeting ended with questions left unasked and unanswered.

Sam and Clare stared at the door after the entourage was gone. Cigi and Parvel cleared away dishes and cups while Zaiyaan crawled around and then stood with the help of tables and chairs.

Over the next few weeks, the Season sisters returned to Cuba and reopened the restaurant. Thomas and David reconciled the investment controversy. Gunther Parsons plotted revenge against Cigi. Parvel and Andre guided the Department of Energy's financial matters with Grendel, Mercy, and Brenda.

Gunther and Andre's android clones remained elusive, while Charles Cook and Charlie returned to operate their solar business in Seattle. The medical androids opened a practice in Alexandria, Virginia, focused on government officials. They removed the memory and thought processes extraction equipment from the hospitals and clinics and installed them in their new clinic. Their mission remained a focal point of their existence. Dr. Sanders and Tatiana Laurent checked on Zaiyaan and Cigi to record their health and progress.

Kelsey Avery and her companion, Jake, returned to Arizona to run Peter's business. A reprogrammed Robby and other guard staff protected against Peter returning. He remained hidden from the public, plotting revenge against his brother and anyone in the government who opposed him.

Sam and Clare returned to Chimacum, Washington, and their small farm. Sam designed anatomical modifications to accommodate Clare's request for reproductive organs and a trip to Arizona to make the changes. Another female reproductive android could sway a shift to the legal status of all androids. Still, the battles began, and the war against institutionalizing artificial intelligent life into human society was far from over.

Ziayaan continued unusual growth and mental development. At his first birthday in 2083, he was as mature as a five-year-old and the almost the size of one. Cigi and Parvel answered Zaiyaan's request for a sibling. They expected a little girl in early 2084. The Dawn of Androids marked a Renaissance for humanity as Congress debated palpable changes to current law.

Peter stayed busy building more soldiers and government clones. Dr. Harper Dillion and RN Paige Turner migrated to Arizona to Peter's facility with one of the memory and thought transfer machines. Peter had what he needed to implement an incursion into local politics and migration into state leadership by manipulating the individuals who counted ballots and certified elections. Peter wanted to replace them before official notifications were sent to voters.

Captain Kristi Tran contacted Ensign Kammi Gines regarding her abilities and the history of her development. The three Coast Guard androids stayed aboard a cutter with new officers and crew that were androids. Military leadership in the Pentagon wanted a robust and positive test supporting androids replacing humans on the battlefield.

As the android incursion into everyday life continued, Cigi and Zaiyaan planned his future advancement into the elite ranks. Was he to become the leader of his mother's species and the beginning of a new world order?

Acknowledgments

Writing a science fiction novel incorporates researching the latest science investigations and imagining what path those studies may follow. I concentrated on stem cells, solar energy, computer advancements, chipping of the brain, and android development. Each of these are active areas of scientific study.

The National Institute of Health is investigating embroyonic stem cells and adult stem cells to better understand disease and serve as accurate screens for new drugs. A third cell, developed from adult skin cells to act like embryonic cells, is called pluripotenet stem cells, or iPS.

An internet article, https://www.nih.gov/about-nih/what-we-do/nih-turning-discovery-into-health/stem-cells, relates the following: "Regenerative medicine is moving toward a day when we can repair and replace damaged tissues. In time, we will be able to make insulin-secreting pancreatic cells, bone cells to heal breaks and defects, and eye and ear cells to restore vision and hearing. NIH researchers are hard at work using stem cells as a powerful tool to study neurological disorders like Parkinson's, Huntington's disease, amyotrophic lateral sclerosis (ALS), and spinal cord injury, to name a few."

I simply imply in my story that science advances the research to actual organ development and transplanting into humans and androids. If this accomplishment happens, then medical science may improve our quality of life over the next several decades.

Solar energy has become less costly and better at trapping the sun's ray for electrical uses in the last few decades. The silicon fibers collect the suns rays and convert it to energy through the photovoltaic process. Cells can be polycrystalline silicon or monocrystalline silicon in the most common form. Recent enhancements in thin film technology are closing the gap in panel development. Materials uses are more durable and flexible. These cells are out-performing polycrystalline silicon cells but have a long way to go to catch monocrystalline silicon cells.

Materials used in thin cells include amorphous silcon, cadmiun telluride, and copper indium selenide. If science continues to develop thinner cells, then it is reasonable to assume a material that can be applied in sheets or like paint is not out of the question.

Applying thin, sheet-like material to cars, trucks, boats, trains, and aircraft, as well as building would revolutionize energy production. Imagination fires the creative nature of humans to make real the science fiction of today.

A third area of today's science is computing technology. We implement binary systems in our laptops, desk machines, and telecommunications devices. The adding, subtracting, multiplication, and divisional mathematical computations that can be found in a binary machine happen at speeds most of us cannot comprehend. The tiny switches that are off or on (zeros, and ones in a binary system) make possible the computing power of the small computers we carry with us, and claim they are a phone. Communication is one feature of a powerful device with which we surf the internet, connect to other devices, and take video and photographs.

The concept of ternary computing is not new or unique. Thomas Fowler built a wooden computing device in 1840 operating a balanced ternary system. The Soviets developed the first electronic system called Setun in 1958 with advantages over binary systems such as lower energy consumption and lower production cost. In 1973, a ternary computing emulator was develped in the United States.

What are the advantages of a ternary system? A balanced system uses -1, 0, +1 as the digits. Calculations can be more efficient than in a binary system. An unbalanced system uses 0, 1, and 2 as the digits producing calculations. Although binary systems dimished the interest in ternary computing, Donald Knuth argues they will come back into development in the future to take advantage of ternary logic's elegence and efficiency.

Several authors use ternary computing in the novels written for science fiction readers. In Robert Heinlein's novel, 'Time Enough for Love', the sapient computer of Secundus uses unbalanced ternary systems. Howard Tayler's webcomic Schlock Mercenry uses ternary systems. The Conjoiners in Alastair Reynolds' Revelation Space series use ternary logic to program computers and nanotechnology devices. My androids use ternary computing to mature emotionally and mentally. It is not a stretch of imagination to imply the power that may be installed into sapient artificial lifeforms.

The fourth area of scientific investigation is installing computing chips into humans to improve functions of the brain and the body. Although, this area is still in infancy, an 2017 article in Forbes Magazine, addresses the interest Elon Musk and Mark Zuckerberg have in a race to get chips into human brains.

More recently, Elon Musk started Neuralink, a company designing and developing ultrathin chips to implant in human brains. The immediate quest is to help disabled people. Ultimately, communicating could change the way we interact with each other.

As I thought about the next area of science in this book, artificial intelligence, the concept of a human-like creature composed typically of non-biologic materials was not enough for me. The integration of human organs and mechanical parts became the model. Whether tissue and non-tissue can meld well enough to develop a hybrid style humanoid is speculative at best. However, people conceptualized much of today's machines and toys decades and centuries ago.

Lie Yukou detailed an automaton in Liezi, written around 250 B.C. Greek mathematician Hero of Alexandria described an automata designed to pour wine for guests. In 1495, Leonardo de Vince designed and built an automaton dressed in a knight's armor and operated with pullys and cables. Nikola Tesla dempnstrated his wireless controlled model boat at the Elecrical Exposition in Madison Square Gardens in 1898. In 1921, Czech writer, Karel Capek introduced the word robot in his play, R.U.R.

Today, companies and research universities are designing and developing human-like robots for educational purposes and interaction with students, the public, and workers. These latest developments show us how the world of automation is advancing robotics to a level that may produce clones of humans so we can work in safer environs and have service work enhance human lifestyles.

I want to thank Rebecca Bauer for her editing skills. She reads each of my manuscripts making cogent suggestions for tightening my writing and improving the reader's attraction to the story. My wife, Sandy Stockwell, reads my manuscripts and encourages me to continue writing because she says I am getting better results from my machinations with the computer keyboard. Susan Wall edits my manuscripts with a keen eye on what readers enjoy.

I use two software editing programs, Grammarly and Prowriting Aid, that correct the rough manuscripts before I send then out to the other eyes. Online editing has improved markedly over the years. I do not accept every suggestion for changes and sometimes I send feedback as to why a certain sentence or use of words needs to remain.

My covers are fun for me to design and develop. I search for royalty free or inexpensive pictures to use. Usually I download from Shutterstock.com. The site has more than enough images and photos for cover design.

IngramSpark is my print distribution site. Without IngramSpark, I would be searching for a vanity press or some other expensive organization and I would not have the distribution connections Ingram has.

Writing, editing, formatting, cover design, and print settup are learnable activities for anyone who wants to write. I wish to thank everyone who has educated me, shown me a better way, guided my work, and supported my writing. Without the hundreds and thousands of followers and readers, a writer might stop entertaining a hungry audience.

Please stay tuned for the next book, Android Incursion.

Sources

- Website: National Institutes of Health (https://www.nih.gov/about-nih/what-we-do/nih-turning-discovery-into-health/stem-cells)
- Ternary computer - Wikipedia article, last edited March 19, 2022
- Website: dsolar, Vitamin D for your business (https://dsolar.co.za/materials-used-to-make-solar-panels/#:~:text=Table%20 1%3A%20Hazardous%20materials%20found%20on%20solar%20 panels.,Sometimes%20found%20on%20solar%20thermal%20sys- tems%20...%20)
- Website: Energy.gov (https://www.energy.gov/solar)
- Could Elon Musk's Neuralink brain chips make us all as smart as he is? - New York Post, April 30, 2022
- Humanoid robot - Wikipedia article, last edited Mar 15, 2022

Biography

Peter Stockwell retired as a middle school teacher in 2010 and embarked on a career telling stories. After 32 years of guiding the minds and emotions of preteen and teenage students, he left the classroom to relax and enjoy the rest of his life with family and friends. Instead, he wrote a book and published it. The fun began when he learned the next step, marketing his creation to the world. He has now written and published 10 books with several more in the future. He writes mystery, crime investigative stories, futuristic science fiction, and inspirational books

He lives with his wife, Sandy, and son, David, in Silverdale, Washington. Five adult children and eight grandchildren are a source of great joy. He is a past member of the Pacific Northwest Writers Association (PNWA), International Thriller Writers (ITW), Northwest Independent Writer Association (NIWA), and current member of Kitsap Literary Artists & Writers (KLAW). He publishes through his company, Westridge Art.

Each month Peter and another KLAW member, Mark Miller, record and produce a television show in which they interview northwest authors, artists, musicians, editors and publishers. Production of the show is in conjunction with Bremerton Kitsap Access Television (BKAT).

Peter enjoys traveling to various parts of the world, usually on a cruise ship. He has visited Japan, Central America, Mexico, Bahamas, Colombia, Ecuador, Peru, England, Denmark, and Norway, . He has been in each of the fifty states of the United States and British Columbia.

Follow him on Facebook and Instagram.

Contact Peter at stockwellpa@wavecable.com
or wrtr14u@gmail.com